JOURNEY THROUGH THE RIFT

CHRISTOPHER HOOTEN

This novel is dedicated to all of those, like myself, who have the persistent feeling they were born in the wrong century.

To learn more about Christopher Hooten and his books, go to his Amazon Author page today:
https://www.amazon.com/Christopher-Hooten/e/B08PMRCR1V

SUMMARY

Horace Bascom was born a hundred years too late. He simply did not fit in the modern world. A recluse, a billionaire, highly educated as a physician and a physicist, he accomplished the greatest scientific achievement of the 21st century—crossing the rift of time into an earlier century. Travelling to Ft. Worth, Texas, circa 1878, he meets a young woman suffering from advanced tuberculosis. This chance meeting changes his life. He races across the rift to bring her life-saving antibiotics and assist in her recovery. However, complications now exist in the modern time-line as leaked financials of H.B.'s vast wealth reach media outlets throughout Texas and his 100-acre ranch becomes a focal point for reporters hawking for a story.

Sinister eyes read of H.B.'s vast wealth and isolation and send forces to kidnap him. However, he has a problem. He must protect the secret time machine from the outside world and yet help the critically ill young woman of another century. He must find someone to help him. Someone he can trust. Someone who can fight to save his ranch and protect the secret locked within his garage. He must leave, take his chances, and again go "across the rift" to fulfill his destiny and save a life.

BREITBART NEWS

"Parallel universes really do exist, according to a mathematical discovery by Oxford scientists described by one expert as 'one of the most important developments in the history of science.' The parallel universe theory, first proposed in 1950 by the U. S. physicist Hugh Everett, helps explain mysteries of quantum mechanics that have baffled scientists for decades...."

CHAPTER

ONE

"What the hell are they doing at my gate on Sunday? Don't those bastards ever take a day off?" He impulsively scratched his head and then spat in the kitchen sink. His spitting and swearing surprised him. He wasn't accustomed to either action. H.B. had left to travel across the rift and had left his hundred-acre estate as a perfect sanctuary of isolation and privacy. On his return, twenty-one days later, he had found it transformed into a parade of gawkers roaming around the premises hawking for a photograph. The onlookers carried cameras with lenses as long as his arm. Where did this sick need to take a picture of him come from? What was the motivation? Horace Bascom bristled at the very thought of their presence.

"Damn 'em," he muttered as he walked through the kitchen and out the back door onto his large sprawling deck. A massive live oak tree held shade on the deck for most of the sunny hours. He plopped down in a deck chair and breathed in the cool early morning air trying to calm himself. The last few days had been pure hell but here on the spacious deck no one could see him. He swallowed hard forgetting, temporarily, the coffee brewing in the kitchen. He had suddenly lost the most cherished possession he had—his perfect isolation. H.B. pinched the bridge of his nose trying to quell a growing headache forming behind his eyes. It was an outright invasion of his privacy but the Facebook generation would never understand.

The initial shock of seeing the media types at his front gate left H.B. confused. He lived on a small country road, unpaved, several miles from Bellville, Texas. The traffic on the narrow county artery was almost non-existent until now, but that had drastically changed. The very evening of his return from the rift, a phone call from David Drake of Drake and Associates, his accountants, explained the reasons for the media's sudden interest in him. His financials had been leaked to the press by a disgruntled employee of Drake's and the release of his vast holdings had stirred the media mob into a feeding frenzy. David Drake explained an internal investigation was ongoing seeking to find the source of the leaker. *It doesn't matter now,* H.B. thought, as Drake and Associates blathered on endlessly about the screw up. The milk had been spilled. The damage was done.

Texas Monthly published the first article touting his vast wealth and the Houston Chronicle had followed up with a huge headline proclaiming him as the wealthiest man in Texas and perhaps even in America. His high-fenced, gated compound and his reclusive behavior drove the media freaks crazy. He was being compared to Howard Hughes. The television stations in Houston found the story of his lifestyle and wealth "fascinating" as one breathless reporter called it. Personal privacy didn't count for much in the new evolving world of social media and their hungry acolytes. The unnamed sources regarding H.B.'s wealth had been unleashed and their forces were formidable. More than his wealth was the fact that he was a recluse, an isolationist, a cave-dweller, as one reporter called him. The media treated him as an oddity. Billions upon billions of dollars stashed away and yet he lived behind a gated fortress with only himself. He was never seen in public and reportedly had his groceries delivered to his back gate. Reporters were becoming so desperate in the coverage of this hermit billionaire that they were inventing fictionalized versions of his life story for the sole purpose of sensationalism. Lies were interspersed with tidbits of truth and the furor had unhinged the last semblance of honest reporting.

The amazing thing about all of this was the fact that H.B. had no idea the depth of his wealth nor did he care. His parents were wealthy as were his grandparents so it was old money, generational money—passed from the past to the future and H.B. had been the sole recipient. His gifts of millions to charity and millions more for college scholarships seemed unimportant in the media narrative. It was his want of privacy, simply to be left alone, that stirred them. Even his vast wealth was secondary to the media wolves.

He slowly walked back into the kitchen to pour coffee and couldn't prevent himself from glancing through the kitchen window again. They were still there. Like piranha waiting for an uncovered leg. H.B.'s road from his massive front gate to his house was "S" shaped and about two hundred yards in length. It was a granite gravel road packed to stay firm in the wettest of weather. His house was only partially visible with large oak trees, thankfully, blocking a complete view of his home.

He noticed only three cars out front. Maybe their interest was waning. It was more likely only the Sunday crowd and it was early morning. He had snapped on his never-used television for the ten o'clock news for the past several nights and there it was, his home, proudly displayed for the world to see. An ungodly amount of time was wasted showing his horses to the world and speculating on what was going on behind his enclosed domain.

H.B. considered the idea of heading out to the gate and riding one of his quarter horses back and forth in front of them, in full public display. The pictures he'd seen on the local networks were dated—from his professorial days at Texas A&M. He quit teaching there dozens of years ago. Yet, the old photos were flashed up as if they were taken yesterday. Let them have some new photos to work with. Maybe that would satisfy their appetite. He finally nixed this plan realizing nothing would satisfy this throng of zombies.

H.B. took his coffee and returned to the back deck and sipped the dark brew. The mockingbirds were flitting in the tree above him singing melodies that would rival Beethoven. The sparrows were just as noisy, but lacked the melodious tunes of the mockingbird. He breathed in the fresh morning air and tried relaxing. It was difficult adjusting to this new changed world. His small ranch somehow had slid, in merely twenty-one days, into an unexplored enemy territory.

His buckskin gelding came walking over next to the deck hoping for a head rub. He was a thoroughly spoiled four-year-old always seeking attention. He was a beautifully proportioned animal representing the best of the quarter horse breed in looks yet he had some other bloodlines mixed in. H.B. wanted his horses living on native grasses and not dependent on a feed sack. Where he had been and where he was going back to, the commissary was the open range. He got up, walked over, and scratched the gelding's favorite places. Scout slung his head nervously as if the gate-crowd had his nerves on edge.

"It's alright," H.B. said, speaking soothingly to the horse.

"We won't be around here for long if we can help it. I know you like it on the other side as much as I do."

H.B. walked inside the house and grabbed his grey Stetson and carried his coffee mug with him to the back side of the barn where his pickup truck was parked. It was a one-ton Ford dually and he started it and backed up so the gate crowd couldn't see. He had a hidden gate entrance on the far backside of his pasture, out of sight, and on arriving he got out, unlocked the heavy chain, and opened it. It was a massive gate, but nothing in comparison to the front gate's behemoth size.

He got out again, secured the chain and lock, took a deep breath as he scanned the horizon, and slowly drove down the bumpy bar ditch where it connected with Coushatta Road. It was a two-football field distance to the small, dusty county road that touched H.B.'s property on two sides. The road was a bumpy and poorly maintained artery which eventually connected to FM 331 going east and Texas 36 traveling west. The traffic was usually light, mostly sporadic, until recently. Now dust clouds and road kill were more the norm. It was a narrow gravel road designed for local ranchers not speeding urbanites. He looked cautiously both ways and turned west thus avoiding passing by his main gate. Hopefully, the gate-keepers would eventually tire of having nothing to take pictures of and pull up stakes. Surely, they had something better to do on Sunday.

JASPER'S OLD-TIME Pit Barbeque was more restaurant than barbeque pit and was the only place open in Bellville in the early morning that served a decent breakfast. It was five miles, as the crow flies, from H.B.'s front gate yet in the eighteen years of his residency he'd only darkened the door once. It was the mecca of gossip for Bellville, Texas, population five thousand. Small town Texas lived and died by the news the grapevine carried. It was the one weed no one could defoliate. H.B. had always avoided gatherings—crowds of any size—but circumstances now propelled him into taking chances in a social setting today. He was uncomfortable but he needed help and he had little time to waste.

He sat for several minutes in his truck trying to calm himself. He wasn't particularly fond of his social awkwardness, but there was nothing to be done. He was the only child of two medical doctors who were gregariously social butterflies. Their gregarious personalities were polar opposites of his. H.B., in his youth, oft times considered himself adopted. How could anyone be so different from his parents? His looks favored his father's and his height, six feet three inches, matched his father's, too. So, he finally reconciled the fact that he was a product of their genetics.

Jasper's was an eatery with its own past. Old George Jasper, the original founder of the restaurant, at one time had been a rather famous character himself. He was an emigrant from Louisiana and thus considered a Coon Ass. It was a common term applied to Cajun Louisianans. From humble beginnings, a tent and a portable pit, George in thirty years had built a successful business. Fifteen years after opening Jasper's doors, a Hollywood film crew stopped by for barbeque and George, himself, convinced a big wig to give him a minor part. The movie was little more than a class B effort, but it made George a household name around Bellville and surrounding areas. The new-found fame and notoriety blurred George's good sense and the movie reels had just stopped spinning when he abruptly left for Hollywood. Well, George's delusions were quickly quashed as he never landed another part and he came home, back to Jasper's, a defeated man. Six months later he passed away in his sleep, and as the grapevine told it, he died of a broken spirit—like an old sheep determined to die—George simply gave up the ghost.

H.B. sat in the parking lot relieved to see little activity. He noticed one pickup truck with a large overhead camper sporting an Alaska license plates. Only a couple of other cars were parked in the gravel lot as few customers appeared interested in such an early breakfast.

Ida Tavish and her friend, Marcy, were sitting in a booth waiting patiently for the busy breakfast run to begin. It was five-thirty and things really kicked into gear around seven. So, Ida and Marcy enjoyed the peaceful lull before the rush. Ida worked Sundays, usually twice or three times a month, just to help pay her utilities bill. Rate increases had started sapping her tiny retirement so she waited tables, gossiped with locals, and visited other blue-haired lady friends. Ida was a plump and full-proportioned woman in her mid-sixties. Her knees ached if she stood on her feet too long. Another waitress would appear at eight, and another at ten, but for now Ida ruled the roost.

Marcy, sitting at the booth with Ida, had been a friend of Ida's deceased mother for many years and now lived out-of-state with a nephew. Marcy was mid-eighties, skinny as a rail, looked seventy at best, middling-colored grey hair, and not enough wrinkles to mention. She was spry and a real firecracker. Marcy spent a month each year with Ida and Ida idolized the woman and her rambling stories about her and her mother's early exploits with men and money. "Oh, those were the good ol' days when boys were boys and girls were girls," she'd say. "Back then," Marcy reminisced of the wild old days, "men were men and the sheep were nervous." Then she'd cackle and laugh with her dentures clicking in rhythm. Marcy's feistiness was good medicine for Ida. Ida was prone to long sulks and Marcy's visits always picked up her spirits.

Ida was picking at a thread on her blouse when she first saw him. The tall cowboy-booted man stood a few steps inside the restaurant entrance appearing uncertain whether to sit down or vanish back out the door.

"Oh, my Lord! Tell me that's not him. Could it be?"

Marcy was paying little attention until Ida's outburst. Her eyes rose to meet Ida's. She saw Ida's face flush red and a gasp escaped her lips.

"What are you saying?" she asked trying to determine what had brought on Ida's exclamation.

"That's Horace Bascom, I think. Dr. Horace Bascom himself." Ida reached for and started fanning herself with one of the menus on the table. The mother of all hot flashes started surging through her body and the increased heat instantly flustered her. She was edging into one of her anxiety attacks that seemed more frequent these days. Marcy witnessed Ida's reddening face and leaned over whispering.

"Honey, you okay. You look like you've just seen a ghost."

"Oh, Marcy it may be a ghost. My gosh! That man never leaves his ranch," she gasped nodding towards the restaurant's front door. Her menu-fanning picked up pace. "He lives behind a huge fence with a gate the size of a freight car. He's a recluse, Marcy. Lives alone, and worth multi-billions to boot. I'm talking billions, girl. Recently, he's made the news all over Texas including Texas Monthly for being so damn rich. I've lived my whole life right here in Bellville and I've never even seen 'im in person. Only pictures, but I know that's him. Sure as shootin' that's Horace himself."

Marcy turned around and eyed the man standing nervously just three steps inside the restaurant. To her he looked way more cowboy than billionaire. Ida's imagination may have run away with her Marcy thought, glancing his way. He was tall, handsome, late sixties maybe seventy, but no more she reckoned. Overall, Marcy felt proficient as a teller of age, especially with men. They didn't have to play the cover-up game that women played. He had removed a rather sizeable cowboy hat holding it firmly in his right hand. Marcy considered that a sure sign of being a gentleman. Manners had slipped from the good old days in her opinion. This Horace fella, if it was really him, had manners. He was no mule in a horse harness.

Ida eventually gained control of herself, sliding her large bulk slowly to the edge of the booth seat, all the while staring at the man. She, of course, had no inkling of how close H.B. was to turning tail and bolting for the door.

H.B. noticed eyes staring at him. He didn't like stares and invariably they made him uncomfortable. Adjusting to a social setting just wasn't his forte. What seemed moments ago to be a good idea had turned sour all of a sudden. *What really was he doing here?* he kept asking himself. The restaurant was large, roomy, and non-intimidating with few customers as of yet, but it was foreign turf to him. A damp sweat was breaking out.

Finally, he took notice of a large woman waddling his way. She went the circle route, and that may have saved the day. He somehow held his ground, fidgeting and waiting, hat firmly in hand and all the time reminding himself that this foray into town was required.

Ida was no less nervous. Her waddle rapidly evolved into a wobble by the time she had closed half the distance. Her heavy legs had somehow gotten heavier and less willing to cooperate. The simple act of balance was not so simple either. The very thought that she was closing in on a man who could practically buy the whole dern planet was intimidating. Ida Tavish, broke widow woman that she was, struggling to make ends meet and barely doing so, would get to say "hey" to maybe the wealthiest man imaginable. Even wait on his table. The very thought all, but paralyzed her. Then it happened. Kinda sudden like. A woozy feeling crept over Ida. *Oh, crap* she said to herself feeling an irregular pulse setting in. *You're not going to faint ol' girl are you? Just a few more steps. Come on, Ida, you can do it girl. Then her face flushed hot again.*

Marcy watched from the booth, seeing the spectacle unfold. Ida reminded her of a sloth dragging her feet, just barely inching forward. She rode Ida relentlessly about her weight but, like Ida's dearly departed mother, she just kept packing it on. Walk. Just walk some every day she had reminded her not an hour ago. Move those tree trunks, honey, and the weight will fall off.

H.B. stood, gawking himself, at the straining, sweating, lumbering red-faced waitress before him. Little beads of sweat lined her brow and her face was flushed and splotchy. Her noticeable anxiety actually had a calming effect on H.B. as his compassion kicked in. Of course, he had no idea he was the precipitator of her nervousness.

"Please take a seat anywhere you like," she mumbled in the throes of her hot flash. Then she managed to add, "I'll bring you a menu in just a minute."

It was Marcy who saved the day. Ida somehow made it back to the booth and collapsed, applying a wet semi-dirty dishrag to her forehead. She quietly prayed for no other patrons to arrive at the moment. She was unfit for duty just now.

Marcy sprang up and took H.B. a glass of water and a menu. She was light and lively on her feet even giving this tall so-called billionaire a little wink when she passed him his water glass. H.B. smiled and buried his face in the menu. Why he's as shy as a milk calf, Marcy thought. His pale grey eyes with thick black eyebrows were a perfect fit for his dark, honey-toasted skin. This man was the outdoors type she surmised. He was startlingly handsome and a man who didn't act like he knew it. She almost danced going back to Ida and their booth. Given the opportunity and forty years younger, she'd chase this man halfway around creation trying to catch him—rich or not.

Ida was still mopping her forehead, attempting to slow her fluttering heart. She was trying to figure out why she was in such a tizzy. She had noticed some dizzy spells recently, but this was a doozy.

"Wow," Marcy exclaimed as she slid lightly into the booth. "That man's good lookin'. He's got Gregory Peck written all over him. Get a hold of yourself, girl. Wonder what it'd be like to catch him. Billionaires don't grow on trees you know—if that's really him." Kiddingly she added, "A woman like you could keep his bed warm, toasty in fact, from the way you're sweating."

Ida was in no mood for humor. She was deep breathing which appeared to be helping. She sometimes worried about her own health and her overweightness especially. A stroke had taken her mother, too, who was also somewhat sizeable. So, she had it in her genes. Maybe there was one lurking just around the corner—lining up an attack in her overworked capillaries.

"Honey, you do need to settle down," Marcy urged, seeing her friend's flustered state. "You pee your drawers and we'll have a real mess. Just keep deep breathing darling. This good looking man ain't gonna bite you."

Ida continued taking slow breaths and sipped ice water sometimes flicking a little finger-full of the water in her face. She could feel things settling down slightly. She almost wanted to test her pulse but thought better of it. Marcy prat-tled on about whatever, trying to take Ida's mind off this Horace guy.

"He's just a human like you and me," she kept saying. "He ain't no different than us. He zips up his britches the same way you and me do."

Marcy finally stood up, tired of waiting for Ida to get hold of herself. She grabbed Ida's order pad and approached H.B. She'd never waited tables, but the science seemed fairly straight forward. The other few customers seemed content enough so maybe Ida's crises would end in time. H.B. lowered the menu when Marcy stopped at his table. Her pencil stood at the ready.

"Short stack with one egg over easy. A couple of slices of bacon, too. Maple syrup if you have it."

Marcy wrote the order down. "How about coffee?" she asked.

"Sure," H.B. said.

"Want any orange juice?"

"Sure, I'll take a small glass."

"Darlin'," Marcy said leaning over to H.B. like the secret of all secrets was about to be revealed. He picked up the scent of cheap perfume as she leaned in close. H.B. nearly fell over backwards as Marcy invaded his personal space. "Your regular waitress over there, Ida, has got herself in a tizzy over you being here. Says you're some rich billionaire. Could I tell her you're not who she thinks you are? I'm not sure she can wait tables at the moment and I'm only her friend, not a waitress. I live out-of-state and am only here visiting."

The question about who he was, popping out of thin air, surprised H.B. He much preferred a life of anonymity yet he'd already been outed in the first few minutes in the restaurant. He had seen his picture flashed on every Houston television station's screen for the past several days, but it was out dated and of poor quality. He was surprised anyone could recognize him from the photo's he'd seen.

"I don't make a very good liar," H.B. said quietly looking towards Ida. She was sipping water and at the same time dipping her stubby fingers into a glass of ice water and flicking them in her face. The sight was humorous, but his growing discomfort voided his smile.

"Would she like me to leave?" he finally asked. "I'd be glad to go."

"Oh, no! Please don't do that, darlin'. That's liable to kill her outright. Best you just hang in. She'll snap out of it I reckon."

With that Marcy bounded off and found the coffee pot, returning with a cup to fill. She carefully poured the steaming hot coffee and smiled at him conspiratorially.

"Why don't you come over and join us?" she asked boldly to a startled H.B. "Poor thing might do better with you sittin' with us. She's just overwhelmed is all. She's in the middle of an anxiety attack which, by the way, she's having more and more of these days. We've got to snap her out of this or she might lose her job. She's only working so she can pay her utility bills." Marcy's last sentence was a direct hit to H.B.'s conscience. A firing was never a pretty thing, especially for someone struggling financially. She instantly saw H.B.'s facial expression soften.

"Why, I'd sure be sorry if she lost her job because of me," he said rather surprised by the offer to join them.

"Well, you just come on along with me, honey, and let's sit with her and calm her flutters. Bless her sweet heart. She's just got to pull it together. The crowds'll be comin' soon and she's all the waitress we have right now."

H.B. surprised himself by standing and following the little

13

elderly lady to the booth. Ida was looking their way and all but swooned seeing H.B. approaching. He slipped into the booth directly across the table from her and Marcy settled in next to Ida. H.B. placed his hat on the booth seat beside him and did a startling thing. He reached over and cupped Ida's chubby wet hand and fingers. This kindly act she would remember for the rest of her life and, initially, did nothing but set her heart racing again.

"Are you okay?" H.B. inquired covering her hand with his. He was not a practicing physician but his medical training kicked in. The red face, the protruding neck and distended veins, the skin splotches, were all indicators of an anxiety attack and spiking blood pressure. Marcy reached over and patted Ida's other hand and cooed pleasantries. Ida, momentarily, appeared detached and said nothing. A man's hand on hers felt good. She couldn't count the years since someone had done such a thing. It was warm and comforting. And the man had beautiful hands.

H.B. continued speaking softly to Ida. Almost whispering.

"Ida, are you taking any medication for anxiety?" he asked. He guessed her blood pressure was spiking off the charts at the moment. He feared a potential stroke. Finally, after several minutes, Ida found her voice.

"No, I'm not, but it seems almost anything can set me off. I kinda get breathless and that scares me. My heart tends to want to flutter."

"Take deep breaths and let them out slowly. In your nose and out your mouth. Please settle down. I'm very sorry if I have caused this."

"It's really not your fault," Marcy chimed in. "She's had a couple of attacks already and I've only been visiting for a week. She just needs to get a hold of herself."

"I'm still a licensed physician in Texas," H.B. said, letting her fingers go, but gently patting the back of her hand. "I'll call you in a prescription that should help settle these attacks down. You need more activity—some form of exercise. Walking would do best. You don't want to have to rely on a pill when there're other ways to solve this."

"I don't have any insurance, doctor," Ida replied letting out a deep breath. "I'm a year away from getting Medicare."

"That's not a problem," H.B. said. "Not a problem at all. The cost will be covered."

In a few minutes, Marcy popped up and brought H.B.'s breakfast to him. Ida continued her deep breathing and her flushed skin gradually took on a normal color. H.B. watched the transition carefully. He wanted to tell her she was dreadfully overweight, but he guessed she was well aware of that.

The few customers in the eatery received refills of coffee as Marcy bopped around like a teenager. She came back to the booth and slid in. She appeared to be thoroughly enjoying her new waitress gig.

"You doin' okay, darling?" she asked sipping slowly on her coffee. "Your color sure looks better."

"I am," Ida replied watching H.B. eating his breakfast. She still couldn't believe he was sitting directly across from her. He was as handsome as any movie star. She couldn't help but stare at him. She'd been watching the nightly news from Houston stations and their prattling on and on about his wealth and self-isolation. Here he was, in the flesh, in her booth watching over her carefully...and those grey eyes!

Marcy, of course, kept the conversation going. "So, Horace, are you as wealthy as they say?" she asked.

"Please call me H.B.," he responded, chewing on a bite of pancake. "These pancakes are really tasty," he added.

"They make 'em with fresh buttermilk every morning," Ida said somewhat put off by Marcy's questioning. Discussing someone's financial status wasn't the way to treat a paying customer. That was a private matter. It could be a point of gossip, however, which seemed to circle in an orbit itself, outside the normal rules of discussion. His immense wealth had always been a favorite subject in Bellville.

Marcy jumped up again and filled the few cups needing coffee. H.B. noticed her engaging in a conversation with a nearby couple. "Those folks are from Alaska," she said as she slid into the booth. "They're sure sweet people."

"Wonder what they're doing all the way off down here?" Ida asked.

"They're here watching Astros baseball. Her husband is a big fan."

H.B. looked over in their direction wondering if they were folks he should talk to. Maybe he could ask them for assistance. They were out-of-towners with no connection to the locals. It would be worth the try.

Lori and Ethan Fowler, of Alaska, had a surprise, too, before they left Jasper's Barbeque. They'd spent the last hour visiting with a tall, engaging guy who raised horses, Lori's favorite subject. Ethan wasn't a natural horseman, but he knew Lori was so they hung around wasting time. He was anxious to drive. Head north. The coastal humidity was about to melt him and Ethan was chomping at the bit to hit the road. A hundred miles north meant less humidity. Two hundred miles meant even less. They were burning daylight. Then the man, calling himself H.B., popped a question. "How would you like to ride one of my quarter horses?" Ethan had tried to dampen the impact of the offer, but couldn't manage it. The man owned a hundred acres and Lori pictured herself riding tall in the saddle smelling saddle leather and fresh air. Ethan only smelled the Houston Ship Channel and overpowering humidity. Lori pushed, so here they were, following the man to his horse ranch, forgetting their day of travel.

H.B. held his breath, even prayed, that the paparazzi wouldn't be at the main gate as they approached. The huge Lance camper the Alaskan couple was driving would never fit through his back gate and he didn't want them alerted to his recent notoriety. Thankfully, they were gone.

They pulled up behind H.B. waiting for the monstrosity of a gate to open. Ethan watched, mouth agape, gazing at the place. The fencing looked to be straight out of Jurassic Park, tall, double thickness, and topped with three feet of razor wire. The gate itself groaned and moaned moving laboriously at a snail's pace. It had various rollers and wheels, motors whirred and strained to complete the task. It had to be remote controlled as H.B. hadn't left his pickup. There was a broad, thick cattle guard under it. The gate must be thirty feet wide, thought Ethan, and weigh in at a ton or more. Ethan had never seen anything quite like it. His eyes scanned the tall coastal grass fields half-expecting to see a T-Rex, at least an elephant. This fencing had to be a bit of an over-kill for a horse pasture. Was the fence designed to hold something in or keep something out? The question crossed Ethan's mind as he drove across the bumpy cattle guard and entered the domain of this elderly horseman. The gate clunked closed with creaking noises behind them as they drove up a small meandering gravel road and climbed a low hill. A ranch-style house, barely visible from the front gate, loomed ahead with various out buildings complete with a rustic barn. Over and around the buildings were scattered large, majestic oak trees providing a canopy of shade. The buildings had the appearance of age--old-fashioned looking and very quaint. Lori practically squealed with excitement in anticipation of her ride. Ethan looked for large, exotic animals or maybe prisoners wearing orange suits. The fencing had him a bit unnerved.

CHAPTER
TWO

T abor Martinez was a thug, plain and simple. He ran his business on the streets of Houston hustling street crimes, drug deals, and heists within suburban homes where lights were low and occupants were shopping or busy at work.

His nickname was Tiger, El Tigre, and he loved it. He had a half dozen sleazy associates coming in and out of the picture assisting to varying degrees when needed. They were low-life types with long, checkered criminal careers. All had done time for their various misdeeds, typical of their trade, and invariably re-entered the work force as career felons.

Tiger periodically checked the Houston Chronicle picking up tidbits here and there to support his lifestyle. Real estate ads were a primary target. He lived, for the most part, in vacant "for sale" homes in Houston's suburbia via the back window and camped out for days quietly spying on neighborhood comings and goings. He snooped and usually preyed by day. Minimally supplied, he could inhabit a property for days unseen and unnoticed. Most hometels, as he referred to them, had fridges and stoves. Electricity was free. With a simple bedroll, a quick removable basket for the fridge, and a gadgets bag, he could vanish into thin air before the front door opened. Plus, he had plumber's coveralls with Tony embossed on the front. It was for emergencies only. Quick on and quick off if absolutely necessary.

His little gang of hoodlums profited from his careful surveillance. He spied on surrounding residents for a few days, learning their travel patterns, and when the time was right his goons broke in and pillaged and plundered. Items were quickly and quietly fenced and profits split. Two old beater vans, Tony's Plumbing plastered on, were used in the heists. Then quietly on to the next neighborhood for another strike. El Tigre, too, was an expert in bypassing home security systems. They rarely functioned as advertised anyway.

El Tigre was tiring of penny ante burglaries. Scanning the Chronicle's Sunday edition, he stumbled on an article about a South Texas multi-billionaire. The further he read the more his interest grew. Horace Bascom, a loner, a recluse, was sequestered behind a large fence and was apparently self-sufficient it said. A man alone, eccentric, and most importantly, tucked away on a one-hundred-acre estate far away from prying eyes. And he was only seventy miles from downtown Houston.

A lot was unknown about H.B. (as he preferred to be called) the reporter admitted. He came from a wealthy family so his massive wealth was unearned. His parents had been killed in a freak aircraft accident in the mountains of New Mexico eighteen years previous. Their then professor-son promptly resigned his position at Texas A&M and planted himself on the family's country property. Their only child, H.B., inherited the family fortune and over the passage of years he had invested wisely. No known relatives. Estate located five miles from Bellville. Raises quarter horses as a hobby. Highly reclusive. Takes delivery of groceries and feed once monthly without leaving the estate. The "lives alone" line caught the Tiger's eye. This H.B. story had him drooling on the newspaper. What? No bodyguards? No gardeners? No servants? This was too good to be true.

MORE SINISTER EYES than the Tiger's read of H.B.'s wealth. Gerard Fremont, a well-known Louisiana thug also read the Chronicle story, his large lips forming the words as he labored through it. His dark, choke-cherry eyes danced in his fat, round head as he read. A recluse billionaire living alone was right up his alley he thought. He had a dozen bone breakers under his command and with the snap of his fat fingers bad things could happen to this rich fella. Gerard had pushed his way around the bayous and swamps of south Louisiana for years and had gained respect the only way he knew how—he bought it. He knew the corrupt politicians. Drank bourbon with the cops. Used dirty money for leverage. Had a half dozen brothels active and running—none legitimate but money-producers nevertheless. The cops knew about them but left him alone. Hell, they were some of his best customers. He sold skin and booze but frowned on drugs. He also owned two large prosperous liquor stores and laundered money through them. He hurt people, sometimes, if they needed hurting. Of course, he hired his bone-breakers. He had a problem, though. Every time he thought about it his head throbbed. It was the United States Government. The IRS. The real crooks in his opinion. They insisted he owed a bundle in back taxes and they were closing in fast.

One of his bone-breakers was a man named Bingo Burns. Bingo had plenty of brawn and, remarkably, a brain to go with it. That was rare in his business. So, he'd called Bingo in for a meeting. Within the hour, the meeting took place.

"Read this," he said shoving the Houston Chronicle story across the table. They had been led by a short-skirted waitress with knobby knees to a dark corner of a dingy Lake Charles restaurant famous for fried frog legs and mud bugs. A blue hue of stale cigar and cigarette smoke clung to the ceiling of the joint. Boggy Montel, Gerard's long-time acquaintance, owned Boggy's and they'd conducted business from time-to-time. It was a small joint and Gerard felt comfortable talking here. The air conditioners were loud enough to muffle the noise of a passing train. He always had a funny feeling eyes were watching him. The damn IRS was relentless. The walls were adorned with pictures of old Confederate generals and charter boat catches.

Bingo read the story carefully trying to determine the point. A Texas billionaire recluse was noteworthy, but how could it interest a man who seemingly had money to burn? He had heard tell that Gerard, known as Big G on the street, could buy life or death with a snap of his fingers. Why would a Texas billionaire interest him? As he read on the answer became clear. It was a bank robbery without a vault. The recluse was cash-rich and seemed to have little interest in money at all. Bingo glanced up and saw black, pig-eyes bearing down on him through a fat, wrinkled forehead.

"What do you think?" he prodded Bingo, hardly controlling his impatience.

"Rich," Bingo replied glancing back at the article. Big G's fingers tapped thump, thump, thump on the table. A waitress

JOURNEY THROUGH THE RIFT

approached, but Gerard waved her off. Bingo finally added. "Rich and isolated. No one else around. Unprotected." He could see he was giving the right answers. Big G smiled. A quarter could slide between the gap in his spacious front teeth and they were stained with cigar smoke and a career of coffee drinking.

"Think of it," Gerard offered turning even more serious. "This guy is a billionaire living secluded. No guards, no guns, no security to speak of. He's an easy target wouldn't you say?"

The boss's eyes flickered a moment for more comment from Bingo. Bingo was a Chicago man experienced, as Big G already knew, in the world of dark deeds and criminal subterfuge. Gerard knew a lot more about Bingo than Bingo realized. He knew his past. At least numerous parts of it. He knew he was born William Devon and had changed identities a few years back to escape authorities. Bingo had spent a couple of years in college as a kid, but was kicked out for cheating. Later, an alleged rape sent him underground hustling for a new name. Big G needed a man with a dark past. They kept secrets. He could control Bingo with this knowledge. He was tired of planning everything himself. The Chronicle story was a golden opportunity. He needed Bingo on his team.

Big G folded his fat fingers over his protruding stomach and focused his liquid eyes on Bingo. Finally, he reached for a cigar, ceremoniously prepared it, lit and puffed, then coughed and blew the blue smoke skyward. Patrons began wandering in for the lunch run and soon Boggy's roared to life. Bingo, again, read slowly trying to absorb the essence of the article under the Big G's watchful eyes. A waitress approached, beer was ordered, and she slinked away sensing that her presence was unwanted at the table. Bingo finally raised his chin and smiled. His thick shoulders lightened and his considerable muscles relaxed. This would take some serious planning so he adjusted his pony tail and slid forward ready to whisper some ideas. Big G leaned in to listen, his lips wrapped around an already soggy cigar.

LORI WAS in heaven as they stood under the sweeping oak trees. A beautiful sorrel was soon tied to the yard gate, saddled and ready. Lori was in a lather to be mounted and off. H.B. appeared around the barn leading two more horses ready for a ride. He had a grin on his face as if handling horses were the joy of his life. One horse was a buckskin, the other a chestnut. They were magnificently proportioned animals, rippling with muscle and obvious good breeding. The horses led obediently eyeing the parked pickup truck and camper. The sorrel swished his tail and jerked his head around at the approach of the other horses. The ranch house and out buildings resembled a western movie set. The lumber used in all construction was roughhewn and authentic. Ethan had a small lumber mill at their Alaskan cabin so he knew a thing or two about rough-hewn lumber.

The ambiance of H.B.'s property openly attempted to capture the spirit of the frontier era. Even his water trough was rough oak and an all wood windmill turned slowly feeding it spurts and trickles of water. Ethan scoured the grounds for a sign of concrete, but found none.

H.B. seemed far more relaxed than at the restaurant. His voice was more settled and somewhat deeper. It had a base tone to it. This was his home turf Ethan guessed. He clearly understood the feeling. He and Lori's remote Alaskan cabin had the same effect on them.

The ride was exhilarating. Riding a well-trained horse through knee-deep grasses was the life Lori longed for. A thundercloud began forming on the horizon, but stayed at bay for the moment. Its cumulus tops building at heights where only jets dare fly. Within the hour, however, the first roll of thunder —akin to the rattle of heavy artillery—announced its presence with ominous warning. Lori stuck to the saddle circling and recircling the hundred acres trying to ignore the storm's approach. Finally, H.B. called the halt and Ethan sighed in relief. Lori would ride through a hurricane. A flash of lightning ripped through the thunderhead and split the thick air. It was high time to head for the barn.

The thunderstorm rumbled closer now as they sat in H.B.'s quaint living room waiting for iced tea. They were both interested by the many artifacts adorning the walls and tables. H.B. had cordially seated them on a cowhide leather couch. The furniture followed the style of the old west—longhorn lamps, antler lighting, cowboy spurs, leggings, and various accoutrements accentuating the life and times of the old west. Nothing modern could be seen except the soft, electrical lighting escaping from hide-covered lamp shades. Rustic end tables, coffee table, rocking chairs, and benches. Highly polished wood with a soft smell of cleanliness and pine polish. The floors were plank and highly glossed and clean. The walls were of knotty pine and spit shiny. Again, Ethan and Lori felt as if they had stepped back into the past. Ethan guessed not a single Chinese nail had been driven in any of the construction, furniture or home.

H.B. delivered the tea glasses and returned to the kitchen momentarily. It was freshly brewed tea, crisp and tasty. He returned carrying a magazine in his hand. He laid it on the coffee table in front of them and smiled. He had a warm smile and Lori smiled back. The interior lighting was soft and dark, but H.B. soon remedied the problem. Bright ceiling lights came on. They quickly saw it was a magazine called Texas Monthly. They hadn't read it in years, living in Alaska, but it was a sacred periodical to Texans.

"Would you mind reading one article in this magazine?" he asked. "I don't want to impose on you, but I'd appreciate it if you would." His voice carried an apology in its tone. Lori picked up a hint of stress, too, in his expression. There was something troubling in the magazine. She could tell that immediately. He quickly added, "It begins on page thirty-six." He wheeled and turned and rode his long stride back to the kitchen and disappeared. They instantly turned to the story. Ethan still wanted to cover some miles before dark so he rushed at first. The intrigue. The startling information within had him rereading it again and ever so slowly. The thunder clapped, but they hardly noticed. Finishing, then rereading it a third time, they sat quietly stunned by the article. Neither spoke. Finally, H.B. returned and sat in a rocker near them. It squeaked on the wood floor as he rocked and looked their way.

"The magazine has most of the information right. It's not purely factual, but close. May I share a problem with you?" He rocked slowly back and forth waiting for their permission. Both heads nodded in unison. Ethan was ill at ease. Lori was captivated.

H.B. told the narrative of his life in soft words and easy mannerisms. It was a tale of a boy, first, then his career as a trauma surgeon and physics professor, and his parent's tragic death in a jet crash--with brief snippets thrown in of his post-career at the estate. It was a man-alone story trapped by wealth, snared by fate, and finally hung by a jury of media-frenzied puppets determined to steal his privacy. He hadn't asked for any of this, but in a sense understood his reclusiveness and vast wealth just added fuel to the flame.

26

"Eighteen years ago, my parents at their untimely deaths, left me roughly $25 billion in assets. It was money passed down through the generations of successful business investments my great grandparents had made and then increased by the wise money management of my grandparents. My parents were highly successful surgeons, my father's specialty being orthopedics. He patented two different models of knee and hip replacement joints and the devices made millions of dollars for them. They continue to earn money to this day. I'm sorry to say, I simply have no use for money, don't like it, and never have. It's the great manipulator of mankind. Washington D.C. is awash with examples of what money can do to a nation and to its people."

H.B. took a deep breath already tired of hearing his own voice, but he was determined to say his piece. He was compelled to tell someone the story.

"I took this wealth to a Houston brokerage and let them run with it. Do what you want with it, I told them. Honestly, I had no interest in it." Pulling a sheet of paper from his shirt pocket, he opened it up for Lori and Ethan to see. He handed it to Ethan. Ethan looked it over and then handed it to Lori. They both were mute at what they saw.

"You see the results of eighteen years of investments. I just passed the $100 billion mark and it's quite shocking to me. I haven't looked at this monthly report in years, but there it is. I have absolutely no interest in it, whatsoever."

"So why are you telling us this story?" Ethan interrupted impatient with the direction of the conversation. It seemed an individual's private business was private and to reveal it was off-character for a man as secretive as H.B. The two somehow didn't fit together. "Lori and I live alone, remote, in a log cabin in Alaska. Off the grid, miles and miles from the nearest road. We have a decent retirement and enjoy our secluded lifestyle as much as you like your secluded lifestyle. If you are unhappy, just leave. With your wealth, you can buy a yacht the size of Dallas and sail the world."

Lori, too, was puzzled by H.B.'s openness. His small ranch was simply beautiful and with a bevy of horses, why would he be unhappy? She couldn't put the pieces together so they made any sense. "Is your desire to leave here?"

"Yes, I need to leave," he said, "but not the way you think. I need someone here to take care of the place. Someone really trustworthy. It needs to be protected and the recent flurry of news about me has complicated things."

Ethan had a sudden desire to get out of the place. Away from this eccentric billionaire's issues and back on the highway bound for Alaska. The word "protected" had taken Ethan aback. Hell, he had fences that looked impenetrable. So, what needed protection? No sane individual could get through. It would take an army tank to break down that monstrosity of a gate. Something was askew, but he couldn't put his finger on it.

To hurry things along and try to get he and Lori out on the road, he offered his solution. "Hire someone to look after the place then. Caretakers are easy to find. Hunting and fishing lodges in Alaska hire caretakers to watch their lodges during the off season. It's a common practice up there. It would work here, too, I'm sure."

Lori added, "H.B., you only met Ethan and me today. We need to be back at our cabin in Alaska as we have several projects we need to complete. We understand, at least to some degree, your frustration in how the news media have treated you. I'm afraid the crazies have taken over, too. We're as old-fashioned as you are in many ways. My advice is for you is to just leave—get away—if that's what you want to do. We have very little to offer, but advise you to simply pull the plug."

H.B. listened and nodded, but his face remained tight and uncertain. He rocked his chair slowly and deliberately. His mind appeared to be a universe away. When he finally spoke, the voice was soft and Lori and Ethan leaned forward straining to hear his words.

"It's the secret I need help with," he said as if a heavy, unbearable weight had suddenly been thrust upon his shoulders. He twisted slightly and stopped the rocker momentarily, placing both hands on his forehead and covering his eyes. The scene touched Lori. His face revealed unspoken pain. He finally dropped his hands and stared at them.

"I want to leave immediately, like the two of you suggested. As a matter of fact, I plan to in the next two or three days, but in a much different way than you might suspect." H.B. paused again and stood and walked a slow, deliberate half circle stopping behind the rocker. "I can't trust a security agency or a firm or a company to do this. I need someone I can trust implicitly. Someone who believes in privacy and the right of an individual to have a secret and who would do all within their power to protect it. An individual with high morals and a willingness to relocate here. I may never return. It could turn into a permanent situation."

"That's a lot to expect of a stranger," Ethan said. "Most people aren't willing to give up their entire life for a job, H.B. It's something Lori and I would never consider, no matter the salary."

"See, that's my problem," H.B. agreed. "It's a lot to ask, but what are the alternatives?"

Lori sat her tea glass down as a clap of thunder crashed outside. "Find one individual first. Trust that individual to find help. Maybe someone they know. Then they could stay here in shifts, like the oil workers on Alaska's North Slope. Two weeks on and two weeks off. With good pay, that could work."

H.B. warmed to the idea immediately. "I have no circle of friends unfortunately. My social contacts are zero. Do you know of someone you might suggest for such a job?"

Lori and Ethan caught each other's eye with the same name flashing in their minds.

"We have a suggestion," Ethan said still looking at Lori. "He's a loner and rugged individualist and probably won't be interested, but trust would never be a problem. He's a rare breed I can tell you that."

"Perfect," H.B. said. "Could you please contact him? I'd like to visit with him right away."

CHAPTER
THREE

He could gut and skin a catfish in three minutes if he pushed it. He had set a trotline in the San Saba River the night before and caught a nice mess of channel cats. Two throw lines, too, had yielded a yellow cat. It was the unsettled weather, stormy evenings that stirred the fish up in the river. Hank Hargrove had developed a tooth for catfish. He should. He lived on the banks of the San Saba midway between Mason and Brady, Texas. His cabin rested off a little caliche road that meandered three miles west of Highway 87. He had no close neighbors and preferred it that way. His was a self-reliant lifestyle. People, he could take or leave. Mostly he left them. He subscribed to two homestead-type magazines, despised the internet and all its trappings, and had a cell phone, but only checked messages once a day. In reality, the speed of modern life had left Hank Hargrove far behind.

He worked part-time and liked it that way. He held to a more leisure philosophy. Tighten the funnel at the bottom and you didn't have to pour so much money into the top. Work could get in the way of hunting and fishing and gardening. He wouldn't let that happen. There wasn't a lazy bone in his body. He just didn't like expending energy in pursuits not to his liking. Hank drove an eighteen-wheeler one week a month delivering sand to various points in Texas, New Mexico, and Colorado. It was a highly specialized sand used by the oil industry. He owned a '98 Dodge truck outright, had a paid-for 700 square foot cabin and fifteen surrounding acres, and held enough guns and ammunition to outfit a small army. He would damn well fight. He had been a Marine in Desert Storm fighting for George H. W. Bush and proud of it. He didn't need any pills or psychological therapy after the war. He fought when the country called. That was his job. Plain and simple.

He fed out two hogs, barrows usually, and butchered them in the fall during deer season. He made his own dried sausage, cured the hams and bacons himself, and tried to put in enough deer jerky to last the year. He allowed himself a six-pack of beer on weekends, but never more. Beer and jerky went well together. Hank killed a half-dozen whitetail deer every year in or out of season. He couldn't tolerate processed meat in any form. Commercial meats had additives and he didn't like additives.

Hank had just turned forty, but looked thirty-five. Dark complexion, heavy dark brow ridges and black eyebrows, he had a beard as dark as Bluto's. If he shaved, which he rarely did, the face looked blue in the beard line. His features reflected some Indian, the genes of which he in fact carried, yet they weren't predominant in his overall appearance. There was no fat on Hank. Muscle, yes, but no fat. He couldn't stand seeing his classmates turn puss-gutted and soft after their high school years. At six foot two and two hundred twenty pounds, his weight had been basically the same since military service. He had played linebacker for the

Brady Bulldogs and was a terror on and off the football field. He liked hitting. He ate it like candy, and no matter the weather, he ran four miles a day to keep trim. He had two acres in garden and what he didn't consume fresh he canned. He had had girl friends in the past, but never anything serious. Most of the opposite sex were too self-absorbed for his taste. He made the perfect poster boy for the lone wolf society.

Hank had met Ethan and Lori Fowler in Alaska on a moose hunting trip. A freak accident had pinned a fellow driver of Brady Transfer Company in a most unfortunate way. Hank was witnessed by several passers-by climbing under the flipped and burning main cab and releasing the injured driver. Seconds later, the cab exploded in fire. For his heroic act of saving the driver, the trucking company rewarded Hank with the hunting trip. Thus, the chance meeting with Ethan and Lori.

A friendship rapidly developed between the mutual remote livers—long distance, of course—Ethan and Lori in Alaska and Hank in Texas. The subsistence lifestyle allowed for a lot of information swapping between the three. None of the three were connected to the electrical grid. Both used wood for heat and cooking. Oil lanterns were the standard issue. Television was ignored for the most part. Radio was the preferred connection to the outside world. Privacy and seclusion the most prized possession.

Hank had paid his dues, however, in a Texas metropolis. After his Marine stint, he worked as a bodyguard for a very long, tiring year in Dallas. He protected a trust-fund playboy with a penchant for sleazy women. The only protection the man ever needed, that Hank could determine, was from STD's and jealous lovers. The man proved to be a hopeless tomcat and a binge spender. His money evaporated within the year and Hank bid him good riddance. Just thinking of the year in Dallas made his head ache.

It was after eight in the evening when he checked his messages. It was Ethan. He'd been expecting them to stop by any day. Hey, can you drive down to Bellville for a day. Call my cell. I'll fill you in.

THEY SPENT the night in their camper in H.B.'s front yard. It was a slightly testy evening. Lori was much less concerned about the day's delay than Ethan. However, it was time to get their garden in on the homestead. Plus, they had plans to add a mud room. Alaska's summers were short. Time was wasting. Driving hard with no delays, Alaska was at least seven days away. The main topic of discussion for the evening was H.B.'s secret, whatever it was. Ethan guessed it was associated with money in some way. A pirate's treasure. Caches of gold coins. Perhaps a huge stash of silver. Something extremely valuable.

"He said he didn't like money, Ethan," Lori said testily as she put away their sandwich makings. "It has nothing to do with money."

"Not paper money, but precious metals. He's the kind of guy who might like the feel of gold. I know I do. He's got a vault full somewhere around here I bet."

"That's not considered a secret, is it?"

"Well, I'd consider millions in gold a pretty deep, dark secret. What else would need that kind of protection? Don't forget these Jurassic Park fences around the place. Still reminds me of a darn prison."

"His secret's not silver or gold or any sort of precious

metals. I'm pretty sure of that," Lori postulated. "It's something entirely different. I just feel it."

"I know what," Ethan said. "He's cloned something. It's in that big attached garage behind the house. Soon to be released on the world."

"Silly, he's a physicist, and retired, too. They don't clone."

"Don't forget what the Texas Monthly article said," he countered. "He was a medical doctor first then turned physicist. Now that's a weird combination. I put my money on cloning."

"Cloning is commonplace now, Ethan. I can't buy that."

"Well, we don't have long to wait. He said he'd show us whatever the darn secret is when Hank arrives. I'm telling you, Lori, these rich folks are strange ducks. I wished you'd just said no to the horseback ride."

Lori's lips tightened, but she couldn't think of a good retort. She was well aware of her weakness in the matter of horses.

Hank arrived at nine the following morning after driving five hours from the Hill Country. He slipped through the chain-wrapped back entrance. Ethan noticed a neighbor lady watching as Hank drove his pickup truck through the narrow gate. The neighbor's house was located about seventy-five yards west of H.B.'s fence line. The woman looked sixtyish and overly curious. Hank got out of his truck after entering and shook hands with Ethan and hugged Lori. Ethan introduced H.B. Hank's eyes took in the high fencing and razor wire. The tall elderly man looked friendly enough. He sure didn't look like a billionaire to Hank, but since when had he noticed what billionaires look like?

A car load of paparazzi had returned and camped out at the main gate, curiously peering within the confines of the estate. H.B.'s house now seemed less important and they entertained themselves taking pictures of the grazing horses. It had grown into a daily routine. H.B. invited his guests in and they sat down at a long, polished wood table. They all shared a round of fresh iced tea.

H.B.'s story, his secret, unfolded in a round-about way. He seemed very reserved, even hesitant, to talk about it at first. He spent several minutes visiting with his guests building his own trust in them again, Lori guessed. Finally, a look of resignation came over his features and he began a long and unusual narrative. It was multi-faceted—sad in some ways— a treatise of loneliness yet complete dedication to a particular scientific goal. Eighteen years, almost a lifetime of rigid discipline with a single objective in mind. Besides, he'd accomplished what he'd set out to do. It was a remarkable success, but success had created another problem. If he used it and did what he wanted, who would guard the home fires? Keep the outside world at bay? Guard the secret for perhaps a lifetime? It would not be a light assignment. He danced around the edges of the secret, but never really gave it. Then he dropped another bombshell. He walked back into his kitchen, entered a closet, and came out carrying a rather heavy cardboard box. He dropped it on the table and opened the lid. It was stacked to the very top with hundred-dollar bills.

"I don't know how much money is in here," he said apologetically as Lori, Ethan, and Hank stared in disbelief at stacks of hundred-dollar bills bulging out. "There's another box back there just as full. I don't want to waste my time counting it, but it's a good many millions of dollars, I think. It's my gift to the person who stays here and protects this estate. Do what you need or want with it. Call it a slush fund if you like. It should come in handy if you have to hire additional help or take any kind of security measures."

The three friends sat stunned by the sight of so much cash. It, indeed, had to be in the millions, many millions it appeared.

H.B. continued, "I have one major account that I intend to sign over, too. It really has all of my assets with the exception of one offshore account that I'll keep for emergency. I want to shed myself of all the funds that I control. I have contacted my accountant and he'll fax paperwork today for signature and the funds will be officially transferred. Do as you wish with this money. I just simply ask for the three of you to help me keep the secret safe. Since the recent media blitz, it may be a larger task than I originally imagined. My gate watchers will eventually leave. Where I'm going, they certainly won't be able to follow."

Hank shifted uncomfortably in his chair. Lori and Ethan's backs stiffened. Just exactly what was this man asking of them? The Fowler's were leaving for Alaska, hopefully today. The piles of cash set everyone's nerves on edge. Storing millions in a kitchen closet? Who would do such an absurd thing? An eccentric billionaire might, and it wasn't in the least comforting. Hank certainly didn't desire nor have any idea what to do with a billionaire's assets. Lori and Ethan had the sudden urge to bolt for the door and seek the safety of their camper. Alarm bells were definitely sounding.

"May I show you my secret?" H.B. intervened noticing his guests' obvious uneasiness.

Ethan fully expected to find the equal of Fort Knox and its vast gold reserves tucked neatly under a vast network of concrete barriers and thick steel doors. They followed H.B. through the kitchen and down a seven-step stairway into a dully lit garage or lab or something. The floors had a smooth concrete finish and shined even in the limited light. The ceiling was tall, perhaps twelve feet in height. The area was large enough to accommodate three or four vehicles. Behind them, from which the light emanated, was an office with a wide entranceway. A very slight humming sound could be detected coming from the office. H.B. had left them there, standing in the middle of the garage/lab, and excused himself. The "may I show you my secret" still ringing in their ears. He peered out the office door and asked them to turn, facing the outside wall. It was a pitch-black wall and then it suddenly changed. A color screen flashed on. It was a very large color screen at that. It was huge and with perfect clarity. In fact, the screen covered the entire back wall. Ethan leaned over and whispered to Lori.

"Wow. This is the best high definition I've ever seen."

The outdoor scene brightened and lightened the garage. In moments, H.B. was beside them.

"Shall we go out?" he casually asked surprising the three.

Go out? The screen theory crashed instantly. This was real live action going on, but how had the door opened? Where were the motors and rollers and tracks that allowed the huge door to open? There had been no sound whatsoever. The grass waved in front of them answering to a soft breeze. Leaves fluttered in the trees.

"Come on. Let's walk outside," H.B. said moving in the direction of the opening.

Lori, Ethan, and Hank still stood firm, stunned not so much by the scene, but by how it had mysteriously appeared. A black, pitch-black opening had suddenly turned into bright daylight—and instantly at that. The inventor of invisible garage doors. There was something odd going on.

Hank stepped first with Ethan and Lori close behind. H.B. walked through the opening, bright sunlight covering him, the wind ruffling his grey hair. Soon the four stood together enjoying a suddenly cooler feel to the air. The grass was browner, too, not as green as in the front of his house.

"Walk with me over here," H.B. said and they followed

another thirty yards to the base of a very sizeable live oak tree
—its outreaching limbs shading a large circle. The air was
remarkably refreshing and cool. Actually invigorating. H.B.
carefully removed a slab of bark to everyone's surprise from
the side of the tree and did something within the recesses of
the tree trunk itself. Shortly he removed a device looking like a
remote control of some kind. They watched in wonder as he
punched in a few numbers and he then returned the device
inside the trunk and carefully replaced the slab of bark.

"Look around you," he said sweeping his long arm in a
rather majestic motion. "I'd like to welcome you to the glorious
year of our Lord, 1875."

With complete shock and absolute awe, H.B.'s visitors
scanned the horizon. It truly was devoid of any signs of civilization. The house, the pickup trucks, the camper, the barn,
the horses were all gone. There were no fences. Nothing. Just
grass and trees and a gentle breeze. Ethan suddenly felt lightheaded. His heart's rhythm was problematic when overly
excited. It was a consistent problem which he usually fought
through. The PVC's (pre-ventricular contractions) kicked in
with a rush. Lori grabbed his arm. Hank the other.

"What's the matter?" H.B. asked surprised. "Is there a
problem?"

"He has bouts with PVC's when he's excited about something," Lori answered. "My heart's about to jump out right
now, too. Let's just give him a minute."

Breathe deeply Lori told Ethan and he dutifully inhaled
slowly. Calm down. Everything's okay. H.B. moved close
checking his skin tone and feeling his pulse.

FOUR

H.B. moved back and forth across the rift several times moving a portable barbeque pit outside, then steaks and trimmings. Hank and Ethan even assisted in moving a picnic table across the timeline. Ethan's PVC's had settled down. The table was stashed in the corner of the lab. Soon oak wood smoke trailed into the blue sky and the mood eased and the tensions dissipated. It was an amazing thing to walk back and forth through time so easily, so effortlessly. Hank, Ethan and Lori fired questions at H.B. and he patiently fielded them. The miracle of the science stupefied them. There was no doubt a scientific genius was at work here. They sat around the picnic table drinking tea, enjoying the cool air, and engaging in a lively discussion.

"I'm sure you've considered all the possibilities this presents?" Hank asked. "Have you ventured over before for any length of time?"

"Yes," H.B. answered. "I spent three weeks in 1878 about a month ago."

The steaks had just been placed on the grill. Every eye

remained on H.B. Surely, he would expand on his answer. Lori's impatience broke the silence.

"Would you mind expanding upon what you've just said, H.B.? Maybe you could fill in a few details?"

H.B. started the story finally. He'd ridden into Old Bellville, circa 1878, just for a visit. It was a small place, maybe four to five hundred strong, at that time in history. The railroad came a couple of years later rapidly swelling the population to over a thousand. He bumped into a couple of young cowboys heading for Fort Worth, needing another hand, and they offered him a job. They were in charge of a hundred-fifty horses and in a hurry. It would be a quick push north then a fast return. They were needed back to help with a cattle drive leaving from Bastrop. No time to waste.

The idea of the venture appealed to H.B., so he signed on. At the time, the news stories about his vast wealth hadn't yet surfaced. Things were still quiet on his estate. He rode back at a gallop, through the rift, grabbing supplies and returned several hours later ready to ride. The drive to Fort Worth had been unremarkable with the exception of one event. A small band of renegades, four in number, tried to commandeer the horses, but they succeeded in dodging their efforts by driving the stock through the night. In a week, they arrived in Fort Worth and delivered the horses to their buyer. Fort Worth was a thriving frontier cowtown of about ten thousand. It was a supply stop for cattle drives heading for Dodge City, Abilene, and points north. This was a booming time for stock drives and the old cow trails were busy. Then the tone of the narrative changed slightly, veered just a bit and his listeners were enthralled. He stayed at a boarding house while in Ft. Worth, Corley's was its name, and the young proprietor was ill—seriously ill with tuberculosis. A most dreaded disease of the day and an unmerciful killer of all it touched. The cure is simple today with

41

modern antibiotics. Trouble is, antibiotics wouldn't be discovered for another seventy-five years. H.B. did not carty antibiotics with him. His heart went out to the young woman. She was already gaunt and pale and her chest rattled with each breath.

During the entire story Lori's mind buzzed with another question. How could a seventy-year-old man hold up to the rigors of the old days? Riding around was one thing, but trail driving was another matter entirely. She'd read a lot about the old trail days and knew it was a tough business. It had to be a trying experience for H.B., testing the edge of his endurance.

H.B. concluded by saying he was heading back to Fort Worth to bring medicine to the young woman. He intended to try and prevent her death. His grandfather had passed away in 1924 of tuberculosis. It was a rather personal disease to him.

Lori couldn't help, but spring the question.

"Did you find your age limiting on the trip?" she asked. He looked to be in outstanding condition, but it was obvious he was an older man. That would have to be a consideration.

"No, not really," he answered. "There's a little trick involved in rift travel. I can adjust the age of the traveler. It was my greatest scientific challenge. It took me numerous years to discover the secret to crossing the rift. It took another five years to perfect the age adjustment, but it works. I didn't want to go back at seventy years-old. So, I was motivated."

"What?" Lori gasped, trying to comprehend what she had just heard.

"Yes," H.B. confirmed. "I went back at thirty years-old."

His listeners were stunned to silence. The science of this was unbelievable. H.B. was an Einstein on steroids!

THE TALE OF H.B.'s secret went on for several more hours, taking up most of the day, but who was keeping time? They were with a man who could control it. Ethan and Lori signed on, so to speak, as associates to the project. They would spell Hank if needed when he wanted some time off. They agreed, reluctantly, to have a large part of H.B.'s fortune signed over to them. It would remain a capital secret. No one need know. Hank agreed to take on the project, too. He would agree to do so with one major stipulation. That he could use the rift himself on occasion. That was easy. H.B. didn't care who used it within the tight circle of his trustees as long as his property was adequately protected. H.B. spent time going over the various settings, the computer servers, the science of his time machine, his rift crosser. Actually, the science was far too complicated to comprehend, but the settings, the adjustments were really quite simple. It could be activated from within the little office or from the oak tree where he'd installed a steel safe, carefully placed within the tree. He had two remotes there, one as a backup just in case. He also had a small cache, an underground cellar, containing a solar panel, a one KW Honda generator, fifty gallons of gas, and various essentials. The remotes' batteries could be charged, but the likelihood of that requirement was miniscule. H.B. had specifically designed and constructed the batteries himself. They were practically indestructible.

Intricacies of the rift were discussed. It could only be used from this one location. So, wherever you went you had to return to his location to return back to modern time. You activated the rift on one side then deactivated it on the other thus removing the screen or opening from view. Various timelines exist in the universe, he explained, thus the capacity existed to use them. The same physical world, but differing realities. The speed of light would be required to time travel in a particular, specific current reality. Not so in crossing his rift. H.B.'s secret opened windows in parallel realities, existing side-by-side with the modern timeline. It was the issue of penetrating various dimensions where only one physical universe existed. The Earth, the very same physical Earth for instance, being occupied by multi-billions of people simultaneously in various realities and in various stages of time. The concept was mind-numbing. Quite surreal.

"What role does God play in all of this?" Lori asked always the good Catholic. "Are we cheating his purpose here? Somehow crossing wires on his plan?"

"As a Christian, that has crossed my mind," H.B. answered thoughtfully. "I would prefer to think he slowly divulged the secret to me for a particular purpose. Perhaps an ultimate plan he has in mind, but think about it. God has the entertainment value, if you want to call it that, of thousands of timelines to choose from. The Bible existed in the 1878 I visited in the same form as today. I bought and carefully read one in Fort Worth. So apparently Christ has visited each rift, spreading the gospel."

"So. we are co-mingling side-by-side without knowing it?" Hank asked. "Can we affect the outcomes, the future of our timeline here by traveling back?"

"No," H.B. said. "That existence is separate from us. Different and yet similar. It's possible you and I might never exist in one particular timeline or another, but the history has evolved very similarly. I noted the 1878 I visited appeared exactly the same developmentally as the 1878 of our timeline. Remember the orchestration of time is being controlled by only the one Conductor. However, how we interact inside it could be dissimilar from one rift to the other."

"I'm on overload," Ethan said throwing up his hands. There was general agreement to his statement. They wandered back into H.B.'s dining room and Lori and Ethan signed paperwork transferring billions under their command.

"We'll extend you a little loan if you need it," Ethan kidded uneasily after the paperwork was faxed. He wasn't so sure that becoming a multi-billionaire was such a good idea.

"Use the money any way you wish," H.B. said smiling. "Just don't let it change who and what you are. I've grown weary of riding herd on it. I still have two off-shore accounts I can use if ever required."

PUFFY EYES WERE a sure sign of a man's extracurricular activities. The lower eyelids drooped slightly leaving a rim openly visible where a small reservoir of tear water collected. The reddish-pink reservoir occasionally needed attention when it dripped down the cheek. They were sad eyes, too. Saddened by the fact that unbridled self-destruction could come in a bottled form: cheap whiskey. He walked with a limp favoring the right side which characteristically changed the angle of his back to a definable "s" shape if you were unlucky enough to be following him. His back pained him, too, as a result of the bearing load gravity placed on him.

He was a middling-sized man structurally yet he carried the normal alcoholic's build: small arms and a robust belly. The belly processed a quart of whiskey daily and sometimes more if his unstable life teetered just a bit. His chronic habit left him debilitated many times when he was needed most. He was a reformed easterner. Distrusted for most part by the citizens of Fort Worth by this very fact. Yet he was by far the best trained and most capable of the eight who called themselves doctors on the banks of the Trinity River. As was his custom, Dr. Jeremy Fields was inebriated, although slightly, when he walked through the doors of Corley's Boarding House. His brain was not yet trapped in a dense fog at 10:00 in the morning. The dense fog settled in later in the day.

Navigating Corley's Boarding House wasn't an easy matter. There was a trick or two the doctor tried evoking, but thus far none of his approaches had worked on Elsa, the overprotective widow woman of the establishment. She was quick to corner the doctor and fired questions faster than he could answer. Plus, she made him nervous with her dark eyes flashing during cross-examination. He normally had two stout belts by this time of the morning, but had held it to one. He was house-calling twice weekly now. The mistress and proprietor of the house had swiftly developed an advanced case of tuberculosis. For some reason her disease was moving rapidly —much more so than most cases the doctor had dealt with. Some referred to it as "galloping consumption." She was an easy victim. Small in stature, thin in build, and made even more vulnerable by the lack of an appetite. She could still walk, but she was unstable. Her breathing was labored and gargling. Her expectorations had become thick and pale pink, the sign that real, live lung tissue was melting away. Damn. Elsa was standing in Jessie Madelyn's doorway, as usual, ready to pounce.

"Well, doctor," she said, her words dripping with sarcasm. "Have you cooked up anything that can get this girl back on her feet? That elixir you left last week scalded her throat. Now she can barely swallow. How do you expect me to get her to eat with a scalded throat? The stuff smells like old whiskey from the bottom of the barrel. I sipped it and it tasted poison to me."

He had brought another bottle of the poison stuck in his coat pocket. In fact, at this moment, he hoped it wasn't showing. "I can lower the strength of it," he said in a weak attempt at his defense. Frankly, in his mind, nothing was going to help the young woman at this point, but Elsa was cocked and loaded for a scrap. Any mention of the disease's fatality would just open him to a scathing attack. He was far too sober to withstand it. He bit his tongue. Elsa didn't appear to be moving away from the door.

"Anything else in that old black bag of yours you tote around? We need action, doctor. I'm damned tired of you dilly-dallying around."

"Elsa," a weak voice called from the background, "don't swear at the doctor. It's not his fault." Jessie Madelyn Corley was gasping for air after the short sentence. Her breathing raspy. Elsa stepped aside and reluctantly let the nervous doctor into Jessie's room. Noticeable sweat beads formed on his forehead as he reached for his stethoscope. He'd bury himself listening to her chest. It was prolonged for a purpose. A brief but needed respite. Elsa stood close by monitoring his every move. There was no change to report. Actually, the breathing appeared more labored. He wouldn't be caught passing on bad news though.

"Appears about the same," he said finally looking for his bag. He spent an unusual amount of time placing the stethoscope just so-so in the worn black leather bag. Visions of slinging back a snort of whiskey clouded his thoughts. He had a small bottle disguised in his bag. Any place short of an open public gathering would do for a shot. His eyelids were weepy and his forehead sweaty. As he rose up with his bag, he reached for his handkerchief to mop up the moisture. The room had grown much hotter and closer in recent moments. Perspiration melted into his clothes. Little dancing stars flashed before his eyes as he fought for composure.

"I'll dilute the tonic," he said grasping for some semblance of authority. "It's the only thing we've got now. None of us have anything else to offer." It was a blanket statement intended to obscure the real truth. The eight practicing doctors of Fort Worth had no real ammunition to shoot at the disease. The disease simply outpaced any known cure. It was a cat and mouse game...and the cat always caught the mouse.

Elsa and Jessie Madelyn both knew the truth. Jessie had buried both her parents within the past year. They had succumbed to the same relentless disease.

CHAPTER

FIVE

I t took five hours to count the cash. Two very large cardboard boxes chock full of hundred and even a few fifty-dollar bills. There was no order to the money. Random stacks mixed and matched. It took a couple of hours just to get some order. The tally came in at just over thirty-five million. Their fingers and eyes were tired and their hands stunk of money. Whew. Lori and Ethan were nervous at the very sight of it. They stowed it back in the closet and drank the stout black coffee Lori had brewed. They sat at the rustic dining table recounting the details of H.B.'s information. The Fowlers wanted to flee the state, H.B. had already fled the century, and Hank wanted to flee back to his quaint cabin on the San Saba River. It had all been a donnybrook, mind-boggling, but Hank was dedicated to protecting H B.'s unique experiment. However, the challenge of protecting the place from hoodlums piqued his interest. Hoodlums at this point were theoretical - stepping back in time was not. Just knowing how to run and operate the rift excited Hank. Not one of them sitting around the table could begin to comprehend the scope of the financial resources that now lay at their disposal. H.B.'s request was simple: protect the premises. Within hours of their discussions, H.B. had left, returning back to 1878 and his mission to help a young woman from the past. They had helped him load his horses, pack after pack, along with several large bags of medical supplies and equipment. With four of his five horses loaded, he then adjusted the settings and walked through the rift and instantly transformed himself into a younger H.B. They all watched with mouths agape. He waved goodbye and rode off as they closed the rift inside the small office.

Lori and Ethan slept in the camper and Hank settled in on the leather couch after nightfall. Hank had hot coffee going at 6:00 when they knocked. "Come in," he hollered. The door had remained unlocked. It was a muggy morning, dew settling in during the night. The Bellville area had its share of muggy mornings. No so in the Hill Country, Hank thought, when he glanced out the door and saw his '98 Dodge covered with sweat. Humidity wasn't his cup of tea, but he'd tolerate it for a while. They sat down talking strategy over coffee and Lori finally got up and searched H.B.'s refrigerator for breakfast doings. There was plenty to eat. She scrambled up a dozen eggs, fried bacon, and toasted bread. There was enough appetite to go around. Not a scrap was left in twenty minutes. Ethan was chomping at the bit to leave town so they went down to H.B.'s laboratory and went over settings and checked their notes on what he'd said. The equipment was turned off totally with the exception of when the rift needed opening. Otherwise, it sat mothballed.

Hank activated it and they spent two hours bouncing back and forth through the rift. It was amazingly easy in fact. You simply dialed in the year, waited an instant, and voila the year appeared through the big screen. Alive and in color. They spent thirty minutes dialing time back until the largest oak tree in the view screen was a mere seedling. That was the glorious year of 1622! In 1621 it had not yet sprouted. They even stepped back through the rift and checked the very soil it would penetrate from. That put the largest live oak in the vicinity at three hundred eighty-seven years old! Wow! What a toy they had. They were like four-year-olds on a new playground. They finally chastised themselves for such foolish play and stopped.

Hank had his horse and trailer in the Hill Country and he needed to tidy up his cabin so it was decided that the Fowlers would stick one final day to allow for the journey. He agreed to leave early in the morning and return the same day. He had a two-horse trailer and figured he'd buy another mount if one could be found on such short notice. An acquaintance in Mason had a nice mare for sale so a brief stop was planned. It was on the way anyway. He grabbed a handful of hundreds out of the hall closet and stuffed them in his pocket. It was a pretty good wad, but he didn't stop to count. The Fowlers smiled. H.B. may have gotten more than he bargained for with Hank roaming around on the back side of time.

Ethan and Lori spent the remainder of the day searching for a security company to come out and set up cameras and monitors around the place. The cameras and monitors were required to be hardened somewhat. In certain locations they needed to be discreet. Being a good ex-Marine Hank had wanted infrared cameras, too. No problem. Tex-Line Security in Houston owned the largest yellow page ad. They agreed to a date and time to meet Hank at the ranch. Would they accept cash? Yes, why, yes they would, without the slightest hesitation.

THE DEPARTURE CAME BEFORE 10:00 in the morning. Hank was outside feeding his horses. He was the owner of a new mare, a four-year-old that Lori wanted to take for a ride. Ethan quickly intervened. Alaska was forty-seven hundred miles away. The gardening season was limited and he always wanted enough spuds in the ground to last the long winter months. June first was the absolute last day to plant. It was eight days away and Alaska was a long way off. Lori capitulated after a couple of long sorrowful looks. Ethan had several thousand hours of logged time in aircraft in Alaska. At one time a friend and he had owned a guide service thus the high time. Lodge work was a time builder and pilot log books got filled. Hank had made it back in the late evening with his horse trailer and the purchase of an aircraft was discussed over coffee. Hank agreed to a tentative schedule of two months on and two weeks off. He desired time at the cabin on the San Saba and a break from the south Texas humidity. Ethan and Lori would fill in and cover the ranch chores for the two weeks.

Ethan refused to fly commercial airliners, hadn't done so in years, so an aircraft purchase appeared imminent. Ethan owned a Piper Super Cub, but it wasn't a long range, any place, any time aircraft. It was a bush plane built for short field take-offs and landings. His plane had tundra tires whose tire size would rival that of a tractor, and it cruised at ninety miles per hour on a good day. It simply wasn't fit for Alaska-Texas commuting.

"I'll get a plane fast enough to get us here in a day," Ethan said as he climbed in the pickup truck. H.B. had imposed this situation on the three of them so the purchase was deemed necessary. He had already called an aircraft broker in Dallas and was stopping by on their way north. A small, fast Cessna Citation would fit the bill. Even a small turbo prop might do. Ethan was so excited he could hardly think of anything else.

"Well, you folks pedal careful on your way up," Hank said hanging on the window. "I'll security up this place and sharpen my knives." There was a dark, black-windowed limo-looking car stopped beside the mammoth gate with a couple of guys wandering around peering through the fence. Hank had been watching them through his binoculars as he groomed and fed his stock. H.B. had reluctantly telephoned his widowed neighbor lady, Katy Kelly, before he left. Her forty acres shared the majority of his west fence. Lori, Ethan and Hank each spent time with her on the phone exchanging pleasantries. Katy, of course, was shocked by H.B.'s call. It had never happened in the eighteen years he'd been her neighbor. H.B. fibbed a bit saying he was bound for a faraway destination and likely wouldn't be back for a long time. Perhaps 1878 could be legitimately referred to as faraway destination though. She jabbered on and on about this and that, but seemed friendly enough. Hank spoke with her the longest requesting her to call should she see any strangers lurking around. She knew the language of a sailor and used it as she vehemently cussed the inept Austin County lawmen.

"Sumbitches just don't give a crap about us out here in the sticks," she fumed in Hank's ear.

"You call me," Hank offered smiling at her response. "Anything unusual you call right away. I'll come a running." The line went blank momentarily as she deciphered the offer.

"Well, uh, thanks, Hank," she said taken aback.

Just before the Fowlers reached the front gate the long black limo crept away apparently in no hurry to leave. Hank rode behind the Fowler's camper on his new mare letting her lengthen her stride to keep up. The gate opened, straining and screeching along. Hank pushed the gate's remote and waved at the Fowlers as they drove away. He looked a moment at the limo and rode their way along the fence line his right arm dangling with a 30-30 Winchester in his grip. He pulled up the mare and stared at the stopped limo not thirty yards away. The front window of the limo was down and the driver flicked a cigarette in the grass along the road. Nothing could be seen inside the dark interior.

"Don't throw your damn cigarettes in the grass," Hank yelled with a strong, challenging voice. "And keep your ass away from the front of the gate."

The limo suddenly sped off spinning its wheels and kicking gravel high in the air. At a safe distance through the dust of their quick getaway the driver raised his hand high and flipped Hank off. Hank nearly sent a shot at the disappearing limo. Why waste a bullet on the bastards, he thought. More than likely, they'll be back.

IT WAS a solid five-hour drive from Bellville to Dallas. They drove Highway 90 to Austin and rode Interstate 35 veering more north than west. The traffic was horrendous. North of Waco it was bumper to bumper to Dallas. Jim Chandler was to meet them at Love Field by his office. Love Field in its heyday was one of the primary training sites for the Army Air Corps during World War II. It was now a private strip serving the suburbs and inner-city travelers wanting to avoid the mayhem of the metroplex and the intricacies of highly controlled air space. They dropped off I-35E and soon found Texas Aircraft

Traders next to a long runway. It was a small building in front of a mammoth hangar. Ethan gazed at the flying activity around him. He was like a kid in a candy store.

Chandler was a tall lanky Texan dressed in the finest western duds. His drawl was deep, his act was all business, seemingly anxious to toss the fish back if they didn't fit his measurements. A camper with Alaskan plates wasn't necessarily the corporate brand he normally dealt with, but he seemed tolerant of Ethan and Lori temporarily interrupting his busy schedule. They could tell he was suffering to be cordial.

"Just what are you looking for?" he asked apparently forgetting their previous conversation. Ethan was about to bolt. They had talked six hours ago. Surely the man had some memory about him.

"Something fast," Ethan said in a snappy voice, "and it needs some range. I don't want to have to refuel the thing every half hour."

"Uh huh, I see," replied Chandler as they started walking back to the hangar. His cell phone rang and he stuck his ear to it. The hangar was expansive with numerous corporate-type jets and turbo props. They all looked fast to Ethan. He wondered how long it would take him to checked out in one. They looked pretty complex and intimidating. Chandler walked away speaking in hushed tones, waving his arms occasionally for emphasis, lighting a cigarette then having a coughing fit. Making some big deal they guessed. There was a smallish biz jet with Cessna written on the side sitting against the back of the hangar and it drew Ethan like a magnet. Lori tagged along watching sparrows fight over nesting sites in the high ceilings above. A splattering of bird crap appeared intermittingly on the concrete floors. The Cessna was a Citation V. It was shiny, sleek, and custom painted a light beige with dark brown and black accents. It looked new, but it was hard to tell as corporate types flew high not choosing to grub around the buckbrush and spruce thickets like Ethan did in his Super Cub. If it wasn't new, it was mighty close to it.

After a good fifteen minutes Chandler finally reappeared and seemed to focus a bit. He lacked stamina for customers wasting his time, however. A quick show and tell should get them out of the way he thought. Hell, he had money to make. This couple had bottom-feeders written all over them.

"Is the Citation for sale?" Ethan growled and Lori grasped his hand to calm him down. Chandler pulled notes out of his shirt pocket and peered at a list as if he might be forced to reveal state secrets. He moved the list in and out trying to get a focus. Ethan enjoyed the comedy. Chandler figured he'd hit them with a high price, scare the hell out of them, and shoo them out. Corporate suit, big Mercedes, and tasseled shoes-- hell he would have rolled out red carpet. He was a lousy actor. Little better than a used car salesman.

"This Citation is a consignment," he finally answered. "Little pricey for you folks I'd guess. Nice low time rig though. Custom executive interior. Long range tanks. Cruise about 390 knots. Fully equipped avionics and latest color radar." He paused from the litany, striking a crooked smile and added, "Gentleman needs $7.5 million." He started walking off when Ethan grabbed his arm.

"Is it open to see?" he asked, rapidly losing patience. Lori steadied him. Chandler looked surprised and disgusted at the same time. What the hell, he thought, and walked around, opened the door extending the automatic stairway. Back to the cell phone for Chandler as Ethan and Lori entered the cabin. Sparkling, luxurious, deep leather furnishings with space to lounge around. Small kitchen, bar combo. Light leather with dark leather mixed. Interior was designed for five or six to travel comfortably. Custom-style layout with even a small desktop, fax and phone hookups. Small, flat screen televisions, two in fact, in recessed cabinets. Stereo complex and sound system. Very nice. Formal yet relaxing. Ethan fell in love with it. Lori was trying out the long sofa.

Eventually Chandler showed up again looking bored with yawning mouth open wide. Several gold crowns sparkled. He was determined to nip these yokels in the bud. Toddy time wasn't too far off.

"Pretty tough to finance one of these babies," he said distracted by a text message coming in. "You'd have to put down a bundle." He couldn't take his eyes off his Apple.

Ethan blurted out. "We'll pay cash. We won't require financing." He delivered the message like a cocky Wall Street veteran. Boy, I could buy this whole damn hangar full if I wanted. "When can you have it delivered to Anchorage, Alaska?"

Chandler reeled a bit, teetered like a man whose wires just got crossed. His mouth drooped open slightly, eyes twisted in a cock-eyed look, chin and lips sagging simultaneously as if the message failed to compute.

He said "Uh," three times before another intelligible word was uttered. "You mean," he stammered and paused again trying to clarify his internal faxes.

"Show me the details in your office. I want to look at the specs, engine and airframe log books. I want to call the owner and tender an offer if all is in order. No intermediaries. He's selling. I'm buying. You'll get your cut when the deal is closed. This is all going to happen in the next hour or I'm driving down the road. No more phone calls, no more text messages, Mr. Chandler. It's time to either shit or get off the pot."

Jim Chandler nearly broke his neck stumbling over his pointy-toed cowboy boots clambering down the jet stairway.

CHAPTER
SIX

What took Ethan and Lori five hours to cover the span of distance, would take H.B. four to five days or more to cross. His horses were heavy laden and needed time to break to the trail. They were city horses in a sense not used to the inconveniences of hard travel and broken terrain. Native grasses would replace the hybrid coastal they were used to grazing. Less protein, less carbohydrates, tougher to chew. Water was uncertain at times. Some of it brackish. Some of it murky. Some of it smelly. Stickers abounded. Mesquite thorns frequent. Weather unpredictable. Ticks could wheedle in if you lolled too long on the ground. Bot flies, stinging flies, horse flies, prickly pear galore – the list of sharp and stinging things went on and on. Everything seemed tougher here, more ready to challenge, willing to advance uninvited, hopeful to gain a reward or seek revenge.

In his previous short trip to Fort Worth a few weeks earlier, H.B. had learned a most valuable lesson: rough customers abounded. The lawless far outnumbered the men who wore badges. Frankly, there just wasn't much law to be found, and those few stayed busy fighting and keeping the peace in fractious, scattered towns. The Texas Rangers, the best-known peace keepers around, were mainly in west Texas stamping out the last renegade elements of various Indian tribes too hostile to settle on a reservation. When they weren't fighting them, they had their hands full with hardened types like John Wesley Hardin and scores of others like him. The war had allowed an open season for hard cases to penetrate Texas' vast regions. Most able-bodied men capable of returning fire had signed on to fight the blue coats. While the men were away fighting, the outlaws and Indians ran roughshod over the state. It was taking time to get civilization civilized again.

The first day panned out beautiful. Since leaving Lori, Ethan, and Hank behind he'd traveled leisurely, keeping the pace slow. It was warm, humid, and still. Even the bug-herds seemed subdued. Mockingbirds flitted through the trees talking their varied language. He had traveled an easy thirty miles and seen not another soul. He cut the trail of a couple of horses earlier in the day, but they appeared to be moving westward. His route would be, for the most part, north. He had ordered fifty rings of dried sausage from Bastrop before leaving the modern era and nooned on a plateau. The sausage was tasty and he easily devoured half a ring. He released and dropped the heavy packs and staked the horses on fifty-foot ropes near a clear running creek. They frolicked a bit, drank deeply, snorted and whinnied at each other, and munched the abundance of spring grasses. Reattaching the heavy packs would take a while, but he wanted to give his animals a rest. He would push them later in the day.

After the brief respite, the afternoon passed without incident. Light clouds gathered to the west, assembled a puffy top or two, and fizzled out without even a single lightening flash. The humidity lessened some as the miles north progressed. As evening approached a touch of cool air started settling in. H.B. was about to pick a campsite when he rode around a low bluff and spotted a cabin, a small barn, and log fencing in the distance. He could see a few acres in cultivation. A small farm. He had no intention of startling the occupants. He was a few hundred yards away when he spotted a man carrying a bucket from the barn. The man stopped, looked his way, and raised his hand in a friendly gesture. H.B. waved back and moved forward. The man waited putting the bucket down.

"Howdy," the man said rubbing his chin and extending his hand as H.B. dismounted. He was as thin as a wire. His clothes appeared well-worn and tattered, but reasonably clean. The shirt homespun. He wore a beard, graying somewhat, and his hair was short cropped. On top of his head sat an aged hat.

"Be glad to have you stay to supper. Wife's a good cook, too. Guess I've got a tape worm 'cause I never get no fatter no matter the vittles."

"Why, thanks," H.B. said. "I'd hate to be trouble for you. You can see I'm well equipped for camping." The farmer had been eying the pack horses.

"Well, you don't travel light do ya?" the farmer said good-naturedly. "My name's Rip, Rip Carter. My wife Jen is in the house cooking supper. Glad for some company. We don't get much by way of entertainment out here."

Rip helped H.B. unload the packs, settle the horses in, and stake them out. There was a spring, fresh and clear, forming a pool near the house and grass abounded there. The farmer's mule brayed and kicked up his heels at the excitement. H.B.'s horses pricked their ears at the unfamiliar call. The gold rim of the sun started dipping below the skyline. An owl hooted in the distance. H.B. dug into his saddle bags and fetched two rings of dried sausage to supplement the supper.

In contrast to Rip, Jen Carter was amply built – more in the pioneer female tradition. Where her husband lacked flesh, she appeared to have muscle. She was medium framed, but not overly tall. Her hands bore the appearance of a worker's hands – thick and strong. She had warm, intelligent eyes and a wide smile. The small cabin had a rough plank floor and was well-appointed and tidy. A pot-bellied stove stood on one end heating a coffee pot. She baked corn bread in cast iron skillets two same-sized ones sealed together providing an oven. There was buttermilk or fresh milk. H.B. loved buttermilk. Rip preferred fresh. The corn bread was supplemented with fried chicken, tasty and tender. The Carter's enjoyed the added dried sausage.

Jen was a talker. She talked non-stop chewing around the words and giving approval or disapproval depending on the input from the men. She, too, was highly opinionated. Rip lit two oil lanterns and shadows flashed about the cabin errati-cally. They had been here, at this location, for two years having emigrated from Tennessee. Jen liked it lonely, away from civi-lization. Rip liked town when he could find one. An irony, H.B. thought. The quieter one liked town, the talker liked the coun-try. She was the farmer, too. She worked the mule team. Rip did most of the building, fences and barn and the house. She was a sage advisor in all matters pertaining to construction, however, according to Rip. Rip stayed out of her way in regards to farming.

"We have a good division of labor," Jen said gnawing on a chicken bone. She finally cracked it and sucked out the marrow, smacking her lips. Her eyes flashed mischievously sparkling like a prankster's ready to pounce.

"Where you headin?" she asked after the table was cleared and wiped.

"Fort Worth," H.B. answered sipping her thick coffee. He eyed the mixture with distrust as the contents quivered in his tin cup. She seemed to be expecting more than a two-word answer. H.B. held his tongue. Jen was born to push and probe.

"You've got business there, huh?" she said hoping for a grain of fodder to chew on. Rip seemed happy to listen and puff on an old corn cob pipe. H.B. might be good for some entertainment yet. Forthcoming or not, his wife wouldn't let a short answer lie, Rip guessed.

A MISERABLE WEEK of losses had gotten the ball rolling. He had gotten roaring drunk at a party and the transgression had cost him dearly. He promptly lost a hundred thousand dollars on a single baseball game. He usually took Atlanta, but somehow found himself, in his inebriated state, riding on the Mets. Well, the Mets weren't a good ride and he promptly dumped the hundred grand. When he sobered up the next morning, he tallied the week's loses and found himself down almost three hundred thousand. He could barely see the figures through his puffy, hung-over, eyes. His head throbbed. His hands shook as he re-tallied and double checked and confirmed the bad news. Then to make matters worse, two of his brothels had been raided in the past week and closed down – the two most profitable ones at that. One of his girls shaken up over being arrested had slipped his name to the authorities so he had an investigator of some kind nosing around. Had already called him twice. Nasty, cocky little pig with an attitude.

Gerard Fremont, Big G, the big cheese in southwest Louisiana was hurting. His once fat bank account was down to its bottom dollar. To top it all off, the IRS audit had gone sour. They wanted another hundred thousand in back taxes on supposed unreported income. Apparently, his sleazy accountant had miscounted the beans. The IRS demanded immediate payment. Their penalties were horrendous and stacking up. He needed money, a lot of money and he needed it fast. He, too, had payroll to make. It had been a long time since he'd felt so desperate. His dirty little empire was crumbling. He dialed Bingo Burns. They needed to talk, he said. Come to my office.

It was Bingo and a big goon named Danny who had taken Gerard's limo at his urging and driven to H.B.'s hidden estate just out of Bellville. It was Danny, a muscle-bound bruiser, who had flipped off Hank as they raced off. Except for this one redneck they'd seen, the place was a piece of cake they dutifully reported. No sweat getting in and out. The fence was penetrable. Too remote to draw attention. The cowboy riding fence looked stupid on his nag trying to act like the Lone Ranger. No problem handling him.

Big G's black eyes danced with delight at the news. Grab the bastard, he said, and bring him to me. Blindfolded, gagged, and bound. Go through the fence, grab the spoiled, wealthy bastard soon as you can. Shoot the damn cowboy if you want, but don't hurt the billionaire. Who do you want to take?

"Danny, me, and one more. I like Little Eddie. He's a cool customer. I'll take him as the third man." Bingo's batteries were charged. He was aching for action. How often do you get to lay hands on a billionaire? Plus, the kidnapping could carry a huge payday. Big G had agreed to pay Bingo a bundle for the delivery.

"Use your brains," Big G cautioned as they left to make final plans. His black eyes flashed in his fat, wrinkled forehead. "This one had better be done right."

CHAPTER

SEVEN

Hank had a blue-tick hound named T-Bone. He liked horses as much as Hank did and usually followed them around lying in the grass, loitering close by, watching them graze. He wasn't a barker by nature, but would give a howl if something alerted him. The van stopping at the gate got a single, low howl. It was Tex-Line Security and Hank punched the open button. They were thirty minutes early, but that suited Hank. He was anxious to get some work done.

Bill and Bob appeared competent types, asking the right questions, looking carefully over the lay of the land. The hundred acres was rectangular. Typical Texas land plot. H.B.'s home was located on the back side or west of center of the property line, more or less in the middle of the land on the north and south bearing lines. Two sides, south and east bordered Coushatta Road, west was Katy Kelly's place, and north was a leased cattle pasture.

Night lighting options were discussed, but rejected by Hank. Infrared cameras and other camera types and listening locations were laid out and approved. Motion detectors, too, were acceptable. Hank wanted it right. No expense to be spared. When can it be done? Hank wasn't interested in sitting at a computer console all day watching for would-be trespassers. He wanted an alert system that discriminated the real from the imagined. He wanted it sophisticated yet serviceable. No rinky-dink project. He wanted a goon alert that functioned, but didn't tie you down.

Hank also wanted the work completed quickly. The Bill and Bob show agreed to start the preliminaries in twenty-four hours with completion within a week, possibly ten days. The completion date was subject to any unforeseen complications that might arise. They would have to overnight different elements of the equipment. Estimates ranged in the two-hundred-thousand-dollar range. No matter. He wanted the stuff hardened, too.

"I don't want some joker with a twenty-two-rifle plunking and knocking out the detectors. I want backups. I want backups to the backups."

Bill and Bob stood engrossed counting their cash, mentally, staring at the largest job they'd ever landed for the company. Their boss would turn a back flip. They were hoping for bonuses. Maybe even a raise. Hank suggested delivering the system on time would earn a tip from him, too. They headed out with a $20,000 cash deposit in their hot little hands. Hank had insisted on calling the number listed on the receipt to confirm the deposit.

"I trust everybody," Hank said while dialing the phone. "After they earn my trust."

THE VERY SAME evening after Bill and Bob sped away for Houston, Katy telephoned Hank excited about two men who were standing near their shared fence line. They were parked beside the road. She had a nervous tone to her voice. The pitch was up an octave.

"They're not on my property, not quite. They're also not on yours. Standing out close to the road. They drove up in a pickup truck – bright red. I watched them at first with binoculars, but it's getting too dark. I've been thinking about letting my two Doberman's out. They've been antsy, my dogs have been. Rarin' to bite someone in the ass."

"Hold the dogs, Katy. I'll check. I'll call you back when I get in. They may be just goofing off, locals messin' around."

"Call any time until eleven," she added. "I hit the sack after the news."

Hank wished the security systems were in. In less than a minute he'd have visuals, audio, and a tracking system up to monitor their movements. No wonder H.B. wanted to leave, he thought. Things appeared to be picking up around the estate.

He grabbed his infrared goggles, standard Marine nighttime issue, his military knife, AR 15 carbine and two 20-round clips. He also strapped to his thigh a Glock 40 caliber automatic. He put a roll of grey tape in a waist pack and snapped it on. An LED headlight also went in. He waited twenty minutes until slap dark and stepped out, melting into the night. It was pitch black. He liked it that way.

THE TIGER HAD HAD one of his most profitable months ever. The last three homes they'd hit were treasure troves. Valuables laying around unprotected. The last house produced more jewelry than he'd ever handled. One diamond bracelet alone brought five grand on the black market. He and his top two thugs had grossed over a twenty thousand in the past month. Cash money. What treasures might a billionaire's house have? He grew dizzy thinking about it. He wasn't above trying to kidnap the man, but casing his pad, seeing what he had, was the main priority. That's why he and Jose had come out – to look it over. Maybe go through the fence and window peep a bit. Check things out. Get familiar with the layout. He had read about the formidable fence so they purchased chain cutters. He and Jose would open the fence, close it neatly, and no one would be the wiser. Piece of cake. The crickets were singing as the night settled in. No traffic at all. It was a quiet Monday night. Everyone was home watching television.

"Is the truck okay?" Jose asked in his thick Mexican accent. Jose had been in the U. S. for five years illegally and liking it. Highly profitable place to reside. He didn't even carry a billfold. No need to. He didn't have anything with his picture on it. He was twenty-five and had never left a trail that anyone could follow. He was smart, street smart, wise to the ways of survival. He was the only one in Tiger's employ who hadn't served time. His switchblade was the only friend he trusted. Its edge was always razor sharp. He spent hours keeping the blade that way. He liked Tiger well enough, but it was a business association. Feelings and friendships could get in the way of business.

A friend of Hank's in the Hill Country always had fun making explosives for special occasions. They were illegal, of course, lots of fun things were illegal. They reminded Hank of the old-fashioned M-80's and cherry bomb explosives manufactured in the 1950's only nastier. Their manufacture halted after children lost fingers and hands through misuse. Bert

White made the explosives and passed them around to friends. He was an older gent living on the outskirts of the tiny settlement of Pontotoc, thirty miles from Hank's cabin. He usually had a box full and they could be had for the asking. His trademark was the fuse in the center, just like the old M-80's, but his did more than just pop. They went boom! His largest so-called firecracker would rattle windows a mile off. Hank estimated its yield at somewhere close to a third stick of dynamite. He smiled to himself as he crept in the darkness remembering ol' Bert setting one off, the big whoppin' mama he called it, in Hank's back yard one fourth of July eve. Bert had grabbed Hank's arm and dragged him fifty yards before they stopped to watch. The explosion blew a three-foot diameter hole in Hank's yard and sent debris raining down all over the place. These were serious explosives. Hank had three of the larger variety with him, tucked away, as he headed to his rendezvous. They were widow-makers if exploded in close proximity to the victim. The concussion of the explosion alone would burst eardrums. They weren't grenade-grade, but close to it.

Hank crept to the chained west side gate bordering Katy's place. He quietly unlocked it, wrapped the chain back and relocked it. It made a light click, but likely undetectable at a distance. He was still at least two hundred or more yards north of the road. A half mile away he could hear a coyote yipping, but it was quiet at Katy's place. He could vaguely see her window lights. He wondered if Katy was watching. It was one of those magnificent nights where the Milky Way painted itself majestically in the sky. No extraneous light shone from any direction. Just darkness. A hand in front of the face would be difficult to see.

He moved slowly on the carpet of grass, stealthily forward, steady and sure of his steps. Hank placed each foot carefully, sensed for objects that might create sound, then steadily applied his full body weight before he moved. He had slipped a heavy pair of wool socks over his boots before he left. Sound would be muffled. He could move very close and they'd never hear him. He wanted to hear conversation. Listen to what the goons were thinking and planning. Maybe get an idea of their objectives.

In less than ten minutes, he could easily detect voices. Hispanic. One voice had a thicker accent than the other. The conversation was still muffled somewhat. They were speaking in low tones. A flash occurred. A cigarette was lit. More arguing and discussion. He wondered at their stupidity of talking in low tones yet engaging the flash of a cigarette lighter. The glow of the cigarette moved erratically. Hank was now less than a hundred feet away doing the Marine crawl in the bar ditch grasses. Another bigger flash, but it was just a momentary one came from behind Hank. He lay lower in the bar ditch, hunkering in the grass, watching. Then another brief flash and the sound of a motor. It was a vehicle approaching down the gravel road, apparently at high speed. The lights now flashed regularly against the shiny chrome bumper of the Hispanics red GMC pickup truck. Hank could hear the road gravel clinking under the vehicle as it approached. The two men ran from beside the fence back to the front of their truck and stood, frozen, waiting for its passage. He heard swear words over the din of the racing car. Gravel clinked loudly. The shrill scream of a girl filled the background. Sounded like a teen frantic with the speed of her driver. Then Hank heard the brakes lock and the vehicle lights go erratic. Followed by another high-pitched scream. The car careened out of control sliding sideways as dust and gravel engulfed it. A metal-to-metal explosion followed. Vehicle hubcaps rattled and clanged. Hank was instantly covered with silt and dust. Then groans and moans. Guttural, incoherent noises of pain. The crickets fell silent in the aftermath. A heavy dust hung like fog over the scene.

Hank raised up and turned on his headlight. He moved towards the moans. The smells of oil, gasoline, and rubber permeated the air. His headlight hardly penetrated the dust. Finally, he bumped into something metal. There was moaning within, but the doors were jammed as he tried opening them. A fire seemed possible as the stench of gasoline filled his nostrils. He couldn't see in the interior of the car as the result of the dust cloud. Then he remembered he'd brought his cell phone. He quickly turned it on and waited impatiently for it to activate. The moaning in the car interior had stopped. He dialed 911. The operator answering the call babbled on asking nonsense questions. Finally, in frustration he hung up and dialed Katy.

"This is Hank. Recall 911, Katy. Make sure someone gets out here fast. I guess you heard the wreck. I already called, but some idiot answered. Get ambulances here fast. Thanks, Katy."

IT WAS A VERY LONG thirty minutes before the first flashing lights approached the accident. Hank had found the boy and girl, pinned in twisted metal. The boy wasn't breathing, the girl was unconscious, but alive. Her limbs, arms and legs appeared malformed so she had serious fractures. Hank found the two Hispanics pinned beneath their truck, one definitely dead as the truck's front tire rested squarely on his chest. The other drifting in and out of consciousness. Hank had tried moving him from beneath the truck, but his screaming stopped the attempt. Katy arrived carrying a flashlight and out of breath. She cussed vehemently the late arriving authorities.

"It's a damn wonder they can find us," she said openly frustrated as flashing lights approached. "From their response time you'd think we lived fifty miles from town."

The dust had dissipated and the carnage nauseated her to the point of vomiting. A fire truck was the first arriver. The EMS vehicle close behind. They needed cutting equipment for the teens, Jaws of Life, so that took another half hour to arrive. The Hispanic man was finally removed from under the truck. He flung Mexican curse words at anyone who'd listen. He was critically injured, though, one leg dangling far to the side and severe lacerations. They finally jacked the truck up to release his deceased companion. A justice of the peace came next. Then, at last, a county deputy appeared with lights flashing. The deputy was roly-poly and moved slowly. He appeared to be put out by the whole event. The funeral home chariot arrived and duly body-bagged and loaded the boy and the Hispanic. Katy gave one and all an earful. She tore into the deputy with a vengeance. The heavy deputy tried escaping. Katy pinned him against his patrol car shaking her finger in his face. Hank knew enough to let Katy go. The deputy finally escaped opening his patrol car door.

"You damn useless doughnut cruncher," she yelled as he rolled up the window.

The deputy seemed disinterested in interviewing witnesses. Hank thought that highly irregular, but it wasn't his business. It may have been Katy's presence that ground the investigation to a halt.

Wreckers appeared lastly, moving the vehicles and Hank and Katy finally walked back down the fence line towards her house. It had been a long, tiring evening. Katy was still hot about the late arrivers.

"It's a wonder you didn't get hit, Hank," she said as they stood on her porch. "You were just plain lucky as close as you were. Were the Mexicans up to anything funny?"

"Likely," Hank said honestly. "They were carrying chain cutters. They never got to use them before the teens arrived."

IT WOULD DEPEND on how morbidly sadistic someone's humor may run, but it could be said, regardless, that "el tigre" Tiger Martinez had a funny thing happen on his way to work. He was lying there, face up, stone dead on a cold slab at the morgue naked as a jay bird. Rigor mortis was setting in, a deep indention in the middle of his chest, tire treads clearly visible. His cohorts in crime awaiting instructions in Houston would never hear from Tiger this night or ever again. The dwellers of Houston's suburbs could breathe a sigh of relief if they only knew the thieving would slow down, if only temporarily, with Tiger out of the way.

Beside him lay a seventeen-year-old high school senior from Bellville. He had been a good quarter miler for the track team and a quarterback, the starter in fact, for the Bellville Tigers football team. His only sin for the evening was driving eight-five miles an hour on a thirty-five mile an hour rural gravel road, and that he wasn't watching the road. His dad had just purchased and given him, two weeks earlier, the new Ford Mustang destroyed in the accident. It was his graduation present, his college car. He had been accepted at the University of Texas in Austin.

Jose, critically injured, would present quite a mystery and

challenge as the Bellville Memorial Hospital staff tried to ascertain his identity as he fought them off when they attempted to cut away his clothes. He slung curse words, Spanish of course, at any one coming near. Finally, a brave nurse plugged him with a needle filled with a strong sedative and he finally faded away. He was far too critical, as was the injured teenage girl, to be handled at Bellville. A medivac chopper landed at the hospital helipad within the hour and hauled both patients to a trauma center on the outskirts of Houston. Jose would die in surgery shortly after midnight. His internal injuries massive. The sixteen-year-old girl, a junior favorite of her class at Bellville, would survive, but with multiple fractures and severe lacerations. Her most severe injury was a partially crushed skull. Luckily, her brain damage would prove to be temporary, but she would forever carry a titanium plate in memory of the event.

IT WAS WELL after midnight when Hank lay down on H.B.'s long, leather couch. He still felt a rank stranger in the house. He wished, for the hundredth time that day, that he was neatly tucked away at his little cabin, tending his garden, on the banks of the San Saba River. He rubbed T-Bone's neck gently, thinking about the events of the past evening. It had been a sobering experience. He had seriously considered the idea of spinning back time, which he knew he could do, and remake – change the outcome of events just passed. He'd move time back to an hour before Katy called and take a walk down the road and scare off the goons before they had a chance to cause trouble. However, H.B. had implicitly warned them about messing with the immediate present timeline, changing the hands of fate.

T-Bone finally relaxed and laid down beside the couch sighing his patented sigh. The house was still. He could faintly hear the crickets singing outside. He forced his eyes closed and tried to blot out the blood and gore he'd seen. He tried to justify, somewhat unsuccessfully, not changing the outcome of the immediate past events. Sometime after 3:00 in the morning, after tossing and turning, he fell into a restless sleep. It was coming daylight when he heard T-Bone at the door, scratching, wanting out. He stumbled into the kitchen and put on a pot of coffee. He added an extra tablespoon to the pot. Hank was in need of caffeine.

CHAPTER
EIGHT

H.B. left the Carter cabin at dawn. He thanked them for their generous hospitality. He intended to push hard on his second day out, but his plans fell flat. Not two hours into the morning, Pretty Boy, his sorrel gelding picked up a limp...a very noticeable limp. H.B. stopped and examined his right fore-leg and hoof carefully and could see no visible injury, but the limp remained and the pace slowed. Pretty Boy's pack was redistributed.

He stopped at noon, reexamined the leg, and guessed them only ten miles from the Carter cabin. The terrain was getting noticeably rockier. H.B. kept at a slow walk, but was forced to stop and wrap Pretty Boy's leg with vet wrap. He kept up, but struggled doing so. It was early afternoon when he decided to pull up and give the hoof and leg another thorough going over. Sure enough, earlier unseen, in the frog itself was lodged a mesquite thorn. It was just beginning to fester. H.B. pulled the thorn allowing it to drain. It was the beginnings of an infection. A shot of antibiotics and he staked the gelding out. Rest would be the best medicine.

He built a hat-sized campfire and watched the staked horses nibble grasses and the evening sun fall out of the sky. By a generous allowance, he had traveled no more than fifteen miles. It irked him to have such a slow start. The late spring evening was filled with chatter. Squawking, tooting, honking, screeching, singing, howling – you name it, the sound was there. Life was out and on the move celebrating the close of day. The horses joined the teeming chorus with snorts and stamping hooves. A coyote yipped in the distance. The mosquitoes started circling prompting H.B. to set up his tent cot. It was a popular contraption for modern campers incorporating a cot system and a tent in one. Nicely waterproof and it kept the bugs and snakes at bay and had legs to ward off ground water. It was surprisingly comfortable. He sat on a log, slapping occasionally, until full darkness settled in. A final check of the horses. Horse thieves were legendary in Texas. His mare Patty Cake was a good alarm. She never failed to notify him of unwelcome company. He put his automatic 9mm pistol inside the tent, two clips extra, and zipped it up. He lay awake listening for an hour and fell asleep as the cool finally settled in.

Two cups of coffee revived him just a bit. Hank had a hunch about something and before the security outfit arrived, he wanted to check it out. He left the ranch and drove quickly to Bellville finding a Wal-Mart open on the west side of town. It was one of those small town stores, the mini-variety. He walked through the hardware section and found the chain cutters. The loudspeakers were blaring an associates' meeting was pending. Employees hustled about swapping the latest gossip. When he drove back through Bellville's town square, he stopped, impulsively at Mama's Square Café and ordered ham and eggs. Hank couldn't remember the last meal he'd eaten. The regulars were there, old timers talking in subdued tones. The table next to him carried the latest news on the evenings' accident. The other Mexican had died. The girl appeared to be making it, but had skull fractures. The town was in shock over the young man's death. The locals considered him an outstanding kid. Why was he driving at such high speed?

He felt better after food in the gullet. A few eyes watched him as he paid out, but for the most part, they were deep in their own world. He sped back to H.B.'s watching the time. He was back before nine. Tex-Line security was due at ten. Hank stopped after the mammoth gate closed and walked to the fence, chain cutters in hand. The two Hispanics had been at the fence, he distinctly remembered, and it appeared their chain cutters may have malfunctioned.

The chain link fencing H.B. had built around his estate was double-layered and thick in diameter. He carefully placed his new cutter on a single strand of the chain link and put his weight into it. He applied full strength. Not a dent. Not even a scratch. This was far from the typical chain link fencing. Some kind of special metal alloy. Hank walked back to the Dodge and grabbed a shovel. If the thugs couldn't cut through it, could they tunnel under it? The first dig answered that question. A heavy concrete footing followed the fence line. Hank dug over three feet deep never finding the bottom of the concrete slab. It, too, was four feet wide. Tons of concrete had been required to secure the fencing down at the base. Very impressive. It would prove very difficult to dig under. Perhaps a backhoe or a bulldozer could do the job. What would be their next alternative? Hank pondered a moment. Parachuting. Sure thing. The goons could drop in by parachute or perhaps lease a chopper. Other than that, penetrating the fence perimeter would not prove easy. Someone was coming, though, Hank could feel it. The question was when and how many?

THE BILL and Bob act arrived at 10:30, thirty minutes behind schedule, with bad news. The news cranked Hank up.

"You boys said seven to ten days. I'm holding you to that."

"We're having trouble finding a dirt contractor on short notice. We have to sub it out. We normally do buildings, homes, and apartments. Open land is different. It's a more complicated project," Bob minced his words with a sheepish look. Bill avoided eye contact with Hank.

"You boys just left with twenty grand cash in your hands. I expect quick action or I want a refund."

"We can't project all the issues. Our boss is working hard to pull it off. Surveillance equipment at the level of sophistication you want is difficult to get. He's ordering most of it from Italy. They're the only ones we know that sell a hardened variety. The same company's responsible for the Vatican's security."

"Here's what we'll do," Hank said with a stern eye. "I want your signatures on a guarantee that all work will be completed fourteen days from today. That's even more time than originally discussed. If that's not satisfactory, I'd like a full refund."

That stunned the boys. Bill walked away punching numbers on the cell phone. He spoke with animation. Apparently, the boss didn't like the idea of the refund. Hank wanted to talk to him. Bill handed the phone over quickly and departed. He didn't want to hear the carnage.

Hank snapped on the phone. "I don't know and don't care how you do this project, but I want a definite time established for its completion. I want your whole team out here, if that's what it takes. I was led to believe there would be no problem getting it done on time. Now I'm getting the run around. I want state-of-the-art equipment and I want it correctly installed. How is that request a problem?" Bill and Bob were taking a walk clearly avoiding the squabble.

Tex-Line's owner stuttered and stammered, even mumbled a bit, and finally started explaining the availability and or lack of availability of certain monitors and equipage. U. S. manufactures had equipment, but most were inferior to foreign design. Italy had the best. Italy's supplier was slow, at times, and it presented problems. Plus, it was very expensive. Governments, not individuals, usually purchased the stuff and the process was a nightmare to get shipped. Italians were never in a hurry which presented another huge problem. They, too, required cash up front before shipping. The cash deposit was nice, but he needed more to get the ball rolling. Hadn't Bill and Bob mentioned a larger deposit was needed to complete the transaction? In a nutshell, the Italians were tough dealers. However, if Hank wanted the best, they were the go-to source. He finally pleaded for Hank's patience.

Hank weakened, settled down, listening to the frustration behind the voice. The man appeared to be making honest efforts to please. "How do we facilitate this?" Hank finally asked.

"We need up front money," the owner said. "Security businesses aren't corporations or governments. We're fairly small operators and fronting money is risky business. We can provide the payment and out-of-country businesses deposit your payment and ship in their own good time. Getting what you pay for is the real issue."

"Do you have a passport?" Hank asked catching the owner off guard. There was a long pause on the line.

A tentative, "yes," was the answer.

"How about I charter you a jet? You fly over and get what you need and fly it directly back. Let's cut to the chase. I'll give you three hundred grand more up front. This is strictly a business trip, but plan an overnight. I'll arrange a nice hotel, y'all eat some famous Italian cuisine, bring the wife and kids, and get back here in a day or two with as much equipment as possible. How does that sound?"

There was another pause. Hank could hear a clicking sound in the background, like a wall clock ticking off seconds. He could hear the owner breathing.

"I'll call you back with an answer in ten minutes. My wife's a schoolteacher. No children. I'll have to try and get her out of class. Is that alright?"

"That's fine. I'd like you to leave as soon as possible."

A semi-retired Boeing 727 freight hauler, chartered from Houston's Hobby Airport, left for Italy two days later. It wasn't particularly licensed to haul passengers, but the owner, offered a nice bonus, conveniently disregarded the requirement. Its destination was Milan, Italy, the home of Guissepe Electronics, the surveillance supplier for the Pope himself. Mr. and Mrs. Henry Pratt were on board. He was the owner of Tex-Line Securities. His wife was a third grade public school teacher in Houston. They had never flown across the Atlantic, never been near Europe, much less flown in a special chartered jet. He couldn't imagine the cost of such an adventure. He really felt like a big shot as the jet lumbered off the runway. Plus, Hank had secured all accommodations in a luxury hotel. They were duly impressed.

CHAPTER

NINE

The trip to Alaska was always interesting, but especially so in late spring. You got to witness spring running backwards the further north you drove. They pounded the road twelve hours a day, at least, sometimes pushing it to fourteen. Ethan was anxious to find an instructor in Anchorage who could check him out in the Citation. He had haggled the purchase price down to 7.1 million, not bad from an asking price of 7.5. A large Dallas law firm owned the jet and were anxious to sell. They'd just purchased a new, fancy, faster model. This Gulfstream bizjet priced in between 30-45 million depending on the model. Ethan had a hard time imagining how anything could be nicer than the Citation V. It would require only one refueling stop between Anchorage and Texas. Likely Calgary or Edmonton, Alberta, would be the stop. Billings, Montana, would work, too. He had already called a friend of his in Anchorage. The friend was busy contacting instructors.

Two and a half days out of Dallas, they crossed the Canadian border at Sweet Grass, Alberta, and over-nighted just below Red Deer. Late in the fifth day, they hit Dawson Creek, British Columbia, the beginning of the world-famous Alaska Highway. Three more days of hard driving brought them to the Alaskan border and within hours were breakfasting at Fast Eddy's in Tok Junction. Pushing it, they would arrive in Anchorage on the ninth day of travel. That was very respectable, considering the distance. After all, spuds were due to be in the ground. Citation delivery was promised on June 7 so they had about a week for dedicated planting. That left Ethan a full seven weeks to get checked out in the new jet. It should be a piece of cake. Anyway, all things with wings flew basically the same.

HENRY PRATT HAD JUST HUNG up after calling Hank's cell phone relaying their Houston departure time, when H.B.'s house phone rang. Hank looked at it suspiciously. But it was only Katy. It was almost noon and she sounded worried.

"Hank, I put a roast in the oven two hours ago. How 'bout an early supper, say three or so. I'd like to just sit and talk a spell. I need to clear my mind. I used to be a competent cook when I had a man around. Hope I'm not out of practice."

"Sure." Hank was thankful for the invitation of a home cooked meal. She lived alone, if you didn't count the Dobermans, and he sensed she wasn't any kind of socialite. Katy was a headstrong woman with of strong opinions, which didn't particularly attract friendships. Plus, she had a mischievous eye likely developed from years of practice. Ol' cut-to-the-chase Katy, Hank thought. Hank didn't want his name on her bad list.

"Come on up early if you want. I always have a cold beer available."

"Well, I might just do that. Thanks, Katy. I'll see you in a while."

Hank and T-Bone walked the hundred-acre fence getting a better lay of the property. It was beautifully groomed. No brush, no limbs, no rocks, no cactus, just lush coastal grass and occasional patches of live and post oak. Hank's horses were on the east end, belly-deep in green pausing their munching momentarily to watch them pass. He stopped a minute and saw Katy in the distance piddling in her garden. The garden appeared oversized for a single lady. Her corn was already waist high. He ambled up the west fence and looked over the smaller chained gate. The chain appeared to be manufactured from the same materials as the fencing. Where had H.B. found such hardened steel?

HANK RAPPED LIGHTLY on Katy's screen door and she let him in. Her house was neat and clean as a pin. No wall to wall carpeting for Katy. Her floors were of shining, polished wood. No clutter visible. She led him through the smallish living room into the kitchen and invited him to have a seat. It was a round, heavy oak dining table. The seats were pillow-cushioned. The kitchen was bright and cheery. Brightened to a large extent by ample windows and a large skylight. Hank heard country music in the background. Katy noticed his ear cocked to the sound.

"I've always liked Loretta Lynn's singin'. Is a cold Coors okay?"

"Sure." The walk of H.B.'s property had sweated him through. He'd even showered for whatever good it did. The air was wet as a sponge.

She sat his beer on the table and walked over and opened the oven. The good smells wafted out and filled the kitchen. Hank's salivary glands kicked in. He was sure he smelled fresh rolls or bread of some kind but held the question. It wasn't his place to pry.

Katy sat down, took a good pull on her beer, and sighed mightily pushing her hair out of her face. She had an equal mixture of grey and brown. It was thick and slightly wavy, rolled into a bun in the back. A widow's peak marked her front hairline. He didn't want to hazard a guess to her age but she looked mid-fifties. Age had been kind to Katy. Light wrinkles, if any, and still a slender and attractive woman, Hank thought. She was fine-featured with full eyebrows. She was makeup free. Her skin dark from gardening. She wore Levis and a cotton shirt. No flip-flops but real boots adorned her feet. She looked as country as the music that was playing.

"Hank, I've talked more to you in two days than I said to H.B. in eighteen years. Can you imagine living next to someone that long without any real conversation?"

"He is a man of few words," Hank admitted. "I have some of his same leanings."

"Well, I don't recommend too much jabber myself but it's been ridiculous. Neighbors should have a few things to say to one another."

Katy took another sip of beer swallowing slowly. "I see his pickup is still here. Has he slipped off yet?"

"Yeah, he's gone," Hank said not wanting to elaborate.

"When are those jerks leaving that are hanging around his gate?"

JOURNEY THROUGH THE RIFT

"Good question. I just told a load of them he was gone. Talk about puzzled looks."

"Ha. I'd like to have seen that. This damn media's gone mad. Sharks. That's all they are. A bunch of damn sorry sharks."

Hank took a drink of beer. It was tooth-cracking cold the only way he liked it. Katy looked over.

"I saw you walking the fences. That's some fence, ain't it?"

"Yes, ma'am it sure is."

"That fence always puzzled me. I have six barbed wire strands on mine and it holds my old Jersey cow just fine. I thought the man was pure nuts when the fence construction started. I thought they were putting in a prison of some kind. It took the contractor three months to finish it. The concrete footing holding the fence is six feet deep. I've never seen so much concrete poured in my life. It would have built Hoover Dam."

Katy stood up and walked to the kitchen window and looked out. "I shudder every time I look out this window, Hank. Thinking of the accident. It was tough to see the aftermath."

"It was," he agreed. Visions of the teens trapped in the grips of twisted steel still haunted him. The pathetic moaning still resonated in his mind.

Katy stayed by the window peering out. She wiped her eyes with her apron and looked in the oven again like she needed to recheck something. Nothing much could have changed in such a short time. She turned and walked back to the table and sat down. Another drink from her long neck.

"I have an unlisted number, Hank, did you know that?"

Of course, Hank wouldn't know such information. His look answered the question.

"Well, I sure got a threatening call yesterday. Who in the

hell it was I don't know? Why would somebody call and threaten the life of a sixty-five-year-old widow woman?" Hank noticed her voice changed. Her throat had tightened. The threat, rightfully so, had scared Katy, and she wasn't the type who scared easy.

Hank's back straightened and he looked into Katy's blue eyes. "Have you called the authorities?"

"Hell no, Hank. There's no real law in this county. The sheriff and his three useless deputies would have a helluva time catching a cold much less knowin' what to do with a threat. They'd laugh if I called. I've jumped down their throats too many times. They'd probably figure I was just getting my just reward."

This information troubled Hank. Two Doberman's wouldn't stop the bad guys. Maybe they surmised threatening Katy would draw H.B. out somehow. They probably assumed Katy and H.B. are friends, bosom buddies, sharing the same fence line and all. If they squeeze Katy maybe H.B. will cave. Not too bright but anything's possible in the twisted mind of a goon.

"How'd the call go?" he asked curious.

"Pretty straight forward. Hello. Yeah, I'm Katy. You know Horace Bascom? None of your damn business. We'll make it our business. Kiss my ass. You want your damn throat cut. You want your ass kicked. You're dead, you bitch. Go to hell. You know, the subtle stuff, typical bad guy routine. I was raised a sailor's brat, Hank. By ten years-old I could go toe-to-toe with dad in the cussin' department. I don't push easy. I apologize for my coarseness. I guess I've never been much of a lady."

"I'm guessin' this all started with the media exposure," Hank said mostly to himself. The goons were drawn to H.B.'s money like buzzards to a carcass.

"Well, the articles even shocked me. I knew he was well set

but never could have imagined he had billions. With the exception of the pickup and his horses, hell the man lived quiet as a church mouse. He'd drive out that damn monstrosity of a gate no more than once a month, usually less, and only tootled around somewhere a few hours. Back in he'd drive and in another month or two, he'd fire that pickup truck up again and go. You talk about a recluse. He'd make the unabomber look like a social butterfly."

Hank couldn't help but chuckle. Katy even giggled thinking about what she'd said. Her expression relaxed a bit. Her lips loosened. She finished her beer and adeptly finished the meal preparations. Hank sat sipping his beer. He kept thinking of how to keep the woman safe. There he sat behind a near impenetrable fence, guns, knives, and explosives aplenty, adding thousands of dollars of surveillance equipment, plotting and planning strategy, and Katy was behind six barbed wires protected by two Dobermans and a Jersey cow. The threats had to be taken seriously. Katy was cocky and self-assured but there was no doubt she needed protection.

CHAPTER
TEN

H ank ate voraciously. He couldn't remember, in recent times, having a better meal. Katy was witty, interesting, and well read. The conversation never lagged. Hank was finally embarrassed by his third helping. The puffy, hot, homemade dinner rolls tasted like a little piece of heaven. Her homemade jam smeared over his last roll thrilled his taste buds. Forget about the surveillance crap, whispered a little voice. Forget about protecting secrets. You're a trained bodyguard. Stay here and protect Katy. Just as long as she keeps cooking.

"You want a cup of coffee?" she asked breaking his culinary dreams.

"Sure, if it's not too much trouble."

"Trouble. What trouble?" she quipped quoting the '70's Jeremiah Johnson movie. She had a hand coffee grinder and placed a handful of coffee beans in and started turning. The product was thick, rich, and tasty. All the more reason for keeping Katy safe, thought Hank kiddingly.

"How long have you lived here?" Hank asked. The coffee aroma filled the kitchen.

"'Bout twenty years," she answered sitting back down. "Two years after we settled here H.B. roared in and started putting up that damn fence. At first, I thought he'd sold it to some prison authority. No one knew what he was up to. Some ranchers raise buffalo around here but they don't require that huge a fence. It was really puzzling. After I found out how reclusive he was I figured it out. It was solely designed to protect his privacy and keep the freaks out. I guess he figured the day of disclosure of his vast fortune would finally arrive."

"I guess you can't hide that kind of money forever," Hank answered.

"Lost my husband seventeen years ago today," she said glancing at a calendar hanging by the sink. "Got killed on an oil rig in the Gulf."

"I'm sorry," Hank replied. "Who'd he work for?"

"Conoco. He'd been working on platforms for ten years. I suspected it'd happen. I just didn't know when."

Hank was unsure if he should pursue her last statement. After a pause he asked. "Why would you suspect such a thing?"

"Drinking had gotten the better of him, Hank. He was sliding downhill. Stayed drunk practically the whole time he was off. He snuck whiskey in his duffle bag out to the rig. It was blatantly against company policy but he did it anyway. I tried to control it. He damned near killed me when I stepped in front of him one time."

A hint of anger and regret settled in her features. She turned the steaming coffee to her lips and took a slow sip. Raw feelings were still there. Old memories that couldn't be laid to rest.

"Conoco found out the truth. His blood alcohol was twice

the legal standard of a DUI, but they still paid a settlement to me. It was very decent of them. I paid off my forty acres, the house, and had enough left to live on. That's why I'm still here. I nearly sold out once and left, but where would I go? I'd prefer living slap dab in the middle of thirty thousand acres, but I settled for forty, 'cause that's all I could afford. I guess I could have done worse."

"Want a piece of apple pie I baked yesterday?" Hank nodded with excitement. Apple pie just happened to be his favorite.

Hank called an acquaintance in Dallas. He had been a fellow bodyguard at one time. He needed advice from a fresh perspective. Someone who knew of other professionals. He wanted someone set up close to the west fence. As close as possible to Katy's house without being on her property. Katy's protection would have to be surreptitious. That, in itself, would be no small trick. The acquaintance gave him two referrals. One was a smart ass, cocky so-and-so unwilling to do anything outside the concrete and pavement of the sprawling Dallas/Ft. Worth metroplex. So much for him. Hank dialed the second number expecting more of the same. A crisp, confident answer on the second ring. Nice guy. Former Navy Seal. Clandestine didn't bother him. Kinda liked the idea. They talked military for an hour. Thirty-five years old, unmarried, unattached, but very expensive. Didn't matter Hank said. Was cash okay? Cash would do just fine. Occasionally, he'd like a little time off. Not much, just to clear his head. They finally agreed on three hundred a day, expenses included. Let's take it thirty days at a time, Hank said. That was fine. Deal done. He'd be down in four days, packed and ready. Hank would let him stay inside his fence, next to Katy's side, and he could patrol from there. The small gate was near. Day time problems were possible, too. It was hard to know what to expect. He could handle it he said. Hank agreed with his confidence. They both knew the routine.

TRENT MITCHELL WAS ALL BUSINESS. Hank liked him from the beginning. As a friend of his from Brady High School used to say, "The boy could savvy coon shit on the pump handle." No superfluous questions. He was intelligent and understood a thug's mindset. He quickly set up a mini-base complete with military-style wall tent, just inside H.B.'s fence and stood engrossed by the security systems quickly being installed by Tex-Line Security. Hank explained the basics and Trent liked the setup. Hank isolated his task specifically to Katy for the time being. Primary responsibility was outside the fence. He'd explain Trent to Katy, even introduce him, and tell Katy whatever it took to allow his trespass across the fence. Katy had shown Hank a .38 caliber Smith and Wesson she possessed. No need to have Katy firing at the good guys.

Katy accepted the idea rather stiffly at first. Hank was rather vague about the details but she finally agreed.

"Katy, we're on your side. Your fence line with H.B.'s seems to be the hot spot. Trent's just helping, temporarily, to secure the place." Hank talked fast. No big sweat. No real infringement on privacy. Just simple precautions. Let's be safe here. We'll outlast the bad guys.

She cussed a little but not at anyone in particular. She actually kicked the front door, but not hard enough to cause damage. She cussed the local laws again finally threatening to call the governor, but she didn't trust the damn politicians either. They're probably all in cahoots anyway. It's all going to hell in a hand basket. Finally relenting, she asked what she could do to help. Give us access, Hank answered. Just around your acreage. Occasionally in daylight but mainly after dark. Thugs thrive in shadows. After all, flies, tyranny, and thugs all breed in the dark. Katy laughed. She invited them in for coffee and they gratefully accepted. The deal was struck.

"Being naïve is a quality admired in a fifteen-year-old girl, I guess, but an old sailor's daughter knows when the skies point to stormy weather." With that, Katy poured their cups full.

DAY THREE WAS BETTER, but not by much. Pretty Boy still carried a limp, hobbling along gingerly on his hoof, and it was still slow going. The weather turned unseasonably cool, growing cold as the day progressed. An early east wind veered to the north now penetrating like it meant business. By mid-afternoon the horses' breaths were blowing steam. H.B. pulled on a heavy sweater, then a jacket. The sky grayed. The breeze became stouter and before long was howling. The change was rapid and the chill deepened. The horses liked it, even Pretty Boy stepped easier, almost losing his limp at times. The evening came earlier than normal with the arriving overcast. The terrain was hilly for the most part broken by wooded areas of thick mesquite and a predominance of scrub brush and persimmon. It was well watered with clear creeks and occasional ponds.

H.B. worked the thickets looking for a protected area to

camp. The north wind had become a worthy adversary in the past few hours. He shook his head in disbelief as a light sleet began falling moments after he unpacked and staked the horses. The sleet thickened and snow mixed in with it. He sat his thermometer out and in ten minutes it dropped to 32 degrees. The north wind was moaning. It twisted through the trees like a snake. What a contrast from last night, he thought, digging for additional blankets to cover the sleeping bag. No fire tonight. The tent-cot felt good. He zipped the windows shut and lit a small lantern. He read an hour listening to the sleet pepper the tent top. He was glad he wasn't out on the treeless plains somewhere suffering through this cold snap. Then a loud crack rang through the woods sounding like a tree limb breaking. H.B. concentrated trying to determine the exact direction. The wind washed the sound making it difficult to pinpoint. He blew out the lamp and blackness surrounded the tent. He listened for the horses. Patty Cake would whinny at any disturbance. He grabbed his headlight deciding to check around. The sleet had stopped but a steady, wet snow contin-ued. He carried his 9mm on full ready. His light would pene-trate only fifty feet with snow blocking its rays. The horses were busy with the grass. He rubbed Pretty Boy's shoulder. He put his arms around Patty Cake's neck and hugged her. She always sought his affection. He walked away satisfied it was nothing. The stiff north wind and snow the only trespassers.

As quick as it came, it relented. The snow had melted by morning and the wind relaxed its grip. No limp. So, H.B. replaced some of Pretty Boy's load and he fell to without much hesitation. The sky cleared by mid-morning and a warm sun penetrated through. All signs of the cold snap disappeared as if it had never happened. The terrain was smooth and traveling relaxed into a steady pace. He stopped for a half hour fishing out another dried sausage to dine on. The horses seemed anxious to go, so onward he went. In another hour he pulled up listening to a keening cry somewhere to his left. It was a wail seemingly from a human voice. The horses pricked their ears. There, another cry, loud and shrill. H.B. pushed Patty Cake and they moved slowly towards it. Again, he heard it. In a few minutes he broke through an opening and saw a large, covered wagon sitting with two mules standing idle close by. Another cry. It was coming from inside the wagon. He approached cautiously within a hundred feet and called out.

"Hello, can I be of assistance?"

No answer. Silence.

"Do you need help?"

Still no sound, but he could hear a rustling inside the wagon. He saw the wagon shaking slightly. He unsnapped his 9mm strap. Best be ready. Finally, a woman's head emerged from the wagon's rear canvass. The head wore hair that was disheveled, stringy, and unkempt. She also wore a pained expression. Eyes puffy from crying. She appeared to be straining for comprehension. She was young, perhaps middle twenties at most. Her tear-stained eyes finally seemed to focus on H.B.

"Yes," she said clearing her throat to speak. "Yes, I need help."

H.B. slowly dismounted and approached the wagon in careful steps. She kept blinking, wiping her eyes, and snuffling. At ten feet he stopped and spoke. "What's the problem?"

Her wits had returned somewhat. "My husband's terrible

ill. He's so hot. Now he's passed out." With that she started sobbing uncontrollably unable to control her emotions.

"How long has he been ill?" he asked trying to get answers.

"Three days now. He passed out this morning early. He's breathing fast and burnin' up."

"I'm a doctor," H.B. said to the tormented woman. It took a minute for his statement to stick.

"Oh, dear Lord," she said stuttering with emotion. "Oh, my gosh. Please. Yes, please, please help." Her face fell into the canvass sheet teetering on the edge of sheer exhaustion.

ONE-HUNDRED-FOUR-POINT-FIVE BODY TEMPERATURE could render a grown man unconscious. All his covers, clothes, bedding was soaking wet. H.B couldn't tell whether the dampness was all sweat or the steady stream of water his wife had poured over him. His pulse raced, breathing shallow and rapid. He was seriously dehydrated and pale. His eyes were unresponsive and sunken back in his head. H.B. left the wagon quickly tending horses and locating medical supplies.

"I'm Esther," the young woman said when he returned opening the wagon flaps. She was beside her husband wiping his forehead.

"I'm H.B.," he answered pulling himself back in the wagon. A short, concise explanation followed.

"I'm using some very new methods in medicine. I'll be doing things you've never heard of or seen, but your husband is very ill. I must act quickly."

She nodded with frightful eyes.

H.B. placed a LED headlight over his forehead and snapped

it on. He had to see. The wagon canvass created a darkened environment. Esther recoiled seeing the light. He continued working. With a piece of twine, he hung an IV line from the wagon ribs and placed a needle in the sick man's arm. The IV flow was begun. Antibiotics, needed hydration, fever-reducing medications. He was guessing the problem was bacterial. Many of the high fevers of this era had that as their root cause.

"Esther, did he complain of any pain before the fever hit? Any specific complaint?"

"No," she replied almost mute with fear. She glanced nervously at the IV bags dangling above her sick husband and the flashing headlight.

He opened the man's shirt and examined him with his stethoscope. His chest was clear, only the slightest hint of congestion. Ester sat back, in a silent state of awe. The light on H.B.'s head was most perplexing to her. H.B. started humming the old cowboy tune Lorena and saw her taut face relax. It was a childlike expression overwhelmed by fears and fatigue. He spoke softly to her in his best comforting tone. She nodded but said nothing. Her weariness had altered her reasoning, dulled her responses. He continued talking, explaining things, what he was doing, why he was doing it. She seemed to be hearing, trying to comprehend, willing to accept, yet bound by uncertainties.

BY NIGHTFALL ESTHER'S husband was fully conscious. He questioned the IV at first, the needle in the arm, a wild look of distrust, but accepted it finally. He was far too weak to resist anyway. Yet he talked. Bart, was his name he said. They came from Arkansas looking to settle in west Texas. Bart talked to a relieved wife who snuggled next to him falling into a deep, exhausted sleep. His skin color slowly returned as the fever came down. His hollow, dehydrated face began filling in. H.B. left in the darkness, finally, to tend the horses and when he returned both man and wife were sound asleep. Their breathing the same, steady, and slow.

By noon the following day, the IV lines were removed and a shot of antibiotics administered. H.B. stayed the second day anxious to leave but unwilling yet to risk a relapse. By the morning of the third day, he departed to the waves of Esther and Bart. They both wore broad smiles. H.B. had helped them hook up the mules and make ready. A rested Esther was funny and witty, even giggly at times. H.B. left them a two-week supply of antibiotics.

"Three pills a day, morning, noon, and evening. Don't stop taking them until the bottle is completely empty."

Esther took possession of the pills, carefully placing them in a small cedar chest inside the wagon. Bart was warned to take it easy for another day or two. The promise was given. They stood by the wagon and waved heartily as H.B. and his packed horses pointed north.

He had practically lost count of the days since leaving Bellville. H.B. pushed hard with rested stock and a silent dread that he might be too late to help the young woman. Three days later, he drew rein on a high plateau overlooking the Trinity River for his first view of Fort Worth. The town of ten thousand bustled below him, raw and hungry for growth. The smoke of a Texas Pacific locomotive puffed in the distance making its way eastward. It was a cowtown of destiny, H.B. thought, but that would be played out in due time. It lay, strategically placed, on the doorstep of western expansion and the burgeoning cattle empire. Fort Worth was the final port of call for scores of cattle herds passing yearly to markets in Kansas and Nebraska. H.B. saw one such herd of several thousand animals grazing tranquilly several miles west of town. Its cowboys, no doubt, whooping it up one last time before facing the many hundreds of miles of empty prairie that loomed ahead.

CHAPTER
ELEVEN

The Cessna Citation arrived one day late on June 8. Ethan and Lori had flown their Super Cub in and waited for it at Anchorage's Merrill Field. Merrill Field was one of the busiest small metro airports in the world. It was located almost in downtown Anchorage and had been the home base for the early pioneering bush pilots first penetrating the remote regions of the Last Frontier. Wiley Post and Will Rogers had landed there as they headed for their ultimate rendezvous with fate near Nome. Every conceivable tundra-tired bush plane operated out of Merrill. The flyers, like their early progenitors, were a unique breed of adventurers, still, that ran the back country of Alaska in their bush rigs. After all, the Super Cub itself was only a Jeep with wings attached.

The Citation V taxied up with its sleek appearance and executive look. The Fowlers were filled with excitement. They had purchased the plane without the luxury of having flown in it. Something Ethan would never do in buying a Super Cub. He had owned several and they all flew differently. Hopefully, all Citation V's flew about the same.

The pilot had overnighted in Calgary because of a minor mechanical glitch. The problem turned out to be a faulty sensor which was easily replaced. He had agreed to take Lori and Ethan for a brief flight but he had a jet to catch heading south at Anchorage International. The Calgary stay had tightened his schedule. The Fowlers climbed in, Ethan in the right front seat with the pilot, and off they took. Wow! It flew like a homesick angel! Smooth, fast, and a joy to handle. Ethan couldn't keep his hands off the controls. The ferry pilot was impressed.

"How long have you been flying?" he asked at one point.

"Soloed at sixteen," Ethan answered. "Flew alone without a license at fourteen."

"How many hours?" he queried.

"Somewhere just over ten thousand."

"That's pretty remarkable. No wonder you handle it so well."

The pilot's seat seemed to fit Ethan's rear end just right, but everything moved fast with it. It was a jet, after all. The ground had the tendency to speed by. Somewhat different than his ninety mile-an-hour Cub. They flew northwest over Ethan and Lori's cabin and out over the Alaskan Range a hundred-fifty miles distant. The climb to fifteen thousand feet was smooth and steady. They leveled out at three hundred seventy knots. What a machine, Ethan thought. He couldn't wait to be the pilot-in-command. He wondered what Bermuda was like this time of year? He was itching for a long trip. Ethan could hardly contain his enthusiasm.

PATIENCE HAD NEVER BEEN a personal shortcoming of Gerard Fremont, the Big G, especially when he was flat broke. Money stress had kept him sleepless for so long he couldn't remember the last time he'd enjoyed a good night's rest. Bingo had been the unfortunate benefactor of the G's restlessness. He wanted action. And he wanted it now. Hell, he hadn't bet on a sporting event in two weeks. Withdrawals from cocaine couldn't have been more punishing. His nervous, sausage-like fingers shook so badly he could hardly hold his cigar.

Bingo, Danny, and Little Eddie had already visited the damn fence and broken two chain cutters trying to get through. That had occurred a week ago. A new plan was being formed to go over the fence but going over was no easy matter either. On the far end of the west fence line, too, was a small hole that had been covered over. Danny and Little Eddie tried the shovel route. They found the heavy concrete in no time. There was no getting under this fence without heavy equipment. Bingo's cell phone rang constantly. The big guy was agitated. Get the damn billionaire. I don't care how you do it, just get the bastard.

Several things had happened on the hundred acres in the course of a week. The three goons had cased the place again in daylight and found a tent set up on the west fence line close to the widow's house. Bingo had been the voice that Katy cursed. She would pay for that. Bingo wouldn't stand a cussing from anyone, especially a smart-ass female. Two large backhoes, earth-moving equipment, too, were on the property and several flag-pole height poles had been set. A myriad of gadgets, perhaps even lighting, were attached to them. *Now what the hell is this?* Bingo thought. His easy hit had become considerably more complex. Bingo assumed the poles housed surveillance equipment of some kind. "What the hell," he exclaimed, for all to hear. Danny and Little Eddie's jaws hung slack as their eyes surveyed the scene. The place looked even more impenetrable. No simple going over, through, or under in the dark of the night. Not unless you wanted your picture taken.

The Big G's reaction was explosive. A flurry of Creole curse words parted his thick lips. A lengthy tirade of foot stomping and kicking followed. His dingy, smoke-filled office took most of the abuse. His long-time secretary scattered for an early lunch. The round face reddened and sweated profusely. He was close to blowing a gasket, Bingo assumed standing back. Danny and Little Eddie cringed in the corner fearing the worse. They'd never laid eyes on the man before. Their marching orders, contractual in nature, always came from an underling. His fit lasted a full five minutes. Then he flopped down in his overstuffed, worn-leather office chair and mopped his dripping forehead with a large handkerchief. His breathing was erratic. He'd sweated through his shirt, armpits moist and drippy.

He dabbed his face and forehead again wiping in circles like a good window cleaner. His broad chest heaved in shallow exhalations. G finally reached down and rattled in his desk drawer chasing a glass and finding his vodka bottle. He filled the glass, drank deeply, and smacked his lips. Another drink and the glass was empty. His eyes focused on Bingo who had carefully watched his boss's rampage.

"What do we do?" he asked as he poured another glass. His tantrum had left him shaky and he bobbled in his chair. He couldn't tolerate complications at this stage. The wolves were at his door, growling, clawing to get in. He desperately wanted this H.B. fella standing in his office begging for his life, offering multi-millions, even billions, for his reclusive sorry little ass. Where there was a will there was a way, and Big G had plenty of will to go around. "Let's see the pictures," he finally said, leaning back.

Bingo connected to the computer in the G's office and displayed the digitals they had taken. His black eyes looked at each picture flashing before him. His fat lips rolled and pursed, depending on the scene he viewed. He belched and emptied the vodka with a particularly long gulp. His nerves had steadied, finally. The vodka carried the hope he needed. It clarified the blurred. Brought a semi-peacefulness to his fat, stressed-out body.

"How do we go in?" Big G asked.

Bingo spoke. "We can't go in unseen anymore. He's hired help I assume. Unless the tent's just a guise. It's now turned into an all-out assault. No more duck and cover. We go in with force or not at all. Maybe one or two more men. We go in by air and we go in ready for action." Bingo didn't blink. This was serious business and it would take a serious effort.

"Tell me, what do we need?" Big G asked feeling the vodka's effects. His eyes intense as a blood hound on a fox trail.

"Four or five men, flak jackets, semi-automatics, ready for action. It has to be fast and furious. Only one neighbor close by. It's a tucked away, lonely place but if there's shooting the local law, of course, might eventually show up. We'll be long gone by then."

"What about climbing the fence?" the big man asked.

"They'll know we're coming before the first ladder is placed. Won't work. We need to go in by air. Parachute or helicopter. Parachuting puts a tough spin on things. We need the activator for the damn gate or we could be trapped inside. Likely, we can get the gate's remote once inside. We need a van waiting outside. Two men in the van armed and ready. They can pick us and the tycoon up. Parachuting is the quietest way in. A helicopter would alert the whole damn countryside."

"There's a skydiving club locally. Owner owes me a favor," Big G said. "Let's get him on board. He's got a plane."

"We need some practice jumps. I don't want the men shittin' their pants on the way down. It'll be daylight and we need to hit the target ready to go." Bingo had already spent considerable time planning the kidnapping, going over each detail in his mind. Gerard shook his head in agreement.

The deal was closed and the go ahead was given. Five days later, after a series of successful practice jumps, a Cessna 206 roared aloft from a remote Lake Charles airstrip carrying four goons, armed and ready for action. The drop would occur from three thousand feet. Low enough to hit the target yet high enough for his boys to get the chutes open. No one would be the wiser. They would float in silent and stealthy. Land quickly, disengage the chutes, and find and claim the prize. Don't hurt the billionaire. However, a little roughing-up is okay. No serious damage, though. He's our meal ticket Bingo had preached over and over again to his thugs. Big G had upped the ante to 75K per man. Success would bring Bingo another 25K bonus. Now that was a paycheck.

A white, unmarked van slipped down Coushatta Road and parked within a hundred feet of the main entrance gate. The driver got out and feigned a tire problem looking down and scratching his head. The van didn't go unnoticed by Hank. A motion detector alerted a vibrating alarm inside his shirt pocket. The Tex-Line systems were now fully functional. He checked the van with his binoculars. He saw Trent standing outside his tent doing the same thing. It could be filled with explosives, Hank thought. A van loaded with the right explosives would likely blow the gate off its tracks. Trent ambled over holding binoculars in his hand.

"What do you make of that?" he asked scoping the van again. The paparazzi had departed two days before apparently giving up on their photo mission. The windowless van presented an oddity, especially at mid-morning on a sunny spring day.

"Possibly explosives. Anything's possible, but who can guess a criminal's mind? I get the funny feeling though that we're the bull's eye for some thug operation."

"What are you thinking?"

"If they blow the gate up with one van then another one is just around the corner waiting to enter. Probably not likely but possible. With the paparazzi gone they're not worried about witnesses. We best prepare for any contingency."

Trent headed for his tent. Hank hurried back inside H. B's house. Their arsenals were checked. Long clips inserted. Extras were located. Auto pistols loaded and ready. Hank put a handful of his homemade explosives in his pocket. His sling shot made a great grenade launcher. He had test shot several, landing them almost a hundred yards for the launch site. Both men put on flak jackets. A hunch made Hank prepare for the worst.

TWELVE

The aircraft circled once and headed off temporarily. The sound of its engine droned in the distance. It was approaching 11:30 and Hank glassed the plane unable to pick up the "N" number. That was odd he thought before it dawned on him. They'd been covered or painted over. The plane's identity hidden on purpose. The red alert went off. Trent ran over where he and Hank had constructed a bunker of sorts out of gravel-filled bags. It was strategically located on the east side of H.B.'s barn, in clear view of the front of the house, protecting the road-side, east southeast to be exact. The filled bags were stacked, double-wide, five feet tall with shooting ports on all sides. Hank had kept a camouflage tarp covering it and another similar one on the back side of the house. Nothing short of a fifty-caliber round could penetrate the thing. Extra clips and ammunition were stashed inside. Even a case of bottled water to last out a long siege. Being that H.B.'s front door was visible fifty yards away, no goon could approach without being caught in the open. It would be a deadly mistake to try it.

Then the distant drone of the aircraft engine grew louder. It was returning on a straight line over the acreage directly from the west. As Trent and Hank looked up the engine coughed, temporarily, as it powered down. One wing dropped slightly, almost imperceptibly and a body dropped out. Three others quickly followed. Chutes, controllable chutes, deployed and their descent started. One chute, however, seemed to behave erratically from the moment of its opening and a terrorized scream from its rider confirmed as much. The erratic parachute started veering off course, angling away from the others. Its passenger screamed at his cohorts in apparent panic, unable to wrest control. Hank and Trent, experienced military paratroopers, instantly saw the problem. Tangled control lines resulting in the top half of the chute not being fully deployed. The lack of lift caused a more rapid descent thus rendering it uncontrollable. Another high-pitched scream as the chute fell out of the sky like a tailless kite.

Hank and Trent watched the show somewhat amused. An imminent, high-speed crash was coming. The three other chutes, functioning normal, appeared on course for their predetermined landing site. Then, inexplicably, the troubled chute dipped sharply to the right, flipping the rider upside down with violent force. It had become a missile now. Dropping at high speed. The rider dangled loosely apparently unconscious from the high G forces. A heavy thud! The body hit with sickening force just outside H.B.'s fence and not more than fifty feet in front of the waiting van. The goon tumbled and rolled from the force of the impact. A puff of dust flew up as the now pulverized form lay limp and still. The remaining chute fabric fell slowly over its victim, now becoming his death shroud. The van stayed put. The van passengers had apparently witnessed the event. Bad guy Little Eddie had been unlucky enough to pick the poorly rigged chute. Jumping from an airplane had terrified him from the beginning, but his fear of heights had slowly succumbed to his greed for money and overcome by harsh threats from his companions. His greedy body was mush now, oozing into the soil.

The three remaining chutes floated slowly toward their target. The riders seriously rattled. The operation was suddenly down to three. Danny, the large-bodied goon, fought to choke back his fears. Bingo yelled encouragement at Danny and Rankin, the other goon. Steady up, boys. The ground was coming fast. They all prepared for landing. The landing had to be soft in the tall, cushy coastal grass.

Hank always liked the role of a prankster. He had stretched an electrified stock wire across the north half of H.B.'s estate, a thin wire practically invisible to the casual observer. His horses had been moved to the north side for safe keeping. The dirt contractor's backhoe, while in service doing Tex-Line's contract, had dug per Hank's instructions, four dozen ten-foot-deep holes varying from six to eight feet in diameter in the south pasture. Using the best military camouflage techniques, the holes had been covered with stretched mesh wire and covered with thin turf. Even a trained eye would miss the pits. They were placed in a random pattern starting about thirty yards inside the fence line. Hank had carefully planned for just this contingency.

They watched the final moments of the descent chuckling at the open arms awaiting the goons. They were heading straight for the jaws of the deep pits. With luck, one or two of them just might get gobbled up by the ground itself on landing. If not, crossing the pocked terrain would be challenging. Likely, probing for pits wouldn't cross a goon's mind, especially with bullets flying.

The first parachute to land, with a semblance of control, was Danny's. He had been the second to exit the plane but his two-hundred-fifty-pound bulk forced a quicker downward trajectory. He slid and tumbled on impact a hundred yards in front of the bunker with a thud and a quick gasp for breath. Then he simply disappeared. The chute remained above ground but Danny had been swallowed. A thin dust cloud appeared above the pit. Then a scream, followed by nonstop yelling. He was disoriented, dazed, and confused. Plus, his right arm was injured with excruciating pain shooting throughout his large body. The hole was dark and hot and he choked with each inhalation. He couldn't see as he pawed the sides of the surrounding dirt in desperation.

Goon Rankin followed Danny. He was determined to make a picture-perfect landing as he'd done on the practice jumps. He glided softly until ground contact and ran, legs churning to match his forward landing speed. Internally, he smiled as he remained upright and controlled the billowing nylon chute as it collapsed around him. He had been too preoccupied planning his own landing to pay much attention to Danny's distressed yelling. Danny was clumsy, Rankin thought. A poor choice for such a mission but he was Bingo's buddy. So, he had kept his mouth shut, feeling fortunate himself for being chosen. *The excitement of the mission, the healthy payday, and kidnapping a billionaire was straight out of the 007 movies* he thought. The landing! Perfect!

Rankin ran beside the chute, unsnapping his harness like the pro he thought he was when suddenly his overconfidence fell, along with his body, into a yawning pit. His forward momentum carried his body over most of the width of the pit before he plunged headlong into the far wall. His head snapped back violently and neck bones popped, vertebrae cracked, and the spinal cord severed instantly. Rankin never knew he hit the bottom of the pit. Never felt anything ever again. The dust and dirt in the hole filtered over him and as he lay unmoving and still. Rankin was stone dead.

Bingo Burns had exited the plane last according to plan. He would view the landing site, survey the area, and take charge of the operation once on the ground. He had two-way communications with the van, at least he would after landing. Unlike Rankin, he had seen the other men disappear in the pits below. It was weird to see the ground swallow them up. He knew what game was up before hitting the ground. Being a novice at parachute control, he did, however, try to orient the landing away from where his hapless comrades had disappeared. He heard Danny's muffled yelling in the final few seconds of the descent but he couldn't let it distract him. He was going to attempt to land just outside the confines of the tall fence. The mission would have to be aborted anyway with Little Eddie likely dead and Rankin and Danny trapped. Bingo looked ahead and saw the tall fence's razor wire looming ever larger. Crap! He was going to hit it. He clawed for the chute's controls and yanked frantically with his right hand trying to change course. He succeeded. His body fell abruptly to the right while the parachute struck the top of the fence. Bingo bounced hard as the parachute cords snapped in response to the force of the impact. Then his body slammed into the tightly stretched fencing, knocking his breath out. His feet, however, never touched the ground. They dangled six feet above the terra firma. The whiplash stunned him momentarily. He fought to disconnect from the harness, kicking and thrashing, trying to break free. He was out of sight of the van, its occupants unaware of his dilemma. His automatic pistol was in a small bag strapped behind his butt. He was trying desperately to reach a knife to cut loose when a voice rang out below him. It carried strong authority, a commanding tone.

"Stop you damn wiggling. Keep your arms high and don't move them. Move 'em and you'll die."

Bingo stopped immediately, bringing his hands high above his head. He could hear the van's motor running, air conditioning set on high. If only he could alert them, he thought. They could stop this damn cowboy's attempt to get him. Then he saw another man below him holding a gun. The cowboy was opening the huge gate now and running towards the van. He quickly knifed the road side tires and within a millisecond was pointing an assault rifle at the occupants.

"Out," he shouted. "Hands up so I can see them, now," he demanded as the door flew open. "Slowly, move slow. One false move and you're dead."

The two thugs exited the van stunned at the sudden turn of events. Their two-way radio, waiting for Bingo's call, crackled in the background. The parachute crash, in their clear view, had panicked them but they waited obediently for a call, but it never came. *Where were the other men anyway?*

KATY HAD BEEN DUSTING kitchen shelves when she heard the aircraft engine shudder and cut power. The Bellville airport wasn't but a half dozen miles away so it wasn't all that unusual to hear airplanes pass over, but she couldn't recall hearing an engine cut out so distinctly. So, she stepped on her back porch and looked up. The parachutes were already deployed. Strange that someone was jumping from an airplane over the top of H.B.'s place. It took a full ten seconds for the reason to register.

"Oh, my Lord," she gasped shielding the sun from her eyes.

Hank had mentioned the possibility to her not a week ago but she didn't take the comment seriously. Now the sky was filled with parachutes.

Katy burst through the screen door stumbling over her Dobermans. She found her Smith & Wesson .38 and checked the loads. Then she ran back outside and watched in horror as the billowing sails descended. She moved to the west fence hearing the screaming of Little Eddie as his fatal plunge came to an abrupt end. The screamer's chute disappeared in a moment and Katy turned her attention to the remaining parachutists. She was sure Hank and Trent were seeing the same thing. Hopefully, they were aware. Katy feeling unnerved, leaned against the fence wire, adrenaline coursing through her body. Her pistol in hand but the arm so weak it could barely raise it.

Then, she witnessed the ground contact and immediate disappearance of the first thug on H.B.'s land. Oh, no, she thought as the second goon landed upright running along folding the chute. He missed the pits, but wait! Whoosh! Then he, too, quickly disappeared below ground. Hanks pits, something she'd made fun of at first, were paying off. The man apparently knew his business. The first rule of warfare, he'd told Katy as she jokingly made light of his "prairie dog town," was to know your enemy and your enemies' potential plans. Thus, the holes were dug.

Then she saw the last flyer to land tangle in the far east fencing and Hank and Trent emerged from the bunker quickly running towards the dangling body. Katy cursed herself for having forgotten the binoculars. She couldn't see clearly. She turned and jogged back to the house wondering if she'd hear gunfire. She didn't. In a few minutes she was back out watching. She saw Hank had captives. Two men, hands on head, walking down the fence towards the hanging parachutist. It was under control. The air assault had failed. Katy's breathing slowed as the adrenaline ceased pumping. Her .38 hung loosely in her hand. Tomorrow I'm buying an automatic shotgun, she promised herself. Things had turned serious around here. H.B.'s quaint, quiet estate had changed. She intended to be ready.

TWO HOURS later the parachute that Bingo bashed into the fence had been removed, shredded in pieces and put away. The white van had been prodded into the barn two rims bumping along on flat tires. Four prisoners were bound and gagged there, too, with looks of disconsolate men uncertain of their future. Danny was fairly seriously injured, not entirely from his fall into the pit, however. Once he reclaimed his orientation in the hole. He had become a raging bull refusing to cooperate and unwilling to surrender his weapons. He pawed and clawed the pit's sides acting belligerent and cursing unceasingly. He even fired his weapons in the air and forced Hank and Trent to stay clear of his random shooting. His injured right arm pained him but not enough to settle him down. Hank finally lost patience and tossed one of his medium-sized explosives into the pit. The explosion was deafening resulting in Danny's immediate cessation of hostilities. The explosion's concussion burst his ear drums and temporarily addled the big thug. Instantly docile and cooperative, Danny emerged from the pit with tear streaks lining his dirty jowls. He was wobbly and barely able to walk. His head throbbed unmercifully. He was a model captive now weeping softly in his suddenly silent, pain-filled world.

Little Eddie's mashed body was rolled up in the nylon canopy of his chute and thrown into the same pit where goon Rankin was rapidly stiffening. Dual goon burial. They didn't deserve any more attention. Six feet of dirt now covered the two thanks to the unwilling but busy shovels of Bingo and the two van crooks.

Trent wasn't a man to question tactics or authority. Especially those of his new employer. Hank was itching to get whatever information he could from the captive goons, especially Bingo, and told Trent he would handle it from here. Trent was hungry and headed for his tent. There had been enough excitement for him for one day. Bingo, as he had heard him called, appeared to be the ringleader so Hank prodded him out of the barn, through the side door, and into H. B's dark laboratory. He parked him on a heavy wooden chair in the middle of the smooth concrete floor. He duct-taped his legs tightly to the chair first, at least a dozen wraps, and all the while pointing a cocked pistol. Then he released Bingo's hands from the handcuffs. Bingo rubbed his wrists working to get his blood circulation going. Hank removed his gag next.

"Put your right hand down on the chair arm," Hank ordered sternly. The hand went down reluctantly. Hank greytaped the right arm down followed by the left. Satisfied, Hank holstered the pistol and pulled his seven-inch hunting knife out of its scabbard. It was razor sharp. Bingo's eyes flashed with hate. Hank's treatment of his friend Danny had infuriated him. Danny was a broken man, sobbing like a child. *Who in the hell did this cowboy think he was?*

Hank's voice altered his thoughts. "Heard some of your bozo buddies call you Bingo. Is that your name?"

No answer. Silence. Bingo's eyes weren't silent though, staring hatefully at Hank. His vengeance-filled eyes spoke volumes but his muteness caused Hank's temper to suddenly boil.

"Bingo, I don't play by any rules. You won't hear your Miranda rights read by me. No Geneva conventions. You're a damn domestic terrorist in my book and your dying would make me happy. Having said that, you damn well better talk to me or body parts are goin' missing. Do you understand?"

Bingo sneered and Hank met the sneer with a forceful downward stroke of his knife. The shiny blade clipped Bingo's right ear taking with it a large chunk. Bingo yelled. The severed ear flopped to the floor and blood splattered. Bingo screamed and rocked the chair trying to force his bonds. Spittle flew from his mouth in vain efforts to escape.

"You bastard. You son-of-a-bitch. You sorry bastard," Bingo yelled a non-stop chorus of insults and expletives. Hank walked off ignoring his spouting off. Just kill the goon kept popping in Hank's head but he needed and wanted the intelligence. He wanted to know the main man who had ordered this assault.

"What finger on which hand do you like the least?" Hank asked after Bingo settled down. Bingo's tirade had lasted a good five minutes. He was met with silence again. Hank had lost all patience. The knife came in quickly and severed the pinkie on Bingo's right hand. The finger fell to the floor joining the piece of right ear. Cursing and swearing ensued again. Blood flowed from the stub remaining of Bingo's finger. The chair rattled, the blood splattered, and Bingo convulsed up and down in a frenzy of anger and pain. After another five minutes of rage, Bingo settled again, a puddle of blood collecting on the floor below his dripping right hand and ear.

"Bingo," Hank said finally. "I'll keep carving until there's nothing left to carve. I don't mind trimming you up like a side of beef. I want information – all of it. Otherwise, you're going to lose one hell of a lot of weight over the next hour."

Bingo was ready to talk. Another quick transformation. He was dizzy from losing blood and parts and knew, beyond a shadow of doubt, that Hank was all business. There was no give in this cowboy. The next question from Hank was answered fully and completely. Names, dates, places. Hank kept notes and Bingo kept talking. It turned into an easy inter-rogation.

CHAPTER
THIRTEEN

Katy called for a pizza delivery. Five of the extra-large supreme kind, along with seven extra-large drinks. Delivery came an hour later from Bellville Pizzeria. The Pizzeria moved faster than the local cops, Katy noted. Hank and Trent delivered four of the drinks and three large pizzas to the POW's. Gags and handcuffs were removed, and closely guarded, they ate like hungry wolves. Even Danny broke out of his stupor and gulped down slice after slice. Bingo ate, too, with his left hand. Hank had bandaged his right pinkie stub finally. The other captives eyed Bingo seeing his partially severed ear and finger missing. It set them wondering about their own fate. They murmured quietly among themselves. Uncertain fate or not, it didn't affect their appetite. Each visited the barn's small urinal under tight guard and returned to be tied up and placed atop spread-out hay. When they were all trussed up, Hank and Trent headed to Katy's for pizza. She reheated it in the oven. Katy was giddy with excitement.

"You boys sure cooked some goose today," she chortled

bringing the pizza to the table. "I like it when rear-ends are busted."

Trent was still amused at Hank's interrogation techniques. Didn't do to scorn Hank, he thought. Talk about attitude adjustment. He fought back a chuckle.

Katy noticed his face. "What are you grinning about?"

Trent finally gave up the chuckle and it surfaced in a deep laugh. "Oh, I'm just rethinking the past few hours. Entertainment's apparently not in short supply around here."

They all laughed at the statement. Hank took a huge bite of pizza, smacking his lips, stringing cheese down the corner of his mouth. Katy giggled again. She hadn't been around feisty young men in years – and certainly never around men of the caliber of Hank and Trent. They were cool professionals. Just go ask the four men trussed up in the barn. She knew nothing, of course, of Hank's interrogation of Bingo.

"What are you doing with the other four?" Katy asked curious regarding their plans.

"Not sure. I've got a plan but I've got to think on it tonight. I'm calling Ethan in Alaska. I kinda think he'll like the idea."

Trent wondered what the plan might be, too. He didn't see Hank turning these jokers loose back into the general population. Plus, he couldn't imagine him caring for them long, feeding, bath rooming and all. He quietly thought the pizza may have been their last meal. Anyway, it was Hank's call.

"What kind of shotgun should I buy?" Katy asked seriously. She was bound and determined to be a contributor. No more running around with a shaky pistol flopping in her hand. She wanted the heavy artillery. Hank looked at her before he answered. Trent was chewing, noncommittal.

"Sixteen-gauge, double ought buckshot for shells, extended magazine. Pump is probably the most reliable. Auto's sometime have a tendency to jam. Stainless steel if you can find one."

"Can you locate one for me? I'm a buyer."

"I'll check around and let you know. They're fairly expensive, Katy."

"I've got some cash under the mattress. Ain't doing no damn good sitting there either."

ETHAN TOOK the phone call from Hank sitting in his cabin watching the Susitna River flow by and Mount Susitna, the Sleeping Lady, turn greener. Spring sprung late in the north country. Ethan listened and heartily approved. *Hell, you run the outfit down there* he said. *Do what you think best.* Actually, Hank's idea was rather intriguing. Even funny, in a rather bizarre sense. It was sure a good way to get rid of problematic goons. Society would be a hell of a lot better off without them. Ethan listened to the full report of the day's events, amazed at Hank's resourcefulness. He agreed that Trent was a good addition. Keep him on full time, Ethan offered. Money wasn't an issue. A good, honest, capable fighting man wasn't easy to come by. With Trent's presence, pressure would be off some for he and Lori when they took over periodically. Ethan would feel safer, honestly, with a military-type around. Ethan and Lori were accomplished hunters but not trained in war games. Offer him a couple of hundred grand a year and hold on to him. It would free everyone else up some. Hank readily agreed.

HANK SPENT HALF the night making preparations for the boys. He'd left off their mouth gags. They sat on the hay, half-dazed when he woke them early. A fitful night he guessed, but all things considered, they looked fairly well rested. Hank had slept on hay before. It wasn't such a bad bed. Bingo still looked rough, caked blood down the right side of his head. It didn't matter, though, what they all looked like where they were going. They sure wouldn't be attending any proms. Danny's elbow was still swollen and sore but not immobile. The other two van-driving thugs muffled themselves in quiet conversation, apparently plotting some strategy. They all were too thoroughly trussed up to worry Hank. He opened the duffle bag of weapons he and Trent had collected from the goons: one forty-caliber, and three 9mm pistols; an Israeli Uzi, 9mm variety; two 223 caliber assault rifles and clips; along with numerous clips and extra ammunition. The Uzi had three 40-round clips and was considered a formidable automatic weapon. Hank would add all of these to his arsenal.

He inquired of boot sizes. What was this moron thinking? Only Bingo took him seriously. Pants and shirt sizes? They listed them as best they knew. What the hell was going on? Trent came in, a minute or two, and left. The POW's appeared thoroughly confused about what the day might bring. They sure as hell weren't expecting new wardrobes.

Shortly after noon, Hank returned to the estate with two duffle bags of clothes, two dozen packages of dried jerky, freeze-dried food packs, and a rather large supply of miscellaneous items including sleeping bags and a large tent. It was quite a collection and the captives looked on with marked uncertainty. One of the van goons, Lopez they called him, had speculated during the night they all would be hung. He set everyone's nerves on edge and wouldn't shut his blabbering mouth. Now the hanging didn't seem likely. Looked more like they were going on a camping trip of some kind. The mood lightened somewhat. There may be a ray of hope.

Hank decided to tell them the truth, at least most of it. It wouldn't matter where they were going. The truth would be completely safe.

Trent was standing guard semi-automatic in hand.

"Change clothes and put on the boots I brought. Load everything you want to take in the extra duffle bags." They quickly followed instructions. The sleeping bags and tent defied logic, however. It had to be an overnighter somewhere. Trent was as stupefied as they were. The mystery deepened and Trent watched and listened trying to pick up clues.

"You're traveling back in time," Hank said matter-of-factly as the goons worked stuffing their bags.

Hell, this is getting good, Trent thought. *Hank hasn't lost it has he?* "You boys know any history?" His slow-minded captives looked up but only Bingo appeared interested.

"I know a little," Bingo spoke up. "Studied it in high school and college." The other goons seemed insensitive to history., or else didn't know a thing about it.

"Well," Hank said in his best professorial voice. "If you weren't in modern times, what era in American history would you like to visit, permanently?"

The question didn't appear to register again with anyone but Bingo. Bingo fell into thought. He was willing to play along. He'd lost a digit and part of an ear not doing so last night. He'd play any game Hank wanted to play.

Trent was in all the way, too. Even though he had no idea where it was all going.

"I've heard about the fight of the Alamo," Bingo finally answered. "I'd go back to that time if I could. Don't know much else about it."

"Do you remember the year?" Hank questioned seeing a ray of intelligence. The other three were clueless.

"Sometime in the 1800's, I think."

Right answer but that covered a lot of years. Of course, Hank knew the answer. "The battle of the Alamo was fought in March of 1836. Travis, Bowie and Davy Crockett died there. They were all put to the sword."

Trent was liking this. For the life of him, however, he couldn't figure where Hank was going. These goons had no appreciation for history. They were simple thugs.

"How about 1825?" Hank asked. "That's a good head start on a bunch of the interesting Texas battles. Plus, the Rocky Mountain fur trade was just opening up. You might want to run up north and see Jim Bridger and the gang." The word "gang" snapped the other three goons awake, at least for the moment.

Hank had led his horses up and saddled them earlier. At the time Trent had wondered why. They herded the POW's out into the bright sunshine. They were all stiff-kneed from sitting so long. They marched them through the lab's side door and into the large, dark room. Trent looked around startled by the size of it. He'd never been inside the structure. Hank fumbled around behind an enclosure and suddenly an image appeared on a huge screen. They all stared. Trent joined the staring. Then the image changed suddenly. Same basic image just brighter sunshine. Apparently, Hank liked this backdrop. Trent couldn't for the life of him guess what was going on.

"Can you hustle these boys out the door?" Hank asked Trent. Trent gazed out of the opening just realizing the screen wasn't a screen after all. It was a door. A large opening in the wall. Odd he thought.

"Yeah," Trent said uncertain of exactly what was happening.

"Just walk them right through the opening and stay put. You won't see any buildings, just the rectangular image of the screen when you cross over. I'm going to get their gear and the horses and be right back. Just take a few minutes." He saw Trent's puzzled look. "You can walk right through it, Trent. It's easy."

Trent wasn't prone to jumpiness, but his gut had suddenly tightened. Something was just slightly out of level here but he couldn't put his finger on it. Nonetheless, he swallowed hard before moving the POW's through. The goons went along by no choice of their own. Trent moved them a hundred feet past the opening and turned around gawking at the weird darkened rectangle frozen in the background. The oak trees remained but different somehow. There were no structures. No houses. The terrain was fundamentally the same yet different. No fences. Trent's stomach tightened even more. *What the hell was going on?*

In moments, Hank walked through the strange rectangular opening leading the gelding and the mare. The mare had several duffle bags tied on. He held something akin to a remote control, made an adjustment or two and the rectangle disappeared. Trent felt the hair on the nape of his neck spring up. The goons looked around, uncertain of their surroundings.

"Welcome to April 10, 1825," Hank announced proudly. "It was a very good year." He quickly mounted the gelding and stood in the stirrups looking over the country then looked down at the POW's. "I'll be back in ten minutes, Trent." With that he spun and galloped over a rise in an easterly direction and disappeared. He was back in less than ten minutes.

"Okay, Bingo, you and one of the other boys climb on the mare. Bingo, you drive."

Bingo hadn't sat a horse in twenty years and only then for a ten-minute ride. He took an insufferably long time mounting the mare, scrambling and clawing to get up. It was a credit to Hank's mare that she tolerated the buffoon. Finally, Lopez made it up with Trent's help. The mare nearly pitched but Hank held her down. Off they walked, Bingo barely in control. In fifteen minutes, Hank returned for the second load. Danny was pathetic. His stiff elbow made one arm barely functional. It took Hank and Trent, in coordinated effort, to get him up on the mare. It was a comedy to watch. The other van driver at least displayed a semblance of agility and swung up easily behind Danny. The horse's reins dangled loosely in Danny's hand. Hank finally gave up after seeing that the man was incapable of handling a horse. Hank grabbed the reins and led the mare away. Danny secured his one hand tightly in the horse's mane, bit his lip, and felt faint. He feared falling and if he did it would surely be his end.

Hank finally got his last two passengers off. Danny taking nearly as long to dismount as he had to mount. Untied, they joined their fellow goons. The four of them stood there looking dumb, eyes cutting around, unsure of what was expected of them. These were street thugs, completely out of their element. Smoky dives, dim pool halls, and back alleys were more their style. Pure and natural Mother Nature was as foreign to them as a plateau on Mars. Hank turned his bay gelding around, ready to spur up.

"These are rough ol' times, boys," he said looking at the bewildered group, "but you're supposed to be tough men. Now's gonna be your chance to prove it." With that he kicked his horse and disappeared over a rise.

CHAPTER

FOURTEEN

I t was tradesman's days in the streets of Fort Worth. Saturday, to be exact, and things were hopping. Buggies, freight wagons, prairie schooners, surreys, all sorts and forms of transports lined the clay-packed, dusty streets. Every conceivable form of frontier conveyance stood at ready. Scores of horses stood idle, their tails swishing the clouds of spring flies looking for something to bite. Mules, too, were well represented. Hitching rails, posts, lantern stands, even other wagons were covered with tied animals. No parking was left. In the midst of the mayhem, gaggles of kids of all sizes and shapes roamed the action-packed streets in search of fun and frolic. Parents, singles, men and women alike roamed the streets, too. There was an unfettered energy. The mother of all shopping and swapping days. Every conceivable item, that 1878 could produce, was available for purchase or even trade in some cases. It was early June now and farmer's produce was just beginning to make it in. Radishes were everywhere and sought by all. It had been a long winter without fresh vegetables and radishes were the first to arrive. More fresh vegetables would soon follow. The early spring rains had been plentiful.

H.B. entered Daggett and Hatcher's Mercantile on Weatherford Street. There was standing room only. The place was jammed with patrons. It was steaming hot and ladies stood fanning themselves, miserable in their multi-layered garments. The men sweated through their shirts. The fog of heat was so unbearable that H.B. abandoned his mission immediately and left Daggett's stepping onto the covered boardwalk. A horse whinnied close by. Another answered across the street. Two dirty-faced kids bumped into H.B., one grabbing his pants leg, playfully chasing each other. The children were oblivious to the adults around them. Their mothers were nowhere to be seen. Every man, woman and child in Fort Worth seemed to be out today.

HE WALKED DOWN BY WEATHERFORD, crossed Houston, and drifted down First Street finally leaving the worst part of the melee behind. The crowds thinned, the streets opened, and he could feel a slight breeze trying to make a comeback. He would shop on Monday he told himself. He should have known better than to try on a Saturday.

Corley's Boarding House was located a quarter mile from the town's center, at the end of First. Traffic was light, a wagon or two, a horse or two, secured here and there. He made his way steadily in long strides. H.B. had been staying at Corley's for the past ten days attending to Jessie Madelyn Corley. She was a very sick young woman. Mostly skin and bones. Her face drawn and withered. Her complexion a pallid mix of mottled grays and blotchy whites. Jessie was suffering the indignity of the final stages of a merciless disease. Namely tuberculosis. There were signs of improvement, tiny signs, but his doctoring efforts had been severely curtailed by the victim's recalcitrance at permitting needles of any kind from touching her body. Her self-appointed bodyguard, Elsa, seconded these misguided beliefs. It had taken H.B. almost a week to convince her to start taking the penicillin tablets. Now, for three days only, the penicillin's army had been on the march. The medical question was simple. Was it too late and was it going to be enough? Her usually inebriated doctor, Dr. Jeremy Fields, didn't even know of H.B.'s medical interdiction. He continually foisted off his snake oil potions on Jessie as the cure-all for all diseases, common and uncommon. At least Jessie had the good sense to pour the stuff out. H.B. smelled the concoction and it reminded him of low-grade kerosene. H.B. suspected the doctor's potion did, in fact, prevent the patient from dying of their actual disease. The snake oil likely did the trick.

His fervent attempts at befriending the young lady and her female watchdog had moved slowly. Earning their trust was no easy challenge. His youthfulness garnered a particular distrust from Elsa for some reason. The methods he wanted to employ were certainly alien to them. New-fangled bunk was Elsa's assessment. And Elsa's opinion counted for a lot at Corley's Boarding House. H.B. had no idea his break in the trust department would come in the next few hours. He would call it a minor miracle later. He was desperate, however, to intervene and take drastic measures to try and save the patient. Valuable hours were being wasted. Any miracle, small or large, he would gladly accept.

Trent immediately headed for the refrigerator and grabbed two long necks and flopped in a chair at H.B.'s long table. He gulped the first beer in two minutes. He screwed off the second cap before Hank sat down and opened a beer. He considered himself calm in most circumstances, capable of maintaining needed focus in times of crisis. His training had been long and grueling as a Navy Seal. He'd participated in Desert Storm, been dropped behind enemy lines in Iraq, operated covertly in various operations around the globe, taken life when necessary, and came close, very close several times to losing his own. However, what he'd just witnessed was inconceivable. His head was spinning, trying to get a grip on the magnitude of it.

Hank sipped his beer, remembering his own experience a few weeks earlier when first witnessing the rift. It lacked an easy explanation and yet it was simple in many ways. It was still difficult to get your arms around such a thing. He could see the look in Trent's eyes. Seeing a ghost would have had a lesser effect.

"Wow," Trent said, wiping his lips part way through the second beer. "I guess I'm wondering if this really happened? Did this really happen?" Trent's brown eyes stayed low on the table as if he was looking for a bug to cross.

"It happened. A time machine, Trent. Straight out of a science fiction novel. That's why you and I are here. The thugs want to kidnap a billionaire, but our real job is to protect H.B.'s secret. To keep the world unaware. Unfortunately, the media maggots brought the buzzards out. That's complicated things." Hank put the Texas Monthly article on the table. "This explains some of it, at least the history of who H.B. is."

Trent started reading. "Wow," he said again after perusing the story. "I had no idea."

"Trent, what would it take to keep you around, I mean on a more permanent basis?"

"How permanent are you thinking?" he asked swigging his beer.

"Well, maybe a year at a time commitment. H.B.'s out there in the past right now running around in old time Fort Worth. We've got to guard the place. Keep the goons at bay. I know the rift changes the magnitude of the job so I thought it best you know."

Trent considered the idea of a more permanent commitment. This place sure didn't lack for excitement. Better by far than guarding a spoiled celebrity or some egotistical multimillionaire. He'd been down that road before.

"Plus, H.B.'s return is doubtful," Hank added. "The goons will keep trying for a while longer I'm guessing, but it'll eventually settle down. I'd like your input and your help, Trent. Plus, we can't forget about Katy's safety."

Hank took a long swallow of beer as his mind wandered back to his lonely cabin on the San Saba. There was a lot of him still there, still working the garden, still taking the long exhilarating jogs, setting trot lines, scattering corn for the white-tail deer. This sweat hole wasn't his country, but he did relish the challenge.

"The thing that worries me the most is somehow letting this secret get loose. It would change the world. No doubt about that. It's a thing that'd start wars, I guess. H.B. feared that possibility."

"I'm in," Trent said without the slightest hesitation. "I especially like scattering these bastards somewhere in the unsuspecting past now that I think about it. Can you believe these clunk heads we just left in 1825? I'd like to follow their journey. Talk about a reality show for television. I doubt they'll last a week but boy what a week it'll be." They both chuckled thinking about it.

"If more come, Hank, let's send the next batch to the Ice

Age. I'd like to see them chunking spears at a cave bear or maybe a sabretooth tiger."

They both laughed. Hell, yeah. The next bunch goes way back.

"Trent, how does a couple of hundred grand a year, cash, sound to you?" Hank asked returning the conversation back to business. "Payable weekly, monthly, whatever pleases you. Plus, occasionally we can play around in the past ourselves. Maybe ride into the Bellville of old, visit a saloon, sit around and take in a little bit of where our ancestors came from. I've always said I was born a century too late. I've daydreamed of living back then."

"Sounds fine to me," Trent said finishing his second beer getting up and walking to the refrigerator for a third. "Three's all," he said reassuring Hank as he carried it back twisting the top. "The second wave may already be on the march. So, let's talk strategy."

Big G's mood swings had become intolerable. His secretary ducked and cowered again and she was growing weary of dodging the outbursts. The man was turning maniacal. She had once been his lover, many years before when she was young and stupid, and when there was some semblance of stability about the man, but that affair had long ago been terminated. She had gone straight, so to speak, even married and now lived with a husband whose temper and behavior more emulated a Boy Scout then the Manuel Noriega she now worked for. Her current husband had been ill for a number of years, however, and she needed the job badly. She wasn't exactly young and beautiful anymore. At one time she didn't need a resume to get a job. She was quite the head turner in her day and by just showing up, wrapped in a tight skirt and an even tighter sweater, an empty desk was usually found, but those days were over. Now they were barely scraping by. Times were hard. Her husband's medications were expensive and she knew the bitter truth; she was no longer competitive in the job market. Yes, Big G had never been a rock, but his blathering frenzy had achieved new levels. He said he couldn't sleep. Insomnia was the least of his problems, she thought. He was becoming delusional. He's on the edge, she told her husband during her extended lunch break. The man's cheese has completely slid off his cracker.

The Big G had tried Bingo's cell phone countless times, with no answer. He fully expected them back in the late afternoon yesterday. What had happened? The drive should have been no more than three, maybe four hours at the most even in the heavy Houston traffic. Pass through the outskirts of Houston, east on I-10, the Louisiana border wasn't that damn far. He'd driven it many times himself. He had been excited all day awaiting H.B.'s arrival. Practically unable to contain himself. A kidnapping ceremony of sorts was planned. With the arrival of the hooded guest and as he settled in his chair, the hood would be carefully removed, toasts to his special guests observed as the billionaire watched in awe and confusion, and then, before the catered meal was served the dramatic announcement would come. He had carefully rehearsed the little speech over and over. "Mister Bascom," he would say in front of his goon audience with as much flair as possible, "this is your last supper. Please eat up and enjoy yourself. No one should have to face their Maker on an empty stomach." Then he'd strike the champagne glass with a spoon, and the caterers would quickly swing into action. Soon, after the meal, the real fun would begin. An old quack doctor-friend of Big G's was on the invited list. Dr. Death was his nickname because of his reputation for being able to incite cardiac arrest without leaving a trace of evidence. The doctor, highly touted and long-schooled in back-alley medical techniques would be patiently waiting to perform his specialized services. He had a bottle of sodium pentothal in his possession to make it happen. The "truth serum" would go to work and account numbers would gush forth and billions of dollars would land in Gerard Fremont's overly generous lap. His long suffering would be over. He could pay off the damn IRS. He could bet again. He could reopen his closed brothels in another town, outside another city. The infusion of funds would make him a force to reckon with.

However, something was bad wrong. Bingo's plan seemed well-conceived and thought out, yet there was no H.B...and not a word from Bingo. He called the flying service and was finally connected to the pilot who flew them. Chutes deployed. Directly over the target. He didn't hang around but he did see the team heading down. The men seemed anxious to go, he said. There had been no hitch, whatsoever, that the pilot could see. Then where the hell were they? Six men just couldn't suddenly disappear off the face of the Earth. Maybe Bingo had betrayed him. Claimed the billionaire as his own prize. Why not? This thought had Gerard Fremont frothing at the mouth.

CHAPTER
FIFTEEN

He fit the left seat better than the right. With many thousands of hours of flying time, Ethan wasn't one to enjoy the co-pilot's seat. He had a smart-ass instructor, a cocky little character who had spent thirty minutes jawing that he qualified as a Citation instructor at their special school for Citation instructors in Oklahoma City. La-de-da. The man's tongue seemed hinged in the middle and wagged at both ends. Ethan finally had enough and with a smart remark of his own cut it short.

"Damn things got wings and a motor, right," he snapped back anxious to get on with the flight instruction. "Most everything flies the same, right?" The instructor sensed the insulting tone and gathered up his courage to shoot back, but at the last moment he held his tongue. Jet instruction students were hard to come by. The pay was the best in the market. No use in getting fired at the onset. He'd milk this dude for all he was worth, stretch the instruction out, find creative ways not to sign him off. He'd pay through the nose for being a wise ass.

After the first few minutes in the air, he knew his instructor-padding-hours scheme wouldn't hold water. The man handled the airplane like a pro. How in the hell did he know so much? He was a smooth operator. A natural. He answered every question, fielded every inquiry, dealt with every supposition with the deftness of an instructor himself. Scott Van Berg had never ridden with such a proficient flyer in his ten years as an instructor. After a rocky start, he decided he best butter this man up. He had to have money to afford a Citation, but he flew into town in a Super Cub. What was a man with this kind of money doing living way out in the bush? He had wrongly assumed this client would have limited skills, but this was no hayseed at the helm. Scott started feeling unneeded and restless. Hell, he could go to sleep on the long deep couch in the back and awaken when they land. Boy, Scott thought as he turned his head and viewed the custom interior, what a nice jet. Maybe Ethan would let him fly it, hauling passengers somewhere, if he, Ethan, happened to be busy. He'd like to do that. He'd even cut him a good deal. With this idea in mind, the cocky instructor had an epiphany. The smart aleck instructor evaporated into the thin air at 14,000 feet.

THERE WAS no love lost between Big G and his Chicago brother. There were only two siblings in the Fremont family and in Gerard's mind his older brother had, over the years, received the majority of attentions. Hamilton had been an all-state athlete, Gerard clumsy with no athletic abilities. Hamilton excelled in academics, Gerard was held back in elementary school and struggled to graduate. Hamilton graduated from college with honors and was highly recruited by numerous firms. Gerard scratched around for years at minimum wage in penny-ante jobs. His parents didn't care. He was the throw-away son. Hamilton the prize, and Gerard was reminded of that very fact at every family gathering. His brother had progressed rapidly in the hierarchy of the business world and in doing so set atop of the organization. The CEO. The top dog. However, there was one small caveat. Hamilton Fremont was a mobster, the top mob boss in a city made infamous by its mafia-style politics. In Chicago listing mobster references on your resume wasn't uncommon. If there were dirty games played in Chicago and there were many, Hamilton Fremont likely had a hand in them. Every goon, thug, street punk, or small-time gangster knew his name. Most feared him. None lived to tell about it if they tried thwarting his many operations. He'd been indicted a half dozen times over the years but the prosecutors couldn't convict him. Hamilton bought juries. Hamilton bought the best legal minds. They all knew the dangers of standing in his way. For the most part, now, city hall let him be. He was good friends with the mayor. He knew how to buy influence.

Big G placed the phone call reluctantly. Two secretaries later his brother answered, a sharp edge to his voice. They hadn't spoken to each other in years. The small talk lasted only a brief minute. If you have business talk, otherwise I have a meeting. Gerard stuttered at first, mumbled a bit, and finally spit it out. Hamilton pressed his ear tighter to the receiver. Yes, he could be interested. Possibly so. Fax the news stories up. I think I've heard about him. Yes, you'll hear from me. Okay. Goodbye. That was it. Big G flopped in his office chair rubbed his wrinkled forehead and exhaled. He had to try something and try it fast. It was his final act of desperation. The mob had been summoned. The faxes were on their way.

THE ENSUING ten days post-goon assault had been busy ones on the H.B. estate. Razor wire now totally encompassed the living quarters, except for three walk-through paths, circling front to back. Trent had broken down and packed away his original tent-camp, driven to the town of Sealy twenty miles distant bordering on I-10, and purchased a new twenty-eight-foot travel trailer. It was totally self-contained, air conditioned, and fully capable of sustaining the onslaught of Houston's summer heat and humidity. Hank had installed a small septic system to support the trailer. It was placed, next to the fence, in easy view of Katy's place of course. Plus, Katy now carried an eight-shot twenty-gauge pump shotgun at her side. Hank couldn't find a sixteen gauge readily available so the twenty-gauge would have to suffice. Katy was a proficient operator of the new weapon, sometimes firing unprovoked at tufts of grass or a misbehaving rock. Save your ammunition Hank had cautioned. Just practicing, she countered, with an accompanying expression of a shot gun rider on a Wells Fargo stagecoach. Double ought buckshot was wildly accurate at thirty yards.

Katy probed, in a roundabout way, the fate of the prisoners. She invited Hank and Trent over for supper, regularly, and the subject never failed to came up. They could tolerate the inquiries. Her cooking was superior.

"They're in another place and time, safely tucked away," Hank said for the second or third time chewing on a delicious piece of Katy's fried chicken. Trent looked off trying to keep a straight face. Hank's expression never cracked.

"Well, when did you do the tucking?" she asked sipping her

iced tea. Katy's binoculars missed very little and she was certain she wouldn't have missed their departure.

"Katy," Hank said deliberately chewing ever so slowly, "even you have to sleep sometime. It probably happened when you were taking a cat nap."

"You think so, huh. Well, you're too sneaky for your own damn good if you think that, Hank. You boys probably stretched their necks in the barn and dropped them in one of them deep holes you got dug. You boys have the makings for a real graveyard out there."

"Would you blame us if we had, Katy?" Hank countered.

"Hell no. I'm just itching to make some contributions myself. Unless you boys are scared of a little competition." They all laughed. Katy laughed along but she was stone cold serious.

Ten days later, at 1:00 a.m. in the morning, a large, heavy van stopped on the gravel road a quarter mile east of Katy's driveway. Three heavily armed men stepped out, flicked their cigarettes on the gravel, and proceeded up the road. The van, still occupied, stayed in place. The three wore dark clothing, had dark painted faces, bullet-proof vests, combat boots, ear plugs, and were wired and miced for communications with the van. They could easily pass for a SWAT team at first glance. They weren't.

They moved slowly, confidently along the edge of the gravel road. Each step deliberate and calculated. All three had previous military training as had their comrades--perhaps their only redeeming quality. However, unlike the countless thousands of veterans peacefully living in American society, this group had put an exclamation mark on their training. They had practiced and fine-tuned their skills. Professionals who didn't ask questions when the dough was right. Two were ex-CIA. Two retired FBI. Money talked and Hamilton Fremont was their employer. This wasn't a killing mission tonight. Simple kidnapping. Just the widow woman. The Team, as they were referred to, had observed through several day's of careful surveillance, the patterns of Katy and her two friends. Katy had made a mistake leaving her home wide open three days ago, walking over to visit Trent and Hank for an hour, and during the intervening time bugs had been planted. Their purpose was general intelligence gathering but the listening devices had quickly proven what was thought to be true. There was a friendship developing between H.B.'s hired protectors and the widow woman. Thus, a vulnerability was exposed. The soft exposed underbelly of a hardened shell. An opening. If her life suddenly became threatened, perilously so, would the event prove beneficial? The bets were it would, and the Chicago boss wanted action. She quickly became the priority. The means to an end. Thus, the plan was formed.

The Team approached slowly, carefully monitoring input from the van. The van was a technological whiz-kid's dream. Loaded with sophisticated cameras, sensors of various kinds and world-class listening devices, it was a 360-degree snoop-ship with practically unlimited potential. The hardened van housed seven monitors coordinating data through a central computer, which instantly analyzed, prioritized, and displayed known and suspected anomalies. It took three highly skilled technological guru's just to stay on top of its uncanny skills at data collection. It even possessed a highly classified ground radar system of Israeli design. Smuggled out of Israel by an undercover agent working with a dirty arms dealer, the radar had made both the agent and the dealer very wealthy. This particular night was so peaceful the radar was ignored. Nothing excited the remaining sensors. The three forward Team members continued unabated.

The widow woman's dogs were the only unknown. They

weren't big yappers, however, so it wasn't likely to be an issue. However, a dog's bark was alerting, and they'd seen Katy blast with her new shotgun. Ha. They doubted the shotgun would even be a consideration. They'd be in quickly, grab the old biddy, and be gone in a heartbeat, and dogs strangled easily. They would die before emitting a single bark.

The Team covered the remaining distance in less than five minutes and paused twenty yards outside the front gate listening to the mouthpieces in the van. One final scan and the all clear was given.

KATY HADN'T SLEPT WELL. Even her Doberman's were restless. She despised shades and window curtains in any form and didn't own them. What the hell was there to see inside of a widow woman's house anyway? The nearest neighbor beside H.B.'s was almost a mile away so what was the problem? Besides, she liked seeing outdoors. Windows were designed to let the moon glow in, the sunshine in, and the breezes through if there were any breezes. What good was a damn window if you covered it, shut it, and decorated it. She hated air conditioning just as much as closed windows. Katy used a rotating fan in the bedroom but only under extreme circumstances. This particular night wasn't an extreme circumstance so the fan was off. In fact, there was a nice, cool gulf breeze pouring through the screened windows making for a rare and pleasant summer night. So, she wandered around, window to window with the Dobermans' faithfully following, peering out into the darkness. However, what she was seeing wasn't total darkness. Hank had insisted on giving her a pair of night vision goggles on a recent visit and she just happened to have them on for a try out spin. They were damn heavy and cumbersome but, wow, what fun seeing things out in the blackness. Downright entertaining. The Dobermans sat down, scratching, watching her movements. Neither had ever been as nocturnal as their mistress. Actually, they were night sleepers, tight sleepers unless startled by a loud noise. However, once appropriately alerted, they would quickly spring into action.

Katy looked out across the back porch, towards Trent's trailer, across H.B.'s fence into the open pasture. She could even make out the swaying grasses as they responded to the breeze. A rare night, indeed it was, with such a cool breeze raking over the countryside, she thought. As a rule, the gulf breezes were hot and muggy, but not this one. The night goggles made it a pleasure to observe. Darkened objects were fairly clear and crisp, easy to distinguish. She liked walking around at night, outside, if it weren't for the dern snakes. Copperheads ruled in south Texas and they were cunning critters. Rattlesnakes were uncommon but still maintained a presence. Other than snakes, Katy feared nothing particularly in the dark. With night goggles she could even see snakes.

The idea of a night walk took hold the more she thought of it. She quickly hustled around, slipped on her Levi's, shook out her boots and pulled them on. Katy grabbed the shotgun, adjusted her new best friend, the night vision goggles a tad, and headed out the back door, her two dogs, Samson and Delilah in tow. She covered the sixty yards westward to the tall fence enjoying the delights of the night. Crickets played, cicadas sang, and an owl hooted softly in the distance. The night sounds always intrigued her. The multitudes of bugs and critters celebrating by singing and calling. The owl's call was haunting and lonesome. Apparently, its mate was answering.

She walked carefully at first, getting used to the contraption covering her eyes, but walking briskly was no real trick after the initial orientation. She was only perhaps twenty yards from Trent's trailer and she didn't want to disturb him. So, she struck south down the fence line thinking of maybe striking the road and walking down it a way. She had a short-sleeved shirt on, Katy wore men's shirts, and the breeze felt invigorating. The walk was actually a God-send. She had the growing feeling of becoming a prisoner in her own home. Trapped by the oddity of the circumstances. Hank and Trent were constantly talking about generic threats in military terms. She had nothing in common with the language, the military jargon, and her dad, the old sailor spoke little in the language of his trade. The Navy was a horse of a different color anyway. Some of the tactical talks made sense to her, but a lot didn't. She respected the job they were doing. Risking their lives for another man's property and land while he was away, God knows where. They weren't normal modern men in any sense of the word.

Not half way down the fence line, a noise different from the usual night sounds alerted her. The dogs' ears pricked up. They didn't bark, just looked, heads raised high. They had built-in night vision after all. The noise came from somewhere close to her house. Not necessarily loud but definitely a discernable noise. She almost released the dogs but thought better of it. They were both anxious to go, see the source of the sound, but Katy held their leashes.

The moment Katy had reached the fence, Hank's vibrating alert activated. The newly installed monitors picked up motion night or day within ten yards of the outside of H.B.'s entire hundred-acre fence line. Hank had insisted the surveillance company do this in order to pre-warn of possible impending problems. Typically, the warning was a deer wandering around, or a possum, red fox, even a flying bat could, and on occasions had, tripped the system. False alerts didn't worry him. He preferred it that way. Hank was on the couch, where he usually slept, and walked over to the screens to activate the infrared cameras. The equipment, especially the cameras, were multi-directional, seek and find equipped, with the ability to immediately hone in on the movement and identify the target.

Ground sonar, the latest development in state-of-the-art surveillance gadgetry, honed in, too. GSS or ground sensing sonar, was new and highly experimental at this point. The researchers called it, and rightfully so, BR or bat radar. The intriguing ability of bats to fly in total darkness catching flying insects all the while doing high speed maneuvers had always intrigued scientists. A great mystery. GSS had been a major research project for dozens of graduate engineering students at Texas A&M for almost a decade. Hank was now seeing, for the first time, the practical application of this extensive research. The GSS system had cost Hank dearly. An old retired professor-friend of his had told him about its development several years ago. A five-hundred-thousand-dollar contribution to the engineering department landed the first working prototype on the estate. GSS had inputted into its computers millions of known objects: size, weight, configuration, conformation, movement dynamics, structural components, mass, density, even down to measuring and determining the size and molecular structure of a single hair on the object. The GSS quickly determined the trip of the system as a human target. One meter from the fence. Initially moving now stopped. GSS mapped and tracked prior movements, too. Canine, two, breed, Doberman. Two dogs. Crap, Hank thought as he watched the continuous readouts. What in the Sam Hill was Katy doing out at this time of the morning?

CHAPTER

SIXTEEN

P aramilitary One and Two stood at Katy's front door while Paramilitary Three proceeded to the back. Para Three spoke quietly. One and Two nodded. Back door secure. The front door took less than five seconds to jimmy. One and Two stormed in flashing headlights for the first time, low intensity, LED's as they progressed quickly to the bedroom location. No one in bed. No dogs. This was reported instantly to the van and Para Three. The van's ground radar now snapped to life. The two moved quickly through the house interior searching every nook and cranny. Para Three reported no exit from the back door. All clear in the back. Para One and Two looked in closets, under beds, even searched for a ceiling entrance and floor entrance. Every possible hiding place was eliminated. The entire search took less than five minutes. The team was baffled. Exit orders were received from the van. They stepped out to Katy's front porch standing idle for a moment. The van's radar was scanning. No readouts or confirmations yet. Where the hell was the old bitch? Para Three moved around the north side of the house approaching the front, visually outside of Katy's view. When Para Three walked through the front yard towards the front yard gate, Katy clearly saw for the first time, a figure in her goggles, a single intruder. Para Two and Three were out of her field of view, still standing close to the jimmied door.

There was the source of the sound. Katy braced for action. The twenty-gauge kicked and she wanted her feet planted firmly. She guessed the intruder was about seventy-five yards away. The nine pellets loaded in 00 buck shells would spread some, not hold a perfect pattern at that distance, but a few should strike the target. She'd shoot damned fast she thought. As quick as she could jack and fire. She'd knock the trespassing, window-peeping bastard down. In the very instant pressure was applied to jack the first round, two other intruders appeared in her line of vision moving off the front porch. Damn. Two more thugs. Now she was really pissed. She had left additional shells in the house. The eight rounds in the gun would just have to do. She fussed, momentarily, at herself for not thinking ahead, for not bringing more shells. She watched One, Two, and Three huddle ten steps from her front gate. They appeared, Katy noticed, to be looking down the road, westward for some reason. Jacking the shotgun would get their attention. She paused and tried to calm down. Her heart pounded in her chest. The dogs, luckily were still not barking, but they tugged for their freedom. She reached down, unsnapped their leashes, but held tightly to their collars. They were restless, thrashing some, anxious to attack, wanting some action. Unknown to Katy, the heavy van's radar was quickly closing in on her.

HANK WAS ten seconds away from walking out to get Katy when the GSS system beeped again. He swore under his breath. New targets. He quickly approached the monitors, spotting for the first time, a lone figure standing on Katy's back porch. What the hell, he thought, in disbelief. Is Katy aware of this trespasser? She had somehow slipped out past this guy. Hank puzzled a moment. The GSS screen indicated Katy appeared to be watching, turned in the intruder's direction, dogs in tow, her weapon clearly outlined. He quickly dialed Trent. We've got problems. Close proximity. Meet you at the trailer. Pronto. Keep very quiet.

Two new banana clips had just arrived for the Uzi, seventy-five rounds each, so he jammed one clip home and grabbed the other. His Glock forty caliber hung on his hip. He strapped on his bag of explosives. Night goggles were in place and another beep. Damn. He needed to go. A quick glance confirmed two additional targets now joining a third. In the front yard, near the gate fence. Crap! Just how many goons are out there anyway?

Hank moved low and swiftly to Trent's trailer, finding him already outside watching Katy and her dogs. Hank held up three fingers and pointed towards the house. Understood. They moved to the small fence gate, the opening lock clicked audibly, and they both prayed for no squeak in the hinges. Luck. No sound emitted in its opening. They could see Katy froze in position, fifty to sixty yards away, shotgun pointing, dogs moving slightly appearing anxious and on the ready. Any moment her location would be revealed and fireworks would erupt. Strategy? Hank waved for Trent to move to the right circling behind the house, in a northward direction. Katy's house would block the goon's view of Trent's approach. Hank immediately moved towards Katy hoping to get her down low, face in the dirt if possible, making her a hard target to hit.

However, she was a woman liking action, Hank thought as he slid quickly down the fence line. She'll be raring to join in and maybe not cooperative, but he had to try. These were obviously pros. He was moments from exposing himself but it was a pitch-black night. The GSS had reported no night vision on the goons. Sound was his concern. It was a miracle they hadn't heard the rustling of the dogs and the fence gate.

THREE EARPHONES on the Team received the message simultaneously. One person on the move. One stationery. Trent was a non-acquisition. The house somehow blocked the radar's penetrating rays thus his presence remained unknown to the van. Para One, Two, and Three were ordered to pull out. The mission commander in the van, the Colonel, he was referred to, had seen enough. Immediately vacate. Had she been tipped off? How had they been found out? Had their bugs been discovered? Many questions flashed through the Colonel's mind as the monitors glowed. Move quickly, he shouted in their ear sets. A third blip has appeared on the screen.

Para One, Two, and Three reached the front yard gate, opened it, and started walking the several yards towards the road when Katy jacked a shell and suddenly opened fire. Samson and Delilah, momentarily stunned by Katy's shooting, didn't chase the intruders. Instead, they spotted Hank, instantly recognizing him and bounded in his direction in a friendly fashion. Katy's barrage continued, wildly blasting into the night, barrel flaming as one round followed another. Her goggles dislodged with the first shot so she shot blindly into

146

the darkness. She emptied the shotgun before Hank could reach her and pull her down – which he did. She fought ferociously mistaking him for an attacker. She flailed her fists, grabbed, and kicked all in the same motion fighting with the determination of a wildcat. Katy put up a valiant struggle all the while Hank held on trying not to cause a great commotion. He was fully expecting return fire at any moment from the goons. Then he heard Trent's gun open fire.

"Katy, Katy, Katy," Hank whispered fiercely. "It's me, Hank. Settle down, Katy."

Finally, she realized it was Hank and she relaxed as Hank released his strong grip.

"Stay down, Katy," he said, "I've got to go. Trent's out there, too. So, watch out for random shooting." He quickly ran forward, striking the road within a few seconds. More gunfire. He could see the flashing coming further down the road. They were returning fire at Trent. Rapid fire. Full automatics. Rat, tat, tat. These guys meant business. Then, in a mere fraction of a second, gunfire came Hank's way. He heard the bullets whizzing over, passing perilously close to his head. He dropped to his knees and put the Uzi to work. It, too, was fully automatic and Hank directed the fire towards the large van. His night vision showed it clearly. It resembled a television crew wagon with antennas protruding. He shut the Uzi down after half the clip expired, tucked and rolled into the bar ditch. He heard the metallic sounds of doors opening and slamming, and in moments heard the increased rpm's of the van's engine apparently attempting to turn around on the narrow dirt road. Hank hurried forward, low in the bar ditch, cautiously but quickly. He couldn't judge if all the goons were in the vehicle or not. More may had exited. The three may have climbed in. Gunfire again erupted. Flashing from the side, maybe fifty or sixty yards from the vehicle itself. The hefty van was now sideways doing incremental forward and backward movements. A deep bar ditch surrounded it on both sides. The van's transmission clanked and ground as rapid forward and reverse gears were engaged.

Hank swung the Uzi up and finished the clip, firing at the bottom of the van, trying to hit tires, perhaps something under the undercarriage. Sparks flew from the ricocheting shells. No return fire at the present. No goons visible in his night vision. Finally, the van's lights flipped on. No attempt at stealth any longer. Turning the lumbering monstrosity around in the dark was proving to be difficult, if not impossible. The nose of the van now sloped precipitously forward, just inches from slipping completely into the ditch. The rear tires were spinning trying for traction, slinging gravel. Hank quickly installed the second clip and ran forward at full tilt now. He could hear his boots grinding the gravel. He saw Trent approaching from the north, moving slowly, cautiously. The van had to be armored. That fact he was sure of. The heavy armor responsible for the weight and bulk of the behemoth added substantially to its clumsiness in close quarters. It was a very large panel van, raised chassis, over-sized tires. Antennas protruded from all angles. Built for a specific purpose. Operations vehicle of some kind, surveillance equipped, heavily protected and armored, but a fish out of water on a narrow country road. Loaded with hefty goons didn't help matters either, Hank thought. He spun in close quarters now behind the van and swiftly tossed one of his large explosives under it. The fuse spewed. Trent stood, not far away, at the ready, watching. Hank moved his direction and braced for the explosion. Boom! Rocks and gravel scattered. Dust engulfed the vehicle. The van rattled and shook. Hank moved in again and tossed two explosives. The van's tires were spinning in reverse, the tail lights blinked through the fog of the dust. Simultaneous explosions. The van teetered for a moment vibrating from the explosives and nosed forward, slowly, inexorably sliding into the jaws of the deep bar ditch. Hank launched another, hitting the roof and hoping it wouldn't fall off. A stunning result. Antennas flew, shards of metal left the top of the van scattering in all directions, electrical cables dangled, sparks tittered and flashed. Aha, the roof was the weak point. Lightly armored if any. One more on the roof and it might open the damn thing right up like a tin can, Hank thought as he tossed again. He could see Trent watching, highly entertained, with his fingers stuffed in his ears to stifle the booming noise.

The second roof explosion was devastating. Its explosive force penetrated downward into the interior creating a strong concussive shock. Eardrums ruptured, shards of metal and debris deeply penetrated several bodies, lungs collapsed, eyes detached from their moorings and swung like marbles on elastic strings, even sinus cavities imploded. Internal and external bleeding hit its occupants. Three of the seven van occupants died instantly. Another would die in minutes. The remaining three were debilitated and critically wounded. The van's motor continued running but the headlights were knocked out. The gulf breezes cleared the explosive dust quickly and Hank glanced southward and saw Katy approaching down the road, shotgun at the ready. The dogs were nowhere to be seen.

"Think they're all dead?" Trent asked standing fifty feet away impressed, with Hank's pyrotechnics. All actions in the van seemingly had ceased.

"Maybe," Hank said pumping his right hand up and down for Katy to see. Hopefully she'd take it for a peace offering and not blast away. She kept moving steadily forward with a death grip on her twenty gauge. "I'm tempted to drop another down the chimney just to be sure. It'll be risky yanking a door open to find out."

"True," Trent agreed moving closer. Katy arrived huffing and puffing, removing her night vision gear and staring in disbelief. Damn, was the only word that passed her lips.

"I'll try pulling the door open," Trent said after a minute's pause as they eyed the van and listened for any telltale signs of movement. "Cover me."

Hank pulled his pistol and brought it up. Cocked and at full ready. Trent yanked and the van door flew open. A body rolled out unconscious or dead, gravity doing its part to release it. The goon's combat boot hung in the sliding door preventing a complete departure. Monitors, at least part of them, still glowed and buzzed on the inside of the van. There was a smell, an acrid scent of explosive remnants and burned wiring emitting from it. Bodies were slumped over and unmoving. All were either unconscious or already dead.

"Last job this bunch will ever pull," Hank stated. His voice quivering in anger. His deadliest moment always surfaced when the enemy was defeated and defenseless. Now, for the next few seconds, he wanted to make sure. Toss in a couple of extra fireworks and let 'em rip. He fought for self-control. Trent recognized the moment, too. Who in the hell in this bunch deserved the privilege of being held a prisoner anyway? Night stalking bastards. Even Katy looked on with cold, deadly eyes. No one could conjure up the slightest pity for these goons.

SEVENTEEN

He nearly lost control of his feet running down the narrow boarding house stairway. The sharp scream, as he sat on the edge of his bed, had come from Jessie's room he thought. However, after opening the bedroom door, a low moan clearly emanated from downstairs. H.B. hustled down the wooden stairway and it clattered and creaked in response. A moan again. The kitchen appeared to be the source. When he reached the kitchen, he saw Elsa draped over the kitchen table. As he crossed the four steps to her side, he saw blood dripping off the table's edge splattering the floor. Two bowls were askew, a butcher knife between them. Elsa's right arm was pinned downward with the left arm and hand extended above her head. Her face and body lay flat against the table and she appeared to be in shock. Moaning again as H.B. viewed the left hand spurting a stream of blood. He quickly tore a kitchen towel in strips and reached for the hemorrhaging hand.

Elsa jerked and moaned. She tried, at first, to fight him off.

Refusing his attempts, but he overpowered her feeble effort and examined the cut. The left palm was a blue color, almost purplish, with a stab wound opposite the thumb. The knife had penetrated deeply, perhaps halfway through the hand it appeared. H.B. quickly wrapped, tightly, the towel strips in circles around the wound. The pressure wrapping instantly curbed the blood flow and Elsa moaned softly. Her breathing was shallow and quick.

A gasp at the kitchen door. It was Jessie. Dressed in her nightgown. Her thin frame looked fragile and breakable. Her features were pale, frazzled black hair, bluish lips. She leaned against the door jam for support, attempting to catch her breath. Rattling noises rumbled in her chest. She was struggling for the required oxygen to stay lucid.

"Oh, my God," she sighed. Her skinny fingers covering her trembling blue lips.

H.B. turned Elsa over on her back, carefully, and left her lying on the table. Elsa's head rolled uncontrollably to one side. The bandaged hand started oozing crimson through the towel. A thin streak of blood trailed down the elbow. "Jessie, come here quickly," he urged. "Please hold her hand up. I need to get my bag."

Jessie wobbled over shakily. Her vision was blurry with tears. She felt faint. A ringing sound trilled in her ear. In her weakened state, even a few more steps to Elsa tested her endurance. She picked up Elsa's hand but feebly dropped it. Her strength was gone.

"Hold the bandaging," H.B. instructed. "It won't hurt to touch it." She did and for the moment seemed in control. Elsa's arm jerked spasmodically. H.B. ran upstairs his clomping boots reverberating through the still house. He grabbed two bags and hastily returned. Jessie was near collapsing when he reclaimed Elsa's hand. Jessie sank exhausted into the nearest chair. H.B. heard the front door rattle open and close. He then heard a rather loud rapping on the door, apparently knocking from within. Jessie whispered come in but H.B. doubted the guest had heard. He was busy unwrapping the bloodied kitchen towel when Dr. Fields peered around the kitchen door.

"Doctor," H.B. said noticing him standing there. "Can you assist me?" Dr. Fields hurried over. "Here," he said directing him. "Place pressure on the cut with the towel for a moment." The doctor complied, exhaling the stale smell of a recent date with the bottle. Elsa's comatose state surprised Dr. Fields momentarily. He had always known the widow as the feisty, incorrigible, Elsa. Capable of neutralizing her opponents with cutting words or a withering glance. He instantly forgot Elsa and her state, however, when he witnessed H.B.'s first injections into Elsa's flesh. Several in fact. Then the speed of the professional dressing and stitching and caring for the wound stunned him. In a matter of minutes, the job was completed. Dr. Fields' jaw dropped open, surprised by the smooth efficiency of H.B.'s fingers. A twenty-first century trained trauma surgeon at work. A look of amazement covered his face.

Elsa gained consciousness with the assistance of smelling salts and looked around groggily. She glanced down at her hand and moaned again. H.B. raised her up from the table slowly and helped her into a chair. Jessie reached over and gently touched Elsa with a tender hand. Elsa struggled to regain her senses, trying to fight off the fog in her brain. Regardless of her efforts, she couldn't remember exactly what had happened.

Dr. Fields stood mutely. H.B. gathered Jessie in his arms and instructed her to hold tightly to his neck. She complied and he slipped his arms underneath her legs and lifted her. She was as light as a feather. As he carried her up the stairway, he could feel her thin legs draped over his arm. She held on tightly, unsettled by the experience. He nudged her bedroom door open with a boot and placed her gently on the bed, carefully fluffing her pillows. When she lay back, he noticed a pinkish blood stain on her nightgown. She had apparently unknowingly expectorated on it.

"Do you have a spare nightgown?" he inquired.

"Yes, why?" she asked weakly.

"You have bled on yours," he said. "What drawer is it in?"

She pointed feebly toward a dresser and bobbed her head yes when he opened the second drawer. She wore a chemise under her nightgown and resisted not as H.B. slipped the stained one off and replaced it. Early rays of sunshine spread through the open window filling the room with light. Sounds of Fort Worth buzzed below them. H.B. walked to the door and paused a moment looking back at Jessie. She was embarrassed by his changing her nightgown and even more embarrassed by the act of staining it. Jessie kept her eyes trained on the ceiling feeling intensely ashamed. She was agitated at her sickly state. Embarrassed by the inability to do even the simplest of tasks.

"Do what you want," she said softly never moving her eyes. "Make me well, H.B. Whatever it takes. I promise I'll mind you, but please do it soon."

IN LESS THAN an hour an intravenous cocktail coursed through Jessie's veins. The needle could hardly find a working vein in her skinny arm and hands. The solution dripped now and H.B. was galvanized to action. Elsa was lying down, resting. Dr. Fields had left mumbling to himself apparently in much need of a drink. H.B. sat with Jessie, on a small chair, close to her bed praying for a miracle. He certainly wasn't an expert regarding infectious diseases but he'd reviewed the medical journals in depth about tuberculosis. This was her only hope. It didn't take an expert to realize that.

Jessie remained lucid, even alert. A breeze played through the window curtains. The heat of the afternoon pounded relentlessly through the thin frame structure of the boarding house. She still felt the heat of embarrassment in her cheeks. At twenty-three years of age, be it a doctor or a man, she'd never had the intimate experience of being undressed and dressed. H.B. was reading a book of some kind seemingly unmoved by the event. She decided a stab at small talk might alleviate somehow her feelings of shame.

"Is it a good story?" she asked as he raised his eyes. Her green eyes remained locked on the ceiling. Her labored breathing and the rustling window curtains the only sound in the room.

"Excellent story," he said. "You might enjoy it, too. I've read it several times."

"What's it about?"

"Some retired Texas Rangers going on a cattle drive to Montana," he answered.

"I've never seen a book that looks like that. It's smaller and thicker than I've seen."

H.B. replied, "It's called a paperback. Easier to hold and less expensive to buy. Would you like to read it?"

"I might," she replied quietly. She was bored beyond belief to be honest. Her bed had become a prison, the center of her sad existence. She felt chained to it.

"If you'd like I'll read to you," H.B. offered. "It should help pass the time. That way I can stay and closely monitor the medications."

Jessie nodded in affirmation, closed her eyes, and began listening to the narrative of Lonesome Dove. H.B. read to her an hour before going to the kitchen. Paula Jane, the young girl who helped around the boarding house, came by and assisted with supper. After a meal of chicken soup and bread, H.B. read for three hours under the lamplight. Jessie listened with rapt attention. But finally tired. The lamp was doused and H.B., after checking on Elsa, fell asleep. He checked in on Jessie several times during the night. She seemed to be resting well.

LORI WAS an easy woman to live with in nearly all respects. However, summer in remote Alaska was considered construction season, but this summer had been different. The early spring trip to Texas had slowed matters. Ethan had been in town soloing the Citation and was spending more time there than at the cabin. Lori knew the summer would quickly come and go and the promised arctic entrance might remain unfinished. She was beginning to be concerned.

Ethan had put in a long day laying out the arctic entrance and had even started framing the six by eighteen structure. It was Friday and he intended to have it dried in by tomorrow. Summers in Alaska meant daylight from 4:00 a. m. to midnight. Daylight seemed endless now so he was determined to make a good showing. Plus, three weeks and counting before they headed back to Texas to spell Hank. Hank was anxious to spend time on the San Saba and leave H.B.'s fenced domain for a spell. The problems there had been ongoing.

It was 9:00 p. m. when he walked in from working and sat down at the table. Their twenty by twenty-eight-foot cabin was built in chalet style and had a twenty by fourteen sleeping loft. It was a perfect size for a couple who were unpretentious. Lori was reading a novel, her favorite indoor pass time.

"I'll have it dried in tomorrow," he said and she nodded approval. He wanted to take a short trip, a break-in flight of some distance in the jet, but he had to be cautious. She would be primed, likely, to disagree. So, he floated the idea carefully. No imperatives. Just small, innocent, declaratives. "What would you say to an overnight, maybe Monday night somewhere? Just a couple, maybe three hours out and back. Return in the afternoon Tuesday and back to the cabin. I want to familiarize myself before jetting off to Texas."

Lori knew his level of competency. He was an intensely agile pilot. He could circle the globe in a plane without ten minutes of preparation. He'd been flying since he was a kid in high school for gosh sakes. The jet was a play toy to him, albeit an expensive one, but she decided to humor him. All this escapade involving their commitment to H.B. wasn't his fault alone. They had both made the call. She knew she shared the responsibility.

Lori raised her eyes from the novel. "Where are you thinking of going?"

"I haven't decided. Do you have some secret destination in mind? I'd be glad to chart the course."

She did, in fact, have a location in mind – Dawson City, Yukon Territories. Klondike country. Diamond Tooth Gerties. A fun little place where the gold rush was king at the turn of the century past. It was now a hub of tourist activity. A day or two there would be fun. So, she floated the idea.

"How about Dawson City? That's a pretty good flight, isn't it?" Ethan had been thinking Seattle but actually anywhere would do. Dawson City would be just over an hour's flying time. They had a nice runway.

"I'll check weather early Monday. Dawson sounds good enough to me." He stood and grabbed a mouthful of sunflower seeds and went back to nailing. Maybe their friends in Wasilla would want to come along. He'd like to show off the jet.

EXPLOSIONS and rapid gunfire were duly reported to the local authorities. The call came in after midnight with only two deputies on duty in Austin County. Bellville, like a lot of small towns, slumbered after midnight. Deputy Cole Lange took the dispatcher's call. He was dozing in his patrol car five miles west of town in his favorite lounging location. Less than a dozen county citizens used this particular road and only in the daylight. Most were elderly and didn't drive at night plus it had no outlet. A perfect place to catch a nap and while away the wee morning hours. Plus, it was a dead time. He liked the graveyard shift. Besides the Doughnut Shop didn't open until 5:00 am. The radio crackled.

Annabelle dispatched the graveyard shift. Six to ten calls were the average between midnight and 6:00 am. She consistently nodded off herself and was startled when the call came in.

"Dispatch," she said groggily trying to clear the cobwebs.

"Hello, can you hear me?" the female voice said.

"Yes, this is police dispatch. I hear you loud and clear."

"This is Lou Ann Turner. I'm east of town on County Road 129."

"Lou Ann, this is Annabelle. I know where you live."

Annabelle had dispatched the graveyard shift for over twenty years and she knew every nook and cranny in the county.

"Hi, Annabelle. Well, Elton and I have heard a lot of shooting and popping going on over towards Katy's place. Woke us up. Several loud explosions, too. We're kinda worried about her."

"Okay, Lou Ann. I'll report it to the deputies. Are you still hearing it?"

"No, it went on for maybe five minutes and quit. It's all quiet now."

"Okay, I'll call a deputy and he'll probably drive out and take a look. Thanks for letting us know."

Deputy Cole Lange cleared his throat and answered Annabelle. Damn two-way radio was a constant source of irritation to him. He hated being on a tether. Annabelle just liked to call to make sure no one slept but her. He had caught her napping once a couple of years ago when he entered the police station and snuck into the radio room surprising her. To her his thoughtless action was an unforgivable indiscretion. To piss everybody off, she'd even key the mic periodically just to make noise and irritate a resting deputy.

"Gunshots and explosions have been reported out west 129," the radio dispatch said. "Deputy Lange, do you have a copy?"

"10-4 that. I copy."

"Lou Ann Turner reported it. Sounded like it came from Katy's place. You got a copy, deputy?" He hated her condescension. He could hear it in her voice. That damn radio room was her ivory tower and she ruled it like the Queen of Sheba.

"10-4, I copy. I'll take a look see," he lied. "Fourteen clear." His patrol car number was fourteen. He didn't give a tinker's damn what happened at Katy's place. She had dressed down every deputy in Austin County a dozen times and the sheriff, too. She was a pure hellcat, a widow with an attitude, and explosions could be nothing but good news for the law enforcement officers of the county. Maybe some terrorists had run over her ass. Ha, ha, ha. Maybe the Air Force accidentally strafed and bombed the damn place. He smiled to himself, yuking at the thought of such an event and tuned down the two-way radio a notch, closing his eyes. He hated like hell to be bothered by Annabelle just when a good dream was unfolding. Maybe he could dial it back.

THEY SPENT an hour pulling the surveillance van out of the bar ditch. The vehicle had the weight of an Army tank. Two of the three remaining thug commandos died during that hour. Only one remained alive but he was mostly comatose, roaming in and out of consciousness. He was hemorrhaging from all orifices, close to checking out. The proximity of the explosives had taken its toll. The second roof explosion blew a three-foot gash through the top of the van. H.B.'s barn now had a new occupant. The new arrival was an electronic marvel laden with high tech wizardry. Trent and Hank spent another half hour trying to decipher all the onboard systems. On the floorboard of the van, Hank spied a small spiral notebook and found it filled with useful information. Dates and places specific to the goons' snooping activities and their subsequent plans for kidnapping Katy were listed. Surveillance information even detailed the bugs installed at Katy's house and their specific locations. *What? Bastards*, Hank thought as he read through it. Evidently these punks were pros but they had still gotten their asses kicked.

Katy stayed with them looking around H.B.'s barn. It was almost 3:00 a. m. but she was too hyped to sleep. She bent over and checked on the remaining survivor seeing if he was still breathing. She was shocked when he grabbed her hand. He was trying to speak. Phlegm rattled in his throat as he worked to clear it. Katy yelled for Hank to come over.

Hank bent over the goon trying to see if he could understand his babble. With much effort, the sound clarified. He could make out words. He identified himself simply as the Colonel. Were his men dead? Yes, Hank acknowledged. How many men attacked them? Two Hank answered. That reply stopped his inquiry for a moment. The dying commando seemed to be pondering the odds. Working on the analysis. *Military training?* he asked. Yes. Navy Seal and Marine. *Why not tell him the truth?* Hank thought. He'd soon be plotting strategy with the devil anyway. Hank decided to do a little fishing of his own. Who hired you? There was a considerable pause. The Colonel's eyes closed, his breathing labored and shallow. Fremont, he said finally. Hamilton Fremont. Wasn't Gerard Fremont the boss? The Louisiana coon ass? No. Hamilton's from Chicago. Gerard's brother. Well, well. They teamed up, Hank thought. So old Gerard brought in reinforcements. As if they couldn't find enough goons in Louisiana. Since the guy was spilling his guts why the hell not ask? How many more are coming? Again, a long pause. Then the Colonel's body shook as a violent spasm overtook it and Hank fully expected him to expire, but he didn't. After several long minutes he became coherent again. He continued talking. Heavy mob involvement. Soldiers aplenty. No specifics but many interesting generalities. Then he shook violently again and this time he didn't make it through. He gargled a minute, choking, and with great effort took one final breath. His eyes rolled back in his head. The Colonel departed for the other side and joined his fellow conspirators. General Lucifer would soon be issuing the Colonel and his cohorts new marching orders.

BODY DISPOSAL WAS FAST BECOMING A GROWING problem at H.B.'s ranch. The seven bodies were stacked like cordwood in the barn and had to be dealt with as daylight brought increased heat and persistent blow flies. Katy finally wandered home to tend to her Doberman's and try to catch a little rest. Hank and Trent had earlier removed the bugs so she began to feel a return of her sense of privacy. The slimy bastards and their bugs made her feel defiled. She took a quick shower attempting to wash away the filth of it all. She couldn't help but have the growing feeling that she was in a war zone now. She walked from window to window peering out trying to anticipate the next assault. Wondering what would be next. She had just sat down with a cup of fresh coffee when the phone rang. It was Lou Ann. Her reputation as a gossipmonger rivaled few in Austin County.

"Oh, dear, we thought something had happened to you."
Sure as hell, took you a long time to check on me, Katy thought.

"All that gunfire and explosions. Goodness sakes, Katy, what was going on?"

"Fireworks, Lou Ann. Plain and simple fireworks. Sometimes I just get the urge to make noise. Hell, you and Elton should have come down and joined in the fun."

There was a pregnant pause on the line. Lou Ann was taken aback. How could anyone do such a thing in the early morning hours when folks should be fast asleep? Katy had always been an enigma, but this was over the top even for her.

"Those loud explosions practically shook our house. I hope you didn't blow something up, dear."

"Oh, I blew plenty up, Lou Ann. I had some old crap stored in my cellar and just decided to blow it to smithereens. Dynamite will do that you know. Scattered it all over creation. It's easier to rake up smaller pieces than haul the big ones." Another long pause. Then a tentative voice.

"Well, bless your heart. We're just glad you're okay. Sure, good to hear your voice." Bullshit. She only called when some tidbit of gossip might be gleaned and shared with the whole county. She'd called a half dozen times when H.B.'s articles first hit the news. Thinking Katy might have some insight into H.B.'s strange ways. Lou Ann was a blue-ribbon pot stirrer.

"I'm great. Couldn't be better. Lou Ann, if you ever need anything blown up just let me know. Okay. It's a great way to release your pent-up frustrations. I feel truly liberated today. Just call and I'll be right up with the explosives."

A weak "okay" then an even weaker "goodbye" quickly followed. Her damn nose should be six-foot-long Katy thought as she swallowed the steaming coffee.

HANK AND TRENT grabbed two shovels and went on a grave digging detail. They dug the rich soil near H. B's estate on the precise date of February 15, 1770. They had both brought their rifles along just in case a roving band of local natives might stumble by looking for trouble. It took most of two hours to dig a large enough hole to accommodate the dead. It was to be a family burial. They walked a quarter of a mile away from the rift entrance enjoying the cool of a February day in the distant past. Just for fun, they brought an axe and cut a gash in one of the smaller live oaks. What would happen to the gash and would it be there in modern times? They'd check it out after the goons were planted. Hank's pickup truck drove through the rift to 1770 without a hitch. The bodies had been wrapped in canvass and were carefully stacked in the grave and covered up without fanfare. The Lord's Prayer was said more for the benefit of the newly fertilized soil than for the occupants interred within. Then back through the rift they drove. Immediately they returned to the burial site in the modern era and found the marked tree. Wow, had it ever grown. The oak had doubled in width and the gash, though long ago healed and scabbed over, was five feet higher and clearly visible. The newly dug grave was, of course, impossible to find having been covered for years with new topsoil and abundant grasses. Amazing, they both thought in muted silence as they walked back to the house. Just knowing that they had been at that particular tree and buried bodies in that specific location over two hundred and thirty years ago was mystifying and incredibly humbling. The unique capabilities of H.B.'s time machine only intensified their determination to protect it.

"I'm worried about us," Trent said chewing an hour later on a piece of charcoal-broiled steak. The steak was delicious and since neither could recall their last meal it was especially scrumptious.

"Why?" Hank asked.

"Well, we've killed nine, dispersed four prisoners in the past and taken no casualties ourselves. War is a numbers game, Hank. Eventually, the roulette marble will drop in our slot."

"I admit we've been pretty lucky. The goons have been incredibly stupid overall."

"True, but when lead flies funny things can happen. Why

they stuck it out in the van and just let us blow the damn thing up I'll never know. I'd rather take my chances in the open, wouldn't you?"

"Yeah, I sure would. I would've never made a tank operator. First, I dislike tight places. Second, the enemy knows just where you're at. I like the freedom of movement. I don't like a thick sheet of steel making my decisions."

"How's your bomb supply?" he asked. Trent turned his tea glass up for a gulp.

"Five or six left. I need to run up to the Hill Country for more. I'll call Bert in Pontotoc and put in an order. I want a beefed-up model, too. One that really goes boom."

"Get enough for me. I hate being left out when the bombs go off. Let's make us a super-sized sling shot. One that can reach the road from the bunkers. We need a good launching system."

"We can do that. I made a nice one as a kid out of inner tubes. It'd shoot a couple of hundred yards." Hank thought a minute about how he had constructed it. "Bellville's got a little charter flying service. I'll get Bert to meet me with the goods at Brady's airstrip. Shouldn't be but a couple of hours flight. He always needs money."

Then the talk turned to Katy. Her living outside the fence was becoming more and more precarious. Protecting her there was becoming increasingly complicated.

"She needs to stay in here," Hank said finally. "Inside the fence. Either that or go stay with a relative for a spell. Eventually, I hope, the dust will settle around here."

"She's a hardheaded woman," Trent offered. Her natural combativeness unsettled him a little. She could just as easily be hogtied and gagged right now or worse had the goons had their way.

"We've got to try. It spreads you and me much too thin to

cover her place, too. Hopefully, she'll understand that. It puts us all at a greater risk," Hank said. "Let's fill her up on her favorite pizza tonight and open the negotiations." The siege likely would only grow uglier. The Katy hurdle needed to be jumped. It needed to be jumped soon.

CHAPTER
EIGHTEEN

Bert was sitting on his front porch watching whitetail deer feed on his corn when the call came. He enjoyed watching the deer nibble at the trough in the late evenings. That's when the heat of the day relaxed a bit and a cool breeze usually found a little energy to stir around.

"Hello."

"Bert, this is Hank. How the hell are you?"

"Gooder'n snuff. Haven't heard from you for a while. Drove by your cabin one day and you was gone. Have you quit these parts?"

"Well, I'm employed, temporarily in south Texas. Say, Bert, I need some more of your fireworks. Have you got any made up?"

"Some, not too many. Whatcha need?"

"I need fifty to sixty of your big ones. I've only got a few left."

"By the way Hank, I've got a new super model. I'm using inch and a half PVC pipe for it. Works great. It's at least twice as powerful as the whoppin' mama you've got."

Hank thought about it a minute. "How about fifty of the new super model, and fifty of the regular whoppin' mama's. I'll pay you cash for them."

"I'm callin' the new one the 'really big whoppin' mama'. You talk about leaving a hole in the ground."

"Bert, I'll take fifty whoppin' mama's and fifty really big whoppin' mama's. I'll pay you five thousand cash for the order. I'm flying up to Brady to pick them up. You'll have to meet me at the airport. Make sure and put them in a cardboard box. I don't want the charter pilot knowing what I'm getting."

There was a long silence on the line. Bert was shocked by the offer. "Hank, that's too much money, way too much."

"My employer wants to buy them, not me. It's not my money, Bert." Hank knew Bert barely scratched along on social security, struggling to make ends meet. He lived on his folk's dilapidated old home place which had been farmed too heavily for too long and now could hardly produce a good blade of grass. For the past five years Bert had deferred the small farm hoping for a comeback. Frankly, the hopes looked dim.

"Five thousand's a lot of money. I'd feel like I was stealing something."

"Bert, you're providing a very important service. Plus, you're taking a risk if anybody ever found out what you were doing."

"I don't put labels on the damn things, Hank. Most of the evidence goes poof."

"Five thousand, Bert. That's my offer. You can take it or leave it."

There was a long pause. Hank could hear breathing in the background. Finally, Bert agreed. "Call me when they're done. Four or five days. Okay. Let me know and I'll fly up. See you soon."

KATY WAS IN A FINE FETTLE. She liked pizza and she seemed to thrive on the excitement, but Hank noticed her eyes betrayed a lingering fatigue. Her brow had deeper furrows, her eyelids reddened and raw by all night sojourns and tiring sentry duty. She was scrappy, though. Hank admired her tenacity. Her spirit seemed indomitable but her body was counting, carefully counting every misstep. She chewed on the pizza and looked around at Hank curious as ever.

"Where'd you bury the crooks?" she asked never missing a chew on her pepperoni pizza.

"We dug a deep hole and they're all happily resting in the hereafter." Hank knew the question was coming. Katy hated to think something would get past her. Body disposal, though never a priority in her former life, now placed high on her list.

"H.B. won't need no damn fertilizer for a long time, I'm thinking." She took a sip of iced tea and smiled. "That soil's getting richer by the day."

"We never invited these fellas to a party. They just keep showing up. Seems like they'd eventually catch on."

"Dumb and dumber, Hank. They're about the same caliber as these damn lawmen in Austin County. It's a wonder they've got the brains to operate their patrol cars with all them switches, and buttons and such. Hell, I've got to give the law dogs credit for one thing, though. They're smart enough to be scared. They're scared as hell of me and they had damn well better be. There's a Chinaman's chance these idiotic goons might develop a yellow streak yet."

Trent and Hank chuckled. Short of an atomic device being detonated, local law enforcement considered Katy's section of

Coushatta Road strictly off limits. They wouldn't chance an encounter with her at any cost. It was comical that a sixty-five-year-old widow, probably five foot five at most, all of one hundred fifteen pounds dripping wet, could inspire such fear in law enforcement, but she did. It was downright comical.

"Katy, you know more are coming. Trent and I've been discussing your safety here."

She broke in tersely. "Don't sweat my safety, Hank. I'm letting these Dobermans' loose next time right off. No waitin' or dilly-dallying."

"They'd be dead now had you let them loose," Hank countered. "Dogs run straight and true to their targets. They're easy to hit. They'll be the first victims."

Katy thought about that for a while chewing more slowly, looking across the table but seeing nothing. Hank was probably right but it seemed wrong that Samson and Delilah were neutralized somehow. They were designed for protection, bred for attack, schooled in the fine art of overwhelming their prey. She had depended on them for a number of years. Now, in a sense, they were almost useless.

"Katy," Hank said breaking into her thoughts. "We're not dealing with a local window peeper or a vagrant slipping around. These are bad men. Bankrolled by organized crime with a specific mission to get a reclusive billionaire at all costs. That van we blew up was a sophisticated craft designed for specific tasks. There is several million dollars worth of snooping equipment housed in it. These boys play for keeps."

"That damned H.B.," Katy snapped suddenly raising her voice level a notch. "Why'd he up and leave and let you handle his problems. It doesn't seem right to me. You boys had better be getting a big paycheck for your efforts and the risks you take. H.B. just cut and ran when it got too hot and heavy. I'd say that's pretty low down of him."

"H.B. hired us and we accepted the job," Hank responded evenly. Trent concentrated on eating, letting Hank try to handle Katy. He wasn't about to let his pizza get cold, and he sure as heck didn't want to tangle with Katy.

"We signed on to a responsibility and we take it seriously. However, you just happen to live next door to a war zone and it's not going to ease up for a while. They've probably figured out the county Mounties don't give a tinker's damn about this little corner of Texas so they feel free to hit as often and as hard as they want. Short of the governor calling in the National Guard, we're on our own, Katy."

Trent burst out laughing turning Katy's and Hank's head. The National Guard, weekend warriors as they were referred to, didn't have a reputation as a fine fighting unit. They'd have trouble not blowing themselves up with their own munitions much less protecting anybody.

Katy cut to the chase when Trent's laughter died down. She knew something unpleasant was coming. She could read it in Hank's eyes. "Okay, Hank. Let's have it. I can tell you've got something on your mind."

"Do you have relatives where you can go for a prolonged visit?"

"Hell no. I have a cousin out in California. I send her a card on her birthday and she calls every Christmas. She'd have a stroke if I showed up. Anyway, California's full of hippies and losers, Hollywood-types. Plus, the damn place is either on fire, mud sliding, sinking into some damn abyss, or choking on its own self-righteousness. California's not for me. Plus, my cousin's a wuss. We never did get along." *So much for that idea,* Hank thought.

"Would you move in with me at H.B.'s? This would only be a temporary situation, Katy. Your life's in danger. Trent and my life's in danger. We're all in danger, and your being here puts all our lives at greater risk. None of this is your fault or our fault, but we've got to prepare. With you inside the fence it makes it easier for everyone and less risky."

Katy looked long and hard into Hank's eyes. There wasn't a trace of hesitation in his voice. She was well aware of the gravity of the situation. Hank and Trent both were professionals and certainly understood her vulnerability. She, too, knew that her vulnerability created a greater risk for them as well. Their genuine concern really touched her. To have a man looking out for you felt really good. It was a feeling she'd never gotten enough of. Her dead husband had never been much of a caretaker. He was always too busy caring for himself. When he was home, he spent most of his time chasing his own pleasures. His turning to drinking and running around on her in the final years had embittered the marriage and destroyed what little feelings she had left for the man.

"It's been a while since a man has invited me as a live-in," she said mischievously. Katy's eyes danced with a coy look. "I've never been invited inside H.B.'s. Is it a decent place? You never know about an old bachelor's habitation."

"It's very nice," Hank said surprised his offer wasn't immediately struck down. "It's clean, and well furnished, and cowboyed up." H.B.'s western motif and memorabilia he greatly admired. He guessed Katy would like it, too. Katy struck him as a western kind of gal.

"Do I have a separate bedroom?" she asked holding a straight face. Trent finally stopped chewing. This was getting good.

"Sure, Katy. Private bedroom and bath. All yours. Trent and I'll even cook."

Trent burst out laughing and Katy joined in. These boys and their jokes. If she depended on them to cook, the pizza joint better stand ready. The local Bellville Dairy Queen would be on constant call. Ha. Ha.

"Okay, I'll do it, but just for you, Hank, because I know you care."

THE ROOM WAS STIFLING HOT. Architecture in the latter part of the nineteenth century left a lot to be desired in H.B.'s estimation. Narrow, tall windows were incapable of capturing a breeze even if there was one. For the past three days, nothing that could possibly pass for a breeze had made a call. Jessie's room was a sweatshop. Dank and humid. Miserable. June's heat was baking them like an oven. H.B. daydreamed of having a small rotating fan stirring around the bedroom. A little generator could run a fan. Maybe there were battery powered fans on the other side of the rift. If he ever made a return call, a fan was first on the list. At this particular moment he didn't care who'd gawk at it. His shirt stuck front and back to his sweaty skin. Jessie, however, seemed to take it all in stride. He read to her tirelessly to pass the long and sweaty hours, and she listened tirelessly. Even Elsa sat in on the reading when she wasn't busy running the boarding house. Her hand was healing nicely and she smiled sweetly at H.B. now. What a difference in her attitude. It was a very pleasant and welcome change.

Late in the heat of the third day, H.B. noticed a subtle difference in his patient. It came in the eyes. Always the eyes. Remembering her dark-ringed illness-haunted eyes were what prompted his return back to Fort Worth to begin with. They had awakened him, those sad eyes, on the other side of the rift on countless nights floating to the surface of his dreams.

Jessie's eyes proved capable of crossing the rift without the benefit of the years of tireless research H.B. had endured. Her eyes pierced time and space effortlessly it seemed.

Just after 4:00 pm, in the hottest part of the afternoon, her eyes softened and the sickness in them seemed to retreat a bit. Like a child's eyes appear after a high fever has finally broken and the illness begins to subside. The intravenous army was marching and winning some skirmishes inside Jessie. The massive medicinal cocktail was, in fact, having its effect. H.B. paused in his reading as he witnessed the subtle change. Jessie turned her eyes to him wondering why he had ceased reading. Gus was charging hard across the Staked Plains in pursuit of Lorena. It wasn't the right time to stop. Now wasn't the time to quit.

"I just need to stretch a minute," he said standing up and walking to the window. Wagons moved along First Street stirring columns of dust around. The small dust devils whirled up the street, following the wagon wheels, like miniature tornadoes. He wandered back to the bedside reaching down into his bag for his stethoscope. "I'd like to listen just for a moment." Jessie turned slightly so he could reach her chest. Even her lungs sounded better. After a couple of minutes, he put away the stethoscope and checked the IV bag. All was well. He had increased the volume of the drip as much as he dared. He checked her hands, the IV entrance, and fiddled with the tape.

"You fret too much, H.B.," she said finally watching him. "You just checked everything an hour ago. Nothing's changed."

"You've changed," he replied looking at her cheerfully. "You're feeling better, aren't you?"

"Yes. Why, yes, I am, I guess. I can't remember the last time I was hungry but I'm starving. Is that a good sign?"

"An excellent sign. An appetite always is. Tomorrow, we

need to walk you up and down the hall a few times. I'll help you do it."

"Okay, but please read now. I'm worried about Lorena. I just can't wait any longer."

H.B. sat down and continued reading. The hours passed as the sun angled to the west. Elsa eventually came in with supper. Jessie propped up and attacked the food with surprising vigor. She quickly dispatched the first helping asking for a refill. Elsa, stunned, hollered for Paula Jane who ran up the stairway clumsily.

"Young lady, can you fill a plate and get it back up here without spilling anything?"

"Why, yes ma'am I believe I can," she answered anxious to please. She was a mature thirteen growing nicely into womanhood. She had been Elsa's salvation, helping run the boarding house as Jessie's illness took over. Jessie smiled at her as she seized the plate and headed back down.

"Watch the stairs," Elsa called after her.

Dr. Jeremy Fields took supper with them a week later. Elsa had reluctantly agreed to the arrangement but only after a vehement protest. Jessie's growing strength managed to soften Elsa's attitude toward the old drunken doctor. Paula Jane was in the kitchen helping and they were using the formal dining room for the event. Elsa groused and muttered bustling about the kitchen and dining room and getting on everyone's nerves. Poor Paula Jane's nerves were frazzled due to receiving a large portion of undeserved criticism. Although, it was a celebration of sorts, the air was tense. Jessie had been detached from her intravenous lines earlier in the day and she felt supremely liberated. The meal was in her honor and the one outside guest she invited was Dr. Fields. Paula Jane was to sit at the table and the invitation had excited her mightily. However, Elsa's criticisms had a dampening effect on the experience.

He had arrived an hour earlier and jabbered nonstop with H.B. He was not inebriated, appeared clear-eyed and smelled fresh barbered. Yet another cause for celebration. He was actually sober tonight. Sober enough to be inquisitive and he directed numerous questions at H.B. and his medical expertise. Quite frankly, every single procedure H.B. performed astonished him, and Jessie's remarkable progress in the past week particularly intrigued him. Patients with advanced tuberculosis were always written off. Death was only a matter of time.

"Germany," H.B. said slightly protective. He was careful to reveal little. "They're on the cutting edge of new medical developments."

"I've practiced most of my career back east. Seems like we'd have heard something about this."

"Well, it's all very new," H.B. offered. "I guess only a few have tried these new methods."

ELSA DELIVERED a platter of hot steaming fried chicken. The kitchen's heat had wet her face and she wiped it with her apron. Paula Jane followed with two bowls of vegetables. Elsa's eyes cut to the doctor and she frowned in disgust. She never bothered to hide her contempt for the man. Jessie crept slowly down the stairway finally easing into the dining room. Dr. Fields looked up and smiled. Amazement covered his face. She wore her new vitality like a glowing aura. H.B. and Dr. Fields rose as one, simultaneously pulling out her chair and helping to seat her. She blushed, slightly, embarrassed by their attentions. Elsa returned from the kitchen issuing orders to Paula Jane in the voice of a platoon leader. Jessie tugged Elsa's arm and talked to her quietly. Elsa calmed but for only a moment.

It was a full five minutes before all were seated. Paula Jane fidgeted in her chair. Elsa dabbed at her brow again. Dr. Field's face was red and small spider veins lined his nose. He had the classic look of a dedicated alcoholic. Jessie called order to the meal and surprised H.B. by asking him to return thanks. He cleared his throat and spoke slowly.

"Father, thank You for the gift of friendship and fellowship as we gather at this table to participate in the wonderful bounty You provide for us. Bless this food, oh Lord to the nourishment of our bodies and to the supplementation of our spiritual growth. In all things Father, Thy will be done. In Your precious name we pray. Amen."

Lowered heads raised in unison, Jessie smiled, and spoons busied filling the plates.

CHAPTER
NINETEEN

The phone call was over in five minutes but the cursing continued for fifteen more. Gerard frowned with the phone stuck in his ear, mopped his brow, chewed wearily on his stubby, damp cigar, and rocked back and forth in his ancient leather chair trying to keep control of his emotions. Listening to Hamilton's tirade reminded him of his deep-seated hate for his brother. The bastard was pure mob, Chicago trained, and steeped in a kill-or-be-killed mentality. He feigned sophistication and refinement, but it was all a cover up. Just a show. He was nothing but a low-life cutthroat. Hell, by comparison, he made a small-time Louisiana coon ass like himself seem like a boy scout. Now he deeply regretted ever calling him. He'd just made another dumb ass mistake. He was beginning to accept his fate as a bumbling fool.

What pissed Big G off was not having been told of the kidnap plot in the first place. He should have known Hamilton operated without inclusion. That was his style, and it wasn't his damn fault the van and Hamilton's men had somehow disappeared. Why the same thing had happened to his crew after they parachuted in. How could he, Gerard, be responsible for something he didn't even know about? The realization that his chances for a big slice of the billionaire's pie was fading fast. At worst, there'd be no slice at all. Damn it! He was tired of listening to his brother's intimidation and blame games. Sure, there was something untoward going on at H.B.'s but how was he supposed to know? Listen, Hamilton my men disappeared, too. You haven't cornered the market on disappearances. He was close to slamming down the receiver when his brother beat him to it. Bastard! He always had to be first.

Big G rubbed his temples feeling the heat of frustration and high blood pressure reddening his face. The cigar nestled snugly in the middle of his frown, and the IRS agents were coming at 2:00 pm. Oh, shit. Now he'd have to liquidate. Sell out. Quit business. The bastard IRS was relentless. His shyster attorney was scheduled to set in on the meeting but all hope was lost. He felt sure they'd cart him off to prison this very day. Big G knew the truth; he didn't stand a dog's chance.

Merrill Field in Anchorage was buzzing. Four planes were in the pattern doing touch-and-goes and a half dozen others awaited taxi clearance from ground control. Typical summer flying in Alaska. Seemed like half of the state's population possessed pilot's licenses and today most were heading somewhere.

Ethan sat with Jess strapped in the front seat. Jess worked on the slope. An employee of British Petroleum for the past ten years, Jess worked a two-week on, two-week off schedule. His wife, Cathy, chatted in the back of the jet with Lori. They were lounging on the deep leather couch trying to look jet-setish, but they were failing miserably. Both were casual dressers clad in Levi's and flannel shirts. They'd been friends a number of years and were born minimalists. The less-is-better lifestyle seemed blatantly ironic resting comfortably in a several-million-dollar Citation.

"How'd you swing this?" Jess asked his curiosity too much to contain. "This isn't a retiree's normal transportation, I'm thinking. Y'all win the Texas Lottery while you were down south?"

Ethan laughed at Jess's attempt at speaking Texan in the middle of calling ground control again. He was impatient to leave. "No, it was bowling for bucks. We hit the jackpot." Jess shook his head at the fiction. Ethan was known as a bucket mouth. He'd get to the bottom of it.

The ascent was flawless. Departure control issued heading clearances and the Citation climbed steadily banking north over the Susitna River revealing a startling view of Mt. Susitna, referred to as the Sleeping Lady. The whisk of the jets only silenced by the occasional chatter in the radio. Ethan banked to a zero six zero heading and passed fourteen thousand feet just as the Talkeetna Mountains loomed below. Cruising altitude would be seventeen thousand feet. The day was clear. To the left of the aircraft, Denali, all twenty thousand feet plus, stuck out like a picture postcard. Ethan wondered how many climbers were on it, going for the summit. Climbers by the hundreds from around the globe clawed their way up its craggy peaks each summer. Denali, the great one, was its deserved native Alaskan name. The national park drew thousands of tourists each year.

Lori delivered two Dr Peppers and Jess and Ethan sipped their drinks. The flight would be approximately an hour. The mountains rolled below. The ramparts unlimited. The views stupendous. It truly was the last frontier. The miles flowed away at a three hundred and seventy knot cruise.

WITH KATY MOVED IN, things seemed simpler. She was a cordial and helpful guest. The kitchen needed rearranging and she busied herself with the task. It had been a womanless house for countless years and signs of bachelorhood were everywhere. She cleaned and rearranged for two days before being somewhat satisfied. The place sparkled and shined. Katy wasn't the kind who sought approval when she charged into action and spread the feminine touch. Plus, her cooking! It was indescribably good. She had a couple of hungry men to practice on which made it all the more fun. Her culinary skills had not rusted from disuse. Hank and Trent jogged daily in the cool mornings trying to wear off some of Katy's calories. They'd balloon up like the Pillsbury Dough Boy if they didn't stay active. Plus, running the fences gave them a chance to reconnoiter a bit.

Katy read voraciously between cooking duties. H.B.'s library was massive and interesting. Volume after volume of western lore and frontier history lined the shelves. It was the era Katy loved best. Best of all, the men weren't stuck on television so long evenings of draw poker were common. Katy had always had a penchant for poker and her chips, many times, outnumbered Hank's and Trent's. She was a canny bluffer. If she won too much, she accused them of being soft on her when in fact they weren't. She was just that good.

After a couple of weeks of peace, the welcome diversion

of poker playing and reading settled in on Katy. She missed her home of course, but she didn't miss the uncertainty of her nights roaming window to window in fear of some unknown threat. She was in the middle of Walter Prescott Webb's history of the Texas Rangers when a distant popping noise struck her ears. The sound wasn't all that close. Was it gunfire? She sprang up from the heavy oak rocker and walked to the screen door. A light breeze was pushing through it. Pop, again. Where are the boys? Then she saw Hank running in a crouch from the barn towards Trent's trailer with a rifle in his hand. Oh, hell, something's up. Hank was traveling low, just above the tall grasses. Then the sound of a ricocheting bullet and a distant popping rang out. She walked further out on the porch and Hank yelled at her, motioning his hand downward. Stay down, go back in the house. Trent's apparently hit and lying by the trailer he shouted. The shooter was directing his energies at Hank now. The popping continued. Katy burst in the house grabbing her twenty-gauge and jacking in a shell. Her heart fluttered in her chest. She could visualize herself as the last standing soldier at Fort H.B. Damn. One down and one to go and dear ol' Katy is next. It wasn't a very comforting thought. Another pop. Somewhere outside the fences, tucked deep in the woods, a sniper pressed his aim...and he appeared to be very proficient.

Hank reached Trent and he was lying just under the tongue of the trailer. Hank noted he was breathing just before Trent turned and gave a thumbs up sign. Trent stayed flat on the ground. Hank belly-crawled next to him.

"Just my shoulder," Trent said. "Hit the meaty part and grazed my neck. It missed the bones I think." Hank saw his blood-wetted sleeve. He checked Trent's neck and confirmed it as a flesh wound. "This boy's good, Hank," he said turning over and glancing at Hank. "Hell, you're hit, too." He saw a red spot below Hank's knee.

"Just nicked my calf. Just a scratch."

"This'll add to our Purple Heart collection," Trent said with a wry laugh.

"Are you good to move?"

"Yeah, but I'm belly-crawling from now on. He's got to be shooting from at least five hundred yards. Just missed my head by inches. The moment I bent down he must have squeezed off the round. Otherwise, there'd be brain matter scattered around."

"I shoulda guessed these sons-of-bitches would try something like this," Hank said. "It's been too quiet." The metal on the trailer released a zinging sound and a pop followed. First the bullet impact, then the sound. The firing continued. Zing and pop. Zing and pop. "How many do you think?"

"One, two possibly. Well, placed. Maybe even in tree stands." The firing was coming from the south, a heavy fortification of trees lined the area. It was a good place to hide with thick undergrowth everywhere. Mesquite and oak lined a small, clear creek. Wild mustang grape vines hung from practically all of the tree limbs near the creek thus sheltering the view of the creek itself. Beyond was a large field where cattle grazed, but were invisible from the road.

"What's the plan?" Trent asked.

"I'll head north, get through the little gate by Katy's and try to get around them. I'll have to stand up to open the gate. They'll like that."

"Let me get to the bunker first. I can spray the trees with bullets. Maybe that'll distract them."

"Okay. Good idea. When I hear you start firing, I'll get the gate open."

Trent crab-crawled away wincing slightly from his

183

shoulder wound. Hank figured they'd arrive at their prospective destinations about the same time. He left, scooting just below the coastal grass level following a northeast direction. The firing ceased momentarily. A good sign the snipers had lost their targets, if only temporarily. Hank prayed for more wind. It would hide his and Trent's passage through the coastal. After a two-minute pause, another ricocheting bullet and a pop sounded out. It wasn't close. Maybe they were shooting at the bunker now. They may have spotted Trent. Hank waited for what seemed an interminably long time before Trent started firing. Rat-tat-tat. Rat-tat-tat. Hank stood, fully exposed, and opened the lock. Rat-tat-tat. He was through the gate in five seconds. The cover fire had worked. The goon snipers had missed him opening the gate, he hoped. With any luck, they wouldn't know he was coming.

It took ten minutes to reach the stand of trees. Trying to remain undetected required passing on the north side of Katy's house and working slowly southward using whatever cover Hank could find. An occasional pop came from the trees followed by Trent's rat-tat-tat return fire, but it was too far away to determine any definite location. The battle continued as Hank worked his way through the trees, found the creek, and crossed it. He was moving westward now inching his way slowly, listening for the sniper's return fire. The creek bank was rather steep and he stayed on a knoll just south of the running water. He could see the field and the Hereford cattle, a couple of dozen, grazing unfazed by the gunfire. He supposed they thought deer season had just opened a little early this year.

The heaviest tree cover was probably five hundred yards in length roughly covering the route of Coushatta Road. In six or seven more minutes, Hank stationed himself in the center of the trees trying to pinpoint the sniper's location. There had been a cessation of firing for the past several minutes. That wasn't a good sign. One more pop and he likely could get a direct bearing.

There was a small dirt road a mile away across the Hereford pasture that connected several small ranch properties. Likely, Hank thought, the assassins had parked there. He was sure they hadn't used Coushatta as their route. Should he head to the road and try and locate the vehicle? Yes, but he'd wait a couple of more minutes first. Two minutes. Then he'd go. He wanted to hear just one pop. One more shot. His adrenaline was pumping.

Then, one pop. Just one. Almost directly in front of him. Very close in fact. Hank re-crossed the creek to the north side and moved into the deep undergrowth. Dead leaves stirred under his feet. It was musty and dark in the matted under-growth. Mustang grape vines grabbed at his gun. He tore through it as quietly as he could but total stealth was impossi-ble. Then he slowed his pace, struggling to control his breathing and listened. He could see across Coushatta now. He was only thirty paces from the barbed-wire fence paralleling the road. He had to be close. Had the sniper heard him? He assumed yes but wasn't sure. Then, in a split second, his peripheral vision detected movement. High in a tree to his right. He instinctively ducked behind a large tree. His instinct saved him. Pop. A bullet embedded in the bark three inches from his head. Hank smiled. The sniper was treed. He had him. He would offer him quarter, but only once.

"You're a dead man," Hank said in a terse voice. "Drop your weapons now and you live. Otherwise, you die." There was a pause. Hank thanked his lucky stars that he was stationed behind a tree thicker than his body. He couldn't safely expose himself but maybe the goon didn't have a perfect vantage point. It was good enough to land a bullet close...ever so close to his head. Yet, he'd take the risk. There was no choice. He had seventy-five rounds in the Uzi. He'd blow the bastard to smithereens. Then a twig snapped to his left side. As the frozen snow betrays the panther's track, so the feeble sound betrayed another stalking sniper. So, there were two, and he was near... very near.

Hank drew a shallow breath and listened with concentration. Brush and vines were particularly thick here and little light penetrated. He waited a painful minute. Then another sound. A crackle of leaves underfoot. Just a few feet away. In an instant, Hank dropped to his knees and faced his stalker. He sprayed in the direction of the sound with unrelenting fire, emptying the clip. Immediately he turned and rolled to his side grabbing his pistol and pointing upward in one fluid motion. When his eyes focused on the sniper's perch, he found him already halfway down the tree moving quickly. He squeezed the trigger focusing on the head and neck. The target was no more than fifty feet away and couldn't return fire with hands and feet preoccupied. Between the fourth and fifth round of Hank's accurate shots the hands released and the goon fell twenty feet to the ground with a heavy thud. The fallen form lay perfectly still. Hank turned quickly to the face the other attacker. He waited several moments, with his own breathing the only audible sound. A woodpecker hammered in the distance. Finally, he released the Uzi's empty clip and installed another. Jacked and ready he stood and peered into the undergrowth. No movement. No sound. He waited a few more moments giving his eyes time to re-adjust to the gloomy undergrowth. He had fired into a tangled patchwork of vines so thick that little visibility filtered through. Then he saw it. A form, a darkened outline of a body, curled in a fetal position, lying on the ground less than twenty feet away. He pointed the Uzi at the form and moved forward cautiously. Dead men kill, the Marines had taught him. They lie in repose and wait.

He was, in fact, very dead. Both snipers were very dead. Multiple gunshot wounds could be listed as their official cause of death but plain ol' lead poisoning would do. Then another sound. Damn, Hank thought. How many are there? The sound was from the direction he had just traveled--to the east. That was odd. He bent low in the vines and waited. Then, a friendly voice called out.

"Hank, it's me, Trent."

"Good," Hank said relieved. "I'm over here. We've got more goons to plant."

"Crap. I guess that's good though. We need to open a funeral home, Hank. At least we'd get paid for our efforts."

"Kinda chancy walking through this heavy brush, Trent. How'd you know I'd won?" Hank asked when Trent walked up to him.

"Hell, I knew that before you left."

KATY HAD chicken fried steak with cream gravy and mashed potatoes ready when the boys returned from burying the goon snipers. She decided not to ask questions about the disposal of the remains. She had heard them in the garage knocking around doing something but she decided to let the topic rest. She hated bitchy, nosey women and she wasn't about to turn into one. They both came in from the garage sweaty and dirty, from digging graves she guessed. Their appetites were strong. Trent's shoulder wound was tender but certainly not serious. Hank laughed about his own scratch.

The chicken fried steak and fixings disappeared quickly. After supper, Katy asked to check the bullet wounds and they complied. She carefully cleaned and dressed them applying antibacterial ointments. Trent's wound was deeper and oozed a clear liquid, but its draining was a good sign. Katy put a light gauze patch over it and let it be. Hank went through the check-list of the fence surveillance equipment making sure it was up and ginning along. They got the poker chips out as dusk settled in and debriefed themselves over the day's events. Hank had an unusual look in his eye and Katy immediately picked up on it.

Hank said, "I'm just remembering what my dear Papa used to say. To kill a snake, you better cut off its head. That way the lower parts can't harm you. That's just what I'm fixin' to do."

Trent didn't need Hank expand on the statement knowing full well what he meant. So, he was going after the top dog. The "he" coon as the old timers put it. If Katy caught the larger point she didn't let on. After a flurry of card shuffling, she began dealing with a more somber eye.

188

CHAPTER
TWENTY

H ank hated traffic with a passion. Traveling I-10 through the outskirts of Houston at 5:00 am was tolerable, but just barely. In four hours, he found a small greasy spoon just outside of Lake Charles, Louisiana, and breakfasted on ham and eggs. Café Hondo's walls were lined with historical information regarding the establishment and settling of the area. The first Europeans had arrived here in 1781 from Bordeux, France. In subsequent years additional emigrants came and in 1855 Captain Daniel Goos established a lumber mill and built a schooner dock later called Goosport in his honor. Timber sales flourished with longleaf pine and bald cypress the main exports shipped by schooner to Texas and Mexico. The town was actually incorporated as Charleston in 1861 later changed to Lake Charles in March of 1867. By 1880 it was the lumber production capital for all of Louisiana. Hank studied the historical bullets that lined the walls wondering what had brought the likes of Gerard Fremont and his ilk to the area. Gambling and gaming was now becoming prominent and had slowly replaced the lumber commerce. Oil and natural gas, too, had been discovered offshore and it had brought workers and revenue into a previously deteriorating local economy. It wasn't a boomtown, but at least its 75,000 residents enjoyed the overall stable financial base that the oil and gas industry brought with it.

Bingo had been forthcoming with Fremont's office address as his tongue quickly loosened with the loss of his finger. He had rattled on and on about Big G's casino, his meetings with him, and the subsequent planning for the eventual air raid on H.B.'s place. He had also mentioned the Big G's IRS troubles.

Hank drove out the Old Spanish Trail Road. He found this section of Lake Charles in various stages of dilapidation. Unkempt buildings lined the road and were mostly boarded up and unoccupied. A convenience store was located on the corner of the block where Gerard's grungy office building stood. Drug and gang symbols covered every wall, fence, and sidewalk where graffiti could be sprayed or painted. A barber shop occupied the lower floor of Big G's office building and Big G apparently was the only other occupant of the place. A broad outside stairway lead to Big G's office and it was unmarked and nondescript. A teen dive boomed rap music next to Gerard's establishment. Scruffy, scroungy-looking teens with billboard tattoos and metal piercings roamed in and out of the place, loitering around in front of the joint. Their eyes constantly scanning the horizon like a cop raid was imminent at any moment. Every other business in the area was closed and boarded up.

Green moss, the result of long exposure to humidity, had colored the sides of Gerard's building giving it a puke-green hue. The upstairs windows were darkened and Hank couldn't make out any interior activity. However, a black limo parked behind the building had Big G's personalized license plates on it. He had watched the place for over an hour and had grown tired of the booming rap music pounding in his ears. Finally, a couple of goons arrived but left after a ten-minute visit.

Hank left his Dodge truck and started up the stairway. Hank's button-down white shirt, pressed kakis, and loafers might be enough to run an IRS con. He stepped close to Big G's office door and slowly twisted the knob. Surprisingly, the door was unlocked. Cigar smoke wafted through the door as he pushed it open. A blue hue of stale smoke floated near the ceiling. The distinct smell of old, musty, carpet assailed Hank's nostrils. Big G had his back to the door, feet on a credenza, puffing away totally oblivious to Hank's entry. Hank cleared his throat. Big G sprang up from his chair almost losing his balance. His bulk teetered to one side for a moment like he might fall over. He was openly shocked to see a stranger just walk in. No one ever came to his office uninvited. Who the hell was this guy anyway?

"Are you Gerard Fremont?" Hank said gruffly quickly establishing authority.

"And just who the hell are you?" Big G almost shouted. His nerves were already shot from his lawyer's lengthy phone call. More bad news from the attorney. The sky was most definitely falling.

"Agent Mulholland, from the IRS," Hank said with added gravity. "I'm authorized to bring you in for an interview." Hank saw the thug's eyes widen at the news. His fat head nodded, then kind of wobbled to one side.

Gerard suddenly felt a wave of dizziness. Oh, shit. They're taking me down, and my damn lawyer just said it would be several more weeks, if not a month or more. He balanced his considerable bulk trying not to fall over. His cigar hung limply in his fat lips sliding cozily to one side. His watered brow needed moping so he slowly removed his handkerchief, hands shaking, and mopped at his forehead. His flushed bulldog face glowed a crimson red. His clogged arteries were under severe stress. Blood pressure skyrocketed off the charts. Marching orders were about to be issued for a debilitating stroke. He was a battered boxer, prepped for the upper cut. To him Hank looked all government.

"Right now?" Big G questioned in a feeble voice tossing in the towel. His eyes burned like hell and water seeped out unchecked. Now he dabbed at them in total humiliation unable to bring the burning under control. His bowels turned to water. He could tell he was close to throwing up. He was in a tight chute, like a fat hog, ready to be butchered. "Do I need to call someone?" he asked in his newly confused state.

"No," Hank stated struggling to keep a straight face. This guy was going to be easier than he thought. "You can call from the offices if necessary."

"Do I go with you?" he asked.

"Yes, and we need to leave right away."

Gerard Fremont lumbered obediently down the stairway, obediently allowed Hank to handcuff him, and obediently parked his over-large carcass in Hank's pickup truck ready for the ride downtown and to the bloodletting he expected. Hank smiled as they drove away looking for the quickest route back out to I-10 East. He wanted to make it to H.B.'s before dark.

Big G finally spoke as they turned onto East I-10. "You have offices off I-10?" he asked.

"We're going to the regional headquarters in downtown Houston," Hank said. The news slumped the Big G further in his seat. With cuffed hands, he dabbed at his eyes and fore-head, trying to adjust to what his new life would be like behind bars. Surely there would be a trial of some sort he thought, but the IRS was a bunch of nasty zealots. No telling what they might do. He wished his damned eyes would quit burning and watering so. His handcuffs were too tight, but he kept quiet. What good would it do to complain?

TWENTY-FIVE MILES on the east side of Houston, with I-10 at a virtual standstill, Hank decided to float an idea at Big G. After all, he had been a model prisoner for almost three hours saying nothing and looking rather pitiful dabbing his sweating face. He was clearly distraught and any chance for leniency he would likely jump for.

"Hamilton Fremont is your brother?" Hank asked as they sat in bumper-to-bumper traffic.

"Yes," came the answer hesitantly.

"So he lives in Chicago?"

"Yes."

"How much do you know about his activities involving the Texas billionaire Horace Bascom?" Big G's fat head turned slowly, looking at Hank and convinced the IRS knew everything about everybody. He feared lying with his entire future at the mercy of the government boys. Hell, they probably already knew the answer. He decided to throw the dice. He didn't like his brother anyway. His answer at least temporarily saved his life.

"My brother's not one to share his plans, especially not with me. We're not exactly tight."

"Did you invite him in on the action?" Hank asked, pointing a hard look at Gerard.

"Yes. It was a big mistake. I'm sorry I did."

"Did you plan the air raid on H.B.'s?"

"No, Bingo did, but he never came back. He just somehow

disappeared." Big G twisted in the seat noticeably uncomfortable. He was a desperate man looking for a break. Anything to help himself. How in the hell did the IRS know all of this?

"Did you bankroll them?"

"Yes, I agreed to pay them."

"Who hired the plane?"

"Bingo."

"Who paid for the plane?"

"The owner of the plane owed me a gambling debt."

"Did you send two Mexicans in a red Dodge truck to H.B.'s place?"

"What?" Big G said surprised. He knew nothing about two Mexicans and a Dodge truck. *Was this another IRS trick?*

"Two Mexicans attempted a break in a few weeks ago. Did you send them?"

"No, I didn't. They didn't work for me."

Hank moved on. The traffic was moving at a snail's pace. "What about Hamilton? Did you know about his assault and attempted kidnapping of an innocent woman?"

"Not until after it happened. I got cussed for it though. He acted like it was my fault." He mopped his brow. Questions made him uneasy. Especially when they involved his brother.

"So, you turned him on to H.B.?"

"Yes, but I shoulda known better. Had he gotten any money he wouldn't have shared with me. He's never been one for sharing."

"Is he still in Chicago?"

"Yes. That's where he lives. He went there and settled after college I guess. Like I told you we're not exactly close."

The traffic seemed stuck in place. I-10 was famous for its traffic snarls close to Houston. It put Hank in a foul mood. He had been fighting the urge to kill Gerard and dump his fat ass in a bar ditch. The thought crossed his mind again. One snarl, one off look, one growl, one scowl would be the man's death sentence. He had a nylon cord in his pocket for that express purpose. This goon bastard could be rendered into lard for all he cared. Being pathetic earned no brownie points with Hank.

"You know his address? Where he works and lives?"

Gerard flashed a look at Hank again. He thought he detected a maniacal look in this IRS agent's eyes. A cold chill cooled his sweating body, at least temporarily. Surely, they had this information. They were just testing him. Testing his honesty.

"Yes, I carry a card in my billfold with his addresses and phone numbers."

"What did you both want with H.B.?" Hank knew the answer but wanted to hear the goon say it. He wanted to hear the confession.

Big G wriggled uncomfortably, sinking lower into the seat. "His money. He lived alone and unprotected. At least that's what the newspaper said."

"Are you planning further raids on H.B.'s?"

"No, no. Not at all," Gerard said emphatically. "I'm done trying. I just tried once and that's all. I'm flat broke or I'd pay you guys."

"What about Hamilton? Is he planning another raid?"

"He may have more planned. He's a hard case. He never gives up. He wouldn't tell me though. He never liked me anyway." Big G quickly surmised the IRS was probably closely connected to the FBI and likely watching them all. They all slept in the same big government bed. Hell, they really do know everything about everybody.

"So, you know nothing more about Hamilton?"

"No, and I'd tell you if I did. He's a stinkin' bastard."

STRESS AND FATIGUE finally took its toll on Gerard Fremont. That and the slow pace of commuter's traffic on a clogged I-10. His fat head rolled and wobbled to one side. It became an inert mass moving slightly, keeping rhythm with the flow of the pickup's movements. He slept in fits snoring loudly at times. His chubby torso bobbed up and down in a rhythmic cadence and then would stop, temporarily, with short gasps and gurgles and restart in rhythm again. His thick lips sagged open and a drool formed on the low side.

Hank was entertained by the scene. Big G's ineptness a classic study, perhaps, in the finer art of goon science. A world of dog-eat-dog where brawn outranked the brain. Predators preying easily on the weak and unprepared, but not so easily on those willing to fight back. *Typical bully*, Hank thought. The bully caves when somebody finally slaps them back.

Finally, traffic thinned and Hank swung right off West I-10 at Sealy and drove north on Texas 36. Gerard stayed in his comatose state until the rattling of H.B.'s cattleguard brought him awake. His dark eyes scanned the landscape expecting to see tall buildings in downtown Houston. The reddish sun was a broad orb in the west now giving the surroundings a pinkish hue. He said nothing as the massive gate closed behind them with its usual clanking sound. Having heard various descriptions and seen photos of H.B.'s estate, it suddenly dawned on him that they were entering his property. He jerked straighter in his seat, lips snapping to attention, black eyes alert with fear. A knot formed in the pit of his stomach. His breathing quickened.

Hank pulled up to the house and shut off the Dodge's

engine. Big G was too stunned to speak. Trent walked up to the pickup carrying an M-16, the 60-round banana clip highly intimidating. His crew cut looked military to Gerard, his chin thick and strong, his demeanor self-assured. A regular damn Rambo.

"Get out," Hank ordered. "Get out and lean up against the truck." Gerard nervously fumbled with the doorknob with his cuffed hands. His already stubby fingers swollen even more now from the hours in the restrictive cuffs. He nearly fell when his feet touched the ground. His right knee was numb and incapable of supporting his weight. He leaned heavily on the door trying to gain his balance. Trent shoved the door shut and pushed his fat ass roughly against the truck. He clung there on the edge of collapse. Hank patted him down and found no weapon. Gerard's head was spinning. Noticing his state of confusion, Hank and Trent grabbed his bulky arms and assisted him through the yard gate and through the house door where Katy stood. Her eyes showed hate one second and pity the next.

Big G led like a chubby toddler teetering for balance. They steered him to the dining room table and he flopped down knowing he would never be capable of rising. His face dripped with perspiration. Hank reached down and unsnapped his handcuffs. This man was no threat. He only hired them. Somehow, he'd misplaced his overused handkerchief. Katy handed him a wad of paper towels and he stroked his forehead soaking up sweat. Katy placed a large bowl of steaming beef stew before him and he stared at it absently. Hank and Trent started eating and he watched them, finally picking up his spoon. Big B held it a while, the spoon, and finally dipped it in for a sample. After the first timid bite, he ate voraciously, smacking his fat lips. The meal seemed to revive the poor goon boss and his face grew more confident with each spoonful. By his second bowl, he finally emerged from his addled state.

GERARD FREMONT SPENT THE NIGHT, restlessly, in the distant past. Hank and Trent set him up under the then smaller live oaks in a roll-away bed and stretched a tarp over all to keep out any errant raindrops. Hank had been generous finding a warm, clear spring evening in way-back-then to accommodate him. Big G stood, dumbfounded by the rustic environment of 1800. He had never been a fan of the great outdoors. A smoky bar was more his style. Big G never fully comprehended what had happened to the house, surrounding fences, and road that he had ridden in on. He only knew he'd never joined the Boy Scouts and had never been on a camp out of any kind. He was a town man. Coyotes were thick as wood ticks and howled their wailing, plaintive songs through the night. He hunkered down with his little bed covers pulled over his large head dreading the coming darkness and wishing he'd never offended the IRS. If this was their idea of a joke he wasn't laughing. He didn't know where he was for sure but he knew he wasn't near a city of any size. Where was Houston? He never realized the night could be so black. The whole experience jangled his ragged nerves and, finally, fatigue pitched him into a fitful slumber interrupted continuously by a chorus of unknown sounds.

It was an old nag Hank purchased for the purpose. The poor old pony probably had a little left to give, but not much. The rider didn't deserve much. Big G was given an old saddle and tack. A rusty carbine with twenty cartridges. A tent and sleeping bag. Ten day's worth of provisions. The biggest challenge was getting Gerard's fat ass in the saddle. It was an immensely comical sight. He had obviously never experienced a horseback ride. He gripped anything in range with stubby fingers afraid of the long fall to the ground. Big G's eyes were round with fear. Here he sat, perched at least as high as two stories up on a beast whose habits he knew nothing of. Hank actually felt sorry for the nag, not Gerard, for having to carry the heavy slug around in the past, but one bright ray of light existed. Gerard would shrink perceptibly in the days to follow. If he survived any time at all, which Hank and Trent seriously doubted, the horse would have a lighter load to carry each day. Hank and Trent flipped a coin on whether to send him back to the year 1500 or 1600. Heads turned out to be 1500 so back Big G went and he nervously fidgeted in the saddle wondering what the hell had happened to his life, his dingy little office and his black limo. The past twenty-four hours had been a blur. Was this some royal joke the IRS was playing on him? If it was he was tired of it. He was most terrified of the fall. The beast he sat on seemed so unstable. One fall would be all it'd take.

"Pull back on the reins to stop," Hank said, grinning as he saw the anxious look on the fat man's face. "Kick the side of the animal to get her started. Pull the rein right or left to turn. It's all pretty simple." The nag turned her lazy head in Hank's direction seemingly comprehending the instructions better than Gerard. Big G was nearing a state of panic.

"You're in some wild old times now," Hank offered with a smirk on his face. "You'll have to fend for yourself. Can't hire someone to do your dirty work now. Besides there's no billionaires around here for you to chase. So good luck."

Stuttering Big G finally asked, "When do I get to go back to Houston?" Houston had to be a safer place to be than sitting uncomfortably on this animal's back.

"Well, Houston's not too far away," Hank said, laughing as he and Trent turned to walk off.

Hank and Trent soon disappeared over the horizon and Big G sat frozen in the saddle wondering which direction he should go. They had blindfolded him until just a few minutes before and he was totally disoriented. When he hit a road, though, he'd ask directions. Surely some agents would be watching him, too. The IRS wouldn't let a man off the hook this easily. His next thought was how to get the damn critter he sat on moving.

CHAPTER
TWENTY-ONE

J essie had grown accustomed to H.B.'s reading and dreaded the ending of the novel. The death of Augustus had been almost more than she could bear. Though she had always been an avid reader, she preferred the melodious, steady tone of H.B.'s voice slowly and deliberately revealing the intricacies of the story. During her week of being connected to the IV drip, great gains in health and happiness seemed have intervened in both her mental and physical state. She would have gone quietly to her end, as her parents had, but she began to feel a robustness for life reasserting itself with each drip from the bag she was attached to. With a child-like faith, she clung to the feeling with a renewed hope that her earthly existence might continue.

As his patient rapidly regained her strength, H.B. walked the boardwalks of Fort Worth enjoying the leisure atmosphere of a surging frontier community. Dr. Fields was insistent on being his tour guide, though no guiding was necessary. The good doctor seemed invigorated by Jessie's recovery and thankfully had lost some of his thirst for alcohol. He still took an occasional nip but steadfastly maintained as much sobriety as possible. He did so for a reason. Sober he was a welcomed guest for the evening meals at Corley's Boarding House, and he had grown quite attached to Elsa's good cooking.

Early summer cattle herds passed through Fort Worth on a regular basis re-supplying their stores for the long push to Dodge, Abilene, Ogallala and beyond. H.B. was in Daggett and Hatcher's Mercantile, piddling time away when he overhead a passing trail boss talking to one of the clerks. He was suffering from a dilemma. One of his swing riders had broken his foot and couldn't continue up the trail. He was already running behind, herding three thousand beeves to the Blackfeet Agency in northwest Montana, and he was looking for a good hand. Needed him today if possible. The clerk appeared to appreciate the foreman's predicament but could offer no advice. H.B. had an immediate impulse to approach the man. One of his lifelong dreams had been to follow a cattle herd up one of the various western trails. His library in Bellville contained a dozen books pertaining specifically to trail drives and their exciting adventures. He had enthusiastically pored over the stories many times. One of his favorite daydreams was to be a regular cowboy, of course, and see the open prairies before barbed wire covered it.

But Jessie's face popped to the surface again in his mind. A twang of guilt stopped him momentarily, just as his legs wanted to carry him forward. Yet her illness was on the ropes thanks to the strong antibiotics she was now taking. Her recovery could go unmonitored by him for the most part. He could leave her an adequate supply of pills so the disease would be in permanent retreat. With these thoughts conflicting in his head, he gathered himself and stepped his lanky frame up to the man and offered his services. The trail boss looked H.B. over with a trained eye, unable to mask his uncertainty. Something told him, and correctly so, this man wasn't a cowboy.

"Name's Orb. Orb Fincher. You from around these parts?" The last man he'd hired three weeks back came out of the Concho River country and looked to be headed for trouble. All he needed right now was another problem employee.

"No, not exactly," H.B. said trying to cover his sudden feeling of inadequacy. "I'm from around Bellville in southeast Texas. Not far from Houston."

"Oh," Orb said still trying to size up the man. He was one of the tallest men he'd seen and likely awkward and gangly he thought. Clumsy didn't go well with a herd of testy steers. He wanted quick men, good horsemen with herding instincts and strong constitutions to handle the rigors of the trail that lay ahead. He'd already lost two men and didn't fancy losing anymore. Fort Worth to Montana was a long trail and something about this tall drink of water set him uneasy.

"You done any herding?" he asked.

"No," H.B. conceded. "I've got my own mounts and they're quality stock. Plus, I'm well equipped." He had no resume in the art of cattle herding. He knew he had little to offer the trail boss.

Orb abruptly started for the mercantile's door, but kindly motioned for H.B. to follow. They left Daggett and Hatcher's stopping on the broad boardwalk facing First Street deftly avoiding the brisk walking traffic. Standing in the bright sun near a hitching rail Orb bit into a plug of chewing tobacco and detached a considerable chunk. He moved the lump around in his mouth and finally spit out a dry tobacco stem not to his liking. Orb was a smallish man likely in the mid-five-foot range. His brow ridges protruded and were covered with dark black hair, but he was sturdy built and looked tough as boot leather to H.B. He had graying hair tufts gathering about his temples giving him the look of vast experience. Despite a broad hat, his face was a ruddy brown brought on by long days of sitting a saddle. It was plain the boss wasn't a man that cottoned to shade. Hell, shade was impossible to find on the open prairie anyway.

"Montana's a long way from here," Orb said, more to himself than to H.B. He looked out across the street moving his chewing cud around like it was a jawbreaker. The streets were lined with wagons and the bustle of mid-morning activity was picking up steam. Orb admitted to himself that he needed a hand and here was a man willing and apparently able to go. The streets were filled with men as far as his eye could see. but they were not the kind of men who wanted to leave kith and kin and proceed with a bunch of hard cobs and wild cattle into a damned wilderness. Yet, he wanted and needed a good steady hand. His Concho hire popped back into his mind. Could he afford to take another chance? His cowboys were pretty tough on a poor hire. He turned and looked up into the tall stranger's eyes. They seemed to be determined, yet kind eyes.

"This drive ain't no Sunday school picnic. There's some hard, dry country up ahead. We're already behind schedule so I'm pushin' this herd from now on as hard as I can. I've taken several herds to Dodge and Ogallala but never beyond. What I'm sayin' is, I don't have time to coddle men and run cattle at the same time. I don't want to be late. I've got to fight a damn blizzard getting there."

"I understand," H.B. said staring down. He wanted to say something but thought a moment before saying it. He had come from a wealthy family but wealth created its own set of sacrifices and troubles. His father had told him one of his grandfather's favorite sayings involved the qualities on an honest man. He decided to say it in his own defense. "My grandfather once said an honest man always finds a place to labor. I think you'll find me to be an honest man if that counts on a cattle drive."

A one-horse buggy rattled up to the hitching post where Orb and H.B. stood, spreading a dust cloud over them. The well-dressed gentleman secured the reins and walked briskly into the mercantile hardly acknowledging their presence. Orb spat a mouthful of dark juice on the dry Fort Worth ground and thought for several moments, his eyes cast in a downward direction. H.B. wondered if Orb had even heard his last statement with the noise and distraction of the buggy. The pause stretched a minute more before Orb spoke.

"I pay thirty-five and found. I've got my drag riders assigned so you'll have to work swing which is lucky for you. Don't mention your inexperience to the rest of the men. They're a nit-picky bunch and touchy as hell. I'm parked ten miles west of town. Circle M herd. We're camped on Little Perch Creek if you know where that is. Chuck's open before daylight. I'll see you in the morning. We'll be rattlin' hooves and horns shortly after breakfast."

"Thanks," H.B. said suddenly startled at the job offer. "I'm H.B.," he said as Orb clutched his hand and shook it. The trail boss's hands were rough as sandpaper and his grip tight as a vice.

"Well, good," Orb said. With no additional fanfare, he walked to a nearby hitching post, untied a nice-looking buckskin's reins, mounted, and disappeared in his own cloud of dust down First Street. H.B. stood a moment, thinking about the decision he'd just made and promptly headed for the boarding house. He had to get packing.

Jessie was in the kitchen with Elsa when H.B. arrived and stated his decision to leave. It took them by surprise. Seemed odd that a physician with H.B.'s apparent skills and talents would head north choosing to chouse cattle all the way to Montana. Dr. Fields had already approached him to join his practice and that seemed to them the logical choice. H.B. wasn't much of a talker, however, so his personal ambitions had never been a topic of discussion. The decision greatly surprised Jessie and created a real uncertainty in the matter of her health. His presence had been a considerable comfort to her through those first trying days as she clung precariously to life and had grown even more dependent as he took over the management of her recovery. His steady voice and particularly his reading aloud had brought a gentle peace into her sick, fractured world. For him to just suddenly up and leave created quite a vacuum in Jessie's life.

"I'm surprised you'd want to herd cattle," Jessie said, struggling to keep her composure. Elsa stirred around the kitchen in her typical way of busy work.

"I'll leave you a large supply of pills," H.B. said. "Take them steadily like you've been doing until the bottle is empty. You'll be fine. I'll likely return in a few months to check on your progress." With that he was gone, clambering up the stairway to his room. Jessie stood quiet for a moment too overwhelmed to answer.

Finally, she found herself on the front porch wiping away tears, upset and surprised at her own emotions. His leaving was so sudden she couldn't get a true sense of her own feelings in the matter. However skilled he might be, she had no hold on the man, but it upset her anyway. Yet she quietly envied his ability and desire to just pull up and go to a wild place like Montana. The tight noose of Corley's Boarding House seemed irrevocably tighter now and she didn't like the feeling either. So, she calmed herself by the little dream that someday with her improving health she, too, might have the freedom to travel to some distant place, but the emptiness remained. It caused a heaviness to form in her heart.

She awoke before dawn determined to say goodbye to H.B. and express her gratitude. After all she owed him her life. Yet she had failed, drowning in her own little world of self-pity and misery, to express her thanks to the young doctor. Jessie shuffled down the stairway carrying a lantern in the darkness hoping to find him on the porch readying his gear. Unfortunately, the porch was empty. Nothing but a neighbor's yellow cat licking its claws, and no H.B. She wandered back upstairs and hesitantly rapped on his door. No answer. She turned the knob and found the bed made up, a bottle of pills lying on top of the covers and a brief note addressed to her. Jessie picked up the note and set the lantern down to read it.

Dear Jessie,

I left early to find the herd. Please continue taking the pills until the bottle is empty. I'll likely check back with you in the late fall. You should return to full health in just a few more weeks but continue taking the pills regardless.

Your friend,

H.B.

SHE PUT down the note and bit her bottom lip. The lantern splashed a backlight around the empty bedroom casting weird shadows. She turned and shuffled slowly down the hall to her room and closed the door awash with regret. She just hadn't said enough to H.B., and now she had let the moment slip away and she couldn't bring it back. Her throat tightened and her eyes watered. She swallowed the regrets and lay back down on her bed and wept.

HE SAW the campfire's smoke two miles away and headed in its direction. In the coming dawn figures could be seen moving around the fire working for position around the chuck wagon. H.B. sat on Patty Cake, his favorite mare, and led a string of his other prized horses behind him. The four others he led were burdened with packs, most of it medical supplies. Finding a storage place was impossible in Fort Worth and leaving it behind at Jessie's wasn't an option. So, he lugged it along, feeling overly encumbered.

He tied his horses thirty yards from camp in a little stand of scrawny post oaks and walked in. He was aware of many eyes watching him. Orb stepped up and warmly shook his hand promptly introducing him around to the other men. They seemed a friendly lot with the exception of one particular hand who snorted and rudely stalked off. He was a thick built man, short, seemingly the same diameter from head to toe. His neck was as thick as a stump. He growled something in the direction of the cook and headed to the remuda looking for his mount. The rest of the men, however, lined up and graciously shook his hand in greeting. Twinks Brady, one of the older hands, commented brusquely on stump's departure.

"He's just a bastard. Don't pay him no mind." As he said it, he shot Orb a quick glance. A couple of the younger hands fidgeted at hearing the comment.

Buster, the chow cook, yelled to line up and the men, including H.B., filled their plates. The men responded more slowly than usual in their various stages of being hung over from a couple of long nights' partying in Fort Worth. Orb wasn't one to try and spoil a young cowboy's fun when the opportunity presented itself. They were planning on skipping Dodge and heading straight to Ogallala before re-supplying. Fort Worth's taste would have to last for a long time.

CHAPTER

TWENTY-TWO

Gerard finally got the old nag moving after flogging her flanks with short kicks and slapping her ribs with the long reins. She was a sway-backed old thing and constantly surveyed her surroundings looking for the nearest barn hoping for a feed bag filled with oats. Unfortunately, no barns were around. The saddle bags flopped, the bedroll waggled, and Big G hung on for dear life suddenly sorry he'd gotten her started. He had enough sense, barely, to know that east was the general direction where Louisiana lay, but which way was east? So, he bounced along, hopefully steering the stiff-jointed old mare in the right direction. He had taken several wraps of the leather reins around his fat hands. The wraps were so tight he soon lost feeling in his fingers, but loosening the reins, he reasoned, would have dire consequences. A spill of any sort could prove disastrous so he suffered the discomfort of the numbness. Soon finger numbness became the least of his sufferings.

The midday sun grew hot and his thighs, sweating profusely, began a process of serious chafing. It was a strange phenomenon and he puzzled over it as he bounced around the uneven terrain in a state of dismay and increasing discomfort. His large butt had begun aching from deep within, and keeping the damn horse going was another matter entirely. It'd stop for no reason and put its head down to graze, refusing forward progress. Gerard yelled, cajoled, cussed, and kicked and finally succeeded in stirring the animal along just far enough to have the whole frustrating process repeat itself again. His impatience with the beast grew as the afternoon heat increased. Big G's wardrobe was sweated through by now and felt glued to his sticky, clammy body. The heat, the humidity, the extreme tension, and the jarring beast beneath him all combined to create a new level of misery. A headache took up residence and throbbed in his temples.

As the afternoon progressed, disorientation as to direction and course of action settled on Gerard Fremont's world like an early dawn fog takes over the morning. The horse wandered aimlessly from one shade tree to another, knowing as all horses do, that the lard ass in the saddle had no clue as to what was happening. Under a leaderless rider, the nag's natural mulishness steadily intensified. Then an unfortunate thing happened. Though in a great deal of pain and discomfort, Gerard somehow managed to nod off. In the process of nodding off, his chubby head failed to negotiate a low-hanging branch, and accidentally raked against a large hornet's nest. The result was instant and catastrophic. The hornets mounted an immediate assault covering Big G's face with relentless attacks. His terrified, anguished screams suddenly awakened the old nag and her bygone days of a quick-starting quarter horse suddenly sprang to life. In three quick leaps she surged into a breakneck run with her rider, unfortunately, totally preoccupied with the hornets.

While flailing at his attackers, Gerard had inadvertently

dropped the reins and he now found himself in a full-fledged runaway. The runaway saved the day as far as the hornet attack was concerned, but a much larger problem now loomed. The horse's acceleration threw Big G back in his saddle as the once lethargic beast came alive. He grabbed in desperation for the saddle horn groping for a hold but in doing so lost hold on his stirrups and one foot slipped loose. Losing the stirrup caused him to tilt to one side forcing him roughly against the back of the cantle. He wobbled, grabbed for air, and with a scream of terror, fell – arms and legs flailing wildly to the hard ground.

He lay sprawled in a heap on the ground. Low groans emanated from his semi-conscious form. He was too dazed to feel much. As consciousness returned, his pain threshold was quickly surpassed and he mercifully passed out. He washed in and out of lucidness over the next hour, finally waking enough to access the status of his injuries. He found his limbs in working order but his right side including the right leg was bruised and sore. His neck was stiff but moveable. His face stung and pained him. It was swollen and out of proportion. No matter how much effort he applied he couldn't manage to get the left eye to open. Then he remembered the hornet attack for the first time. He cussed the hornets under his breath.

Gerard turned on one side wishing it were cooler when something poked him in the ribs. He flinched in pain and looked up with his good eye blinking into the bright blue sky trying to make out who or what had poked him. That's when he saw three dark faces. Men with fearsomely savage countenances staring back down at him. They jabbered a language he couldn't comprehend. He cupped his hand over his seeing eye attempting to block the sun for a better look. Something struck him as abnormal. He'd never seen men who looked like this. Then a weird thing happened. Suddenly, they grabbed his arms, both of them, and pulled him roughly to a nearby tree and helped him lean against it. He sat there feeling dizzy, sore and disoriented noticing the one man standing close by while the other two walked towards his horse. They approached cautiously making hand signs to one another. Good. They were going to help him catch the damn miscreant he thought. To his immense surprise, they instead fitted arrows in their long bows and took aim. Before Big G could even raise a protest, the arrows flew and struck the horse's neck. The horse squealed, reared on its hind legs, and started pitching frantically. More arrows. Another in the neck, and one burying itself high in the shoulder. The horse staggered, snorting loudly, lowered its head, and fell hard to the ground. Big G sat stunned by what he'd witnessed.

The two strange men ran to the fallen animal and immediately started hacking away at the meat. Even before the horse had yet to finish its death kick. Soon one let out a howl, a high-pitched triumphant yell and the man next to Gerard answered in kind. He immediately ran to join his comrades. Large pieces of meat were stripped and eaten raw. One of the savages opened the horse's body cavity and soon entrails were scattered over the grass. The animal's intestines were systematically cut into strips two to three feet long, reversed quickly stripping out the dung, and then rapidly gulped down. Their dark, nearly naked bodies soon turned crimson from the horse's blood as they danced and gesticulated around the feast. The spectacle nauseated Big G having never observed such strange behaviors. Then the realization struck him that this could all be just an act of some kind. Probably IRS agents out to make an impression on him. If that was the case they were certainly succeeding. He'd heard some pretty wild stories about crazed government men wreaking havoc on private citizens by bizarre and even illegal means. Their behaviors were unchecked and vicious because they answered to no one but a few of the big boys in Washington. Surely Agent Mulholland would eventually blow a whistle or raise his hand and the ordeal would be over. His conversion was complete. Big G was born again! He'd never again cheat on his taxes. He'd even fire his damn incompetent accountant.

THE CESSNA CITATION settled into a long approach under the Texas sky and set down gracefully at Brenham airport. Hank waited near the runway to gather his two Alaskan friends. Brenham was twenty miles from Bellville and the only airstrip in close proximity with enough runway length to accommodate the jet. They all talked non-stop as they drove down Texas 36 towards Bellville. Hank filled them in on the latest developments including the depositing of Gerard in the past. Ethan talked excitedly about the thrill of flying a jet, their own jet, all the way from Alaska. Lori asked for more information on this Gerard character Hank had mentioned.

"The man thought we were sending him to some remote IRS camp for wayward taxpayers," Hank laughed. "I kid you not. He never got a handle on what was really happening."

"You've sure cleaned up a lot of trash, Hank. Plus, a few mercenaries thrown in. I'm not sure the past will ever be the same." They all laughed. "Any trouble as of late?" Ethan asked hoping secretly for a little action. After all, H.B.'s estate had been the scene of almost non-stop goon activity.

"No. It's been quiet for the past few days. I imagine Hamilton's planning something, but I'm not sure what."

"Are you planning on heading to your San Saba cabin?" Lori asked knowing Hank would be anxious to get home.

"Maybe. I might have another plan though. I'll talk to you about it over supper." Lori looked at Ethan, briefly, wondering what was up. Ethan moved on to other subjects.

Katy and Lori hit it off from the moment their eyes met. Katy herself wasn't anybody's baby doll so an experienced bush woman homesteader instantly piqued her interest. The two of them fell into long discussions about the intricacies of remote living and its long and short comings. It sounded like Katy's cup of tea so she and Lori sat around the small kitchen table in deep discussion, drinking iced tea, isolated from the men. They weren't particularly interested in war strategy.

"So, you make your own sausage?" Katy asked interested in the finer points of remote living.

"Yes. Ethan gets a yearly moose and we raise a hog to make dried sausage. We do forty to fifty rings yearly. It's never enough. We kinda ration it throughout the year."

"I've never tasted moose," Katy offered. Lori immediately rummaged in her backpack sitting beside the table and came out with a vacuum sealed bag. It contained two strips of dark-colored meat.

"Try this. When we're not eating sausage. We're eating moose jerky. We usually carry a supply of one or both when we're on a trip."

Katy eyed the jerky with light trepidation and carefully took a bite. She chewed slowly measuring the flavor. "Wow, that's delicious. How do you prepare it?"

"Salt, pepper, and alder smoke. All natural. No additives. Can't beat it, can you?"

"My, oh my. That is tasty. Is all moose this good?"

"Absolutely. Moose sure beats the taste of store-bought

beef. It makes a great roast, and stew, too. Ethan loves moose chili. We hardly ever buy commercial meats."

Katy chewed and savored the deep, rich flavor. Nothing any store carried could possibly come close to tasting this good. She wanted more. Lori gave her another piece and she bit into it with great gusto. Wow. She wanted her own moose.

"I guess you know it's been a virtual war around here," Katy said, as she chewed the jerky. "Seems like it's been one attack after another, and to think those news stories started all this mess. I'd like to stake out those damn reporters who wrote the articles so the goons could target practice on them for a while."

"They don't give a whit about anything but selling papers, Katy. Journalism has sunk into the garbage heap. It's just cheap, tabloid pop-culture crap slanted primarily to liberal east and west coasters. Ethan at one time was a journalist. Now he won't even watch a broadcast or read news reports. They're all going broke anyway. The sooner the better for us."

"Tell me something," Katy said, suddenly looking serious. "What ever happened to real men? I mean men like your Ethan or Hank and Trent. The Gary Cooper, John Wayne type of men. Hell, most of 'em now are just pure candy tails. A lot of 'em even talk like girls. I've heard their manhood is getting smaller. Do you think that's true?" Lori giggled. Nothing subtle about Katy. She'd charge right into battle. No subject was taboo for her.

"Men have changed," Lori said, acknowledging Katy's observations. "No doubt about that. There's definitely more beta males than alpha males these days, and tons of weird freds out there. I'm talking really strange ducks. Real men scare the media's beta-types. A manly man these days is a coveted prize for girls like us but they've got a great big bull's-eye painted on them by everyone else."

Lori stood up and walked to the kitchen window and looked out. Razor wire seemed to be the predominant feature of the landscape. Bunkers in the front and rear of the house reminded her of a war movie set. Too bad such a beautiful place had to take on the appearance of a battle zone. "I get the funny feeling that I'm behind enemy lines here, Katy. What makes people think they deserve something they never worked for? I still feel wrong about flying around in a jet H. B.'s money paid for."

That was news to Katy. Hank, of course, wasn't one to divulge many details.

"I now know what Davy Crockett and Colonel Travis must have felt like at the siege of the Alamo," Katy said. "We've had air assaults, land assaults, sniper attacks. You name it and we've had it. Snipers wounded both Trent and Hank last week. It was a close call, Lori. The spy equipment Hank installed is nice but not bullet-proof. The snipers climbed tree stands outside the compound and took aim from five to six hundred yards out. They were accurate, too."

"Ethan did say it was a close call."

"It was one hell of an attack. They shot from so far away you could hardly hear the report of the rifle. Knocked Trent down by his trailer. Shoulder wound. Hank made it to Trent then circled behind the critters after Trent made it to the bunker."

"Did Hank get 'em?" Lori asked. Ethan hadn't filled her in on all the details.

"Got 'em both. The bastards. I'm mad at H.B. though for packing up and leaving. I'd never guess the man would cut and run out like he did. Hell, he hardly ever left the ranch before."

"He had some very urgent business on the other side of the rift," Lori said, still looking out the window at the newly installed coils of razor wire. *What had they all gotten themselves into?* she was thinking and the statement just slipped out. Then she realized after she'd said it, that perhaps, the rift was unknown to Katy.

"Rift? What rift are you talking about?" Katy inquired with a puzzled look. Lori bit her lip. She figured Hank had told her about H.B's time machine. How had they been able to move the goons around to the past without Katy's knowledge? If anybody could be trusted with a secret it seemed to Lori that Katy would be high on the list. After all, her life was on the line as much as everyone else's. So, Lori spoke the truth. The narrative took some time to tell. She went back to the original meeting at the barbeque pit and outlined the subsequent events. Katy sat and listened, wide-eyed with disbelief.

For the first ten minutes, Katy thought the account was surely fictional. Lori was just having a little fun spinning a yarn and it was a good one, too. With Katy's long history of being H.B.'s neighbor, and considering his overall weirdness, pieces of the puzzle did seem to make sense. The man certainly was unusual and secretive, but a time traveler? Come on now. Let's get real.

Lori plugged along, though, spinning the intricacies of a web that left Katy incredulous. Rich, yes. Secretive, yes. However, a mad, time-traveling scientist transporting himself to the past was a reach. It was just a little outside of Katy's imagination. Lori finally ended the fantasy by taking a long sip of tea and looking Katy in the eye. Disbelief was written all over her face.

"Well, that's the story. Believe it or not that's why we're all here. Honestly, I'm sorry we had to come. South Texas is a far cry from Alaska and combined with all the attacks and the razor wire strewn around everywhere absolutely unnerves me."

Katy slid her chair back from the table. She liked Lori and

didn't want to hurt her feelings. It wasn't that she was insensitive, but hell, she wasn't the one telling this outlandish story. Anyway, she could play along just for the fun of it.

"How about someone taking me back in time then? Just a little peep. A brief visit." Ha. It was time to fish or cut bait. This would get Lori squirming.

Lori immediately stood and walked into the dining room. She could hear the men grow quiet as Lori spoke. Then an audible murmuring. Hank appeared at the door. He had a serious look in his eye.

"Katy, don't you think some things are best to be left unknown?" The question angered her to begin with but the way he said it instantly flared her temper.

"Not when my ass is on the line, too, Hank. I'm good enough to live in this armed fortress, be the chief cook and bottle washer, give up living in my own home for a man I rarely spoke to or hardly knew, sacrifice my freedom and my lifestyle but not trustworthy enough to know the whole story. Doesn't that strike you as a bit odd? If Lori's story is true, I might just faint away, but I'd sure as hell like to have the chance."

Hank softened a bit. Katy's eyes danced with fire as she fidgeted in her chair. She certainly had a point. "Where do you want to go?" he asked.

"What do you mean?" she fired back.

"What date back in time? Choose a time period you want to visit."

"Oh, hell, I don't know, Hank. Well, wait a minute. I just read a history of Austin County and Bellville's early days. The railroad came in 1879. How about 1880? I'd like to ride horseback into Bellville and see an old-fashioned steam engine locomotive. Can you do that, Hank, for an old gal like me?" The jig was up now she thought. Put up or shut up time. Hank didn't blink. He wore his perfect poker face. He turned and left the kitchen.

Lori wandered back in the kitchen and sat down. Katy sat sipping her tea with a smug look on her face. She could hear Trent and Ethan talking in low tones. Lori returned to the kitchen and refilled her tea glass.

"Men strike me odd sometimes," Lori said, sitting down stirring her tea. "We're in charge of rearing infants into boys and boys into men yet they somehow disconnect themselves from the very source that nurtured them. No man that's ever bore arms did so without a mother behind them. Their strength on the battlefield is our strength. Their wars are our wars. Yet, they still lose sight of the better part of their nature. I think they just forget where they come from." Katy slowly awakened from her haze of disbelief. The realization dawned, without anyone having to say more, that this whole time travel thing wasn't, in fact, a hoax. Lori had spoken the truth. She was aware of a quickened pulse inside. Her throat tightened as she spoke.

"Did Hank leave?" she asked, not hearing his voice in the dining room.

"Yeah. He's outside saddling the horses. I guess you're about to take a ride."

Katy bumped her tea glass and it spilled with a splash over the side of the table. She reddened with embarrassment.

CHAPTER
TWENTY-THREE

Karankawan tribesmen had the reputation for partaking of human flesh. Of the many sub-tribes inhabiting the Texas coast in 1500, the Capoque tribe was perhaps the most vicious of them, known to regularly dispatch rivals of nearby tribes and cook them up in an open pit. Protein in any form was welcome to the Capoque and an actual tooth for human flesh had developed amongst them over the generations. Gerard Fremont would likely be no exception. Their Brazos River encampment was only five miles away, so one of the three savages was quickly dispatched to get assistance in packing the considerable quantity of meat from this strange animal. Once their appetites had been satiated, the two remaining natives dug through the tied-on baggage chatting gibberish and occasionally pointing at Big G with their bloody fingers as they scattered recklessly his few worldly possessions on the ground. A simple zippered canvass bag required long moments of intense contemplation. Of all the items and deep mysteries that Big G's baggage imposed, the rifle and knife seemed to pique their fascination most of all.

The rifle was tossed back and forth between them in toy-like fashion. Even Gerard was no ignoramus in reading what he was witnessing. It finally dawned on him that the carbine was an unknown item to them and their total lack of knowledge of its use and purpose was obvious. *Where in the hell had the IRS imported these boys from?* he thought. Some remote Amazon tribe he reckoned. He'd seen a television show about them once. They were dangerous as hell as he could recall. That thought chilled him momentarily. Right now, Louisiana seemed a far piece away.

Gerard had managed to stand up finally, sore leg and all and he watched the Indians from the shade tree where they'd drug him. A deep feeling of horror had settled on him. His body was sore and ached and sweat dripped from his face but the hideousness of his savage visitors sent chills through him. The knife Hank had sent along now attracted their attentions as the gun was tossed gingerly in the grass and they worked feverishly to slip the knife from its sheath. The sheath's snapper took several minutes to decipher and once unsheathed, the sharp edge was admired accordingly. They went immediately to the disemboweled horse and practiced with its keen edge. Then a squabble broke out among the two, apparently over its rightful ownership. Just before they came to serious blows, more Indians appeared, five more in all, carrying crude packs for transporting the meat to camp. They all stood around the carcass for a moment, admiring the mountain of meat and jabbering and pointing at the horse's head and pulling on its mane. They behaved as if the horse was a totally unknown animal to them. Big G looked on in growing wonderment.

One of the five new arrivals had several large feathers in his topknot and noticing Gerard standing near the tree, approached him slowly speaking gibberish and carrying an unusually large spear. The tip of the spear carried a sharpened stone and he gestured with it threateningly as he closed the thirty yards with feinting pokes and barking noises. Big G cowered and held his stubby hands up in a defensive posture. The naked savage seemed completely fascinated by Big G but not necessarily in a friendly way. He circled the small tree in a hopping, jumping, strutting dance. His chant was loud and to Big G unintelligible. Gerard turned as the savage circled trying to keep the man's hideous figure in front of him. Shortly, all seven savages joined in the game and circled him singing, barking, shouting, and dancing.

Big G's blood pressure spiked as their chanting and yelling intensified. He began to feel lightheaded. A fainting spell was close at hand he feared. His legs grew numb. His eyelids fluttered. Then nausea swept over him. Overwhelming uncontrollable nausea. His stomach did a back flip and he puked suddenly, sending it splashing near his tormentors. He had always been prone to strong projectile vomiting and he performed this feat over and over again. The natives watched the exhibition wide-eyed. Then Gerard's knees buckled under the stress and he slumped forward finally hitting the ground with a thud. He could now smell the soil where he lay and the stench of rotten puke that mixed with it. The smell brought an urge to retch again but all he had left to offer were dry heaves. His eyes were closed tightly but he could still feel the strong presence of these terrible, screaming men. He feared opening his eyes. Somehow, he felt safer with them closed. Whatever horror awaited him, he preferred not to see it coming, and there seemed to be a little safety here behind his closed eyelids. Like a child with the covers pulled over its head, he felt a momentary sense of security amidst these savages.

He lay curled up in a fetal position in the stinking stench of his stomach contents, eyes tightly closed, actually calm in the moment. Damned if he'd open his eyes again and view these hideous beings. The very moment Big G determined to keep his eyes closed, something very strange happened. A quick blow to the chest. Someone had kicked him he thought and it hurt but not so much as a feeling of uncomfortable pressure, but he could tell there was something wrong. He couldn't breathe right. Yet the breathing crisis passed quickly as a warm sensation spilled through his body and a buzzing sound came into his brain like the simultaneous playing of a thousand crickets. The crickets played louder now and the warm sensation spread. Gerard thought to open his eyes now for just a peek but couldn't get them to open. Oh, hell, he weakly thought as the buzzing increased. It was getting warmer and darker now. Why worry? Things seemed so peaceful. He had lost all worries and concerns. The crickets suddenly ceased their playing and a blacker darkness closed in. A permanent darkness.

The Capoque tribal sub chief pulled violently to remove the stone-tipped spear from Big G's ample chest and screamed his cry of victory. It was indeed an eerie call as the others joined in chanting their war songs. It was a surprisingly easy kill. The weird white-skinned fat man hadn't even fought. There would be much feasting in their village tonight. Even the elderly would have plenty. Thus, the sub chief quickly organized the disembowelment and quartering of Gerard for the convenience of distributing his fleshy proportions evenly on the Indian pack boards.

DUST WAS AN EVER-PRESENT element of the trail. The wind's intensity steadily increased as the first day's trail unfolded. It was a dry, northwesterly wind and by the time they nooned, Buster's wagon sheets billowed and bulged like a schooner's sails. The noon fire was built in the bottom of a dry creek bed, but even there Buster struggled to warm the stew. The men grumbled about the wind, Buster cussed it, and the Stump set off by himself in a sulk. No one paid much attention to the man. Over his brief tenure, the men had already grown indifferent to his surliness. Twinks Brady was the only one who aggravated over his behavior and appeared to be spoiling for a fight. Orb avoided the man like a plague. H.B. couldn't define the rub but it was clear the man was the Concho hire and seemed determined to not fit in. Cody Meyer, a friendly young cowboy, mentioned his name as Cobb Pickens.

"He's a shooter," Cody said, as he leaned in his saddle and rubbed his horse's neck. The cattle were crossing a steep creek and were bunching up in the narrow passage thus slowing the herd. "There's trouble brewin'," Cody reiterated with an added emphasis. "Captain Brady ain't tolerant of his type." H.B. had never heard the reference of the captain applied to Twinks Brady. Cody readjusted his hat and H.B. retied his bandanna carefully. The dust gritted in his teeth, his eyes stung and felt dry, even his hat had small lines of dust coiling along the brim like so many little snakes trailing from front to back.

"Where'd he earn the title captain?" H.B. asked. The Civil War's end had sent multitudes of officer-types back into open western society at-large. There were lieutenants and captains and majors and colonels spread throughout the south and west now. All keeping their military ranking as part of their name. It wasn't so much an ego thing as it was a matter of pride. Pride in their service in the war against northern aggression. They had no intention of letting anyone forget about it either.

"He was a captain in Robert E. Lee's forces and fought numerous engagements in the war, including the battle of Bull Run. Entered service with the Texas Rangers later and served as a captain for a good many years. He's a tough man." Cody continued rubbing and massaging the horse's neck.

Orb rode up and stopped, watching the steers slowly funnel across the creek. The relentless wind and its accompanying dust was just another inconvenience of the trail. It was expected, occasionally, but it made for miserable travel for man and beast alike. Orb spit a mouthful of tobacco juice watching it spread and disintegrate in the wind. He released his bandanna and shook the dust out of it. He stood in his stirrups and surveyed the crossing scene before him. The cattle moved slowly yet doggedly into the stiff north wind.

"Nevershed warns of a storm coming tonight," Orb said spitting again. "Hope it ain't much. I'd like to cross the Red for once when it's not on a rise." The Texas-Indian Territory was separated by the Red River, notorious for cowboy drowning and cattle bogging. Even in the best of conditions, it was a chancy, temperamental stream whose mood could never be predicted. It could be crossed with little or no trouble one day and the very next day be a trail boss's nightmare. Working cowboys hated it. Shallow, unmarked graves of unfortunate drovers lined its banks. Rumors had it that no one could cross the river without stepping over the grave of a comrade. "We'll bed 'em early and try and hold them down. Nevershed's rarely wrong about the weather."

Orb rode off to meet Twinks Brady who was riding his way. The two met and spoke briefly. Orb then headed towards the crossing. Twinks rode over to where Cody and H.B. sat.

"This is a fine profession," he said, pulling up the reins on his horse. "Where else do you get to eat grit all day, smell cow shit all day, and witness the never-ending flow of the ass-end of a northbound herd? I should've been a gambler. Whore sittin' on one knee, clean shirts every day, plenty of whiskey to drink, and a bed to sleep on under a roof that don't leak. I'm beginning to think Mother Brady did raise a foolish child."

Cody smiled. H.B. had to acknowledge the fact that his first day of trail driving hadn't been necessarily a pleasant one.

"Nevershed and his damn weather predictin'. You got a good slicker, H.B.?"

"Yes, I do." Most if not all cowboy slickers were yellow in color and highly functional. However, he had a Gore-Tex rain-coat straight from the twenty-first century. He hoped it proved to be workable.

"Eat grit all day and suck rain all night. I guess I'm too damn old for this job. Chousing cattle all over creation ain't my idea of a good time."

"Maybe Nevershed's wrong," Cody offered, trying to lighten the mood. Twinks was on the prod and the dust and wind hadn't helped matters. At best, weather on the range was always unpredictable, but he had to admit, Nevershed's predictions had been true as a rule on the trail.

"How can it turn wet when it's so damn dry right now? On these plains you got to be ready for everything. After this drive I'm finding me a rocking chair, a roof, and a plump little woman to snuggle with. Some gal's bound to want an old worn out Texas Ranger like me. Hell, I don't even snore much, do I Cody?"

"I ain't ever heard you," Cody lied afraid to admit otherwise. Actually, he was a noisy sleeper rattling along like an old locomotive in his bedroll. No one had enough starch to mention it as fact though. Plus, the normal trials and tribulations of the trail provided enough sleeping potion to counter an accomplished snorer like the captain. It would take a cannon blast to arouse most of the hands from the scant comfort of their robes.

"Women don't cotton to a man who's noisy at night," Twinks continued like an expert on the matter. He reached in his shirt pocket and pulled out the makings for a roll-your-own. In less than a minute he had it rolled and struggled to light it in the stiff wind. The bottle-necked cattle moved at a snail's pace. Leisure moments were a scarce commodity on a cattle drive so the three men enjoyed the momentary slow down. Twinks slipped his right boot out of the stirrup and propped it over his horse's neck. He deeply inhaled the cigarette smoke with a reminiscent expression.

"I met a gal in Uvalde once that I think liked me. I caught her lookin' at me when I was waterin' my horse. Me and Pat, another Ranger ridin' with me, had just hauled in three stinkin' horse thieves and there she was just standin' by the water trough as pretty as you please. I'll never forget that pretty face. I meant to look her up after delivering those damn horse thieves but never did. Kinda sorry I didn't. I never forgot that look she gave me."

Cody looked at H.B. as a soft smile formed on his lips. Captain's reputation as a fighter was renown and as a result was heralded in most quarters as a hero in the state. He had also taken a big bite out of the last Indian stragglers and slave traders that raided out of strongholds in the lonely plateaus of the Staked Plains. Tales of his fighting exploits even trickled down to deep south Texas where Cody lived, but he'd never heard a single story about his being a lady's man of any kind. Cody suspected he was in over his head in knowing a woman's intentions. Even men with finer honed skills than could be found on this cattle drive had failed in reading the many and varied turns in a female's way of thinking. Captain Brady knew his way around a Colt and a Henry repeating rife better than most men could even imagine. His skills didn't seem to run along the line of knowing what a woman's look might add up to.

Twinks relaxed and smoked. The steers trickled slowly down the narrow draw in ones and twos then climbed the steep bank in no particular hurry to face the unrelenting north wind. Orb was on the other side of the creek with a cowboy named Travis Strayhorn pushing the mulish animals up the long, sloping terrain. The western sky already had a reddish hue painting the horizon, bespeaking the possibility of Nevershed's prophecies. H.B. scratched Patty Cake between her ears and she pushed her head up against his hand requesting a harder rub. A gust of wind tore through the three men suddenly kicking dust in all directions. Twinks cussed. Cody tightened his reins holding his mount steady. Patty Cake seemed undistracted by the wind, totally engrossed in H.B.'s affections.

"I guess I'll go help push up the drags," Twinks said, tossing his smoke to the ground. "Way I'm feelin' right now I better not run into that bastard Cobb Pickens. He needs his lard ass kicked." With that he kicked his horse into a trot and headed towards the back of the herd.

Orb led them to bed ground two hours before the sun found the rim of the world. The sun looked muddy and weirdly enlarged by the undulations of high-flying dust. The light, what light could penetrate from it, was reddish and the landscape and grasses and cattle and cowboys hued red as a result. It was one of the strangest sunsets H.B. had ever witnessed and he sat transfixed atop Patty Cake watching it unfold. The wind had finally settled somewhat but its ravages had not been forgotten by the rarified atmosphere that surrounded them. As the sun nestled down even further westward the red intensified until it finally turned russet and then lavender in its final moment before extinction. Then the enlarged, blood-red orb hugged the skyline for a few brief minutes painting the ground gloriously with its brilliant crimson brush strokes. Buster's dinner bell clanged to life and awoke the observers of the unique experience to the reality of growling stomachs. The stew pot steamed and the cowboys held their tin plates at the ready. The only cowboy missing from the crowd that lined up for supper was, of course, Cobb Pickens. Orb asked around and no one had seen him since mid-afternoon. Nevershed claimed to have seen him some time, on the east side of the herd, during the creek crossing. No one could recall seeing him since. The men talked in subdued tones regarding his absence as the first night herders rode out to tend the cattle. Far to the north, farther then some men's imaginations, the first flashing signals of an approaching storm appeared. Orb watched with trepidation as he poured another cup of coffee. He then issued orders to the cowboys to rope up their night horses and prepare for the inevitable. The oracle of weather, Nevershed, was proven to be right once again.

Within two hours of first sighting its approach, the rolling thunder rattled like the sound of an old potato wagon traveling down a bumpy road. The long day's combative wind had withdrawn now and an eerie calm sent Buster's campfire on a straight trajectory to the stars...and there were stars! The ones that could be seen occasionally over the relentless flashing in the northern sky. The men stood at ready around the campfire waiting for Orb to deliver their orders. Orb had ridden out to look over the bedded cattle and would return shortly with detailed instructions. Buster's coffee was black and stout to compensate for the night's promise of no sleep. Every cup steamed and every eye watched the gathering thunderheads seething and boiling. Twinks Brady shook his head wondering how fate had seen fit to place his feet on this path.

"Looka there," he said, pointing a crooked finger at the bulging, boiling mass of clouds. "Hell, look at how green it is. Damn straight sign that hail's comin'. Check your hat straps boys. It'll pulverize your topknot if you lose your hat. Hunker down, boys, we're in for a siege." The hands quickly obeyed his warning. Lightning flashes spread, filling the east-west panorama with streaks of thousands of super charged wiggly electrified snakes. The roar of the storm grew by the minute. Then a flash revealed Orb's return to camp and he sat his horse looking at the wide-eyed men.

"Everybody in the saddle. We can't control what's coming but let's hold the cattle as best we can. Stay in twos. Make sure you've got your six-shooter so you can turn the leaders. This is going to be a big one." H.B. knew his reference to turning the leaders meant an impending stampede. Burning gunpowder in front of the charging beeves sometimes assisted in milling them thus negating a five or even ten-mile run. Scattered steers could take several days to round up.

The men tossed their coffee, made for the saddled night horses, and quickly left for the bedded cattle. Cody and H.B. teamed and took an easterly direction, settling themselves fifty yards from the nearest steers. Most of the steers were still down, nervously chewing their cuds but each ensuing lightning flash revealed an increasingly unsettled herd. Cody checked the loads in his Colt and tied his hat straps tight under his chin. H.B. followed his lead and pulled his Gore-Tex rain coat out and slipped it on. A mile distant the lightning flashes revealed the wind stirring grasses and rattling leaves of the scrubby oaks. The roar of the approaching storm became deafening.

CHAPTER

TWENTY-FOUR

Hank walked in wearing cowboy boots complete with jingling spurs, faded Levi's, and a pistol dangling from his hip. He wore a light flannel shirt, a tall Stetson hat, and was carrying a light coat. What the hell? Katy thought looking him over. It was ninety degrees outside and he's carrying a coat. I didn't request a trip to the ice age.

"Katy, you best dress for the period, I guess. You have any western duds?"

"Yeah, I got plenty of 'em but why the coat?"

"Let's go back in February. I'll choose a cool day. I don't want to melt with this humidity around here." Katy was ready for cool weather, too, so she headed for her house in a daze of excitement, Hank accompanying to change clothes. The late June south Texas heat and humidity enveloped her and she was dripping wet as she and Hank walked back to H.B.'s. Hank thought she looked remarkably nice in her new outfit.

"You know I'll cause a quite stir in the 1880's dressed in pants. I'm liable to get stoned for my sass."

"I'll try and hold them off," Hank said, as they led the saddled horses towards the double door, lab-garage entrance. The premise of what they were supposedly going to do seemed like the plot from a science fiction novel to Katy. Dress up in western duds and head back nonchalantly into the past like it was just another Saturday shopping trip to town. The idea was so surreal, so fantastic, that she couldn't get a handle on it. Once inside the strangely lit garage, she grabbed Hank's hand and squeezed it tightly.

"Is this real, Hank? Are we really doing this?"

"Yes, Katy, but it's strictly up to you. It's your choice."

"Am I the only one that thinks this is just a little crazy? I mean, hell, this is just a pretty bizarre deal to have sitting five miles from podunk, little Bellville, Texas. Are these powers something we should be messin' with?"

"I can't answer that, Katy. I just adjust the settings and it all happens. This is all H.B.'s creation. He built it to suit his wants and needs. I guess it was his life's work. The rest of us are just keepers of the secret. It's engulfed my life as well as Trent's and Ethan's and Lori's. Had the thugs not attacked you, you could have avoided being swept up by it. Now it's too late. I thought I could protect you from it but it's no use. The rest of us made the choice to be here but you didn't. You just happened to be his neighbor."

Hank's revelation surprised Katy. So, he had envisioned protecting her not only from the attacking goons but from the clutches of the scientific miracle she was about to witness. He hadn't wanted her life endangered by the knowledge of its existence. He had been secretive for her own good for a very valid reason. The more she knew, ultimately, the more she had to lose. The very thought of his protecting her caused her heart of swell and her eyes to tear. She pulled his arm to her and buried her face in the soft cotton of his shirt sleeve. Her tears flowed into its fabric. Hank draped his arm over her shoulder and comforted her. He wasn't sure of the precise feelings that stirred her but he felt compelled to soothe them. Katy finally raised her head, wiped her eyes, squeezed his hand tighter and braced her boots on the slick concrete floor. Her eyes adjusted to the lowered light.

"Well, I'm ready, Hank. Let's go take a look at yesterday."

Hank walked to the back of the garage, entered a side room and returned in a few moments. The big screen, huge and brilliant in color snapped to life with the bright sunshine of a February day. The two horses stared at it as transfixed as Katy was. Hank grabbed the horses' reins and approached the portal as casually as he'd stroll to a Sunday picnic. Katy flinched a little, held back momentarily, watching Hank and the horses walk through as easily as they would through an open garage door. Hank turned the horses around and waved to her standing in the present, while he waved from 1885. A sudden flush of emotion started her heart racing and she walked, cautiously forward, urging her feet take each step. Her willpower faltered again just at the entrance of the portal and she paused. Hank could see her standing there, indecisive, and he smiled broadly. Somehow his smile comforted her. Then her feet stepped through. To Katy, the event was mind-boggling. Yet once across the portal, the exhilaration of having crossed the uncharted boundaries of time immediately replaced her fears. She took a deep breath as the portal screen disappeared and her eyes surveyed the surroundings. Oh my, was her first thought. What have I done now?

She sat Hank's mare like a veteran equestrian and handled her with a deft hand. Hank noticed her riding skills from the moment she sat the saddle.

"What year did you put us in?" she asked, as they went into a slow lope in a westerly direction.

"1885. The first railroad arrived in the winter of 1880. I thought I'd let the town grow up a bit."

"It was the Gulf, Colorado, and Santa Fe Railroad. They've even got two newspapers going in Bellville in 1885. Do you know the names of them?" she asked, her tone cocky. It was a cool, clear, crisp day in mid-February and Katy drank it by the bucket-full.

"I see you've grown cocky with a little history readin'," Hank responded smiling. The horses were as frisky as they were with the feel of cool air, open terrain, and a loose rein.

"I'd rather see history than read it," Katy said with a look of excitement on her face. The ride felt like a jaunt back to a fairy land where all things were possible. It reminded her, too, of her first trip to Disneyland with her father. There was a bubbly, child-like feeling surging within her breast. It was exhilarating. Thoroughly wonderful. It was hard to contain herself.

"Hank, are you feeling the sense of freedom like I am? I've never felt this fine. This alive. Do you feel that, Hank?"

Hank looked at her grinning. She had no idea what he'd done. So, he let it be. She'd find out soon enough. "It's great, Katy," he answered seeing her sparkling enthusiasm. Her spirit, her enthusiasm was what Hank admired about her the most. She was an indomitable woman, he thought, and her exuberance for life was only one of her charms.

"Where did you learn to ride?"

"My dad's way of making up to me for being away on long Navy cruises was to buy me a pony. I rarely sat a saddle though. A bridle is all I needed."

236

After about a mile's ride they saw a horseman cross a knoll to the north and head their way. Likely a local rancher or farmer Hank thought but unsnapped his holster as a precaution. As the stranger approached, he noticed a Winchester resting lightly across the saddle pommel. Hank reached and unsheathed his Henry repeater. The stranger noticed his action and slowed a bit. Hank levered in a cartridge. He carefully released the hammer and let it down.

The stranger's horse slowed to a trot and he pulled up ten yards away.

"Howdy," he said through a stern face. He was pig-eyed and greasy haired. His lips were thin and tight. "You folks from around here?"

"Not too far from here," Hank responded fingering the Henry's hammer. Where they lived clearly wasn't any of his business. The stranger wore a dark, floppy hat, with loose hair dangling out from the sides. He appeared to dislike both barbers and bath water. The Winchester was firm in his hands.

"I'm missin' three horses off my place. I spotted tracks headin' this way so I followed. Looks to me like someone run them off."

"We've not seen anything," Hank answered beginning to feel edgy. The man just didn't have a rancher's look. He carried a heavy sidearm. The stranger's eyes moved to Katy and lingered too long. The look immediately incensed Hank.

"We've got business in Bellville," Hank said, his voice quivering in rising anger. "You best be huntin' your horses rather than wasting time with us. I expect you'll want to get going." Hank cocked the Henry with an audible click. It was a clear challenge.

"Now hold on just a minute there," the stranger said raising his voice an octave. His back stiffened in the saddle. "I hope you ain't tryin' to tell me what I ought to be doin'."

"Your business is your business. You're the one that rode up to us, if you recall."

Hank had found many items of western memorabilia in H.B.'s sizeable collection back at his house and had enjoyed poking through them. Before leaving, just for the fun of it, he had pinned on a Texas Ranger badge for the sole purpose of teasing Katy. It was polished to a shine. Katy hadn't noticed it yet, and obviously neither had the stranger. So, without hesitation Hank decided to push a bluff. He gave the badge a full display. It glistened in the bright morning light and he saw the man's eyes collect it. The stranger's stern face registered a slight change. The message was received. Hank decided to push it.

"I'm on urgent state business but the constable in Bellville needs to know if there's a chance rustlers are working the vicinity. I'd be glad to pass on the word."

The insolence remained with the stranger. "Now, wait just a minute here mister. I'm the one missin' the horses. I can talk for myself if need be."

"Well, that's good. You do that fella. Now you need to move along with that nag of yours. My patience is wearing thin." Hank's eyes grew cold with contempt.

The stranger's jaw tightened with Hank's statement. He could hardly tolerate this smart ass lawman trying to order him around. Who in the hell does he think he is? Badges didn't make anyone bullet-proof. He cut his eyes again in Katy's direction. His expression was easy to read. The stranger's horse slung its head impatiently as a long pause ensued.

The man fidgeted slightly in his saddle contemplating action. Hank appeared ready which tempered his actions somewhat. He felt he'd been called out and even belittled. Badge or not, it was hard to ride away from a cocky law-dog bastard. Killing him, just now, might not be easy. The stranger liked the odds stacked more in his favor so finally, with a sneer, he loosened rein and moved away slowly. Hank followed his every move. Two hundred yards away he topped a grassy knoll and disappeared. Hank watched a few seconds longer and slid the Henry back in its leather scabbard.

Katy turned to Hank still stunned by the man's belligerence.

"I'd say that was pretty close, wouldn't you?"

"Yeah. It was pretty close. He wanted a fight and almost got one."

"You think he may still try something?" Katy asked still stunned.

"It's hard to say. We'll watch out coming back through here. He's likely a professional back-shooter."

They spurred up to a fast lope, pointing towards Bellville. The further behind they left the stranger the better she felt.

"I could feel death in the man," Katy said, as they stopped and let the horses blow on a slight rise overlooking the little town. "Oh, by the way, what kind of state business are we on?" Hank turned and flashed Katy his badge. She gave him a startled look.

"So, I'm ridin' with Ranger Hank, huh," she laughed as she studied his shiny badge.

Hank unpinned the badge and stuck it in his vest pocket as they rode into the outskirts of the small town. A tall church steeple dominated the western edge of the community. Several wagons inched along the main thoroughfare as they followed them into the little berg. One wagon in particular was heavy laden with fence posts and rolls of coiled barbed wire. Hank observed the slow-moving wagon with some regret. In just a few years the open range would disappear and freedom of movement curtailed. The one defining feature of the past most admired by Hank was the fact that the liberty of movement still existed.

Katy gawked at the sight of the frontier settlement. They walked the horses, slowly, in the circle of plank-board stores that defined the center of town, the square so to speak. It wasn't sizeable really but had two hotels, the Bellville Inn, and the Tavern Hotel on opposite sides of each other. Both businesses had prominent signage advertising bath houses, barbers, and eateries.

Bellville's two weekly newspapers were almost side-by-side with only a general store separating them. Both the Bellville Standard and the Austin County Times looked prosperous and competitive. The Wild Rose Saloon's piano player banged keys sending a tune through the batwing doors of the establishment. It seemed a bit early for piano playing. Katy's eyes flitted around absorbing the scene. A half dozen wagons with an admixture of mule and horse teams were tied up in various locations. Two larger freight-style wagons were located in front of Miller's Mercantile being loaded by strapping lads. Next to Miller's was a small bakery and the smells of fresh baking bread reached Katy and it stopped her in her tracks. She pulled up and pointed her mare to a hitching rail and promptly dismounted. Hank followed and dismounted, too, wondering about her intentions. The town square had six-foot boardwalks connecting all the businesses. The Germania Bakery had tall letters painted on its plate glass windows touting fresh bakery goods. Katy was impressed. She was hungry and had a strong desire for a slice of hot, fresh baked bread.

They both tied up while speaking and stepped on the sidewalk. Katy grabbed Hank's hand and held it excitedly. Her heart thrilled at the scene, the feel, the raw robustness of a surging frontier community. She felt like a kid again and she stared through the picture window noticing her and Hank's reflection. She had pulled her hair back in a pony tail just before leaving H.B.'s and she checked its status. She'd hung her hat on the saddle horn. Looked fine. Then she noticed something. What? A surprised expression formed on her face. She stared in stark disbelief, walking several steps closer to the window. Two stout women were busy serving customers inside from behind a waist-high counter. Katy's look turned incredulous.

"Hank," she practically shouted turning abruptly to face him. "What the hell's going on? My hair's changed color," she shrieked. "Why has it changed to dark brown? Am I seeing it right? Tell me, Hank, please, and don't you dare lie."

"It's dark brown, Katy," he said enjoying her startled moment. "Very dark brown actually."

She grabbed his arm roughly again and pulled him down closer. Her breathing was shallow and rapid. "Something mighty weird is going on, Hank. What's happened to me?" she almost screamed. Luckily no locals were close at hand to witness Katy's outburst. Hank gently grabbed her arm and tugged her back off the boardwalk stopping beside her mare.

"Take off you riding gloves, Katy. More than your hair has likely changed."

Katy peeled them off as if both hands were on fire. She looked down in stunned silence. Their youthful appearance astonishing her.

"Oh, my Lord. What's going on?"

"H.B.'s invention has a wonderful twist if you want to use it," Hank said, as he steadied her with his arm. "It can adjust your age, too. You're twenty-five years old, Katy. You're somewhat younger than I am now. I guess I should've asked your permission, but I wanted it to be a surprise."

Katy tugged at his arm absently in a semi-dazed state. She could feel her heart pounding in her chest.

"For God's sake, Hank. This is a whole lot more than a surprise. Oh, crap! Look at me. I'm shaking like a leaf. You mean to tell me that machine of H. B's reverses age and ships you back in history at the same time?" she gasped and made sure of her footing. Her legs felt wobbly with excitement. "That's unbelievable, Hank. Unbelievable."

Just as she finished, a man and woman stepped out of the bakery looking their way, pleasantly, until the woman observed Katy in pants. A female dressed in pants and displaying herself in public was such a shock that a sneer immediately transformed her face. The expression bespoke volumes as she stared directly at Katy, unable to break eye contact. Finally, the man pulled the glaring woman along but she continued throwing furtive, disapproving glances over her shoulder. Katy wasn't too shocked to take note of the woman's scornful expression. Hank braced her up by one arm as she slowly gathered her wits.

"I fought like the boys as a kid, Hank. A regular hellion I was. I'll probably have to kick some frontier broad's snooty ass before the day's out. I have no tolerance for a catty, judgmental female. Especially one who has ten pounds of bloomers wrapped around her butt."

"Katy, now keep your cool," Hank cautioned. "You've got to remember we're in their world now. Seeing a female in pants in this era is totally scandalous. Remind yourself that we're foreigners in a foreign land. We knew you would attract a lot of attention. You just have to deal with it."

"Damned if I'll wear a dress and all that crap they put up with, Hank. No matter what. I never liked a dress with the cold breeze blowing up my legs. There ain't nothing beneath a woman in a dress but open air. I don't know how the hell women tolerate them present or past. Wear one a while and you'll know what I'm talking about."

"Just keep calm," Hank said softly trying to settle Katy. She was clearly on the prod and spoiling for a fight. The already rambunctious Katy, revitalized with youth and ready to thump someone. Hank was determined to slide in and out of the lazy little berg without creating a major disturbance. It was a relief to see the sidewalks nearly empty of patrons.

"If we go in they'll stare, Katy. No way around that. You want me to get us a roll or pastry or whatever they have and bring it out?"

"No," she said emphatically pointing through the window. "I want to sit down at that little table in the back with the red gingham tablecloth and enjoy a cup of coffee and eat a hot roll or slice of bread. That's all. Is that asking too much?"

Hank wasn't sure how to answer. It wasn't such a simple black and white matter. A simple yes or no was fraught with potential complications. Katy wasn't the submissive type and they had entered a woman-submissive past. She was highly opinionated, headstrong, and willing to mix it up with all comers – male or female. Perhaps the mores, standards, and beliefs of where women stood in the society and culture of 1885 wasn't ready for the likes of a Katy.

"Katy," Hank said firmly. She raised her head and looked into his eyes, fire dancing behind her pupils. "Let's go see the locomotive if one's around and meander around for a while and head back home. I'll take you to that little doughnut shop in Sealy and we'll have a pastry and an espresso and talk a little philosophy. Your pants won't draw a single look or comment. Does that sound okay to you?"

"Will I be twenty-five there or sixty-five?" she asked testily. She saw Hank's expression tighten with the question. She noted his discomfort. As a youth and practically her entire adult life she had survived as an island unto herself. Self-actualized. Independent. Her rough and tumble marriage hadn't changed that. So, the thought of considering someone else's feelings, especially a man's, had never had been of paramount importance. Few men she'd ever known really deserved or earned her respect, but with Hank it was different. She didn't like being at odds with a man who fought one skirmish after another, risking his life, for her safety and well-being. For a man who fought so well, he, too, seemed to possess a gentle spirit. A smile slowly replaced her fiery look.

"Sixty-five," he said quietly. "We can only cheat going back not forward as far as I know. Maybe there's a way to do it but H.B. didn't explain the whole process. I just went back and followed the commands he entered turning the clock back on himself. He clicked in thirty. I clicked in twenty-five and it worked."

"So, I was a guinea pig, huh. You experimented on me. I was your test subject."

"No," Hank countered quickly. "I tried it on myself a couple of times, first. I knew it would work."

Katy half-smiled enjoying the moment. Hank seemed endlessly patient with her ranting and raving, but he wasn't easy to outmaneuver. She liked it that he was a thinker as well as a doer. She seemed to have always clawed her way through life. Hank, in stark contrast, was a careful planner and initiator.

"Let's go in," she said grabbing Hank's hand. "I'll make nice, I promise. They'll be staring wishing they were as brave as I am. They'll all want a pair of tight-fittin' jeans. I may set up shop right here sellin' lady's blue jeans. I'll make a mockery of their uppity-up ways, and I could get rich, too, you know."

"We're already rich, Katy. H.B. left more money lying around than any ten people could ever spend."

"What do you mean we're rich? When did I get an inheritance?"

Hank squirmed at bit. "Well, I've got a pocket full of gold coins from this era. I should have enough to buy you a roll and some coffee. Are you ready?"

She slipped her hand inside his arm as Hank led her to the door and opened it. The door squealed on its hinges and a large woman behind the counter looked up. Hank immediately noticed her wowed expression but a broad smile followed her initial shock.

"May I help you," she said in a strong German accent looking first at Hank and then Katy. Katy remained close to his side returning the woman's smile.

CHAPTER
TWENTY-FIVE

The thunderstorm delivered on its promises. The puny efforts of the drovers were quickly overwhelmed by the sheer force and magnitude of the storm. Orb soon discovered the maelstrom more than a match for his wits and the combined force of drovers he marshaled against it. Though youthful, Cody's experiences trailing cattle had paid off. H.B. felt lucky to have his expertise as all hell broke loose with the storm.

The roaring noise took on the sound of a thousand rumbling locomotives and the cattle rose from their bed ground and started milling. With a clattering of hooves and horns, they stood as one against it. At first confused, the beeves now appeared to be marshalling their forces. The brilliant light of the lightning flashes displayed a cattle herd primed and ready to bolt. Then to make matters worse, there was a sudden thumping noise. A loud thud here and there. H.B. couldn't discern the source. Then it quickly became abundantly clear. Hail. Hail the size of pullet eggs started raining down. Slow-paced at first but it was enough to unhinge an already nervous herd. Moments after the first hail stone dropped, the cattle stampeded with the main column of animals charging eastward. Amazingly, in one flash of lightening the steers were milling and nervous, and in the next flash they took flight like a retreating army. So instead of heading, H.B. and Cody found themselves heeling a racing herd.

They were left behind in a matter of moments and keeping up proved impossible with the long-legged steers. They truly were animals bred to run. South Texas cattle were of mixed breeding. Their skinny, deer-like cousins splashed through the muddy waters of the Rio Grande from Mexico and bred with the larger, beefier Texas cattle. The result eventually became known as the legendary longhorn. Mexican horns and legs. Texan in flank and frame. Cowboys revered the animal because you could drive it twenty-five miles a day through tough terrain and adverse conditions and the beasts would actually gain weight. So, the marriage of the two breeds was a blessing instead of a curse. The one exception, of course, was when they stampeded. Then and only then did the cowboys curse their speed.

Soon, however, the cattle, their breeding, and their general direction of stampeding became only of secondary concern. The hail storm rapidly intensified and began sending sheets of hail stones with incredibly destructive force. The size of the hail grew rapidly and finally the battering became so intense that Cody and H.B. had to take cover. The ground quickly became littered with white stones. Some were the size of a clenched fist. A tree could provide some protection but they were the favorite targets of lightning bolts. So, they both dismounted and sought shelter next to the suffering and panicked horses. Finally, Cody suggested uncinching the saddles and pulling out the saddle blankets to cover the horse's heads. H.B. expected Patty Cake to protest the action as he pulled the saddle blanket over her head. The mare was highly agitated and began to crow-hop. Between the darkness and H.B.'s soothing hand she began to settle down.

As quick as it came, the hail subsided and sheets of rain replaced the ice. Then the wind returned with renewed force. Remounted they pursued the long-departed cattle at a steady lope. The wind and rain raked them, tried tearing them from their saddles, but at least the hail had stopped. H.B. could barely see through the waterfall that gushed over the front brim of his hat. They plodded on into the darkness each buried in his own thoughts, silent. As becoming of most top hands, Cody accepted the storm like just another inconvenience expected of the trail.

The wind subsided after midnight, but the rain continued to pound them unmercifully. After a couple of hours of trailing against a strong prevailing rain, they met Nevershed doubling back towards the original campsite.

"Goin' to check on Buster," Nevershed shouted over the rain. "Orb thinks he saw a cyclone headed that way earlier. I'll catch back up." With that he spurred his mount to a lope on his mission to find the chuckwagon.

The lightning flashes faded away to the south and the night turned pitch black. H.B. silently hoped Cody knew where he was going. He had long since lost all sense of direction. The rain let up after three in the morning and turned to a misty drizzle. Everything was soaked. The horses dripped water. H.B. could feel water in the seams of his hat, but his Gore-Tex coat seemed to have kept him dry. For that he was thankful.

"Hard to see anything in this infernal darkness," Cody said pulling up finally. "We should see some light in a couple of hours. Let's get off and rest the horses. We'll need 'em fresh for later."

They trudged along in ankle-deep water waiting for the

first rays of morning. Finally, after what seemed to H.B. an eternity, a pencil-red line formed in the east. Just as they were remounting with enough dawn to see, Nevershed rode up.

"Camp's okay. Buster's cussin' as usual. He's got a bad case of red ass. Some of his flour got wet."

"We're not but a day or two from Doan's Store. They'll have some," Cody said reassuringly.

"I tolt him that very thing but he wouldn't listen. He's too damn bullheaded."

Two LONG, exhausting days in the saddle finally had the herd trail-ready again. Orb, usually light-hearted and good humored, fell into a sulky mood barking orders and riding the men. It wasn't his usual way but the leaden skies and intermittent drizzle would test any man's resolve. The men fell into a deep gloom and the soggy campfire and wet sleeping rolls did little to ease the tension.

"Best be watchin' your back trail," Twinks Brady cautioned, as if they didn't have enough to worry about. Muggy weather and chasing stays had a way of dulling a man's senses. "We ain't seen the last of Cobb Pickens. That bastard's slinkin' 'round. You can bank on that."

"What's he hangin' around for?" a tallish, lanky cowpoke named John Henry Sodke asked. "Ain't nothin' here for the likes of him."

"His blood's up," Twinks barked back impatiently at a man who'd likely spook at his own shadow. "He's a vengeful type. He'll kill for the pure pleasure of it. There are some men like that and he's one of 'em."

Orb was standing outside the shadows of the campfire listening. His schedule to Montana was being tangled up in one mishap after another and he was having to struggle to keep his mind right. The ill winds had been blowing and he was upset with his own dark mood. Frankly, he'd never been prone to such a thing, but it seemed impossible to meet his obligations when they wasted countless days handling one calamity after another. Missed days of driving turned into weeks and weeks into months. Seasons didn't wait. They came and went no matter the circumstances. Each day missed was another day gone never to be gotten back. The big cold was coming to Montana whether the steers arrived or not. Fighting these gloomy thoughts, he walked back into the circle of the campfire, reached down grabbing the coffee pot, and refilled his metal cup. The men got quiet in his presence knowing he'd been overly touchy of late.

He stood after pouring his coffee looking around at his hands. They're just boys, he thought, for the most part. Trying to do their job, and he knew he hadn't been contributing to their stability by being hard on them. His noggin had been filled with too many doubts and fears and one of the thoughts that continually surfaced was Cobb Pickens. Knowing that he was the one who hired the man in the first place galled him to no end.

"Best be listening to the captain," he said addressing the nervous group. "Make sure you've got your loads ready. He's likely a back shooter, too, so be aware of your surroundings. If anyone sees the man don't approach him. Get me or Twinks if you can. Night herders had better be extra wary, too. I'm setting a guard in camp for the next few nights. He's liable to try and slip in and out unnoticed."

"He'll slice your throat right where you're sleepin'," Twinks added for emphasis. "He's sure 'nough a slinky bastard." That statement sent a shudder through the men. It was one thing to keep a watchful eye out during the day but having a man's throat cut in his own bedroll was downright scary. There was general relief that Orb was posting a camp guard. The cowboys slept like dead things after long days in the saddle and weren't likely to hear an intruder. Buster was up many hours during the night clanking pots, coughing and stirring the cook fire but he could easily miss an intruder.

On the morning of the third day of stoppage Orb finally ordered the cattle off the bed ground and they proceeded north toward Doan's Store and the Red River. The weather remained soggy and damp. Spirits were at boot level and seemed to sink with each muddy step. Orb's mood, however, had brightened somewhat in his attempt to rally the men. He had finally come to peace with himself and the expectations of the drive. It was a subtle but substantial change in his philosophy. Did he drive the cattle or did they drive him? Fretting over forces he couldn't control had ruled too long over him. He'd do the best he could do with what he had, period, and no amount of worry could change the inevitable outcome anyway. Besides what was a little snow? Most of the south Texas cowboys had never even seen the stuff. He'd like to be the man to introduce it to them if it had to be. They could buy heavy coats and extra blankets in Ogallala if needed. One way or another he'd see them through to Montana.

OVER THE COURSE of the next hour a growing kinship developed between the two stout German sisters, the proprietors of Germania Bakery, and Katy. Hank did the ordering, Katy held on to his arm, and Freda beamed at them both from her square, red face. Helga, equally broad and red, moved in and out from the back room of the bakery tending ovens and wiping her sweaty brow. Both sisters spoke a heavy German accent indicative of recent immigration. Both were talkative, robust, bustled with activity, and cut a rather large swath.

Hank and Katy took their seats with a gingham tablecloth beneath them waiting for Freda to deliver hot buttered bread. Freda waddled over and it being a quiet moment for the thriving bakery engaged Katy in a conversation.

"I like what you're wearin'," Freda said, emphatically pointing a plump finger at Katy's pants. "These heavy dresses get in the way of the stoves. Poor Helga caught on fire just last week pulling out the bread. We want to know where to find some of those?"

Katy glanced at Hank and answered. "Some stores around Houston have them. If I knew your size I'd get you a few pairs. I could measure you with some twine."

"Oh, wonderful," Freda exclaimed shouting for Helga to come over. "She can get us some pants just like hers. Whatcha' think about that Helga?"

Helga shook her head excitedly. "Yeah, yeah. We like your pants."

"Do you think pants might scare off the customers?" Katy asked amazed they were even interested.

"What do we care anyway," Freda intoned. "We bake just for the fun. If they don't want our bread that's fine with us. They can take it or go away from it."

Katy took her first bite of piping hot bread and knew immediately the customers would keep coming regardless of their attire.

"Wow, this is delicious. Wonderful in fact."

Both Germans beamed with pride.

"We use the old country recipes. Passed down from our mama," Helga said.

"Delicious," Katy added. Hank took his first bite savoring the flavor. They both had cups of steaming hot coffee waiting on the table. The German girls stood close by watching them eat, enjoying their response to the bread.

The German girls had plenty of gumption and were a truly spirited team. Customers trickled in and out carry loaves of hot bread while others sat at the tables eating and drinking hot coffee. No one else took much notice of Katy's attire and that was fine with Hank. Katy ordered a second slice and savored it slowly. The bakery was warm and the smell of fresh bread filtered throughout the establishment. The jovial mood of the Germans was infectious and if a droopy lip entered the bakery. It was quickly transformed into a smile. Katy relished the atmosphere.

"Oh, Hank, I can't get enough of this place," she said leaning over. Her brown hair glowed as radiant as her face. "There's just a feel about it I can't describe. Do you feel it too?"

"Yes," Hank admitted. "I think its as much the good smells as anything. I'd be as big as the German girls if I worked in here though. I couldn't stay away from the bread."

Katy laughed. "I sure like Helga and Freda. Now they've got the spunk. Too bad that's missing from where we come from. People have lost their spunk, don't you think?"

"For the most part that's true. Fewer have it, that's sure."

"Well, I like spunk. I like drive. These gals here just sparkle with it."

Freda approached them with a fresh pot of coffee and filled their cups. Her face glowing like a coal in a campfire.

"Stays hot in here," she said, setting the coffee pot down to wipe her brow. "Feels like my folk's sauna back in the old country. Hot and steamy. You want one more slice, too, Hank?

Just got my special pumpernickel out of the oven. Piping hot and ready. I know you'll like it."

"Sounds great, Freda. I'd like to try it." Rye had always been a favorite of his. Hank's mother baked it for him occasionally as a kid and he'd never lost the taste for it.

Freda laughed with her huge bosoms bobbing as she waddled off to slice the bread. She soon returned with a large, freshly buttered slice. The rich rye aroma wafted to Hank's nose and he wasted no time digging in. Freda stood close monitoring Hank's response.

"Best bread I've ever tasted. Delicious, Freda. Absolutely delicious," Hank said, barely able to inhale between bites. It was, indeed, rich, dark, and highly tasteful. There were certain flavors in the bread he couldn't identify but they blended into a delightfully sumptuous treat. Freda walked away beaming and on the prowl for other satisfied customers.

As the mid-morning run at the bakery slowed down, Katy took Freda and Helga, individually, to their living quarters in the far rear of the bakery and carefully measured them using twine. They, too, liked Katy's denim shirt so she measured their back, bust, and length to try and determine a fit. The Germans were stocky and thick but didn't run to fat. They had an abundance of muscle with arms rivaling a man's. Katy quickly surmised that if a scuffle ever broke out in the bakery, she'd want them on her side.

Hank lingered for a while waiting for Katy and finally went outside and walked the boardwalks checking other stores on the square. He entered Miller's Mercantile and found himself examining the various tools and implements. He found them to be not only sturdy but of surprisingly high quality. It took only a glance to see they were much superior to those now found in the average 21st century hardware store. Handles were stronger, longer and heavier built. Axe blades were razor sharp and appeared to be made of quality steel. Men of the field and farm of the mid-1880's required good tools to ply their trade and they certainly were readily available.

Miller's also sold guns so Hank spent several minutes looking over their selection. A sleek Colt revolver particularly caught his eye. It was a special edition forty-four caliber beautifully scrimshawed with shiny mother-of-pearl handles. It was an exquisite piece for the era. He asked the clerk the cost and was told this particular model was especially expensive. Fifty dollars would buy it which included a tooled leather holster and accompanying belt. Hank's fifty-dollar gold piece quickly left his pocket and was plopped down on the counter. The clerk threw in two boxes of ammunition to boot. Hank quickly removed his double action six-shooter and promptly strapped on the new Colt. He felt like a gunfighter with the new sidearm in place. The clerk wrapped Hank's other weapon in brown paper and tied it tightly with twine. Hank strutted out the front door feeling pretty full of himself with, perhaps, a little added swagger. Katy had just exited the bakery and scanned the boardwalks finally seeing Hank. She half-trotted up to his side. The new revolver immediately caught her eye.

"Gosh, Hank. You're lookin' pretty sharp with that new pistol. Can I see it?"

He carefully slipped it out of the holster and handed it to her.

"It's not loaded, Katy. Look at the scrimshaw and those genuine pearl handles. Quality work, and it has marvelous balance. I wonder what it's worth on the other side of the rift?"

"You're not planning on selling it are you Hank?" Katy responded surprised at his question.

"Absolutely not, but it would be interesting to know its value."

"What'd you pay for it?"

"Fifty bucks including the holster, belt, and two boxes of ammunition."

"I'd say that was a pretty good deal. You ready to show me a locomotive? I heard a whistle blowing a few minutes ago. Helga says the train's due around noon but the time varies. We'd better get a move on though."

The train was just pulling in when they arrived and Katy's eyes went wide looking it over. It was a small station with only one attending ticket agent who served in various capacities including baggage handling. There were only two freight cars and a smaller passenger car. Two riders stepped off. The conductor was out stretching his legs and Katy asked him if she could board the car and look around. Of course, he said proudly explaining the car had just arrived newly constructed from the east coast a few days ago. In fact, this trip was its maiden voyage. He boarded behind Katy and Hank and gave them a full tour explaining its various accommodations. It was, indeed, luxuriously appointed including a small dining area and wash room facilities. A half dozen berths were available for anyone who wanted to lie down.

The conductor's face bespoke the pride he felt for being the man in charge of such a superior luxury liner. Katy pulled and tugged at Hank wanting to immediately purchase a ticket for the train's next destination. The conductor was certainly taken in by Katy's beauty and charm and her daring boldness for wearing pants like a man. If this was the coming new fashion for women, he was perfectly willing to second the motion. He was so taken that he offered a free pass to Katy to ride and return from any destination in which he was the conductor-in-charge. Hank interceded but Katy weaseled a rain check out of the conductor who confirmed the complimentary ticket with the attending agent.

After an hour of touring the train, including a thorough examination of the steam engine, Hank finally prevailed and coaxed Katy away. Hank, without saying so, wanted to return in full daylight in case they had another encounter with the stranger. So, they rode slowly southeast over the rolling hills of post oaks and springing tall grasses. Katy felt light and happy although she carried a burden on her heart. Frontier Bellville had struck a strong chord in her. So much so, that riding away from it was about the hardest thing she'd ever done. Somehow it seemed to fit her she thought. It was her era. Her time. The quaintness of the small town filled a void in a way she couldn't explain. Freda and Helga had seemed to be kindred spirits. There were no such women like them on the modern side of the rift. That was for certain. Their vigor for life was like a fresh breeze cooling and inviting. The pace of life here, too, was slow like thick honey. The feeling of being somehow misplaced in life by some quirk of fate, a feeling Katy was all too familiar with, had retreated for the moment and for the first time she felt like she belonged.

Hank rode along scanning the horizon for trouble and quietly noting Katy's internal struggle. He half way expected to hear the crack of a rifle from the vengeful stranger they had met this morning. He dutifully stayed away from the thicker clumps of post oak groves where a back shooter would likely slink around. It was reasonably easy to do with the countryside offering spacious openings to pass through. He couldn't prompt Katy to even trot the horses so they pranced, snorted and whinnied, straining to break into a lope in the cool, spring air.

The sun had a good afternoon slant on it when they reached H.B.'s secret tree where he had stashed the time traveler's devices for activating the rift. Katy sat in her saddle watching Hank open the safe that had been carefully inserted into the trunk of the largest oak tree in the area. She had been fighting tears the whole ride out and her emotions were raw. Finally dismounting, she walked to Hank as he readied the remote device for activation. The cooling evening air should have been stimulating but she felt none of it. Her thoughts were in turmoil. She grabbed his free hand and intertwined both of her hands in his. He stopped his setting adjustments abruptly.

"Hank," she said clinging tightly to his brown hands. "There's just so much evil on the other side. The Devil rides my back there. He does, but the burden seems lifted here. I'm misplaced over there, Hank. It's plain and simple. Over here I finally found my home. Are those bad feelings to have, Hank?" Katy's face frowned in confusion.

"No. I don't think they're bad, Katy. I have some of the same feelings, too. However, responsibilities and commitments call us back. I've committed to protect and defend H.B.'s place and that's what I aim to do."

Katy's mind ran to fear for him. For Hank. A pervading worry had been growing inside her. Thinking about it made her legs light and wobbly. She was suddenly weak and needed to sit down. Hank noticed and slipped his free hand around her waist and held her. Her breathing grew shallow and quickened.

"Oh, Hank," she said fighting for control. "Perhaps you can't kill all the evil that lurks over there. I fear the evil might prevail and win in the end and somehow take you with it."

"There's enough evil to go around everywhere, Katy. Don't forget our encounter this morning. We were close to gunplay within ten minutes of landing in 1885. There're bad hombres on both sides."

"Oh, my God," she said, leaning against Hank and enjoying his strong arm around her. It was so comforting to have him there. She felt safe and secure in his arms. "I know now why this secret's worth protecting. Heaven's sake is it ever worth protecting. I've got a whole new appreciation for H.B. now. His genius offers a new life for me I could never have dreamed existed, but my question is, is it worth your life, Hank? You didn't sign a death warrant, did you? No one can ask that much of a person."

Hank looked off into the distance watching the grass tumble and roll with the late afternoon breeze. A red-tailed hawk circled high above them hoping for a meal before dark. They'd stirred up a half dozen rabbits riding back so the hawk's chances were good.

"I knew the risks, Katy. I always calculate the risks before I commit to a job. You match your skills and wits with the risks you face every day of your life. There's no assurance of the outcome. You just attempt to stack the odds your way. That's all, Katy. I'm just a hired gun in a sense. That's what I've done in the past, and honestly, I like doing it. I like the adrenaline rush of hunting a man that needs hunting. Killing a man that needs and deserves killing. I guess I'd make a perfect bounty hunter."

"Hank, Hank, Hank," Katy said feeling his warmth against her skin. "You like to act like you're meaner than a snake, but I know better. You just take your job too seriously, that's all. Hang around me awhile and I'll show you what it means to be a real hard ass." They both laughed holding on to each other.

"Listen, Hank. Freda and Helga offered me a job. What would you say if I decided to accept it? Would you let me go back? They've got a spare bedroom. They've got a huge living quarters in the back of the bakery. It's very nice actually."

Hank thought such a proposal might be coming. Katy seemed entirely taken by the bakery and the little town itself. She would certainly be safe there, in comparison, and the issue of Katy's safety preyed a good deal on his mind. Hamilton Fremont's soldiers would soon be marching again. Taking their evil plans to the next level.

"I wouldn't try to keep you from going, Katy. You're free to choose your life over here or over there. I have the money to send you anywhere in the world on the other side, however. Anywhere you want to live, safely, if you'd like. Choose the location and you can go. We have several millions of dollars at our disposal to do just that."

"Hank, the big bad world over there has nothing to offer me. I'm comfortable here. For the first time in my life I feel like me. You know what it's like not to feel like yourself for your whole entire life? It's weird but that's how I feel. Today for the first time in my life I actually felt like I fit. Finally, my square peg fit the square hole of Bellville, Texas, circa 1885. That's a first for me, Hank. Even in pants I felt completely at home." Hank laughed out loud and Katy giggled with him. "That's why I'm so irascible over there," she added. "Notice how sweet I am over here." Another laugh.

"Katy, you do beat all," Hank said squeezing her waist with his strong arm. "Well, we're not heading back right now. It's getting late. I'll bring you back to Old Bellville in a day or two."

"Oh, I can't go back just now, Hank. I've got clothes to buy for the German girls. I've got a pocket full of string measurements. I don't intend to disappoint my new employers."

With that, Hank promptly opened the rift. The square portal appeared, and they walked across into H.B.'s garage horses in tow, holding on to one another's hands.

CHAPTER
TWENTY-SIX

To the surprise of everyone, the Red River crossing went without a hitch. The brackish red water was up some but not enough to thwart the long-legged steers. Buster brightened significantly after re-supplying at Doan's Store. Flour was the staple of a cook's life and without it grumpy only got grumpier. Plus, he smoked a short stem corn cob pipe and coughed incessantly. He only slept short periods at night waking to choking fits brought on by his breathing difficulties. The absence of sleep wreaked havoc on his normal touchy mood. It had been five days since the disappearance of Cobb Pickens. Twinks Brady continually warned the boys to be wary.

"Let your guard down and you'll be takin' a dirt nap," he cautioned the first night after crossing the Red. "He's behind us or in front somewhere. Just because you don't see 'im don't mean he ain't out there."

Orb had the habit of scouting far ahead during the day looking for dry bed ground and the least challenging water crossings. They were now crossing Indian Territory, the Oklahoma country, and the Salt Fork of the Red River lay ahead. It was steep-banked, treacherous, and notoriously swift. Orb rode in after dark with his horse lathered in sweat. He immediately sought the cook pot and filled his plate with beef stew. He had a strange look in his eye. Twinks gathered in the expression and fired a question.

"What's out there you don't like, boss?"

"The damn Salt Fork's almost out of bank and that's saying a lot for her. The Colorado freshets have the water surging." Orb kept his eyes down stirring the stew around in his plate. Buzzing mosquitoes had the men slapping their faces. Twinks read the untold story in Orb's expression.

"Ain't no river drawing that tight look, Orb. You best spill it for all of us. These boys have already fretted themselves into a case of the drizzlin' trots anyways."

Orb took a small bite and rolled the meat around in his mouth awhile like it was too tough to chew. He was still trying to tie together what he'd seen. Making sense of it was no easy matter but the warnings were out there. Of that much, he was sure.

"Cut the trail of some shod horses up ahead a ways. I know Cobb's track so one of 'em is his. He's got some companeros with him now. Seven other men as best as I could tell."

"Why hell, that butters our biscuit," Twinks said loudly without thinking.

The cowboys around the fire suddenly grew uneasy. One scoundrel was bad enough. Seven more constituted a formidable problem. Twinks took a long drink of coffee, regretful of his outburst and swirled it around in his mouth before swallowing. John Henry, more prone to fears than most, lost the coloring in his face. Buster coughed and stirred the stew pot glancing over where his ten gauge was leaning. The crew was as quiet as church mice each thinking his own thoughts. Just as the weather had finally cleared, another dark shadow had arisen. Cody Meyer shuffled from one boot to the other observing the round eyes of fear in the crew. He was the polar opposite of John Henry in the fear department. He had a fair dose of self-preservation but had never feared a snake until it bit him.

Twinks was properly entertained by the fearful expressions around him. Their looks of fear were rapidly disintegrating into expressions of pure terror. Nevershed shuffled around in his dirty clothes getting more coffee. He'd earned his name honestly by never tainting his naked hide with soap and water. His scruffy appearance and soiled clothes, too, reflected his disdain for cleanliness. Hygiene issues aside, he was a sage advisor to Orb. Rumor had it he was a decorated war hero with medals in his saddle bags to prove it.

"Boys," Twinks said before someone fainted and fell into the campfire. "Cobb's got him a small army and they're on the prod. He's after something more than just us. He's wantin' the herd I reckon or at least part of it. An easy way to gather cattle or so he thinks. They're likely gun hands and not afraid to use 'em. They probably don't think we know about 'em yet. So that's our edge."

Orb finished his plate and walked it over to the wash pot. Travis Strayhorn, the horse wrangler, had just walked in from checking the remuda and noticed the unnaturally quiet cowboys around the fireside. A few of the hands were muttering to each other in nervous tones. Buster added a log to the fire. Embers floated six feet high in response to the stirring of coals. Orb walked slowly back to the campfire and poured out his coffee. He wanted to talk to Twinks and Nevershed alone so he moseyed out to his horse to pull off the saddle hoping they'd follow.

Orb turned his horse loose in the remuda and circled

behind the wagon and relieved himself. He stayed outside the circle of the fire trying to get a plan of action together in his mind. He'd fought in the great war, too, and seen armies and men rise and fall. He'd witnessed the sheer terror of battle. His men were not fighters, he knew that for sure. They were just good cowboys and as competent as could be expected in their given trade, but most hands carried their six-shooters for snakes or belligerent badgers and in some cases just for show. They weren't good shots as a whole and under pressure of battle likely would miss more often than strike their target. They weren't man killers for sure and weren't expected to be. There were only four repeating rifles in the whole outfit, too. Nevershed, Twinks, and H.B. carried one. He, himself, carried a Henry but many times left it in the wagon with Buster. That would have to change now. Twinks and Nevershed finally found him standing in the darkness.

"What do you think?" Orb asked Twinks as he moseyed up. Nevershed was close behind. The campfire's light flashed ominously around the huddled up and nervous cowhands.

"Take the fight to them. Don't wait 'em out. Do the unexpected, Orb. That's the only chance we've got. They'll start picking us off one by one or strike when we are least prepared These boys are about ready to shit their pants as it is."

Nevershed quickly agreed to the plan. "Can't wait. We got a chance by hitting them fast. Otherwise, we might as well just sign the herd over and head on back to Texas."

"How many and who do we take?" Orb asked still uncertain about attacking. He already knew the answer more or less. Cody, Twinks, Nevershed, and himself. H.B. was an unknown quantity. Yet he did carry a long gun. The rest were untested for sure. Maybe H.B. would loan his gun to Cody since he didn't have a rifle.

Twinks fired the answer. Just you, me, and Nevershed.

Maybe Cody. The boy's steady but I don't know his fightin' skills. I like H.B. He's a thinker and not prone to fears that I've been able to pick up. Plus, he's mature. All the boy's been run out of him long ago, and he's got the good sense to carry a rifle. Maybe he can even use it."

Nevershed nodded his head in agreement. He liked the philosophy of first strike. The Southern boys were always ill equipped and undermanned in the war but they won more than their share of engagements with the Union boys by hitting hard at odd hours and in odd ways. Even trained gun hands could be put to flight by a well-planned surprise attack.

Orb voiced another of his concerns. "Are we sure of their intentions?"

"Hell, Orb. You know the answer to that. They're a gun outfit. Cobb's nothing but a sorry back-shootin' snake. Likely the other riders are as bad if not worse than he is. I could feel something wasn't right ever since we left the Concho country. They're low-down cattle thieves lookin' for a big payoff. We're workin' for them right now, Orb, as they reckon it. They're the owners just as sure as I'm standin' here letting' us do the drivin'. Plain and simple."

"What do they do with them once they get 'em? They can't sell this road brand in Dodge or Abilene or even Ogallala. The buyers would know."

"They'll split off pieces one small bunch at a time, Orb. You know how their kind work. They'll sell a hundred head here and fifty there until they're all sold off. They'll move 'em east a ways and scatter the herd to small buyers. No one will be the wiser. Especially if we're all dead and buried."

Ranger Captain Twinks Brady knew the outlaw's way of thinking better than anyone else in the outfit. His read of tough men had thus far been highly accurate. He'd hunted down too many of them not to know their schemes and motives Orb guessed. Orb's mind swirled with concerns more so for his men than the cattle he drove. Hell, cattle could ultimately be replaced but not the boys in his employ. He'd rather be a disgraced foreman and hand over the whole damn herd than lose a single hand in a fight they neither invited nor signed on for. He knew several of his cowboy's families, some even from his home county in Goliad, and he didn't want to face their mothers with the news of them dying in some useless skirmish with outlaws. Losses due to the normal rigors of a tough trail were expected and even understandable to some extent, but battle deaths, death by bullets and violent means put a different spin on things. Mothers didn't accept those reasons easily. To Orb, just seemed out of bounds and unreasoning to risk his employees for the likes of Cobb Pickens and his cutthroats. The whole thing put him in a quandary and he knew he stood responsible for the hiring of Cobb. Twinks took his last sip of coffee and tossed the grounds in the dirt. Buster wandered around the chuck wagon glancing their way with a questioning look about their discussions. His eyes moved back and forth to his ten gauge furtively as if he might need to dive for it at any moment. The camp's tension was so thick you could cut it with a knife. Nervous men made for nervous cattle, too. That was a basic law of the trail.

"Okay," Orb said convinced suddenly to action. "Let's take it to them. Strike hard and fast. Let's put these bastards away."

Orb Fincher was a fighter by nature. Twinks and Nevershed both knew that, but those tendencies had been shelved for years now for a more peaceful existence in deep south Texas. Sure, an occasional brush with an unruly character occurred in Goliad but not frequently. Most grown men there had been to the war and witnessed firsthand too many maimed men. In settled times, they were unlikely to invite it upon themselves. Most were busy raising families and trying to carve out a living in the rough, post-war environment. Carpetbaggers had ridden roughshod through Texas spreading the disease of mistrust and planting seeds of discontent. Finally, the state of Texas had swung up and out of that sorry miserable system called Reconstruction and seemed on course to prosperity now. Though nests of men like Cobb Pickens still existed, lurking like cottonmouths, ready to strike. Young Rangers straddled their horses and hunted their kind relentlessly and would finally, in the end, win. The Army was of little assistance, unfortunately, in most cases throughout the wilds of west Texas. They were always too preoccupied with their own protocol and command decisions to field a consistent, valid force. They weren't in Texas now anyway. They were in Indian Territory, which was known for its lawlessness. It was a perfect setting for Cobb Pickens and his band to do their dirty deeds.

Twinks posed a question bringing Orb out of his thoughts. "What about Cody and H.B.? You want to talk to them?"

"Yeah, let's do it."

Twinks walked slowly to the fire and Cody and H.B. dutifully followed him past the rim of the camp's light. Cody more or less guessed what was about to happen and was hoping to participate. H.B. had no idea what might be in store.

Orb led the discussion with Twinks and Nevershed pushing in close.

"We're going to hit Cobb and his nasty bunch and see if we can rout them. The three of us will do it but we'd like to have you two if you're willin'. There's gonna be a fight, no doubt about it. These men have designs against us and the herd. I notice you have a rifle, H.B. If you don't want to fight with us we'd sure like to borrow your weapon, but that's up to you. Of course, you're welcome to join us."

H.B. was struck momentarily speechless. He'd never really

267

contemplated being involved in a preemptive strike against a group of men, outlaw or otherwise. He wasn't necessarily against such a venture if their very survival depended on it. However, a sneak attack against a body of men who hadn't displayed any aggression struck him as wrong. He promptly voiced his concern.

"Does cutting the trail of a group of shod horses constitute a provocation to the level that requires us to kill them? Or at least try to kill them?"

Twinks was angered by the question. He could read sign as well as an Indian and knew the prophecies that each trail rendered. It was, to him, as clear as the stars that hung above him. What was easy for him to understand, however, many times evaded other men.

"H.B.," Twinks said, curbing his anger somewhat, trying to be patient. "We're being trailed, stalked if you will, by men with bad intentions. Take a look at the campfire over there. Some of those men gathered there won't be there in a few days. One or more will be missing if we let Cobb and his cut-throats carry out their scheme. They're planning to steal this herd, or try to, and young men will die tryin' to defend it. Some of us standing here probably won't be around either. They'll get us because they'll lay a trap and we'll step in it before we know it's there. H.B., I've led men to their deaths before, and I don't like it either. To save our lives and the herd we've got to hit these devils first."

Nevershed nodded his agreement at the statement and Orb looked away into the darkness wishing fate hadn't dealt him this particular hand. It placed a weight on his drooping shoulders and he didn't like the burden.

"H.B., all I ask of you is the loan of your rifle for a few hours," Orb said finally. "Cody needs a rifle for this engagement. If you would do that, I'd sure appreciate it."

Orb's humble request whittled away at H.B.'s concerns. He was surrounded by men who apparently knew their business and knew all too well the dangers. He cautioned himself against carrying the excess baggage of his past life – burden himself unnecessarily with standards from the other side of the rift. The Twin Towers had fallen in New York City for some of the same reasons. Prove it before you can stop it. It's difficult if not impossible to prove the erratic behavior of men and what they might do before it happens. Thankfully, political correctness in decision-making hadn't wormed its way into the society of this century. Orb, Twinks, and Nevershed were thoughtful, intelligent men as far as he could tell. Though he'd been with them less than two weeks, they had proven their competency time and again. It was time he trusted their instincts. H.B. knew all too well his instincts were sorely lacking and weren't tuned and honed for this era.

"I'll join you," he said suddenly with a firm voice. "I have other weapons for us in my gear. Cody's welcome to use any extra weapons I have."

Orb's startled look was only surpassed by Twink's stunned expression. Cody smiled and quietly said "thanks" to H.B. Nevershed's steel gray eyes never blinked. So, now it would be five against eight. The element of surprise, hopefully, would even up the remaining odds.

CHAPTER
TWENTY-SEVEN

J essie Madelyn stormed out of the back door with Elsa in hot pursuit. The old frame door rattled as it slammed shut. Elsa was yelling and Jessie was trying to ignore her. Paula Jane stood behind Elsa wondering what the ruckus was all about.

"It's too late in the season to plant a garden," Elsa cautioned, loudly standing on the small rear porch of Corley's Boarding House. "It'll just burn up, honey. We're getting plenty of vegetables in town."

Jessie continued her journey to a small patch of ground that used to be her parent's gardening plot. It needed hoeing and weeding but the soil was rich and in need of seed. Elsa finally stomped her foot in disgust and returned through the door. The young woman was foolish, she thought, and less and less controllable as her health improved. It frustrated Elsa to no end. Paula Jane slipped inside a doorway mouse-like not wanting a confrontation with Elsa. She had been the victim, on more than one occasion, of Elsa's venting wrath. She possessed a sharp tongue and the woman's looks could freeze water. She

270

remained hidden until the coast was clear and slipped out the back door feeling safer outside. She observed Jessie already whacking away with an old hoe at the weeds. The heat of a Fort Worth summer day was just taking hold and Paula Jane felt a bead of sweat pop from her brow. Even standing in the shade, the heat was difficult to bear.

Jessie noticed Paula Jane and waved her over. Paula Jane considered Jessie a valuable ally and they talked often about things she couldn't reveal to her parents and certainly not to Elsa. Jessie was younger and had an appreciation for the wayward thoughts and emotions of a rapidly maturing thirteen-year-old. At least Jessie was sensitive and considered her opinions. Her mother always seemed too busy raising her rather large brood of younger brothers and sisters to talk seriously to her, much less listen. Jessie never laughed or made fun of her behind her back when she shared her private thoughts and dreams. It was nice to have a confidant who'd just listen and not necessarily stand you up in judgment.

Paula Jane walked over to Jessie, noticing the sweat dripping from her face. Jessie stopped hoeing for a moment and leaned against the handle. The garden site was in full sunshine and the sun was unbearably hot.

"I won't last long out here," Jessie admitted. "The heat's almost ready to bake me."

"It's awful hot," Paula Jane agreed using her apron to wipe her face.

"I'll start to work earlier tomorrow. The morning cool will help." Admittedly, there wasn't much of a morning cool in a Fort Worth summer. By nine things grew stifling hot. Even the wooden hoe handle was hot to the touch.

"How's your parents' garden doing? I haven't visited with your mother in some time."

"Everything's up and going. The tomatoes are blooming

but no tomatoes yet. Corn is waist high, maybe taller. My dad works it when he can. They keep him jumping down at the hotel."

Since the Texas and Pacific Railroad's line reached town, the local economy was hopping. The hotels were full. Even Corley's Boarding House was on overflow. The carpenter's hammers rang out trying to keep up with the rampant growth. The days of a calmer, quieter Fort Worth that Jessie remembered from her early youth were gone. The Iron Horse had forever changed that. Plus, the cattle drives brought an influx of rambunctious cowboys to town. Even occasional gunshots sang out when their riotous celebrations carried them too far. New deputies had been installed to keep the peace and provide a safe distance between the rambunctious young drovers and the local citizens. Local merchants wanted the lucrative trade of re-supply for the trailing herds but their commerce added burdens to the local peace officers. Dr. Fields constantly grumbled that the city fathers were too lenient on the drovers.

"There's got to be a better way to deal with them," he said, recently as his biscuit sopped up Elsa's gravy. The good doctor had taken up permanent residence at Corley's and seemed to be on course to turn his drinking habit around. Jessie harped on him, in private, about his drinking and it seemed to be taking effect. Plus, his curiosity about H.B.'s magic pills had piqued his interest in medicine again. He was very disappointed when he heard of H.B.'s departure a few weeks ago. He had many more questions to ask.

"Are you sure he's coming back?" Dr. Fields had asked of Jessie countless times. Jessie could only confirm that she thought so. He certainly had given indications of returning. Her heart, too, ached that she hadn't properly thanked him for his effort and the many hours he had spent nursing her back to health. She had planned words to tell him but the words and her true feelings were left unspoken. Somehow, she had slipped inside her own dark, sick world and had grown self-centered and childish. Just thinking about her rude behavior and lack of thankfulness towards H.B. and his miracle cures caused her throat to tighten and her eyes to tear.

H.B. HANDED Buster a hundred pinkish pills in a bottle and told him to take them, by swallowing, three per day. Buster, usually grumpy and busy tidying up after breakfast, glanced at the funny little container hollow-eyed without immediately responding. He was shocked by the thoughtless intrusion of this new hand onto his hallowed turf. He was in half-stride when the tall hambone had stepped right in front of him like he owned the place. Breakfast cleaning was a serious matter and he was in no mood to banter with the cowhands. He scorned clean up as did most cooks and a serious confrontation was in the making. Who in the hell did this tin pan greenhorn think he was blocking his path and handing him these ridiculous-looking pebbles. Buster was trying to come up with a scornful dismissal when H.B.'s voice again broke the silence.

"Your lungs are rattling, Buster. If you'll swallow one of these three times a day you'll eventually stop coughing and be able to sleep at night. You'll only get worse if you don't follow my instructions."

Buster listened impatiently, so upset by the uncalled for instruction, that he almost turned and tossed the bottle into the coals of the morning fire. The cowboys had already scattered taking the herd off the bed ground, spreading them out for grazing. So, what the hell was this guy doing standing here?

273

Buster studied the bottle again as the faint rays of morning sun cut through the prairie grasses. His temper was building fast and due for an explosion at any moment. Sure, he felt a deep rattle, a continuous itching in his lungs, and he constantly fought the urge to cough. He knew the disease that had gotten a hold on him but couldn't bring himself to admit he was a lunger. The end would most likely come in some sanitarium for lungers. That dismal thought had scared him into the shakes at various times. It was a lunger hotel that you checked into but never checked out. Or when you did it check out – it was always feet first.

"How in the hell do you know?" he snapped in a gravelly voice. This foolish jawing was fixing to stop. He'd kick this tall bastard in the nuts if he had to. He didn't like any man blocking his path much less during clean up.

H.B. quickly played his trump card. "I'm a physician, a medical doctor, Buster. I know what you're suffering from and what will cure the disease. Do as I say and you'll feel better in a few days. Otherwise, things will grow increasing unpleasant. If you wait too much longer, I won't be able to help you." H.B.'s voice was steady, firm, and authoritative.

A doctor? This tall cowboy was a doctor? It took him a moment to digest this unexpected information and try to make sense of it. Could it be true? Buster's jaw grew slack as the strange idea of it rattled around in his noggin. Even his greasy, matted, grey-brown head stopped shaking momentarily as his temper dampened slightly. This new revelation had startled him and he didn't startle easy.

"What the hell are ya doin' way out here?" he asked raising his voice. "Don't your types like town where there's peoples? Ain't much doctoring to do way out yonder here."

"Take the pills, Buster," H.B. said forcefully. "Forget the questions. There's life for you in that bottle. I've heard you for the past two weeks struggling to breathe. You need help now. Do as I say. Swallow one pill morning, noon and night."

Buster seemed actually moved for a moment. H.B. stepped a foot closer. Buster looked up with glaring eyes not liking the fact he was being cornered. He especially didn't take to being pushed.

"You do what you want, Buster. If you don't want your life, hand me the pills back. I'll give them to someone else who will use them. They're too valuable to lose."

Buster gripped the bottle in his thick, hairy hands trying to reason through these odd developments. Admittedly, in the past several weeks, even months, he'd never really felt his old self. His wheezing chest grew tighter and heavier each day. His energy seemed sapped and draining quicker now. He struggled to place one foot in front of the other as the long hours of the trail passed from darkness to darkness. The demands of a chuck cook never ended regardless of how he might feel. He had hungry men to feed. Fires to build. Mules to harness. Pots and pans to clean and put up. Bumpy prairies to navigate sometimes in the darkness. Sometimes in howling winds and rain storms. The demands were never-ceasing and highly burdensome even on a healthy man. No matter his trials and tribulations, a line of needy, hungry men always lined up with their forks and plates in hand several times a day.

"Your choice, Buster," H.B. said and suddenly spun around and walked away in strides only a tall man could manage. "Take one now," he said yelling back over his shoulder as he grabbed his horse and swung up. "Swallow it with coffee or water but get it down."

Buster stood stock-still tightly grasping the bottle trying to make sense of what he'd been told. Finally, he pulled out of his stupor. His disbelief over a doctor being on the drive and the idea that these strange, pink pills could cure him bordered on crazy in his book. Regardless, he regained his composure and quickly slipped the bottle in his bulgy pants pocket and proceeded with his tasks. H.B. spurred out and was almost out of sight before Buster raised his eyes and saw the man melt into the far dim-lit horizon. Without anyone's eyes to witness and a little more careful thinking, Buster opened the bottle, fingered the pink pills with his thick hands and on a sudden impulse tossed one back in his and swallowed it. He chased the pill with a mouthful of cold coffee. Oh, what the hell, he thought, might as well give'em a try.

Twinks was an excellent tracker if pressed to be and Orb was his close second. Cobb Pickens and his crew of misfits weren't worried about the trail they left behind so it didn't take a lot of tracking to locate them. Eight heavily armed men weren't about to hide in the shadows and duck around like scared children. Their mission was plain and simple and it didn't matter a tinker's damn who knew about it. The herd was theirs to take whenever they chose. Earlier in the day they'd run into a family of sod busters traveling through Indian Territory and had terrorized them to a state of tears. In the end the couple had lost almost everything eatable to Cobb's bunch and were left in rough country with so few supplies even the mice abandoned the wagon. Doan's Store was the nearest re-supply and, barring mishaps, it stood more than two weeks away. They callously took most of the settler's cooking utensils including the woman's most prized possession – her deceased mother's cast iron frying pan. Her husband could strike no defense against the surprise attack as he was hopelessly outnumbered and merely tried comforting and protecting an over-wrought wife who screamed and cursed for all she was worth. To cap off the foray, the criminals took his wife's second-most prized possession: a dozen, fat laying hens. They carefully crated the chickens in Missouri, their point of origin, and coddled them daily making sure of their survival. His wife had finally consented to leaving their old milking cow for the sake of speed, but wouldn't even consider parting with her "girls" as she called them. Starting over in the Texas without a chicken flock was unthinkable to her.

The following night, around a sizeable campfire, Cobb and his crew dined on fried chicken and laughed loudly reliving the incident. The woman's prized frying pan and cooking accoutrements were promptly abandoned after the meal's preparation.

"That ole' bitch were a screamer, weren't she?" Cobb intoned gulping down his last bite of chicken. "Her cussin' and carrying on over them damn chickens and fryin' pan made me want to wring her neck."

Cobb's other scruffy companions greedily cleaned up what remained of the chicken cracking the bones and sucking out the marrow. To a man, all were in a jovial mood having eaten so well on a lonely prairie where pickings were usually slim.

"Sodbusters don't deserve nothin' in my book," a smallish dirty-looking old man chimed in with a gravelly voice. His face favored a shriveled pea pod and he carried a large scar across most of it. It was a nasty, crooked scar that ran from the right eyebrow, slashing across the nose, stopping finally at the corner of his mouth on the opposite side. His scarred half-face sagged grotesquely to one side. The hideous old wound gave him the odd appearance of being out of balance. He wore a tall, dirty chimney hat and answered to his most distinguishable feature, "Scar." He was considered highly dangerous even by his present rough company because of his sudden and unpredictable mood swings. His severe mood swings had earned him a wide reputation in the unsettled regions of the Concho River country. In a word, his fondness for burning living things, especially humans, sent chills of fear up the spines of those who had the good sense to fear the man. It was widely known, in the parts where he roamed, that he fed his sick psyche on the pleas and screams of burning victims. He'd torch anything that moved or didn't move. His sick mind had lobbied hard to burn the settlers whose chicken they ate and would have prevailed had it not been for the fear of setting the surrounding prairie on fire.

"You can burn everyone, of those damned cowboys, one at a time if you want, Scar," Cobb said noticing Scar's sulking attitude as he sat alone at the far end of the fire. "One at a time or the whole damn bunch at once. Don't matter to me."

Outnumbered, outgunned, and overruled by the majority he rode with, Scar had already hatched a deadly plan to kill his sorry comrades for not letting him burn the couple. He didn't like being thwarted when a good burning was at hand.

"I tolt ya, we shoulda burned the bastards," he muttered through his few remaining blackened teeth and chicken-greasy lips. Revenge would ultimately be his, he thought. He'd been openly cheated, denied in his demented way of thinking, of being able to hear those burning screams he so fervently craved.

The present campsite was ground zero as far as Orb was concerned. The cattle had been held in close proximity to the camp with, luckily, abundant grazing available. A fresh water pond provided adequate water so the steers were obliged to stay near it. Twinks rode in a few hours after dark having observed, in close, the goings on of Cobb's group of cutthroats. It had been easy to infiltrate the area with four-foot-tall grass surrounding the camp and a rather deep gully to crawl through. They were no more than seven miles from the cowherd and, besides, had started a substantial campfire for all to see. They were so sure of themselves they hadn't even bothered posting a guard. They yipped and howled and quarreled never knowing they were being watched. Twinks had bellied in through the small gully snubbing his horse off a quarter mile away. He sat in a clump of grass not forty feet from their camp with his pistol drawn and his ears open. One of Cobb's desperados came within ten feet of Twinks taking a piss in the grass, unaware of his observer. Twinks considered the accessibility of campsite, the ease with which he had approached them, and the growing inebriation of the group as a good omen for what was to come. A drunken bandit made for an easy target.

"Bastards are laughing about some poor settlers' couple they just hit and left without supplies," Twinks said, as he dusted himself off and filled his plate and coffee cup. He was openly riled about what he'd just seen and heard. Most of the hands stood back in the shadows not wanting to face the captain when he was riled. He was considered by the men to be only slightly less dangerous than a wolverine when on the prod.

"Sons-of-bitches are a ruthless lot. Ol' Scar's with 'em. He's one of the worst of the hold-overs from the ol' bad days. Hell, the bounty on him alone could retire a man. You boys ever heard of Scar?" Twinks asked scanning the shadows. No one volunteered an answer. Twinks stirred his stew around on his plate looking sadly reminiscent, his eyes watching the steam rise.

"We nearly nailed the ol' turd several years ago out close to the New Mexican border. Would have, too, but he knew watering holes and we couldn't find 'em. He'd just burned a settler's shack with them still in it. He's bad, bad news, boys. I just heard Cobb make him a solemn promise that he could burn us all at the stake." There was an immediate group shudder where the cowboys lined up in the shadows. "Come on out and socialize," Twinks commanded. "No need to pee your pants. The bad guys is gettin' bull drunk right now. You ain't gonna be their target. Not tonight anyhow."

One by one the hands started moving closer to the fire like shy children. Twinks gulped his stew and swigged his coffee. Cody, Orb, and H.B. had ridden south a few miles to test out some new guns H.B. had shown them. Nevershed stood close to the fire apparently unmoved by Twinks story. He knew Scar. The bastard had killed his half-brother many years ago close to San Angelo. He and two other half-brothers had chased the lunatic for two months seeking revenge for the murder. They had cut a broad swath through deep west Texas tracking a hard trail to follow. The outlaw and his two companions left little sign in the rocky ranges and craggy valleys. Starving, the brothers had barely made it back to San Angelo in a fierce snow storm. Scar had disappeared, evaporating into the far reaches of the all but impenetrable Chisos Mountains. It was rumored he was raised from early childhood by the Lipan Apache. Thus, his knowledge of the area and his ability to travel an almost waterless frontier.

Orb had placed three men on night guard before leaving. They had nearly stampeded themselves when Twinks loudly rode up, insensitive to their fears. The night guards rode out reluctantly fearing with certainty their end was near. The men had even drawn lots as to who would go out next if the three unfortunate night guards ever returned. Deep down, most of the group questioned the idea of confronting a tough gun outfit in the open prairie. Travis Strayhorn, the assigned Segundo when Orb was away, feared being encumbered with responsibilities he couldn't possibly fulfill. What if the attackers never returned from the fight? That thought alone caused a complete loss of appetite. With a large knot in his stomach, he had stiffly protested to Orb, but to no avail. How could they be expected to perform duties with the core of the outfit missing?

It was nearly midnight when Orb and company rode in. Cody wore a broad smile and swaggered to the coffee pot as if all dangers had instantly evaporated. None in camp had bothered to try sleeping and Buster had, thoughtfully, kept a fresh pot of coffee on the fire. Twinks had cleaned his rifle twice, the smell of fresh oil permeating the area. Orb even had a look of confidence as he asked Buster if he had a cold biscuit to chew on. H.B. stayed in the background, gripping his coffee cup, glancing up occasionally. Twinks quickly filled them in on the location of Cobb's camp and its assailable positioning.

"They was practically drunk when I pulled out. They was draining two fat whiskey bottles and raising hell amongst themselves. Ol' Scar's along, Orb. Saw 'im myself. Can you believe it? He's been needin' killin' for thirty years."

Orb knew of the man and had heard of his exploits. Rumors of him floated the many miles south to Goliad County on the usually reliable telegraph of trail messengers. He was a murderous scoundrel with a penchant for torture.

"Surprised he'd leave the mountains," Orb said chewing Buster's biscuit.

"Hell, he's so old he farts dust, Orb. Probably can't climb anymore. Cobb's men ain't fond of 'im. He sat off by hisself pouting and cussin'."

"I owe him one," Nevershed said with a voice as cold as ice. The comment caught everyone by surprise. All eyes turned his way.

"He done ya wrong?" Twinks asked as a deep silence reigned.

"Kilt my brother a good spell back. I tracked him for a long time but damn near died doing it." Nevershed's eyes stared unblinking into the fire seeing only the coals of hell. His facial expression was set in granite, rigid and unmoving. "I'd like the honor of killin' im, Orb. I'd be much obliged if you'd allow it."

"Hell, school kids could sneak in on this bunch," Twinks chimed in. "Got a gully leadin' right to their camp. Tall grass all around. I'll take ya right to 'im. I sat on their front porch in my rockin' chair and they never knowed it."

"Let's do it then," Orb said with a stern look. "You can kill that ol' man, Nevershed, and as many more as you want. I think there's enough of 'em to go around. We got a rustler's moon to guide us and Twinks can put us on their doorstep. Let's get the bastards and send them to hell where they all belong. I reckon Lucifer's anxious to get some fresh recruits."

CHAPTER
TWENTY-EIGHT

T rent all but ambushed Hank with the news. Hank was in the process of deactivating the rift when Trent rushed into the lab, a look of concern on his face. Katy was looking down at her newly aged hands, trying to get accustomed to sixty-five again. "We've had visitors most of the day," he said matter-of-factly. "Pretty heavy-duty surveillance. Cameras clicking from every angle they could find. Weren't afraid of us knowing about it either."

Hank looked up from the computer, punching in the final commands.

"How many?" he asked as the rift window closed.

"I counted five. Ethan thought he counted six, but that's not all of it."

"Well, what is all of it?" Hank asked.

"Ethan and Lori have to leave. Someone's broke into their cabin. Their nearest neighbor checked on the place and found the door jimmied. They're worried about what's missing, if anything. What's got them concerned is the fact that crime, break-ins and such are unheard of as remote as they are.

They're wondering if there might be a connection between their trespassers and Bellville."

Highly placed spies, capable, talented espionage agents of the mob likely rivaled the FBI or even the CIA for covert operations. What they couldn't get spying they purchased by buying info from a shadowy underworld of for-hire informants. Money bought information and information transformed itself into power. Hamilton Fremont was a man on a mission and his momentum was building. His incompetent brother had started a ball rolling that had to be stopped. A couple of weeks of peace and quiet was turning out to be only the hush before the storm. It wouldn't surprise Hank if the man's tentacles had already reached Alaska.

Katy overheard Trent's news and walked away fearing what might be coming. She already sorely missed 1885 and the feisty German girls. Admittedly, she missed being twenty-five again, too. Not that sixty-five was such a horrible age, but, damn, she'd choose twenty-five over sixty-five any day of the week. You'd have to be nuts not to.

Katy walked into H.B.'s kitchen and saw Lori sitting there, coffee steaming in her hand. Her expression was miles away, as far away as Alaska likely.

"Someone's entered our cabin, Katy. I feel so defiled you can't imagine. I'm tired of this whole mess. I'm sorry we ever got mixed up in this affair."

"I know how you feel. Goons crawled through my house like they had the right. I still feel like just burning the place to the ground. To top it all off, there were bugs planted all over the place. Eavesdropping on me. Can you believe that? You and Ethan better have your place swept for bugs, too."

Lori dropped her head to hide her tears. Katy walked behind her and rubbed her hand across Lori's tense shoulder. The stress was easy to feel in her knotted muscles.

"Let it go, Lori. You can't change things by worrying yourself to death."

"But there's no telling what they've taken, Katy. Our whole life is there. Everything we have, our privacy, our precious cargo of pictures and family keepsakes that can't be replaced. Some sneaking, no account, sorry criminal has run their grubby hands all over everything. I can hardly bear the thought of it."

Tears started streaming down Lori's face. The images of a creeping thug slinking through her cabin couldn't be erased. She was emotionally drained, and she was mad as hell. She kept picturing herself as being there, catching them red-handed and pulling a trigger until the creeps were blown away. Seeing pieces and parts dissected off their sorry asses. Somehow picturing that image comforted her in a way. She was surprised at her own vengeful attitude and the visuals that flashed in her mind. Surprised that such a violent act against another human being helped the pain subside, but it did. A justifiable homicide.

Katy massaged Lori's taut muscles in her shoulders and neck trying to ease the tension. Lori lowered her head and breathed deeply feeling the pain lessen beneath Katy's strong fingers. They could hear Trent and Hank in the dining room talking in subdued tones. Ethan had driven to Brenham to ready the jet. Privately he feared that someone could have sabotaged it. He had already arranged for an aircraft mechanic to check it out. If they knew where his cabin was then it was possible they knew about the jet. Nothing was off limits in the criminal world. Perhaps, even his cell phones were tapped. Perhaps a locating GPS had been placed on the Cessna for whatever reason he couldn't surmise. Slowly the peacefulness of his Alaskan retreat seemed to be slipping from his grasp. A new, dangerous world now surrounded him and Lori. He had desperately tried to console Lori and minimize her fears when they first heard the news of the break-in. Now he was having trouble getting his own fears under control.

Katy left Lori for a moment and walked to the kitchen window to look out. It was a bright, late afternoon, the razor wire surrounding the place glistening in the sun. Her overwhelming sense of misplacement returned as she viewed the present. She was in the wrong place, at the wrong time. An era past was her home now. In a world filled with uncertainties, she was certain of that fact. Hank had promised to return her. That was a promise she intended to see that he kept.

She walked into the dining room and stood, feeling strangely out of place. Hank glanced up and easily read her face. He always kidded her about the openness of her expressions. Trent's and Hank's conversation lulled as they watched her standing there trying to gather her thoughts. With Ethan and Lori pulling out, Trent had taken the liberty of hiring his brother, Trey, to back up their team. Trey had been a grunt infantryman in the regular man's Army for six years. He'd served in Desert Storm and had polished off his fair share of bad guys. He'd gone through sniper school and graduated first in his class. He's thinner than me, Trent had just been telling Hank before Katy's arrival, but mean as hell. Works cheaper than me, too. Hank had already countered Trent's offer to his brother. Double the money. That's the least of our problems.

Hank stood and walked to Katy's side. Trent watched the stress on Katy's face reckoning that the womenfolk were coming apart at the seams. Lori had been a nervous wreck since the break-in news, and Katy, usually a pillar of strength, appeared openly shaken. He had to admit emotions were running high for all concerned. Trent saw Hank reach for Katy's hand and whisper something to her. Her expression remained unchanged.

"We'll head back tomorrow, Katy. Let's leave very early and get the shopping done for the German gals. We're probably in for some activity around here. So, let's get an early start."

Katy leaned her shoulder against his saying nothing. Words, always her most reliable companions, seemed to escape her for the moment. She desperately wanted out but her heart was torn, too, at leaving the guys behind. She felt, in some ways, like a traitor. It especially bothered her to leave Hank. She would physically be only five or six miles away but separated by the vast gulf of time. One hundred and thirty-plus years and that seemed incomprehensibly distant to her. Actually, downright scary when she thought about it. Uncertainty settled in her like a long winter chill.

"I don't know, Hank. I fit there I guess but I'm unsure now. I'm not a quitter. I don't like going AWOL. I was raised to stick."

"You stick over there, Katy. We'll be fine over here. Trent's brother's coming and he'll back us up. Anyway, I intend to come over and eat some more of that good pumpernickel bread."

She tugged at Hank's hand and they walked out onto H.B.'s front porch. The sun was setting low on the horizon. A red hue washed the western sky. Bullbats roamed the skies above them, spinning and diving and calling.

"Hank, Chicago's no place to go hunting. Those folks are tough customers."

Katy always knew more than Hank intended. She had her own methods of surveillance. Her intelligence info was pretty near accurate.

"Katy, I've always been perfectly honest with you. That's where the snake den is. The head snake lives there. Maybe, just maybe I can convince the head snake to let us be. Otherwise, we may exist in a perpetual state of war around here. I'll hate

Chicago like I hate all cities, Katy, but this is one battle I've got to fight."

"Hire it done, Hank. You've got the money. Hire a hit man."

"I've thought about that, seriously, but there's risks. It could leave a trail and a good hound dog might sniff its way back to us. Then all bets would be off. I don't want to go to war with the whole Chicago mob. I'd have to hire an army."

"I know how good you are, Hank, but they're good, too. That's the business they're in. Knocking off folks and spreading mayhem and misery. They're some mighty onery bulls in that herd."

Katy was right, of course. Chicago wasn't Hank's country. Mobs weren't his business. Hoodlums didn't roam the wilds around his little cabin on the banks of the San Saba River. This was definitely the major league, but he'd been planning this for some time now. He already had a lot of intelligence, had been gathering it for some time on Hamilton Fremont. He'd hired a private eye in Chicago, through a friend of a friend in Dallas. Very discreet. No trail, no tracks to follow. Cash only: $25,000. The investigator was a very good operator. Retired FBI. Knew his stuff. He had produced numerous photos, places frequented by the mob boss, patterns and habits, number of bodyguards, work location, the works. If Hamilton Fremont was anything, he was highly predictable. His regular routine changed little. Both limos he used now had small tracking devices already installed, inconspicuously placed under and around the inside rear bumper, hotwired to the taillights. The tracking gizmos were too small to be a bomb and so did not attract the attention of the Fremont goons who gave a cursory inspection of the limos on a daily basis. Hank had meticulously studied the data, had a plan, and he had no plans to change it. Help would arrive soon in Trent's brother. With at least the two of them on duty, Hank would take leave for a few days and go do his hunting. The Windy City would have to accommodate, at least temporarily, a new sheriff in town.

H.B. PASSED water next to Twinks who was doing the same. The horses were properly staked a long mile away, out of nickering range. H.B.'s reluctance to carry out the deed they were about to do surfaced again with increased force. "Thou shalt not kill." A commandment from the Bible and something he took literally. He couldn't get his mind around the justification of killing another man – outlaw or otherwise. He hadn't come back in time to go on a killing spree. His identity was a physicist and, secondly, a physician. A healer. He'd worked as a trauma surgeon for three years of his surgical residency. Gunshot wounds in and around Houston were common in the emergency ward. They weren't a pretty sight to see. Bullets did a lot of damage to the human body. Now he was about to inflict gunshot wounds on eight men, only one of which he'd even met. Even the irascible Cobb Pickens didn't deserve death, or did he?

"What makes a man capable of killing another man?" H.B. asked only vaguely aware the question had parted his lips. His mind was in a turmoil and his pee only dribbled.

"Don't know," Twinks said slightly amused by the question. He'd taken life and plenty of it. Killing was many times necessary and justified as a Ranger. Wearing the badge allowed it and even required it when some gang or egotistical outlaw thought they could out fight the Rangers. Oftentimes they succeeded. He'd never really thought about it much though. It had to be that way in the matter of taking another man's life or it'd drive you plumb crazy. Over the years you scabbed over, the hide toughened, and you took killing as necessary in the rough settings where lawmen were outnumbered a thousand to one. He carried three wounds where outlaw lead had tried to take his life as he and a few others attempted to keep law and order on the frontier. It was the country you traipsed through that invited the problems. The law breakers needed open country to work in. They needed freedom away from witnesses that might testify.

"Taking life is not easy for me," H.B. said, having a serious problem trying to squeeze out his full bladder. "I know evil exists. I know men sometimes deserve to die for their deeds, I guess. I have trouble being the judge and jury. Seems mighty high handed and uncivilized to me."

"Hell, this ain't no civilization out here," Twinks said, slowly buttoning his pants and waving one arm in a broad swath as he turned to face H.B. "If it was, Cobb and his kind wouldn't be around. They don't fancy being where there's any numbers to oppose them. Outlaws is basically cowards, H.B. They're like a school yard bully waiting to catch someone smaller, someone unaware, someone incapable of self-defense. They like striking when a man's back is turned. Back shooters. They're the kind that bring a knife to a fistfight. They don't operate in a civilized manner. They don't know how. Out here you best be judge, jury, and executioner. Otherwise, you're not goin' to last long. They're brutes, violent men, pert near a subspecies. They are a sight worse than cannibals, H.B. At least the cannibals eat their victims."

Twinks paused a moment letting his words settle in then added. "Sometimes we have to adopt their philosophy for a spell. We become one of them so to speak. Speak their language, take their habits, adopt their methods, but we're still civilized when the shootin's over. We can never be like them.

The reason you feel the way you do right now proves my point, H.B. They've never had a single moment of remorse for taking an innocent life. Think of how many innocents those men have already killed and will kill in the future. What we're doing is a positive step for decent society everywhere. Never forget that."

Twinks felt his own uncertainty in spite of his lecture to H.B. He had given the same speech, basically, to a young Ranger named Billy just before they hit a nest of horse thieves along the Rio Grande some years back. The Mexicans had been raiding over the border relentlessly pursuing horseflesh to sell to Maximillan's soldiers as they readied for war. The Mexican raiders had turned violent when settlers started fighting back and dying in the process. Billy had turned white as they made plans that day for the ambush. He had spent most of the afternoon vomiting up his socks as they waited high in the rocky crags for the cover of darkness. Billy was just a kid. It was his first assignment as a Ranger; he was barely eighteen years old. Of the ten men under Twinks' command, there was only one fatality for the Rangers during the successful raid. A stray bullet, fired from a fleeing Mexican's revolver, had struck one of his men square in the chest. Unfortunately, the one Ranger hit was young Billy. Twinks had held him, elevated from the rocky ground, trying to comfort him in his final moments. The young boy tried to speak, wanting to say something in the throes of his dying, but his efforts were unsuccessful. Twinks lost sleep for a year regretting Billy's death. Maybe he should have left the kid in camp? Maybe the speech had been wrong to give? Maybe the damn Mexicans should have stayed on their side of the border? In the matter of Billy, the maybes had never been fully reconciled inside Twinks.

"Do these men really need killing?" H.B. asked, searching for the least bit of reassurance. His moral clarity was in a jumble, his judgment clouded. He was shaking in his boots thinking about being only a mile away from the most decisive moment in his life. Here he was in another time, another long-passed century, about to shoot at men not even from his own era. He was a cheater, in a sense, skipping like a rock into the past to commit an unimaginable act. Why had he come back here to begin with? Was this his higher purpose? Wasn't he ordained, in a way, to be here? Surely God had gifted him, granted him, the ability to go where only His angels dare travel. Wasn't all he was experiencing and wanted to experience in the past simply manna, a pure gift from his Maker? Was this God's way of testing him? Testing his heart, testing his mettle, testing his morality? He was switching from being a cowboy, which he had dreamed of being, to a killer. What gave him the right to decide who lives and who dies? When he signed on with Orb, even when he had traveled back to Fort Worth, it had been to help mankind, prevent suffering, cure a deadly disease in a young woman. The requirement to take another's life, especially preemptively, had never crossed his mind. Now a new reality dawned, and the awful weight of it pulled at his heart.

"H.B., I'm letting you know they need killin'. They gotta die to prevent others from dying. Those cowboys back there holding the stock aren't killers. They're all good boys mostly from good families with mothers and fathers and sisters and brothers much like them. They're mostly here for some adventure and trying to survive some of the hard times we face on the trail. Hell, they face dangers every day. I can't prepare them for the likes of Cobb and his cold-blooded killers. These boys ain't Rangers. They are just cowboys doing their job. This is one time you've got to buck up and quit over-thinking it. Cody's troubled, too. So don't feel alone. None of this is easy for any of us."

Orb, Cody and Nevershed walked up after a final check on

the horses. H.B.'s stomach was tied in knots, still churning inside. The slightest provocation could have him heaving on his knees. He buttoned up, fumbling with his pants placket, still unable to pass all his water.

Orb spoke in low tones as they all came to a huddle. They were so close H.B. could smell the breaths of the others. He took deep, slow breaths trying to quell his nausea.

"Twinks leads and we'll follow one step behind," Orb continued. "Pay attention to all sound. Step heel to toe to lessen the noise. Raise and lower your feet slowly. We ain't in no hurry here. There's effort in a good sneak so prepare yourself. We're goin' in real close on 'em. When we get ready we'll form a line, side by side facing their camp on my orders. Drunk or sober, they'll likely be returning fire. Shoot standin', then kneel if you want. Keep blazing until you're sure we've taken them out. Presumed dead men are the deadliest of all. Don't forget that."

There was a naked pause. The lone call of a coyote somewhere in the distance broke the absolute silence. Cody was fighting down his own queasy feelings. His knees were shaking and wanted to buckle, especially when he stood still.

"Check your weapons," Twinks said. "Make sure you're ready." He added, "Nevershed, Scar's likely on the right as we face 'em. East side. I doubt he moved much from when I last saw 'im. You take the east side of our skirmish line." Nevershed nodded but said nothing. Another silence.

"Cody, H.B., are you in?" Orb knew the two men where unsteady, filled with uncertainties. No doubt close to balking. It was a pre-battle thing that happened even to tested veterans. He needed to know their state.

"I'll make it," Cody said shifting his weight from one foot to the other. He said it with a total lack of conviction, his words rolling off a dry and thickened tongue.

"What about you? H.B.," Orb inquired. Buster had quietly passed word to him moments before they left cow camp that the tall greenhorn professed to be a doctor. Orb doubted the information as credible. Buster, at times, tended to be a bit windy.

H.B. took a deep breath and his throat tightened, but he managed to speak.

"I'm still not convinced I have a right to be here. I'm not entirely sure how I feel about all this."

"You can stay here if you want. No hard feelings." Orb said it in a chivalrous manner bespeaking an acute awareness of H.B.'s misgivings.

H.B. straddled a steep divide. One way led down a slippery slope where his morals, ethics, and the very fabric of his faith would be compromised. The other way definitely would let his friends down. Perhaps even endanger the young men back at camp. His life had been formed around the precept that turning the other cheek was admirable if possible. Love thy enemy. Yet, now, either path led to some losses or potential losses. There would be no going back once he started down either path. He'd already taken on the responsibility of introducing advanced, state-of-the-art semi-automatic weaponry to this century. He was deeply culpable, already directly connected to what was about to happen. He had done so in the good faith that by helping it would secure victory for his outnumbered comrades. He swallowed hard, finally, trying to summon his courage. He nodded a stiffened neck a few degrees forward and backward.

"I'll make it," he said unsure of who had uttered these words. Surely the statement had come from him, at least it seemed to be so. Had he said that?

Twinks suddenly turned, tired of the palaver and angled for the gully. The men fell in and were soon moving down the middle of the small ravine in slow, well-placed steps. Cody's determination was wavering. Cowboying was what he knew and loved. He knew a heifer from a bull and could sling a rope better than most men. He could single handed throw a steer in a matter of seconds with his lariat. He could dance a waltz on a horse and could green break a rank bronc in a day, but he'd never killed and had never really wanted nor had a desire to do so. He trusted the company he kept and he trusted their judgment and he especially trusted Orb. They were neighbors. Family friends. Goliad County citizens, but he couldn't kill the feeling he had.

H.B. stumbled along, trying to stumble deliberately, feeling almost outside of himself. All the while his legs kept moving although they didn't seem under his command. Forces beyond his control were at work here. Yet, he didn't want to let anyone down. Didn't want to be a disappointment to anyone, but the voice that had answered Orb's question just a few minutes earlier couldn't have been him speaking. Something had jumped over his conscience, moved past his judgment, and recklessly wiggled his tongue on its behalf. Now his legs followed the same strange utterance that had escaped his mouth. He was a mere chip in a stream carried along by the forces over which he had no control.

The night breeze stirred the tall grasses sweeping occasionally below the shallow gully. Two coyotes now played a yipping serenade in the far reaches of the open prairie. One calling and the other answering back. The moon's half circle hung like a crooked tooth high above them, white-washing the scene with its light. It was peaceful, serene, a world bathed in a soft backlight. Certainly, a land of contrasts. The pit viper lurked there waiting for the unwary. Carefully lying amongst the peaceful slow moving grasses. Ready to strike. Now two-legged predators slipped through the moonlight casting weak shadows, making their way along a meandering path. Playing the favorite game that men often played since the dawn of time. Participating in just causes that justifiably filled graveyards, chiseled tombstones, and made mother's weep. A great irony in the peaceful light the lone moon sent earthward on this particular night. The tall cowboy from the future writhed in his soul yet followed obediently.

CHAPTER
TWENTY-NINE

The trip to Chicago proved to be uneventful. Although Hank was in no rush to get there, he knew that time was of the essence. Katy had been in old Bellville for ten days now. Safely tucked away working with the German girls. The sisters had cried with glee when Katy arrived. Their clothes fit perfectly, believe it or not. They chatted excitedly and bragged of their fashion rebellion and promptly returned to work freshly decked out in their new duds. They were ready to show off their bulging bosoms and broad, voluptuous hips. At first, the oh-so-proper bakery cliental nearly bolted for the door so shocked were they by what their eyes beheld. Then, they seemed to accept it, more or less, as the day wore on. Actually, it was good for business as if the Germans could stand much more. Men roamed the sidewalks trying to think of new reasons to enter the bakery. They came to gawk, hardly hungry at all and spent their money just to see the sights.

And this new gal, Katy, well she was young, shapely and willing to advance the cause of liberated women for all to see. She was in and out and around the tables talking and laughing and charming all who came. Men were simply unable to wrest their eyes away from her. Her enthusiasm was even more captivating. For them, dodging stares, quick admiring glances, and whole-hog looking became their new fashion. Spring fields might go unplanted with Katy around. The local black-smith spent so much time in the bakery the first day he left two horses unshod and tied behind his shop.

The local constable patrolled only on the bakery side of the square it seemed now. Surely if some conflict were to break out in the sleepy little town, it would be near the bakery he surmised. The result of this decision caused his stomach to hurt from eating so much bread and pastries. His feet hurt, too, from standing upright so long. In the little closet of an office he inhabited, he normally had his feet propped up six of the ten hours he was on duty each day. His new routine was taking its toll.

And the women came now in droves to the bakery for their own reasons. For some it was to spy on their husbands to see where they might be loitering these long spring days. For others it was to simply observe. These three sinners, the local women's sewing circle gossip concluded, had not only eaten from the tree of knowledge but had consorted with the serpent himself. All sorts of evil was about to befall them if this was allowed to continue. Under the direct bullying of their female flock, Bellville's two most reverend pastors, Preacher Jim Davis of the Baptists and Pastor Curtis Fritz, Methodist, went together to witness the sin in action. Every eye in the bakery watched them as they seated themselves and partook of bread and coffee. Katy herself served them and did so with dignity and grace. Preachers or no, tight pants or no, button shirts or no, their hearts were won over by the young woman who waited on them and saw to their every need as if they were family. When they finally left the bakery, extending their stay as long as humanly possible and expanding their stomachs to the very limit, they left converted pastors themselves. The watchful eyes of the men and women who occupied their pews on Sunday followed their exit carefully. Oh, they'd have to play along a little with their respective congregations. Maybe mount a few light criticisms and slanted remarks, but there'd been no fiery sermons over the girls and their new choice of dress. Why Jesus himself had visited the homes of sinners hadn't he? The sinful tax collector, Matthew, for example would be one to name. Sin was an active, living thing. It wasn't always a passive impulse resting in the shadows ready to pounce. It had to be watched and inventively so, so a strategy of countering it could be adopted. One had to confront sin directly, openly. Both good pastors would soon pledge, heartily to their followers, to visit the bakery as often as they could and bear strong witness to the misguided and lost souls of the poor girls. Judge not lest ye also be judged took on new meaning for Preacher Davis and Pastor Fritz. The creed, the commandment, now became an oft quoted defense.

HANK STAYED to the back roads routing to Chicago. At least as much as he could. Cracker Barrel restaurants were his only diversion on the main thoroughfares. They were a favorite of Hank's serving delicious breakfasts which he ate regardless of the time of day. They were, as a whole, friendly places with good smells and a touch of small town about them. Hank loved biscuits and they produced the flaky kind his mama had been so consistent at serving. Eagle Lake, Illinois, was his first destination. It was only a blink of a little community on a county road ten miles east of Interstate 57 and barely twenty miles from the beginnings of Chicago itself. One mile further east, as the crow flies, was the border of Indiana. Eagle Lake was comprised of one small café, called the Bear Den, a convenience store, and of all things, a tiny barber shop, the proprietor of which looked ninety and appeared to be too feeble to heft a pair of scissors, much less control the turf of a full head of hair. Hank had done a minimum amount of research and had called the convenience store manager inquiring about storing his Dodge truck there. A couple of hundred dollars for three days storage behind the store was quickly accepted, no questions asked. Hank switched plates on the truck, prior to calling a cab, using one of the van's licenses now stored in H.B.'s barn. He concealed the Dodge plates under a tall hedge in loose dirt. He would later replace them.

It took thirty minutes for the Yellow Cab to arrive with a rather defensive female at its controls. He stated his destination watching her examine with critical eyes his meager luggage, a stuffed bag, and his worn Levi's.

"Downtown Ambassador," she said with a hit of sarcasm. "That's a really upscale place. You sure you want to go there?"

Yes. That's where I want to go. Thanks. Hank kept his tone civil.

Hank knew the routes, had carefully studied city maps, and his driver successfully skirted the direct connecting streets opting for a more circuitous approach. The meter clicked happily along gaining a healthy margin of profit for its driver. Finally, after two fakes and a long pass, she chose the right street and deposited Hank in the drop-off zone of the hotel. Hank smiled, paid the fare, and stepped out into a breezy, cool, mid-summer Chicago morning.

The Downtown Ambassador Hotel was, indeed, an opulent structure emulating a monarch's palace from a third world country. Tall arching columns of marble covered the front reaching high into the thin, blue air. Six-foot-high polished brass letters proudly announced itself just in case some peasant might wander near the doors and accidentally stray inside. The foyer was ridiculously large and overwrought with polished granite floors. In fact, it was so cavernous a little league baseball team could safely play a game inside. Around the center foyer pedestal, like spokes of a wheel, lounges appeared with overstuffed chairs and couches. All deep leather, of course, and here rich, red carpet took over to comfort the weary traveler. Bell boys and girls hopped to and fro ranging wide and far to meet each spoiled consumer's every need. Large growing plants, actually trees, lined any space available giving the place a noticeable safari accent. Hank glanced up into their tall branches expecting to see a monkey in flight. There was no doubt that a number of small mammals could escape the best of hunters here. The wealthy were at home here, each dressed to suit their over-rated egos. No eyes met his as Hank approached the check-in. His Levi's were way under the dress code thus he had to be low class and not worth noticing.

Hank had reserved the room under the alias of Lee Barnes. He had bullied the reservationist a bit not giving a credit card number to hold it. Thankfully, she was an intern, on her first day of duty she said, and Hank had pulled it off. She said it would be held until noon only. He was an hour early. Shelly was her name. Hank was hoping she would be present for his check-in. As he approached the polished granite counter, four hotel employees stood behind it. A young female turned and met him by the check-in computer greeting him with a strained smile. Intern in broad letters with a much smaller Shelly printed under it was on her nameplate. He was happily surprised.

"Lee Barnes, Shelly, how are you?"

"I'm fine, Mr. Barnes," she said startled he called her by name. Most of the cliental they served didn't stoop to mention first names. Especially, when Intern was attached to it. "Do you have reservations?"

"Yes, Shelly. I spoke with you last week." The other three counter employees appeared preoccupied, one with a client checkout in progress. As Shelly punched in the name her eyes twitched in nervousness. She looked quickly to one side as if she anticipated watchful eyes.

"Mr. Barnes," she said in a lowered voice. "I see you're paying with cash?"

"Yes, and I would like to pre-pay, if possible," Hank said matching her low voice. "I'll make no phone calls and I promise not to use room service. I do all my dining out."

"Do you have identification?" she asked shyly, as if she anticipated a problem.

Hank offered her a driver's license, a perfect replication yet a bogus one, for Lee Barnes, Dallas, Texas. Shelly took the driver's license, glanced at it, and immediately handed it back. She was obviously unnerved by accepting a cash only, pay-in-advance transaction. Likely some vague hotel policy was being broken. Her initials accompanied the reservation and by reneging her superiors would certainly find a transgression. Work had been hard to find. She needed this job. She was single, trying to save for college, and didn't want to hit the streets to find employment again.

Hank flashed his widest smile seeing her squirm. Two of the front desk employees, with stern looks, walked to the back leaving only Shelly now and the checkout next to them in progress. Hank carefully handed her an envelope with two thousand dollars in cash. The room he'd reserved for three days went for four hundred per day. That would leave Shelly an eight-hundred-dollar tip. She fidgeted as she nervously counted the cash, never pulling it from the envelope. She actually counted it twice her fingers fumbling through the bills. Finally, after the second count, she raised her eyes ready to speak when Hank stopped her, finger over his lips. She knew instantly why he'd hushed her. Shelly paused, slightly shaking, and handed him a registration form to sign. She turned and keyed the room's entry card and handed it to him. Hank smiled, again, and left for the elevators.

HAMILTON FREMONT FANCIED himself a blue-blood mobster. He occupied the penthouse floor of a 20-floor designer office building barely a rock's throw from the broad waters of Lake Michigan. Highway 41, which ran north-south along the lake's shore, bordered the core of the rich business district with the city's coat and tie crowd lurking there. It was the habitation zone of the highly successful, upper-crust types who drove black BMW's and kept the doormen hopping. The Hancock Towers stood proudly on the very beginnings of Lincoln Avenue and its designers had carefully planned it so. It gave its high paying occupants an unobstructed view of the mighty lake and the sailboat traffic that frequented its summer waters. The Hancock stood only four blocks from the massive Sears Tower.

The office building was the home of the largest law firm in Chicago. James, James, and Gindel held onto the lower floors and above them the Chicago Board and Stock Exchange resided. The top floor or penthouse suites, in rarified air, was occupied by Mr. Fremont himself and his minions. Fremont

Investments was a cover, an apparent honest business, and Hamilton himself was accepted generally as an exceptionally rich executive living on a golf course and frequenting the social circles of the wealthy and famous. If he had dirty laundry, it went unmentioned and was conveniently put aside and then forgotten. After all, a biz jet, two limos, and hefty political contributions was the Chicago way of buying influence and power. The FBI nosed around occasionally and even tested the indictment waters but Hamilton's twentieth floor housed his own cadre of personal lawyers and they had succeeded, at times with supreme effort, to keep him from behind bars. For Hamilton, dealing on the fringes was his way of life. He was deeply involved in the Chicago drug trade and owned, by hook and crook, a good-sized chunk of it. He had hundreds of mules working the streets, distributing the goods, collecting the money. If you were a good mule, you'd scratch out a living. Cheat once and you became a dead mule. Life was cheap in the world of Fremont and sudden disappearances weren't all that uncommon under his employ. Lake Michigan was deep and lonely with a piece of concrete chained to your ankle.

Hank was dressed as a jogger. It fit him perfectly. He could run five miles and still keep his pulse honest. He had always been a magnificent specimen thanks to a healthy, vigorous lifestyle. He knew no one, short of a highly trained collegiate athlete, could stay with him at the running pace he could maintain.

The private investigator had provided him with a mountain of intelligence to digest. It was money well spent. Hank wanted to confirm the evidence thus he watched the Hancock Towers from a small bistro across Lincoln Avenue. It was a busy place with broad sidewalks and throngs of harried office dwellers darting to work. He had jogged there, from the hotel two miles distant, barely raising a sweat. It was his first morning on the streets and he wanted to witness firsthand the tight schedule that Fremont supposedly kept.

Limo arrives at 10:00 in the morning sharp. Two beefy types step out glancing around, but never really seriously observe the surroundings. A third stout bodyguard then exits and opens the limo door. He stands close by the door while the original two walk slowly towards the office building entrance. They can't actually clear the way, as there's far too much foot traffic to accomplish that, but they appear to be watchful – awaiting their boss.

Finally, Hamilton Fremont, himself, steps out, straightens his tie, smooths back his hair, and struts toward the entrance. The P. I. said he took an average of fourteen steps to reach the doors. Hank counted fifteen. One goon following, two goons covering the door and seeing him through. The limo departs and Hank watches his GPS locator gizmo confirming the departure. From its bumper location transmitting perfectly, Hank had also tracked it arrival. Setting at a small round table, the bistro was the perfect place to witness the comings and goings of his target. Hank would hit him there, somewhere between those fourteen or fifteen steps. He'd hit fast and hard. One more day of observation would do the trick. Fremont followed a tight timeline and was never behind schedule. He was a man with a mission and he was on time doing it. Tomorrow, Hank would be jogging by when Hamilton walked those fourteen or fifteen steps to the office building. Day Two would be the set up for Day Three. He wanted to be close enough tomorrow to smell the man's foul breath and watch up close and personal as his self-assured swagger propelled him to the open door.

THIRTY

A hundred yards from Cobb's camp Twinks and Orb called a stop and everyone stood quiet for a moment. They were listening. Trying to discern any movement or rustling in the camp. Any slight sound could signify someone was alert to their approach. Night sounds of the expected variety certainly could be heard. The hooting call of a prairie owl, the stirring grasses waving and whooshing softly to an unseen breeze, the melodious crickets playing their fiddles, and the seemingly ever-present distant yipping of the prairie's coyotes or song dogs as the cowboy's called them. The scroungy occupants of the camp appeared still and unmoving.

The outlaw's horses, conveniently, had been staked a fair piece behind the camp removing the one thing that could warn the outlaw gang of danger. Orb and Twinks, acting as scouts, noted nothing unusual so the approach was ordered cautiously forward. Steps were more carefully placed now, only inches apart, as the final distance was negotiated. The moon had passed the apex of its nightly circle and now was slanted slightly westward. The star herds shined like miniature jewels covering the top half of the night yet were subdued just a bit by the moon's glow. The sights, the sounds, the serenity of this early morning hour would normally have had a calming effect on men like H.B. and Cody, but not on this night.

Rationalizing the coming event, the thought of shooting, and subsequently killing sleeping men destabilized its normally soothing effects and forced pounding heartbeats in both men. The coming attack, did affect their metabolisms differently, however. H.B. had felt chilled, almost cold as the sneak progressed whereas Cody had been sweating profusely. The chilled-feeling had tightened H.B.'s leg muscles and the possibility of leg cramps seemed possible, even imminent. Cody's body, by contrast, just perspired. Sweat dripped in his eyes causing them to burn. He used his sleeve often to clear his eyes. Both men, at times during the duration of the hike, felt emotionally drained and insecure in their ability to perform expected duties. Then, just in the depths of questioning one's ability to act, for some unknown reason, something strange happened. Even more remarkable, it happened almost simultaneously for both men. The fog of uncertainty lifted and simply blew away. Just as their clarity of purpose returned, Orb halted the group and before them, not twenty paces away, dark figures of sleeping men lay. Some appeared wrapped in light blankets, while others slept without the benefit of any covering at all. The men, as best as could be discerned, were all snoring to some lesser or greater degree. At twenty paces, the sound of their snoring even rivaled the singing of the crickets.

Orb organized his line of attackers silently with Nevershed standing on the east side. His target, Scar, looked to be laying nearest the fire curled in a ball and snoring loudly. The fire, of course by this time, was nothing but dim glowing coals. The glint of two empty whiskey bottles discarded near it reflected the moonlight. For the first time, faint stirrings of grazing horses could be heard in the deep background. The next sequence of events moved rapidly. Orb and Twinks, followed closely by Nevershed, raised their weapons and waited for Cody and H.B. to follow their lead. They quickly did. They had been told to shoot first toward the center of the camp and move outward if necessary. Twinks and Orb were to fire left of center and move inward as the shooting continued. Nevershed was to shoot right to left making sure, first and foremost, that Scar's nasty existence be terminated. In a short two seconds after their weapons were raised, all hell broke loose.

After the battle, while discussing the attack's finer points, it seemed as though Orb and Twinks fired at precisely the same moment. H.B. never heard but one explosion coming from his immediate left before he commenced pulling the trigger. Then all he could hear was a continuous chorus of gunfire. Nevershed seemed to be firing slower than the rest but his accuracy was unquestioned. Cody fired rapidly, wildly at first, and his shot placement reflected his hurry. One of his targets actually got his hand on a six-shooter and squeezed a round off before succumbing. His effort was in vain hitting nothing but unoccupied air. H.B.'s first target rolled to one side but soon stopped moving. After the heat of the melee, H.B. thought he, too, had fired a few rounds at the one outlaw getting off the only return shot. Organized shooting quickly disintegrated into random firing pumping already dead forms with more lead. Twinks and Orb seemed to rake the camp with gunfire over and over again in remarkably fast order. Then as quickly as it had started, the firing ceased. Smoke from the gunpowder hovered momentarily and spread itself in the night breeze. Absolute silence reigned in the camp itself but the outlaw's horses weren't silent. They had panicked. Stake pins were in the process of being tugged at or already pulled. Screaming whinnies arose to a frenzied pitch then the sound of horse hooves pounding the prairie followed as they made their escape. Just when the horse sounds had faded into the distance, H.B. rocked the entire gathering to its core. The ghastly apparition of a recently dispatched outlaw would have had no less effect. He promptly flipped on a bright LED headlight placed over his head and shined it directly into the outlaw camp. Twinks jumped back temporarily and in his initial fright even turned his gun on H.B.

"What the hell's that?" he said clearly shaken. In all of his full life's experiences he'd never witnessed such a startling thing. The other company stood no less shocked.

"Called a headlight," H.B. said nonchalantly and strolled calmly towards the camp. The rest stood stock-still, watching the amazing glowing beacon. The light rays were the strangest sight they'd ever witnessed.

"A what?" Orb managed to ask taking a few indecisive steps towards the camp.

"A headlight," H.B. called back. He wanted to check their victims to see if anyone was alive. It seemed only fair to check. Finally, H.B.'s companions followed, uncertain about approaching the strange light. H.B. was moving from one form to the other checking for signs of life. The others stood, mouths agape, watching the strange glow lighting the darkness.

THE FIRST SURPRISE was they counted seven dead outlaws, not the eight they expected. H.B.'s bright light quickly revealed this troubling fact. It appeared that one, Buster Cobb to be exact, had somehow managed to escape. The general consensus among the leaders, Twinks and Orb that is, was that he probably had left camp for some reason and wasn't even there when the fighting started. Twinks had positively identified him earlier in the night. Later it was discovered that Cobb's saddle was indeed missing and he had likely departed just prior to the attack. How and why that had happened was a mystery. Twinks wanted to immediately strike out for him but Orb nixed the idea.

"Cobb can't hurt us now. He's alone. He ain't no good unless he's got some cutthroats to back him."

"I'll go it alone," Twinks said pleading his case. "I'll be back in two days with his topknot, Orb. He needs killin'."

"That he does, Captain, but we need to move our steers northward. I've got to have all my hands. If we cut his track again I'll send you after 'im."

Twinks groused and grumbled but respected Orb's decision. Although he could easily follow a warm trail. Cold trails were a different matter. Cobb was plenty slick. He could still cause misery for the outfit.

In further checking the bodies, Scar was found riddled with lead. He died in the fetal position curled around an old Colt Dragoon six-shooter he kept close by. The smell of stale whiskey emanated from his scruffy carcass. Saddle bags and saddles were strewn around with no organization in the camp. They were a ragtag bunch apparently far better killers than campers. Twinks, now trusting H.B.'s strange light, searched the saddle bags finding mostly cartridges and little else of value. All guns were collected, along with the ammunition. Two saddles were particularly fancy ones adorned with Mexican-style silver conchos. Orb decided to take them along. Maybe one of the cowboys would want to switch out. Only two decent ropes could be found and they were included in the booty. Twinks latched onto the best of the saddlebags.

They spent a few minutes lining up the bodies beginning to

hear the faint buzzing of the first circling blowflies. There would be no burials. No one had brought a spade with the general consensus being outlaws didn't deserve such dignities as being planted in the ground.

"Coyotes will dig 'em up anyways," Nevershed said, "them and the badgers. Might as well make it easy for 'em. The buzzards will be pitchin' in, too, I reckon."

Not burying them, regardless of reasons, seemed wrong to H.B. but he kept his own counsel.

They walked back to their staked horses and headed for the herd arriving just at dawn. Travis Strayhorn, with no witness present, went behind the wagon and wept in relief at seeing the party return unharmed. The ordeal had been a nightmare for him imagining his responsibilities increasing a thousand-fold. Buster served breakfast as appetites increased after hearing the good news of the successful attack. The men talked, laughed, and poked fun at the very fears that mere hours ago had paralyzed the group. For them now the sky was clear, the early summer sunrise warming, and the way to Montana now seemed paved with tall grass, soft pastures and easy living. Cobb's escape, of course, was puzzling and a cause for real concern but without his motley crew to back him up he seemed only a minor irritation, akin to unwanted mosquitoes, in the larger scheme of things. Twinks held the boys' rapt attention around the breakfast fire, retelling the entire episode in graphic detail. Before long, however, Orb ordered the men back to their duties and the camp settled into its normal routine. The steers were off the bed ground grazing north through Indian Territory. The boss herdsman hurried them along wanting to cover at least twenty-five miles of the long remaining drive to the Blackfoot Agency.

Day two went as planned. The limo again arrived precisely on time. Hank left the bistro early and crossed the street to position himself for the jogging approach. He was surprised at how easily he got within five feet of the man as he made his way the fourteen steps to the open doors of the Hancock Towers. The three large bodyguards seemed rather lackadaisical in their protection of their thug boss. His walk, in downtown Chicago, from limo to building apparently wasn't considered a threatening zone. Hank jogged slowly, cutting between the single tail guard and his employer for the sole purpose of testing the reaction. No one seemed excited by his intrusion thus sealing the deal on Hank's hit strategy. Tomorrow would go fundamentally the same but with a different outcome if all went as planned.

Hank took his time covering the two miles to his hotel. He stopped by a Starbuck's on Lincoln Avenue and ordered a large espresso mocha sipping on it as he walked. He almost wished he'd done the deed today allowing his escape from the big city sooner. Traffic snaked along the tangled roadways snarling itself with late-arriving inbound commuters. Sidewalks were pedestrian rich, each scurrying to their pre-ordained destinations. The hustle and bustle of the masses sent his hackles up. Even with the prevailing breeze off Lake Michigan there was the stench of the city floating in the air. Hank's mind went back to his and Katy's last ride to old town Bellville. The open sky above so blue you got dizzy just looking at it. It was so refreshing, remembering his and Katy's trip, riding fresh horses into the new country of the past. The red-tailed hawk's call beckoning from its high vantage point. The freedom and openness of 1885 was appealing and calling to him. Yet, here he was having to do a dirty deed in the very armpit of a decadent society spiraling rapidly into its own cesspool.

He was a half block away from the Downtown Ambassador, his thoughts elsewhere, when he noticed something troubling. Shelly, the intern receptionist of the hotel, nearly bumped into him going in the opposite direction, tears streaming down her cheeks. She was clearly distraught. Hank immediately turned around convinced he should follow her. She didn't seem to notice his presence, or anyone else's for that matter. She stopped at a street crossing weeping silently when Hank stepped close to her.

"Shelly, may I ask why you are so distressed?" Hank said in a soft, calming voice. He didn't want to alarm the already emotionally stressed-out young woman.

She turned and looked at him her eyes red and swollen.

"It's you. It's you," she said sobbing and unable to keep eye contact. "You just got me fired from the hotel. They caught my mistake. I shouldn't have let you prepay."

"That's very inconsiderate of them," Hank answered quickly. "I'll go see the manager and get this straight right now. You only did what I requested."

"No, no. I'm not ever going back there," she whispered through a tightened throat. "They were so mean and nasty to me. I can't believe they were so rude."

The light changed to walk but Hank put his hand on her elbow helping Shelly aside, keeping her from being trampled by the press of foot traffic. She stumbled along, as he helped her, almost unaware of where she was going. Soon they were standing close to a small café, The Hole in the Wall, so the sign said and Hank gently guided her towards it. She didn't resist, sobbing ever more loudly. Hank stood with her just outside the café holding her arm, trying somehow to comfort the distraught girl. She sobbed on and on and finally pulled a linen handkerchief from a pocket and blew her nose, her hands shaking as she held it. Hank stayed with her. In what seemed to Hank to be a very long time, Shelly finally gained control and actually made her first genuine eye contact with him.

"Would you come into the café with me a moment and sit down?" he asked. "I realize the request may seem slightly irregular to you but I'd like to help if I may. Since I'm the one responsible for you losing your job."

Shelly nodded her head, sniffed a few moments more, wiped her eyes and with Hank's helping hand they found a table nearest the front window. The Hole in the Wall was a small place with a dozen tables at most. It was mid-morning so the noon rush wasn't yet on. It was only half full. A waiter approached quickly, then noticing Shelly's distress stood back, uncertain what to do. Hank motioned him forward.

"Coffee," Hank said and Shelly nodded in agreement. The waiter left promptly to fetch their order.

"It's really not your fault," Shelly managed to say between sniffles. "I just messed the whole thing up."

"Again, you just did what I requested. Do you have a line on any other job?" he inquired.

"No. It took me a long time to find this one," she said after a rather long pause. "Jobs are hard to get for someone with no real experience. I'm just trying to save up so I can go to college."

"Are you from Chicago?" Hank asked. Somehow, she didn't have the look of an urbanite to him.

"No. I'm from a little farming town in Indiana. Only two stop lights. My parents are farmers but farming's been tough lately. Dad and mom are just scraping by as it is. There's no money left over for college."

The coffee arrived and the waiter quickly left. Hank stirred in sugar and cream. Shelly seemed uncertain what to add to hers.

"Do you not like coffee?"

"I do, kinda, I guess. I usually get something at Starbuck's when I can afford it. I'm not used to taking it straight."

Hank smiled to himself at her response and handed her the creamer and she dutifully added a goodly portion followed by a generous supply of sugar.

"Most of my friends drink coffee without sugar," Hank admitted. "I've got to have it sweet."

"Me, too," Shelly said looking slightly calmer. At least her red eyes weren't streaming tears at the moment. Hank watched her as she stirred the coffee. She had the look of a country girl, unsophisticated and unpretentious, and definitely out of her element. He doubted, however, that she really understood that.

"Where do you want to go to college?" Hank asked trying to keep the conversation light.

"Oh, it doesn't really matter. I had hoped for some scholarship money but the high school where I graduated didn't have much to offer. My mom and dad never went to college so they don't know the ropes about college. My older brother's in Iraq with the Army so he couldn't help." Shelly took her first sip, blowing the hot brew first, her high cheek bones blushing pink.

"Did you make good grades?" Hank asked.

"A's and B's," Shelly said pulling her linen hanky out again and wiping her nose. She had long blond hair, natural blond, Hank thought with almost black eyebrows. Her facial features were thin, thin nose, deep-set eyes, and a pretty light complexion. Light makeup most of which had washed away with the tears. Shelly wasn't a phony. Hank's conscience was really pricking him over his involvement in her firing.

"How do you afford a place to live? It isn't cheap living in a city like Chicago."

"I'm living in a room at an old school friend of my mom's. I help with the groceries and try and help pay the utilities. She works in a beauty shop. She's kinda weird though. Comes and goes at all hours. She has some strange-looking friends, too."

"Is it close by?"

"No. Ten blocks, I think. It's a pretty good walk from the hotel." Mentioning the hotel made her sigh heavily. Then she straightened her back and sipped at the coffee.

"Are you hungry?"

"Maybe. I guess so. I haven't eaten since early this morning. Only a Pop Tart."

"I'm sure we can find something better for you to eat than a Pop Tart." Hank waved his hand and the waiter approached carrying the pot of coffee. "Bring us a menu, please."

SHELLY ATE LIKE A CHAMPION. She looked half-starved to Hank and proved her worth by eating a large stack of pancakes, covered with strawberries and cream. She relaxed, even became animated and funny. She openly admitted her fears to Hank, an almost perfect stranger, and that alone showed her lack of street sense. She was a perfect victim. She had only been in Chicago a month so her guardian angel had been providing cover.

"Are you partial to Illinois?" Hank questioned as she took her last full bite of pancakes. She wiped her lips with a napkin and looked up.

"Oh, no. I don't like the winter all that much. Illinois and Indiana get very cold. I would rather live in the south."

"Any place particular?"

"Not really. Just south. Texas maybe. I read Old Yeller and Savage Sam in school. Sounds interesting down there."

Hank smiled. Pure kid. Just a young, impressionable kid.

"How about attending college in Texas?"

"I wouldn't have the money to travel that far. I barely had enough money to get here." She raised her eyes watching the turmoil on the sidewalks just outside the café doors. She had a lonely look about her. Sadness crept into her eyes again when the thought of losing her job re-crossed her mind. She'd never experienced a firing. Actually, she'd never held a real job so it would have been impossible to have been fired. She sniffled, digging for her hanky. She hated to crawl back home defeated. Shelly feared being trapped there more than living on the streets of Chicago for some reason. There was a lot of the past in her home town but no future she knew of. Only if you were a larger farmer did you stand a chance. Her parents had a small acreage and almost starved most years. It wasn't such a great life either. She'd witnessed too much desperation in her parent's eyes trying to provide when there wasn't anything to give.

"What about attending college in Texas?" Hank pressed. Perhaps he could get her imagination stirring again.

"Can I call you Lee?" she asked finally coming out of her reminiscing.

"I won't answer to that name," Hank stated remembering that was his name on the hotel register. "Call me Hank."

Shelly looked quizzically at him a moment but quickly accepted Hank as his name. "Hank, I don't have the money to attend college right now. That's why I was working. I have to save up first."

Hank knew the real truth about that. She'd never save enough. She'd get swallowed up by something or someone and never escape the city's confines. The snares were already set and waiting for her. Hidden pitfalls that even the wary, trained eye might fail to negotiate.

"I'll pay your way through college, Shelly. No strings attached," Hank blurted. "I know plenty of colleges and universities in Texas. Trip's paid, college paid, and I'll even buy you a nice vehicle to run around in. What do you think about that?"

Shelly's mouth dropped. "What?" she finally managed gaining control of her sagging jaw. "Pay my way?"

"Yes, Shelly, pay your way. All the way until you graduate. My gift to you for doing what I asked when I asked you to do it."

"I've been raised not accept a stranger's offer," her voice said but her eyes remained sparkling, excited.

"And that's a very good philosophy," Hank added. "I'm not your typical stranger, Shelly. I got you fired. It's the least I can do for you."

"But that's too much," she said still wearing an incredulous expression. "You can't owe me that much."

"I have the money to help you. I believe you'll be a very good investment. Keep your grades up and I'll keep you in school. Will your parents accept you going off to Texas?"

"They'll like it more than my being in Chicago. My dad had a fit when I came here."

"I'm on you dad's side. No one belongs here." Hank reached his hand across the table. An empty plate of pancakes lay below it. "Let's shake on it. Remember a handshake is a binding contract that you'll succeed in college. Do we have a deal?"

Tears filled Shelly's eyes but this time they were tears of

joy. She reached across and delivered a firm handshake. Her face blossomed with a smile. "When do I go?" she asked obviously anxious to test the validity of the offer.

"Do you drive?" Hank asked.

"Why, yes," she said slightly insulted by the question. She may be from Hickville, Indiana, but they do issue driver's licenses there. Actually, she considered herself a darn good driver.

"The reason I asked," Hank said noticing her expression, "was that I wanted to know whether you wanted to fly to Texas and then buy a car or if you wanted to drive down in your own vehicle? One that we bought here."

Shelly sat a moment stunned by the sudden turn of events. It seemed to be too good to be true. Drive down? She'd never left Indiana with the exception of coming to Chicago and she'd ridden a bus here. Driving alone to Texas seemed a far reach. This was all happening pretty fast.

"How'd you get here?" she asked.

"Drove my pickup truck," he said.

"If you don't mind, I'll ride back with you. I've never even thought of riding in a jet."

Riding with him seemed irregular. Hank heartily disapproved of the idea.

"Shelly, it's not wise to ride a long distance with a single male, even one of my age. Even with someone you think you might know and trust. You'll enjoy the plane ride. I'll get you a ticket in first class. Once in Texas we'll select a school and get you transportation. Is that a deal?" He offered his hand again. She thought a minute and shook his hand with enthusiasm.

"Let's call and get a reservation. We've got a ticket to buy. Do you own a cell phone?"

"Yes, but it's a cheap one."

"Let's get you an updated phone, first thing. We need to be

in contact. Then I'll use your phone to call your dad and mom. Do you want to go home for a visit first?"

She thought about Hank's suggestion a minute. "No, I just left. I'll head south if you don't mind." She broke out in a huge smile as the slow realization set in that all of this might actually come true. "Oh, I almost forgot," she said apologetically looking at Hank. "Thank you so much for the tip. I felt so guilty taking it but I didn't know what else to do. That's a huge amount of money. I almost forgot that I'm a rich girl now."

CHAPTER
THIRTY-ONE

S hooting someone at point blank range opened up a set of potential hazards to the shooter. Hank had carefully explored each possibility over and over again. Did Hamilton Fremont wear a Kevlar bullet-proof vest under his suit as he strolled amongst the common folk? Highly unlikely. However, Hank's intentions were not to shoot for body mass so it really didn't matter. He had a police model Smith and Wesson caliber 38 that would suffice. His intention was to shoot, point blank, at the base of the skull thus eliminating any possibility of missing. Plus, he didn't want any collateral damage like an inadvertent bullet fragment striking an innocent victim. Having to exchange fire with one or more of the bodyguards was possible but not likely. His strategy was speed and surprise. That would be hard to counter with beefy bodyguards who appeared to be lackadaisical in their guarding duties.

Hank wanted only one casualty to occur on Lincoln Avenue on Day Three. Pedestrians would be in close proximity to the assassination thus Fremont's gunners, even if they got around to firing, would have to be cautious slinging lead indiscriminately. Hank's best guess was that he would be ten to fifteen yards away, running as only he could, before the goon guards collected their wits. The element of surprise was an amazing antidote to even the best bodyguard preparedness. Fremont's guard dogs appeared to do everything by rote. They had obviously become too comfortable with their duties and, thus, were unprepared for the unexpected. That's how the best trained horse throws an unprepared though professional rider. That's how a goon boss can get eliminated. Expect the unexpected--even plan for it.

Hank had already pre-determined his escape route. It would roughly be a square S route following the patterns of various alleys and main streets. On Day One he had perfected the route running the course at different speeds to eliminate the possibility of having to stop. Of course, he bypassed street lights and any normal stoppages that the average city jogger might observe. A dumpster two blocks away would get the top cover midnight blue jogger's suit revealing the bright yellow second suit underneath. The same dumpster would also get the flak jacket Hank wore. The phony driver's license had already been destroyed. Just his remaining cash stayed with him in the pocket of the yellow suit. Approximately a mile away, just off the jogging trail next to Lake Michigan, he would hail a cab for the long ride back to his pickup truck. In less than fifteen minutes from the hit he should be in the back seat of a cab heading south on Highway 41. In one hour, roughly, he should be departing his parking area in the Dodge truck. That is, if all went according to plan.

Hamilton Fremont arrived as usual at 10:00 sharp. Bodyguard Goon One and Two behaved as expected and preceded their boss to the door. Goon Three followed at a reasonable distance behind thoughtlessly watching his own feet and not watching his boss. Hank struck with a cool and deadly precision. He closed the last twenty feet between himself and the target traveling in a fluid, easy trot. In the last ten feet, he brought the weapon up in ready position and cocked the hammer. On Hamilton Fremont's tenth step after leaving the limo and five steps from the entrance of Hancock Towers, the 38-revolver delivered a deadly round to the base of his rather sizeable skull. His forehead literally exploded as the bullet passed through skin, hair, bone and brain and exited with explosive force just below his hair part. The skull literally collapsed from the sheer force of the point-blank shot. One of the bodyguards, unknown to Hank at the time, was Fremont's nephew and close confidante. The shock and awe of blood and brain matter literally spraying Fremont's nephew caused an immediate reaction. In the extreme panic of the moment, he screamed frantically for someone to help his uncle. His high-pitched scream caused Bodyguard Two to fumble for his semi-automatic pistol unable to put in into play. Bodyguard Three, lumbering behind the victim, reacted to the nephew's scream thinking both his boss and the nephew had been somehow shot simultaneously. He ran to assist the screaming and panicked nephew, only to be roughly pushed away by the same. The shooting had occurred while his head was down and vaguely saw a figure pass by but could not, even when pressed later by Chicago police, identify the color of clothing the assassin wore. Bodyguard One and Two could render no serious description other than the fact that a pedestrian, apparently a man, had run up and done the dastardly deed. It took two other witnesses at the scene, including Hamilton Fremont's limo driver, to piece together the fact that the attacker was wearing some kind of jogger's apparel. No one could remember the color he wore but described the apparel as dark with the hood pulled up. Hair color, facial features were nondescript. Hancock Tower's one outside security camera had been on the blink for the past several days and captured no video.

Chicago police and city detectives fumbled around the crime scene for a few hours after cordoning it off finding no evidence whatsoever with the exception of one bullet fragment and Fremont's biologics. The bullet had first exploded the mafia bosses head then exploded itself on impact with the office building's marble exterior. Exact caliber of the round would never be precisely determined from the fragment. Later, however, according to official police reports, the damage to Fremont's head indicated the use of a smaller caliber bullet. His burial casket was never opened.

As the police investigation turned in circles in front of the Hancock Towers, Hank was changing his license plates in the back parking lot of the convenience store at Eagle Lake. He had decided to stop by Shelly's hometown in Rainsville, Indiana, and visit with her parents. The phone call he'd made with her new cell phone hadn't gone too well but he still wanted to reassure her mom and dad of her safety and her subsequent college attendance. Four days from now, he was to meet Shelly at Houston's Hobby Airport and get her college career on track.

COBB PICKENS HAD LIVED on pure dumb luck most of his life. However, luck had deserted him in regards to his headaches. He had been plagued with severe headaches since early child-hood. They didn't come often, but when they did, they hit with a vengeance and always at the most inopportune time. As the two whiskey bottles were being passed around camp by his motley crew, he felt the beginnings of the headache start just after his second turn at the bottle. The pain always centered first in the front of the head and progressed slowly along the top of the skull until it reached its full, almost unbearably painful zenith square in the back of the head. Spikes of pain, at times causing bouts of nausea, often ran far down the neck in its final excruciating stages. The headaches came for reasons Cobb could never fathom. However, over the years he had found that by bathing his head in cool, or preferably cold water, oftentimes the worst of the symptoms, puking in particular, could be somewhat curtailed. The very moment that former Ranger Captain Twinks Brady led his attack group down the small ravine a short mile away, Cobb Pickens was saddling his horse, pulling its stake and riding out in search of a cold water creek he and his men had crossed an hour before making camp. They'd watered their horses in it, filled their canteens, and sauntered along another hour before deciding to settle down for the night.

It was a small inconsequential creek but Cobb recalled its water to be cold, probably bubbling up from the source of a deep-water spring. His head was splitting, hurting so intensely that by the time he mounted his saddle he could hardly ride. In desperation, he did ride slowly into the night with each falling hoof sending a jolt of pain through his brain. Five agonizing miles later he stumbled onto the creek's glimmeringly cold waters and fell into it dunking his head far under its soothing waters. Over and over again, for as long as he could stand it, Cobb submerged his splitting head hoping for some relief. Finally, in small, miniscule increments, the headache's intensity began to recede. The nausea in his stomach settled a bit, and after an hour of practically living like a frog under the cold waters, he rolled to his side and tried to rest. As he lay there listening to the gurgling of the creek water, he heard what he thought might be the sound of distant gunfire. It was a thin sound, carried away by the incessant prairie breeze and muffled somewhat by the water. He was too tired to take much note of it and closed his eyes hoping for the last of the pain to eventually drain away.

At dawn, almost an hour before sunrise, Cobb clawed his way into his saddle and rode the back route he'd ridden earlier in search of the creek. Fatigue weighed heavy on his eyelids and he could barely keep them open. However, he did see a horse grazing with its pulled night stake a couple of miles out and wondered how it had gotten loose. As he closed on his outlaw camp, he then noticed an unusual number of turkey buzzards circling directly overhead. Even with his depleted energy reserves he rallied himself to pay closer attention to the surroundings and scanned the horizon with tired eyes. Then he witnessed the reason for the buzzards. In the last fifty yards before camp, he saw hordes of flies covering his sleeping men. Only they weren't sleeping. He pulled rein and sat in stunned disbelief, his eyes finally accepting what was true. Lined close together, side-by-side, only bloody corpses remained of what once were his men. Two coyotes shooed the millions of flies momentarily as they fought over one of the corpses' tender morsels. Cobb wavered in his saddle at the startling sight, growing dizzy suddenly. The camp was a mass of bloodied bodies and he slowly counted seven. No one had survived.

Using all of his remaining strength, Cobb stood tall in his stirrups and scoured his surroundings for any sign of the attackers. *Who in the hell had done this?* he asked himself. *What had happened? Who could take a gun outfit like his so easily?* His brain was too tired, his skull too tender to field the questions but they came nevertheless. Seeing the bloodied bodies of his comrades rolled his tender stomach again and he felt bile rise in his throat. He took one last look at the sorry sight, glanced briefly into the distances and spurred his horse into a slow lope in a northeasterly direction. This was too much. He was too tired to try and figure out what had happened. Whoever it was could still be close by so he pushed as hard as he could trying to put miles behind him. He stopped at the cold creek again, filled his canteen, watered the horse, and kicked into a steady lope.

Somewhere out there, in front of him, was Dodge City. He'd get there one way or another on his own. His dreams of taking a cattle herd had vanished for now, but other opportunities would come sooner or later. He considered himself a damned good gambler if given half the chance. Dodge was full of gambling opportunities he'd heard tell. The law was light and easy there compared to Texas. Law dogs could hardly be expected to quell free-spirited men like himself anyway. As the miles passed under him, he started feeling just a little of his old self again. Cobb pushed as hard as he dared and nooned under a scraggly little bush standing hardly higher than his head. It was shade on a prairie and he longed for a nap. Maybe with a little rest, he could think better. His mind seemed bogged in quicksand. Maybe he could make sense, later, of the events of the previous night and the sights his tired eyes had seen. So, he slept long and hard. When he awoke, the sun was hanging low in the west, only an hour away from settling itself down for a long night's rest.

THIRTY-TWO

S helly Stark walked off of Hobby's concourse in new Levi's with nothing but smiles. She beamed radiantly with a carry-on bag dangling from one shoulder and a new suitcase full of college clothes on the other. They were new purchases in Chicago. Hank had left her another five-hundred-dollars for shopping purposes and she excitedly outfitted herself. Katy hugged her warmly after formal introductions, as Hank had just fetched her from Old Bellville and the German girls, temporarily, to help him settle Shelly in. Brenham Junior College's second summer term was about to start and Shelly was scheduled to enroll. She seemed to be floating on air as her eyes took in the scenes of a busy metropolitan airport. It was a hot and typically humid day in Houston. A regular mid-summer steam bath was in the offing but nothing could dampen Shelly's enthusiasm.

West I-10 carried them to the outskirts of the city, out to Katy's namesake – the town of Katy. It was really a far suburb of Houston with little but concrete and pavement in between. Car dealerships lined the highway and Hank had already, secretly, decided to try and lobby her into a pickup truck. He favored the larger four-door Toyota but a combination Ford-Toyota dealership would provide Shelly with a choice between the two. She didn't need much encouraging to settle for a truck either, but she liked the Ford F150 four-door, short bed. It was all about colors for Shelly and the bright red Ford with luscious grey interior won the day. She cried with joy when Hank handed her the keys.

"Oh, my gosh," she gasped as her hands shakily held on to the new keys. "Is the truck really mine, Hank? Oh, my gosh."

"Ford's a great truck," Katy said enjoying the moment immensely. The kid in Shelly shined brighter than the young adult she really was. Katy always admired that quality in a young person. Not a pretentious bone in her body. No wonder Hank had taken to her.

"Oh, my gosh," she repeated for the third time.

I-10 finally ran into Texas 36 at Sealy and a right exit had them on the road to Bellville and the very next stop, twenty miles farther, was Brenham. Shelly was to check into her dorm room by 4:00 pm, so their schedule was rather tight. Katy rode with Shelly trying to help her navigate in Texas. The dorm director, a very nice elderly lady, had placed Shelly with a second-year student, soon to be a transfer to Texas A&M. She, too, was a farmer's daughter from Waxahachie and was serious about her grades. It would be good grounding for Shelly. Debbie Zorn, the new roommate and Shelly Stark, fresh from Chicago, seemed to hit it off immediately. In only a matter of minutes after settling in, the two new roommates struck out in search of pizza in Shelly's new truck. Hank and Katy laughed as they drove away from the college. It had been fun allowing themselves to be caught up in the giddy excitement of college-age girls.

"I like youth," Kay said beaming. "Dial me back to nineteen

for my return to Old Bellville, Hank. I may be too long in the tooth as a twenty-five-year-old."

Hank cut his eyes towards her not believing his ears. "I think twenty-five suits you just fine. You're still way too full of yourself at twenty-five," he said jokingly.

"Just look at the energy of those two college kids. I wished I'd had the chance to attend college and make something of myself. My dad didn't think it was much of a priority for girls to attend. He was from the old school. It would have been a big deal to me though. I'm sorry he thought that way."

"Well, I went and look at me. I'm just a high-paid military-type always spoiling for a fight."

"Fiddlesticks. That's not true," Katy retorted on the defensive. "You're soft as kitty fuzz, Hank. Gentle as a lamb."

He laughed heartily and Katy joined in. She had a way of reading him differently than most people he knew.

"Hank, you think things will settle down now that ol' Hamilton's out of the way?"

"I sure hope so. I don't want to go goon hunting again in Chicago. I've about had my fill."

"Come stay with me in Old Bellville, Hank. It's such a lovely place. The pace of life is so different, so charming. Yet there's an energy about it. Something I can't put my finger on. In the short time I've been there, they've come to accept me more or less. I lived most of my life, my previous life, in New Bellville on that damned old dusty county road and hardly anyone there ever took me seriously."

"Oh, they took you seriously, Katy. You can trust me to that."

"Hell, they're all scared of me is all. Just a crazy old broad. I couldn't get anyone's attention unless I threatened them or blew something up."

They laughed again. Katy in her familiar habitat started

becoming the old Katy again. She was fun either way but in Old Bellville something softened her, rounded off the rough edges Hank thought. The old stiffness departed as her years rolled back and her youth returned. She always had a special spark about her but the Old Bellville spark was different somehow. Still, there was no such thing as a tamed Katy though, that was for sure. The modern world had heaped a weight on her shoulders she didn't carry lightly. Hank even noticed the difference in himself when he was across the rift. A safe haven of sorts. A port of safety in the stormy seas of cell phones, internet, and the incessant, relentless pounding of television and radio waves. The twenty-four-hour news cycle. Media prejudice. Men and women mixed up about who and what they really were. Just plain steak and potatoes. Old Bellville was the way Hank liked it before pop culture, wokeness, and political correctness started convoluting the system.

"I'll visit you more now," he said, smiling. "Trey and Trent likely will be able to handle things. Hopefully, it will be more peaceable."

Katy had never intimated the great torment she'd suffered while Hank had been in Chicago. When he returned, and she first saw him tying up his horse in front of the bakery, she almost lost it. She squealed so loudly the customers were wondering what had caused the commotion. She ran out to greet him as if he'd been gone a year. Tears of relief filled her eyes as she held on to him on the boardwalk.

"You'll just get tired of me hanging around," Hank said, bringing her out of her thoughts. "I'll probably get on your nerves or just bore you."

"Hank Hargrove, you're anything but boring. I just might get tired of you hanging around too much," she said, laughing and punching his shoulder. "Better watch your step. You might just get run off."

Shelly called them just as they entered the outskirts of Bellville offering left over pizza. No thanks. We're almost thirty miles away but thanks for thinking of us. Just a cute, thoughtful kid about to embark on her new life. So excited she could hardly talk. She'd make something her parents would be proud of Hank figured. He had liked her parents even though his visit had been brief. They were people of the soil. Good, solid, plain folks with callused hands and honest intentions.

INDIAN TERRITORIES WERE primitive lands inhabited by natives on the verge of being herded onto waiting reservations. In the matter of a short generation, the various tribes were losing that which they'd clung to for countless generations – the right to occupy the land of their ancestors. On the second day after the outlaw attack, three skinny braves appeared begging for beef. Buffalo, their mainstay for those many generations, had been almost annihilated by skin hunters and the bleached buffalo bones that littered the prairie bore mute testimony. Northern herds still hung on precariously but the southern herd had been decimated to the point of extinction. Twinks, riding point, had encountered them first and understood their signing. They desired several beeves, they signed, their families were poor and starving. Their hunts had been unsuccessful. The wind had smothered their corn with blowing sand. From the skin and bones that stuck out from under their meager clothing, there was probably more truth to their story than fiction. Orb rode up as Twinks signed back. They had one old musket among them and it appeared far too rusty to be a working firearm. If they were representative of the rest of the tribe, they couldn't put up much of a fight. Their hunting skills had probably grown rusty as the buffalo disappeared. They looked half starved.One brave tried getting too familiar edging in between Twinks and Orb attempting to touch their saddles. Lice were more than likely on the ready to jump ship and settle on fresh meat, so the two of them moved back a safe distance. A crippled steer lingered in the rear each day, usually showing up after dark, so Orb pointed the way and the Indians set out on their bony horses to claim it. Orb followed along and charitably gave them another steer that had wandered in a few days earlier. It was a stray from another herd and carried an unfamiliar road brand. The animal was a large, healthy specimen. They immediately started driving the gift steer seemingly forgetting about hunting the crippled one.

This particular night camp, as a result of the Indian visit, was a lively one with the cowboys jawing about the encounter. Half of the boys hadn't even seen the poor, emaciated braves but that did little to dampen active imaginations. Twinks decided to take advantage of the keen anxieties presented by the redskin visit. Stories of wild Indians and rough old times were bantered around as preparations were made for a poker game. Buster had, by pure luck, found an old dead stump in a nearby ravine so the campfire roared with unusual brightness. The prairie was usually stingy with its wood.

"Again," Twinks said, picking his teeth methodically with the sliver of a sharp green briar, "you boys is getting the drizzles over the wrong thing. Them poor devil injuns ain't dangerous, they're just hungry. Beggars is all. That ol' gun they packed likely wouldn't fire. It's just carried long for show and bluff."

Buster clanged pots and pans in the background letting the boys know that at least someone was still working. Fire sparks danced in the air ten feet above the burning stump spreading fire flies and cinders galore. Bo Davis, the young kid of the outfit, struggled to roll a smoke with only minimal success. He mumbled under his breath as his unskilled hands failed him at each attempt. Bo rode drags with Nevershed and carried a hue of trail dust. He always looked like Buster had just rolled him in flour. No one could guess Bo's true age and even he didn't have a clue. The best estimate was fifteen but the herders weren't known for their skills in age guessing.

"Hell, I'd join a circus if I could guess ages," Twinks said, when John Henry first postulated on Bo's age. When discussions waned around any late night campfire the mystery of the boy's age would usually surface for lack of anything else. It was just something to think on. A little diversion from the ordinary yarns they spun.

H.B. sat against his saddle watching the poker game get started. He enjoyed the intricacies of the betting strategies, especially bluffing. Twinks was a bluffer of the first degree and carried most bluffs to a successful conclusion. His dour expression never changed when cards were in hand. Whereas most of the other men couldn't pull a bluff as their faces were as easy as book pages to read.

"Why, I had a better hand," was the common lament when Twinks cleaned someone out and then let on what he held. Debts were very complicated as Twinks already owned various saddles and most of the tack. Several men just used them, on temporary rental, hoping for a chance to redeem them in a future game. Bo Davis wasn't allowed to participate in the poker games because his skills were minimal and his betting style extravagant. He did watch carefully trying to pick up the game's finer points.

The ever-present breeze of the prairie for some reason ceased this evening as a settling calm prevailed. Orb stayed in tonight, close to the fire, enjoying the comradery of the camp and feeling somewhat relieved over the turn of events. Normally, he patrolled with the first guard and sometimes the second and as a result slept less, on the whole, than even Buster. Actually, his rigid work schedule seemed to agree with him.

"When I was just a sprout, maybe fourteen or fifteen, my Pa and I took a trip out to the west Texas area," Twinks said in a reminiscing mood as he meticulously moved cards around in his hand. "We was starving in Lampassas, very drouthy, nothing to eat for the few cattle we had. He'd heard they was good grass out in the Tom Green country so we struck out. We was on the trail nearly a week, starving ourselves, tryin' to get there. We'd been followin' the banks of the Colorado River but the trouble was there weren't no Colorado River, just pockets of brackish water puddles filled with boilin' nests of cotton-mouths. Hurrah! My Pa said when we finally hit a branch of the Concho, leading to Tom Green, but it wasn't no better. The country was burned up. So poor a chigger couldn't make a proper meal."

Twinks dropped two cards on the discard pile waiting for his turn to draw. Travis Strayhorn, perpetually slow at selecting cards, studied his hand like his life depended on it.

"By late evening, of the third day trailin' the Concho, we found a little cabin, small corrals close to it, and a couple of young settlers holed up inside. It was a hot day in mid-May but they was shut in like a blizzard was blowing. The man of the house seemed talkative enough but the young woman was hollow-eyed and quiet. She had a scary, not-really-there look about her. Anyway, we took a light supper as they looked about starved out. The cabin was stifling hot and the misses stumbled around in a somewhat addled state. Being uncomfortable and as night was falling anyway, my Pa made an excuse to leave but the misses screamed like a scalded cat. The very first sound she made was this weird, shrieking scream. My Pa and I stood paralyzed at the cabin door stunned by her caterwauling."

Travis finally flung his cards down and the dealing continued but interest had been lost in the game. Players and spectators alike paused and waited.

"Well, we walked out and settled our ponies promising the strange woman we'd sleep just outside their cabin walls. Pa wouldn't sleep inside though the misses pleaded with us to. We guessed the young woman was just plumb loco. As we was rollin' out our bedrolls, the man of the house stepped out pulling an old calf hide chair along and flopped down like a fool right next to us. Odd behavior but the evening had already had its share of odd behaviors. Anyway, there we sat cross-legged on our bedrolls wondering what would happen next. We didn't have to wait long. The young settler started telling a story my Pa couldn't give credit to. It was sure some kinda strange tale."

The campfire partisans were quiet as church mice. Twinks glanced at his draw cards as if the poker game had suddenly become his focus. The other players fidgeted nervously some having abandoned their cards on the blanket in apparent disinterest. Orb pulled on his corn cob pipe hoping Twinks would speed his delaying tactics up. Bo Davis sat transfixed, forgetting the need to roll his Bull Durham, his eyes following every move the captain made. Twinks reveled in a captive audience. He was a Ranger by trade but a performing stage actor by nature. Even Buster had stopped his dish rattling and moved closer to listen. Nary a sound could be heard with the exception of the crackling campfire. Twinks moved cards around in his hand arranging and rearranging their order. Finally, after what seemed an eternity to his avid listeners, he cleared his throat and started the story forward.

"Five miles further down the Concho River," the nervous young settler told us with tight lips, "is a family that helped us survive when we first got here a year ago. We had almost nothing but the clothes we wore, not much else. They were a comfortable family with three strapping boys, a large cabin, corrals, barns, and outbuildings. Their cattle were fat and well cared for. They had mules and chickens. Heck they even raised hogs. They were kind enough to loan us one of their milking cows for a season after our old bossy had dried up."

"Thinking back about the generosity of his neighbors, the young settler's emotions got out of hand, momentarily, and his eyes watered," Twinks added. "After a long pause and mumbling quietly under his breath, he was able to continue. "My wife and I rode over to visit them three days ago. We was invited over to eat fried chicken. Margaret, the lady of the house, fried the best chicken I've ever ate. So, we came hungry and looked forward to the visit. What we found has my wife scared clean out of her wits. She mostly just babbles now. I just today heard her talking to her long dead ma like she was sittin' in the cabin with us. She believes ghosts took them. I'm afeared she's losing her mind."

"Tears welled up in the settler's eyes and a quiet sobbing started. My Pa looked my way and feeling sorry for the man carefully put a question."

"'You've not said what you found?'" Pa asked, curious about fate of the family.

"We didn't find anything," he sobbed. "That's just it. We smelled the fried chicken through the open door of their cabin and after calling out and getting no answer we finally just walked in. What we saw was seven plates set and ready on the table. Fried chicken still steaming in a pan on the very same table and hot cornbread, too. Our friends were gone, their boys were gone, all gone. We hollered for them. Checked the barn and outbuildings finding everything just so. I mounted and rode in circles around the place expecting to see signs of a struggle, signs of a kidnapping, maybe Indian sign. There weren't no blood, no unusual tracks, no struggle. We finally left confused and scared leaving the fried chicken to grow cold. We weren't about to touch it! The stock appeared to be okay. His horses, his mules, his hogs, even the chickens seemed to be fine. All his tack was hung up and in order. Even the man's rifle, the six-shooter, the shotgun were all there. Nothing was gone."

"Have you tended to their animals?" my Pa asked suddenly worried about the stock. Penned animals needed looking after.

"No, I haven't been able to leave my wife. She's too fretful, too scared for me to go anywhere."

"Pa told the settler to go in and comfort his wife. Before daylight we pulled out heading down the Concho. Pa suspected Injuns had swept in and snatched them. They was thick as fleas in those days and bold as brass, but he wanted to see it with his own eyes. Sure enough, we found the cabin and what the distraught settler had described to us to be true. Fried chicken was still in the pan growing stale with flies buzzing around, plates still on the table ready for dishing, cornbread dry as a bone, but no human sign. The horses, mules, and hogs sure enough needed tending. We worked around the place for a couple of hours and then Pa and I searched high and low for any sign of the folks. There weren't any. They'd just evaporated, disappeared just like the settler had said. There was no sign of hostiles either. We rode four or five miles in a circle lookin' and never saw a thing. Never cut a trail."

The mysterious disappearance of the settlers had all the cowboys spooked. It was hard to credit such a strange turn of events. Nevershed, usually silent during campfire bull sessions, stood close to Buster and tossed his cold coffee in the surrounding grasses. His high-pitched voice screeched and the jittery men raised their eyes surprised to hear him speak.

"Them was the Ratliffs," he said, with authority slowly shaking his head. "Heard about 'em disappearing back when I was runnin' freight wagons years ago out of Fort Concho. Family just up and vanished just like the captain said. Soldiers out of the fort talked about finding their abandoned cabin and how it had started fallin' apart finally. The fort soldiers never bivouacked anywhere's near the place. Folks say the place is haunted."

Bo Davis checked the shadows behind the chuck wagon feeling the small hairs on the nape of his neck stand up. A chill crept down the length of his backbone feeling like cold water dripped down it. John Henry, already possessed by fears of spooks and specters, felt a strange uneasiness settling in. He cursed himself, silently, for not having left the fire before hearing it. His night dreams oftentimes took the form of nightmares. This incident would only add to his already troubled sleep.

Cody Meyer, not often a participant in storytelling but an avid listener, seemed inspired suddenly to tell his own tale. "My Pa witnessed a disappearance as a young man. He's never forgot it neither. I'm here to tell ya it's the living truth according to him." His beginning lines immediately grabbed his listeners' attention.

"Orb knows about this one. 'Cause it's told as common knowledge around the Lavaca country." Orb nodded his head acknowledging the event Cody was about to tell. He'd remembered hearing about the strange happening years before. "My Pa, just a few months before he married Ma, had attended a barn raisin'. He and about twenty other locals had labored into the middle of the afternoon on the far edges of Lavaca County putting the finishing touches on a family's new barn. The couple and their children were fairly remote in them days, located a good many miles away from their nearest neighbors. The woman of the house was a noted cook so all the men were anxious to volunteer their labor in exchange for her fine vittles. Well, all the men having worked hard all day, crowded in the house at mealtime and lined up to get served. Pa said they were all starvin' hungry. Just as the serving was to begin, she asked her twelve-year-old boy to take two pails out to the well and fetch them full of water. He was barely gone a minute or two when a surprised yell came from outside. The men, so says my Pa, charged out of the house pistols drawn and rifles cocked expecting an Indian attack or something akin to it, but they didn't see no Indians nor no renegades. Nothing unusual. What they saw was one full water pail sitting by the well and the boy and the other pail missing. Several men approached the well fearin' the lad had fallen in. At that very moment a woman's shrill scream came from the cabin's door. The woman of the house had charged out and was pointing up wildly towards the clouds, shrieking in terror. The men all looked up seeing but not believing. Above them, with one pail in hand, was the boy being yanked by some unseen hand into the clouds. One hand was above his head like a rope was attached, while the other hand held the pail and dangled down. In a moment, the boy disappeared silently swallowed up by the grey clouds."

Cody paused a moment catching his breath while the cowboys held theirs. "Well, you can imagine the shock by everyone who was there. The boy's mother collapsed, fainting dead away. The boy's father reached her side eventually, but himself was so addled, he was of no help to her. All the other folks just stood there in total disbelief at what had just happened and what their eyes had seen. The men nervously tried comforting the distraught family but were so confused themselves they were of little help. They eventually left, leaving the meal getting cold on the table. The woman never recovered and never spoke another word. She went stark raving mad and finally starved to death. Her husband later threw himself down the very well his son had been taken from. Thus, leaving their remaining children orphaned."

Cody paused again mildly surprised by his own narrative skills. He had a rapt audience and felt the power of his own words, for the first time in his life. He viewed an engrossed audience and felt the influence he momentarily exercised over them. It was a keen feeling.

He continued. "My Pa, to this very day, refuses to let any child fetch water from our well. Occasionally you can catch 'im lookin' upward, towards the sky, tryin' to make sense of the boy's disappearance. As Orb is my witness, this is a true story as seen by twenty solid citizens of Lavaca County. To this very day, no one has ever seen or heard from the lad who was pulled by some unseen hand into the clouds that day."

The men turned their curious and apprehensive eyes on Orb who dutifully nodded in agreement confirming the story. Orb promptly tapped out his pipe ashes, disappearing into the darkness, and left the cowboys to ponder these two very strange stories. Uncertain eyes glanced around the campfire unsure as to what might lie beyond the fire's glowing ring in the unknown darkness. The Indian incident seemed to be of much lesser importance now. Whole hog disappearances had now taken center stage and there was much to digest, much to contemplate, much to consider around the fire that night. Night herding had instantly grown unpopular again as each hand departed for their duty with a renewed belief that this old world offered many unsolved mysteries. Especially when an innocent youth and even a whole family could simply evaporate suddenly in thin air.

CHAPTER

THIRTY-THREE

Cobb rode through the dark evening and early morning hours placing the north star ahead of him and slightly to his left. This would satisfy the route he wanted to follow to find Dodge City. He felt rested, finally, after the tension-filled night of an agonizing headache and the shock of finding his gang murdered by some unknown assailants. The moon was strong enough to reveal terrain so he gave the gelding his head. The prairie air grew cool in the hour before dawn. As the coolness settled in, he stumbled on a fast-flowing creek. Scrub brush lined the little oasis clinging precariously to creek bed and seemingly holding its own in a place where only the vast prairie grass flourished. Cobb walked his gelding into the creek and sat in his saddle, eying the surroundings. He had no idea the plains were so vast and so empty. A full night in the saddle had been unremarkable by the very fact that the rolling grasslands replaced itself over and over again, mile after mile, with exactly the same country he'd just passed through. The monotony of the terrain had caused Cobb to doze intermittently waking only to realign the north star in its proper position. Had it been cloudy Cobb would have stayed put. The plains, themselves, provided him with no sense of proper direction.

The gelding eased out of the creek bed and he decided to follow it until sunrise since it seemed to roughly parallel his chosen course. Cobb held his mount, now to a cautious walk, as the moon had set and the darkness before dawn made gullies and ravines imperceptible. A simple gopher hole could cripple a horse and being horseless in this vast expanse of nothingness would almost certainly prove deadly.

PEARLY FAKES and his brothers Remus and Roscoe had pulled off the job of a lifetime. They'd pert near wore out their horses getting away from where they'd done it. Word trickled down to them at a faro table in Dodge that a Wells Fargo stage carrying a bag of gold nuggets was trailing its way down from Ogallala, Nebraska. It was bound for Dodge City to be shipped somewhere back east by rail. It was being carried, under heavy guard, from a mining district in North Dakota Territory. Only problem, according to the old geezer who told them about it, was that the Northern Cheyenne were on the warpath and had attacked the stage a few days back killing all the guards with the exception of the driver and the shot gunner. Pearly, the eldest and leader of the Fakes brothers, didn't credit the information as reliable until the old gent produced a rather substantial nugget the stage driver had given him for helping to repair a broken wheel.

"How far back are they?" Pearly asked his mind working fast. His platinum-colored hair at birth had earned him the unlikely Christian name of Pearly. His mama couldn't be convinced to name him otherwise since his almost translucent top not reminded her of the one piece of jewelry she owned and treasured – an heirloom pearl necklace handed down to her by her long-departed mother.

"Three, maybe four days I reckon," the old timer said loosely having had several jiggers of whiskey. "They 'as jist resting thar horses a spell when I seed 'em. Been a long trip I suppose with them Injuns hittin' 'em."

Pearly siddled up to the bar and bought the old toothless coot a bottle of whiskey. Before the old man had downed his last swallow, Pearly, Reemus, and Roscoe Fakes were on the back trail looking for the stage. Two days later they found it.

They rode ahead of the stage route on the bumpy trail where Remus lay down and faked an injury. The stage driver pulled reins looking down at a man in their path appearing to be seriously injured. Remus moaned the most sorrowful of moans. His persistent howling and moaning eventually brought both stage driver and gunner down from their perches to assist. Pearly quickly dispatched them from a nearby clump of brush as they bent over trying to assess the extent of Remus's injury. The brothers had creatively covered the front of his shirt with fresh rabbit blood and the two drivers had easily taken the bait. Two heavy saddle bags full of gold nuggets were found stowed away in the strong box and now, nearly a week later, they were camped on the same little creek Cobb Pickens was following up in the dark morning hour. They had charged south with their ill-gotten booty heading for Texas as fast as their horses could travel. Pearly, always a nervous robber, felt certain they were being followed. His lazy brothers didn't share his fears and slept like dead things each night. After all, the pace of their flight from the robbery had been brutal. This particular morning Pearly was waiting for enough light to move around when he heard the unmistakable sound of an approaching horse. He grabbed for his six-shooter and stayed quiet, waiting, having to listen to the low rumble of his brothers' labored snoring. Sure enough, moments later, the silhouette of a horse and rider appeared on the horizon and Pearly fired away dead certain he was shooting the one who had been following.

Cobb Pickens hadn't suspected campers on the creek and was completely caught off guard by Pearly's first volley. He'd not seen a living soul since leaving the carcasses of his own men rotting in the sun and had no idea he'd blundered into someone's camp. Pearly's first round, fired at close range, struck Cobb high in the right shoulder and Cobb, in half a doze himself, was almost knocked out of his saddle. He grabbed for the saddle horn completely stunned by the sudden gunshot, trying to steady himself. Profanity crossed his lips when a second round left Pearly's revolver and struck the calf of his leg. His horse reared, startled by the sudden explosions and bright flashes, and almost unseated Cobb again as he clawed to stay atop his panicked mount. A third flash in the darkness meant another round was coming. The bullet whistled so close to Cobb's head he could feel the whisper of the lead's passage. Finally, with a valiant effort, he gained a degree of control over the frenzied gelding spurring him into action. A fourth round sang out and as it did Cobb heard yelling men from the camp of his attackers.

In the confusion of the moment, Cobb had been unable to pull his own pistol. When he did finally extract it, he stupidly dropped the gun, fumbling it as his gelding bolted into a wild run. He cursed himself for his carelessness and clung to the rein – his head pounding to the rhythm of his horse's hoof beats. Cobb could feel the warm, sticky blood running down his shirt and a hot stinging sensation in his shoulder. His calf he knew was hit, too, but the only sensation he felt there was numbness. A woozy feeling began to overtake him just as his horse grew winded and slowed its pace. The light-headedness quickly intervened with his already befuddled thinking and clouded his judgment. Try as he might, he couldn't recollect how far back or how long ago, now, he'd been shot. The sun glared in his eyes, by now riding rather high in the sky, when he spotted a grove of trees far ahead. Yet after riding towards them, the grove of trees never materialized and Cobb finally realized that it was only a mirage.

His vision wavered and finally blurred and just as it did an odd thing happened. He woke up from the wavering feeling to find himself on the ground surrounded by tall grasses. There was a strange high-pitched ringing sensation in his ears. Cobb couldn't summon the strength to stand up so he lay where he had fallen trying to clear the cobwebs from his brain. The cobwebs stayed and he passed out again as the ringing in his ears and loss of blood took him away. When he awoke it was to another shock. He was no longer on the ground. The grass had disappeared and the empty prairie with its accompanying mirages had gone the way of the grass.

He awoke in a dirt house, to his consternation, with dirt floors, and the unreal sensation of silty sand trickling down from the low ceiling above. He tried to get his bearings, to make sense of it all, but still his thinking was muddled. He could see well enough but when he attempted the slightest movement his vision blurred and he was forced to lie still. The sod house was quiet, engulfed in silence, but his nostrils picked up the dank, musty smell that only a soddy could produce. He forced, again, the merest of movement and again his eyes lost focus. So, he lay quiet, which was the only way he could lay, trying to replay the timeline of the past day's series of events. Cobb could remember tidbits at best, snippets of scenes but that's all. He clearly recalled the explosions, the flashes of light, of someone firing at him and the sensation of being wounded but that's where his memories faded. Vaguely he recalled lying in tall grasses but couldn't remember when or where or for how long? A dense red fog had settled in his brain and nothing, no matter how hard he tried, seemed to clear it away.

KATY ALLOWED herself only one night in the modern era. She met Trent's brother, Trey for the first time and could instantly tell they made for a very competent security team. Hank wanted the razor wire to disappear from around the immediate vicinity of the house but decided to wait a week or two for further developments. It seemed offensive, suddenly, to have H.B.'s hundred acres looking like a maximum-security prison. Perhaps Hamilton's demise wouldn't deter the thugs he'd already hired. Maybe they'd freelance a hit against the place. Who could fathom the workings of a criminal's mind? Best be wary and plan likewise. The prevailing atmosphere that had dominated for so long, that of imminent and certain attack, had been quashed somewhat. The evening's discussions around the supper table were lighter in mood and joke telling took the place of serious strategic planning. They would not be an easy target with three capable men on patrol. Plus, the sophisticated security equipment had proven to be failsafe for the most part and adequately hardened against most antagonists, short of a howitzer round.

Katy cooked for the hungry men, and happy to do so. She liked watching appetites satisfied and seconds asked for. She appreciated the lavish compliments on her culinary skills and even whipped up two apple pies for dessert. Trey and Trent wandered, with overfull stomachs, to the living room turning on the television in search of an Atlanta Braves baseball game. Hank headed to the kitchen to assist in cleanup. Katy found the private moment with Hank irresistible to lobby for a new life on the old side of the rift.

"Hank, come live in Old Bellville with me," she said, as she dried a frying pan. She left the emphasis rather light, not a demand but a quiet request. Hank wasn't the kind of man you could push too hard, but he could be nudged a bit she thought. She knew he longed for the simple life away from all of the incessant buzzing of electronic gizmos, surveillance cameras, and high-tech wizardry that surrounded H.B.'s estate. She had witnessed, first hand, the peaceful, easy expression that changed his eyes the moment the rift was crossed. He was a different man there, as she was a different woman. It wasn't easy for him to leave his post and she understood that. His commitment to H.B. and Ethan and Lori ran deep and was governed by values the average man wouldn't understand. He ascribed to rules, followed a code of behavior and conduct, and didn't cave to the pressures that brought down so many. However, under all his tough and many layers, Katy knew a gentle spirit lived. After all, men who fought and wore the uniform and ascribed to such values as he did, did so in search of an ultimate peace. In her mind, that peace lived in Bellville now, circa 1885. It was right at his fingertips. Just waiting for his arrival.

"You mean you're inviting me to share your living quarters, Katy?" he teased, wiping bread crumbs off the counter.

"Oh, Hank, take me serious. Trey and Trent can handle this place now. Hell, you've killed off most of the country's more interesting criminals or sent them back in time to God-knows-where. Most of the bad guys with enough salt or stupid enough to try and penetrate this damned fort have been neutralized. I'd say the threat level around here is a pale green at most."

"I admit it's likely to settle down, but there might be another skirmish. We've just got to hunker down and see. Let's be patient, okay Katy?"

Katy wiped a bowl and placed it in the cabinet. Hank cleaned counters and shuffled silverware into the drawer.

"How often will you be coming over?" she asked in all seriousness.

"More than you'll probably like," he answered.

"I doubt that," Katy snapped. "I've managed to tolerate a fair amount of your company."

"Well, you've heard the old saying that fish and company start stinking in three days." They both laughed. Hank could easily find a place in Old Bellville. If not, the hotels always had space Katy thought. Deep down she still feared for his life here at H.B.'s. She'd witnessed too much, heard the sounds of battle, not to feel that way. The place seemed to attract goons like honey attracted flies. The media spin of H.B.'s wealth and reclusiveness had started a death spiral for so many now. A stray bullet could still find the best professional. No one was completely bulletproof.

"Come stay with me, Hank," she said, getting as close to pleading as she dared. "It's where you belong and you know it. Don't be hardheaded like me. You've got more class."

"Katy, you say the darnedest things. I told you I'm coming but it'll take time for this place to settle down. Let's not take any chances. There's too much to risk."

"I hope that includes your own life, Hank. How many times are you willing to risk that?"

H.B.'s mind relived the moment his finger started pulling the trigger against their would-be assailants. He recalled, vividly, the cursing, drunken men as if it was replayed in slow motion as they died in their bedding, lying exposed, totally unaware of what was happening under the innocent moonlight. They never stood a chance against the withering firepower that was delivered that early morning. The right and wrong of it plagued his mind no matter how busy he was herding rebellious steers along. Almost more surprising than the attack itself, was the way, he himself had reacted to the incident. How moments before the fighting started his own mind cleared and the butterflies that crawled and wiggled in his stomach just magically dissipated. His own reaction, his psychological and physiological toughening had appeared at the very last moment. That which paralyzed him instantly swept away. It was a phenomenon he'd never experienced. So, the intricacies of the event and his emerging as a full participant played out continually in his mind.

Certainly, he had faced life and death decisions in situations before. Three years of surgical residency and many months as a trauma surgeon trimmed away, eventually even hardened, his reaction to the near-dying and desperately injured. The turf was different in the emergency room. The choices different. The surgeon's charge was to save not destroy life...to do all within ones power to prevent death. Yet, here, he had crossed the line forever it seemed. Made the decision, assisted even, in the decision of others to take out men he didn't know nor had ever met. It was the kind of thing that hung around in a man's mind no matter how busy the body was. A cantankerous steer could never eliminate his thoughts of culpability in the whole matter. Justification was the problem. Like a black and white steer who constantly challenged him this day. It was in one sense black and white. The black side being a dark and dastardly deed profiting no one. Sin in its purist form. The white side being noble and necessary to prevent future loss of life and to save a valuable herd. A purely preventative measure. The two arguable sides of the issue could never be fully reconciled in H.B.'s way of thinking. It was an enigma. One he would likely never sort out.

CHAPTER
THIRTY-FOUR

L um and Etta Haney walked into their sod house and found Cobb conscious, for the first time in three days. They had moved him to their bed when they first brought him in after carefully tending to his wounds. Etta had made a pallet for them on the floor, near their patient, so she could monitor his condition. His blood loss had been copious. So severe, in fact, that at first little hope was held out that he would survive. He made it through the first day, then the second, and now appeared to have awakened from his deep sleep. Etta quickly walked over to him surprised and thankful to see that his eyes had finally opened. Lum walked in the door carrying a basket filled with vegetables to their rough plank table.

Etta looked into his face still seeing Cobb's glassy stare but yet she caught a glimmer of awareness in his eyes. She bent over, close to his face, and whispered softly. Then he blinked his eyes, one time, slowly, appearing to have heard her voice. There was some measure of understanding. Yes. Yes, he was coming back. She was now sure of it.

It was Cobb's paleness that had frightened them. He'd lost so much blood when they found him and he seemed perilously close to death, and for the past three days she'd tried feeding him broth unsuccessfully. She had carefully raised his head, meticulously patient in her efforts, and placed spoon after spoon in his mouth only to watch it dribble back down his chin. Etta had finally cried in frustration. She had nursed many wounded and sick creatures back to health but yet this wounded man, who desperately needed sustenance to survive, refused to swallow. Oh, but now he was awake. Maybe now she could get him to take her precious, life-giving broth.

Cobb saw the woman's face, leaning over so close, even heard her speak but didn't feel compelled to reply. Her sweet smell so close to his nose even overwhelmed, momentarily, the musty smells of the sod cabin. He stared at the ceiling seeing only dirt staring back. He wanted to be away from here. He didn't want any damn sodbuster's help. He cursed himself, silently, for having gotten into such a predicament. His growing hatred succeeded in wresting his mind further awake, but he didn't let on. He'd hold on to himself.

Etta instructed Lum to build a fire and soon heated the broth. She came to Cobb with a bowl filled and spooned, carefully, a portion into his mouth. He swallowed. Not that he really wanted to, but because the reflex seemed to require it. Etta was tender but forceful in her insistence and Cobb responded mostly through thirst and the sensation that he'd choke if he didn't swallow. Her persistent patience overcame his feeble resistance. Soon the bowl of broth disappeared. She tenderly placed his head back on the corn shuck pillow and seemed genuinely thrilled at her success. Cobb lay still fighting the urge to curse aloud, shout profanities at the damned sod ceiling and the sod busters within. She'd won this time. One for the soddies. They better damn well not get used to victory. It wouldn't last for long.

TWO DAYS later and after too damned many bowls of soup and broth to count, Cobb shocked his caregivers by managing to sit up on the edge of their bed. They had been outside for a spell doing chores, he guessed. His efforts to get up from the prison of their bed had been rewarded. Cobb peered up at Etta as she shuffled to him with a look of concern on her face. Inwardly he sneered at her approach but he forcefully controlled cursing the woman. She was a beauty and to some extent her good looks helped settle his hate.

"I felt good to move," he said, looking around the room not wanting to look directly into those caring eyes. At first when he sat up things grew fuzzy for a few moments but the fuzziness just as quickly departed. He looked over at the man and saw him fussing over his vegetables again. A sodbuster's dream. A field and a vegetable garden. Watching the ass end of a mule all day. It for sure and certain wasn't Cobb's idea of a good time.

"Please take it easy," Etta cautioned. "Don't try to do too much."

"I'd like to walk," Cobb said, suddenly and started trying to get up. Lum dropped the basket and rushed over to steady Cobb. He was able to stand momentarily, with great effort, and then flopped back down on the pallet exhausted. The fuzziness returned and then faded again. Cobb wanted to curse but held it in. The couple stood above him with looks of concern on their faces. Cobb felt bound, in a sense, but couldn't conjure up a single warm emotion for the young couple who seemed determined to help. They may or may not have saved his life but he'd be damned if he was going to be beholden to a couple of stinking sodbusters.

"I'm Lum," the young farmer said, "and this is my wife Etta." Cobb already knew their names from eavesdropping on their conversations. He'd faked sleep, even fainting spells, to listen in to their private talks.

Cobb nodded his head but didn't say his name in return. They finally let him be after a few moments.

They fed him a supper of chicken soup and boiled potatoes. His appetite was sharper and she offered him corn bread of which he ate an ample amount. Cobb could hardly keep his eyes off the young female farmer. Her hair was the color of corn silk with eyes as blue as the sky. Her lips were full with the upper lip slightly up curled. She had her hair tied back in a pony tail and her skin was a reddish golden brown. She had fine lines, Cobb thought, and were she a mare she'd be the most stylish one in the corral. He watched, observing Etta unabashedly in total disregard for what Lum might think. All Lum did was chew the dry corn bread and wash it down with creek water – the whole time a vacant look on his stupid face. How did this yokel rate such a beauty? Where had he stumbled on to such a prize? A sporting girl with her looks in woman-hungry Dodge could make a man rich right quick. He couldn't get rid of that thought. She'd be a real money-maker.

Over the next couple of days Cobb's strength returned and he was able to walk around the little dirt-floored soddy and even walked out to check on his horse. He was glad to see the animal was uninjured. Lucky to have not been hit by the wild gunfire. Etta fretted constantly and Cobb returned her thoughtfulness by tossing dark, insolent looks her way. He didn't give a damn for a fretting woman especially one who thought she was his own personal caretaker. When they were outside working, Cobb rifled through their meager belongings looking for a gun or anything else of value. He found neither but did find, finally, a rather nice gold watch in working order. The couple, with all that Cobb could see, owned a total of two mules, one old shovel-nosed plug of a horse, three pigs, and a few dozen chickens. Slim pickings but what the hell. They were sodbusters. They never expected much. Lum spent most of the long, hot mid-summer days grubbing and pulling stumps while Cobb watched his young wife with growing interest.

Cobb's major concern was he couldn't find a gun. How could anybody be outside a settlement some distance or within one for that matter without a gun? At least they should have a varmint gun. Finally, as the days passed, Cobb found an old wooden box under the couple's bed and inside it lay a rusty shotgun and a dozen shells. His first impulse was to take the gun and immediately kill the two sodbusters and be done with it, but he decided to wait a few days more. Bide his time and wait for his strength to return.

Cobb's restlessness, nonetheless, grew after the discovery of the shotgun. His insolent looks had slowed Etta's fretting but not stopped it. The mother hen in Etta irritated Cobb to no end. The wounds, Cobb knew, were more superficial than serious with the shoulder wound being the one that had bled him out. As the long hours passed, Cobb hatched a plan to kill Lum outright and force Etta to go with him to Dodge. He finally scotched the idea as her witness to the murder, even in lawless Dodge, could hang him. The beauty of Etta and her shapeliness clouded his judgment. He knew he couldn't kill her easily because of her beauty, but if Lum suffered an accident of some kind the door would be opened for Cobb. The problem was arranging an "accident."

As the afternoon wore on and Cobb racked his brain trying

to figure out an accident scenario, something happened that solved his dilemma. Cobb was inside the cabin thinking so hard that his brain hurt when a loud ruckus outside caught his attention. He heard Etta scream, the sound long and filled with anguish. Cobb hurried outside to see the reason. Etta was running towards Lum seeing him wrapped in a mass of tangled reins and being drug, tumbling over and over, by a frightened mule team. Cobb figured, at first, the mules would stop on their own. After all, they were prone of laziness, but Etta's frenzied screaming seemed to spur on the runaway mules. Lum's body appeared loose and rolling; he was apparently unconscious from the dragging. The plow flopped and tumbled along still hitched to its tethers. The sight was humorous to Cobb and fraught with opportunity and he laughed, under his breath, as he watched the scene unfold. Cobb watched the frenzied mules, flopping plow, and the unfortunate farmer disappear over the edge of the field and into a wooded area. Etta had fallen to her knees in the middle of the field sobbing and wailing in desperation. Cobb walked slowly back to their tumble-down old shed with a plan forming in his head. He deliberately took his time getting his bridle and saddling his horse. The woman's screams and sobs continued. Finally, he swung up and rode past Etta and her wailings and headed towards the woods. She stood up as he passed wiping her wet, tear-stained face with her sleeve. Cobb ignored her. The last thing he wanted to do was deal with a hysterical female.

A half mile down a long sloping hill and a couple of hundred yards in the woods, Cobb found the two mules standing peaceful-like fluttering their long, floppy ears. Still tangled in the reins lay the semi-conscious sodbuster moaning in low tones. His breathing was regular and his eyes open but he looked stunned, at least temporarily, by the ordeal. Cobb, a plan already hatched in his twisted mind, looked around after he dismounted and seeing no witnesses, other than the distant figure of a distraught woman, tightly placed his hand over the nose and mouth of the injured farmer and clamped down. Lum was too feeble to put up much of a fight over his smothering. He raised his arms, grappled with Cobb's hands weakly, but soon succumbed to his loss of oxygen. Cobb kept his tight grip until the death twitches ceased. There, he thought, satisfied with his effort. The problem was solved. Etta was now free to go with him. What a splash she'd make in Dodge. She'd be worth far more than a damned troublesome cattle herd anyway. A broad smile cracked his face as he remounted and headed towards Etta trying with supreme effort to twist his beaming smile into a troubled and sympathetic frown.

JESSIE MADELYN CORLEY looked in the mirror and was pleased with what she saw. Her face had filled out and browned in the hot Texas sun as she spent more and more time weeding her late planted garden. Elsa continued to warn her about the imminent failure of the enterprise, but regardless of her criticisms the vegetables were growing quite nicely. For some reason the early summer's heat had given way to a more moderate, and thankfully, a rainy mid-summer. Though rare for Fort Worth, the combination of cool and wet that is, Jessie welcomed it with open arms. She didn't necessarily want to prove Elsa wrong in her prognostications, she just wanted to prove she could succeed at something she'd never tried before. Even Paula Jane slipped out occasionally to assist in the venture. Unfortunately, getting past Elsa's watchful eyes proved to be difficult.

Paula Jane's hormones were on a tear so she talked nonstop about the things any young, insecure teenaged girl would talk about. She wasn't necessarily boy crazy but they certainly were shadowy forms dancing in the background of her mind. Soon enough they would erupt into flesh and blood lads and have to be dealt with. Jessie was far from being an expert on men. Oh, she'd had a visit or two from potential beaus in the past but nothing very serious. Her pursuers were mainly silly boys unable to figure out the finer art of courting and romance. Then the dreaded disease had struck. Tuberculosis had taken the front seat in all of her affairs – boys or business. Now the magic pills H.B. had left had robbed the disease of its power and it lay in retreat. She wheezed no more. Coughed no more, and she felt healthy and whole again. As complete as a young woman should feel at the ripe age of twenty-three. Ah, yes, her age was another sore spot for Elsa. Hearing Elsa talk about it you'd think she was ancient. Over the hill. Men want young women. You've waited too long she warned. You'd best get out and look around. Beggars can't be choosers you know. Jessie knew she wasn't going to throw herself at the first eligible man that came along – no matter what Elsa said. There needed to be a friendship, a feeling. Tell Elsa that and you might as well be talking to a stump. Elsa's fletching drove the arrow straight to the heart of every matter. The world to her was, in fact, black and white, even when it came to men.

Dr. Fields came hobbling out to the garden wiping his brow as the sweat poured down his face. He smiled at Paula Jane and frowned slightly at Jessie.

"Jessie, it's too hot out here. Sunstrokes aren't all that

uncommon young lady. They've killed full-grown, healthy men you know."

"Well, I'm a full-grown healthy woman, Dr. Fields. Surely you know that women have more stamina than men." Jessie didn't know any such thing but she enjoyed floating ideas around. Who knew for sure? She was sure the good doctor wasn't an expert in the field. Though he may proclaim to be.

Paula Jane piped in. "She rests in the shade sometimes doctor. I fetch her water when she asks me."

Dr. Fields' eyebrows knitted together not convinced in the least of Jessie's safety. The young woman had been deathly ill just over two months ago, and now she's out here slaving away in a vegetable garden hoeing weeds? To what end? It couldn't be good for her this early in her recovery.

"Jessie, take a break will you? It is miserably hot right now. The garden will survive without you tending it for a spell." His pleading, concerned expression encouraged her movement to the nearest shade tree. She daubed her forehead to keep the sweat from stinging her eyes. Dr. Fields and Paula Jane followed her over jockeying for position under the scant shade of a small mesquite. Dr. Fields' breathing was rapid like he was the one who'd been chopping weeds. Elsa suddenly peered out the back door watching the group loitering under the shade tree. She'd been busy, in the hot kitchen, preparing supper and her temper was perking along, too, slightly hotter than the outside air temperature. She called, with a touch of anger aimed at Paula Jane who ran quickly and guiltily in Elsa's direction. The door slammed and Paula Jane disappeared inside. Elsa raised her chin, angled her head upward in a delicate movement of chagrin, gathered up her skirts, turned and grandly swept back into the kitchen. Dr. Fields remained under the thin shade sweating profusely under thick layers of both clothes and fat. Elsa's cooking and his keeping the cork in the bottle had caused him to fattened up like a gopher.

"Elsa's looks could sure freeze water," Dr. Fields pronounced looking somewhat worse for the wear. His clothes were rumpled and creased. His hat was sweated through. Over the course of the past several weeks his medical practice had blossomed due to his sobriety and a very small, white lie. Sober he possessed excellent bedside manners and the pressures of the practice had mounted. He was noted as a Yankee practitioner, up on all the latest medical developments. Unbeknownst to Jessie, he had quietly claimed at least partial credit for her remarkable recovery and new-found health. He secretly hoped the tall, young, gifted physician who'd given Jessie the miracle pills would soon return. Tuberculosis patients were lining up now expecting something similar to Jessie's medical miracles. Yet he had nothing more to offer really but his tired old tonics and a dose of strong encouragement. His ruse wouldn't last forever. He'd be found out, and his patient's expectations were growing daily.

"She can be difficult," Jessie admitted.

"I sure hope young doctor H.B. returns soon," he said, wistfully looking towards the house but only seeing trouble in his future. "I surely can use some of those pills he gave you."

"I counted today. I still have just over a hundred left and feel great. Take what I've got."

"I'll not do that," Dr. Fields answered firmly. "Those are yours. After all, you said he told you to take them all. You're still taking them, right?"

"Yes, but I'm sure I'm over the worst. Maybe they could help someone who needs them more than me."

"Jessie, those pills were meant for you and only you. He'll be along soon, I'm sure. You'd better follow H.B.'s advice. He knows what he's doing."

Mentioning H.B. struck a chord in Jessie's heart. A feeling of regret settled down over her There were words left unsaid between them and if he ever returned, they would be spoken. She had quietly sworn an oath to herself in that matter. Her severe illness, at the time, was an excuse she used for being thoughtless, but she knew the real truth. She missed his tender, caring voice as he read during those long hours to her in the confines of her dank and dreary bedroom. He was there during her lowest moments, her worst time. Patiently tending to her as she quickly approached her end. He was kind. Always positive. Encouraging her when death seemed to be pulling her away. Oh, yes. She longed to see him again. Jessie would make her feelings known to him.

CHAPTER

THIRTY-FIVE

I n matters of Indians and thieving renegades, things seemed to settle a bit. Stream crossings stepped front and center and were another matter entirely when it came to trailing cattle. The Washita River proved to be deep yet narrow and had amazingly steep, slick banks to clamor up. It wasn't out of bank but freshets in the high country had it surging. After the Washita came the North and South Canadian streams and they offered their own special version of "hell" on the range. The South Canadian proved to be the most cantankerous and dozens of cattle bogged in its bottoms. Orb stated the river would "bog" a saddle blanket and the statement proved accurate. Hours of labor were required to free the cattle from its sandy suction pits. Finally, after wallowing in the mud for half a day, all but an unfortunate few were safely across and Orb managed a smile again.

The miles passed under the steers' long legs and with the exception of tricky water crossings the range was open and lush. The weather, mid-summer now, was hot with skies blue and prairies so endless it strained your eyes to try and see

363

across. Mirages danced their dance of deception floating up hither and yon as the sun's heat reformed the distant landscape. Lakes appeared and disappeared just as quickly. Trees dotted the skyline temporarily only to be gobbled up by the grassland's endlessness. Buster cursed and swore having to burn buffalo crap for firewood, barely scraping together enough dry tinder to cook coffee and meals. The mood was light amongst the hands, finally, having made it unscathed through the unpredictable Indian Territory. The land of beyond, the land of the Shining Mountains seemed more accessible now. The Blackfoot Agency in Montana wasn't so much a distant dream but a potential reality. There were miles and miles yet to go, incredible spaces to cross, but why not celebrate the distances already traveled. Optimism wasn't such a bad thing now, was it? Moods and cowboys are changeable critters. A dark cloud loomed on the horizon and it wasn't in the form of a coming prairie thunderstorm.

Twinks Brady riding point scouted ahead several miles when Orb was taken away on another mission. This happened to be one of those days. A cloud of dust had been spotted in the rear of the Circle M herd, several miles back, so Orb had taken it upon himself to ride the back trail and see who followed. He had left just after Buster clanged the dinner bell and wasn't expected back until well after dark. Cody's natural position was on the west side of the herd, in the front point position and he first saw Twinks charging towards him waving his hat excitedly. Cody's impulse was to ride out and meet him halfway but decided better of it. The cattle were calm and docile yet anything out of the ordinary could change a fickle herd. So, he sat in his saddle watching Twinks flail away at his horse's flanks racing his way. Twinks blew in at full steam throwing a cloud of dust and dirt clods as he dragged his mount to a halt.

"Bugs is comin'," he said, in a near panic with both his and his horse's eyes rolling. "I ain't never seen nothin' like it."

"Bugs?" Cody asked incredulously. Twinks was the steadiest hand he knew. What the heck was going on here? He'd heard a few strange pronouncements in his time but this one beat all. He couldn't make any sense of it.

"Best circle the steers and get 'em stopped," Twinks yelled as he spun his sweated horse around not waiting for Cody to ask questions. "Doubt they'll like what's comin'. Slow 'em down, Cody. I'll ride on and tell the rest of the boys."

With this cryptic explanation he spurred his lathered steed and bolted away. Cody sat puzzled a moment, wiping his brow with a dusty sleeve, watching Twinks fade into the distance. Travis Strayhorn galloped over with a tight look on his worried face.

"What's happening?" he shouted as he pulled up showing the beginnings of a panic.

"Not sure," Cody said. "The captain said something about bugs. Said to stop the herd."

"Bugs?" Travis said his eyes casting about wildly in the direction Twinks had ridden in from. After a few moments of hard looking, he did see something. It was on the distant horizon and growing larger by the minute. It was something odd indeed. A gyrating mass of a cloud yet it didn't seem to be a cloud at all. Its bottom was dark and foreboding yet immediately above it was a perfectly clear sky. How could that be? Travis thought. Watching closely, it wiggled and spun and turned strange circles like a living thing.

"Good God Almighty," Travis shouted in a startled voice. Cody pivoted his horse to see. "Looka yonder."

Cody stared in mute disbelief. It took a moment before the realization bore in. He was looking at a moving wall of insects. Mountains and mountains of bugs swirling like a prairie whirlwind towards them. They filled the horizon from west to east and they were moving towards them at breakneck speed. He'd heard tell of such happenings but never thought he'd witness the event first hand. Cody froze, momentarily, then quickly tightened his hat string and pulled his reins up tight.

"Grasshoppers," he yelled as he spurred his horse into action. "Come on, Travis. Let's try turnin' the leaders and circle 'em. We best get a move on."

MILLIONS AND MILLIONS of grasshoppers descended on the cowboys and the herd, in biblical proportions. Buster battened down the chuckwagon in a desperate attempt to make it grasshopper proof, but nothing could be. Any crack, any slight entry and they wiggled through assuming proprietorship by the fact of their sheer numbers. Buster covered, closed, shoved and pushed things around to protect the foodstuffs and cooking ware from invasion, but they invaded anyway. Finally, defiled and discouraged, Buster simply crawled on the wagon seat to wait out the indignity of it all. When he sat down on the seat, scores of grasshoppers crunched under his buttocks. To hell with 'em, he thought pulling his handkerchief over his face for protection. Hoppers covered Buster, his hat, his handker-chief, his arms and hands and legs. The wagon sheets were black with them. The prairie was black with them. The sky was black with them. The mule team suffered the plague by twisting their floppy ears in vain attempts to loosen the crit-ters, but it did little good. A thousand replaced the thousand they shook free.

Cody and Travis turned the leading steers and started the

cattle milling just as the cloud of grasshoppers arrived. The steers, though restless at first, accepted the fate of the bug cloud like all other unfortunates caught up in their path. They kicked and pitched and shook but found their efforts unrewarded. The hoppers covered the steers, by the thousands, from hock to head munching away with their ravenous appetites. Cody and Travis sat together, covered with the confounded critters, feeling completely helpless. Things on the prairie, Cody thought in utter frustration, had a way of taking over a body as he flapped his arms in circles trying to dislodge the grasshoppers. They seemed to be consuming the very fabric of his shirt. Rivers, thunderstorms, wind, quicksand, rattlesnakes, Indians, and bad men waited in the tall grasses for the unwary. Rough trails, narrow ravines, deep gullies, rocky outcroppings, dust storms, and cantankerous and stampeding steers competed for your attention. Each time a peaceful moment seemed at hand, a new malady, a different challenge, a new threat waltzed in. To relax a little and smell the roses was a sure invitation for another of the trail's many dooms to unfold before you. It kept the cocky somewhat humble, and lest you forget, the innocent gopher hole and a stray lightning bolt were always possible. Nature had its way of being peaceful one moment and a tyrant the next. The grasshopper plague was just another calamity in its bag of many tricks.

H.B. sat astride Pretty Boy witnessing the world's take over by grasshoppers. The Bible's reference of the locust plagues came to mind. He snugged his hat down tight and drew the tie cord tight. Pretty Boy seemed resigned to endure it. He shook his head, stomped his hooves, and shivered his hide trying to dislodge the creepy crawlers. H.B. tightened his bandana around his face, finally, to keep the hoppers from entering under the brim of his hat. The steers stopped walking and moseyed in half circles trying to figure out which way to face the plague. The steer's stringy tails switched in vain attempts to fling the millions of trespassers away, but the trespassers stayed and kept increasing in numbers. They grew so thick that H.B. had the strong sensation of smothering. The bright shining daylight ceased to shine, turning strangely dark. The sky and soil and air became literally choked with bugs. The grinding noise of their mandibles and their buzzing wings sang like a stiff prairie wind.

Then, in what seemed several hours but was perhaps only thirty minutes, the light reappeared slowly. When H.B. could see a slight distance in front of him, he was shocked to see the grass was gone. Only a short stubble remained of what had been eighteen-inch tall, lush prairie grasses. Thousands of grasshoppers were still present where millions had been. The toll of their passage was the destruction of anything edible. H.B. noted several holes in his shirt sleeves where the grasshoppers had chewed through. The steers sniffed at the ground curious about the hoppers that remained yet puzzled that their food supply had so rapidly disappeared. Cody finally rode over shaking bugs from his hat.

"You ever seen anything like this in all your born days?" he asked, picking bugs loose from his horse's mane. Every step of the horse's hooves crunched as if they were walking on egg shells.

"Can't say I have," H.B. answered removing his bandana. A grasshopper crawled under his hat brim and he grabbed it and slung it away. In the distance, they could see Buster knocking bugs off the wagon sheets with a stick. His efforts were being rewarded somewhat but hundreds remained locked and holding. His cursing was inaudible at the distance but his moving lips betrayed his unending use of expletives. Twinks rode up shaking his head.

"Wonder what's next?" he asked sticking his finger through a fresh hole chewed in his shirt. "I guess we're lucky the herd didn't stampede. They were as dumbfounded as we was."

Cody continued pulling hoppers from his horse's mane and H.B. did the same for Pretty Boy. The skies were beginning to gain sunlight and look blue again. The sun took on the glint of a normal mid-afternoon.

"There's a little creek a mile or two ahead," Twinks said, pointing north. "Maybe there's enough grazing for the night. Ain't enough here to feed a herd of jackrabbits. Cody, you and H.B. and Travis head 'em that way. I'm gonna get Buster settled down and we'll be along. I saw a little stand of dead wood there. Pile it up for Buster. He seems a mite frazzled."

ORB ARRIVED after midnight wearing a long face. H.B. had just come in from night guard and saw him standing with Buster at the fire. H.B. unsaddled, turned Pretty Boy loose in the remuda and walked to the fireside. He needed a stout cup of Buster's coffee to shake a bothersome headache. Orb was talking in low tones as H.B. poured his coffee.

"He lost his other son last year. He drowned crossing the Canadian," Orb was telling Buster. "This boy's all he's got left."

H.B. took a sip of coffee hoping the caffeine would go to work quickly. Coffee was usually a sure cure for him. Orb raised his eyes to H.B. with a questioning expression. He had a pained look on his face like he had a toothache working.

"Buster tells me, H.B., that you mentioned being a doctor. I kinda take what a man says to another man as a private matter and I'm sorry to ask. There's a boy bad hurt in the herd behind us and most likely he's dying. Do you know something about doctoring?"

H.B. took another pull from his battered tin cup and slowly nodded. As much as he wanted to stay away from being Horace Bascom, M.D., he wouldn't hide from the truth. If he could help a seriously injured young cowboy he'd do so willingly.

"Yes, I'm trained somewhat in medicine. What happened?"

"Well, the damn grasshoppers spooked a cowboy's horse and he got throwed and gored by a steer. He's lost a passel of blood and got a big hole in his side. I doubt he's got a chance but anyway, I had to ask."

"We've got to leave immediately," H.B. said, taking another swallow. "Time is of the essence. How far back is their herd?"

"No more'n ten miles, maybe less. I'll guide you if you're willin' to go."

"I need the bags out of the wagon, two of them in fact. We'd better get going."

Orb carried the largest bag and at first his mount balked at the unaccustomed burden. His mare finally accepted it begrudgingly. They rode through the stillness of the early morning hours still hearing the crunching sounds of the left behind grasshoppers under foot. Orb told of the trail boss, Gene Terry, and his elder son, Alex's drowning this summer past on the Canadian. Gene Terry was from Bexar County, Texas, an acquaintance of Orb's, and was bound for Ogallala with two thousand heifers, cows, and a mix of breeding bulls. It was a starter herd for a determined rancher in Wyoming Territory. Bill, Gene Terry's remaining son, was the cowboy who'd been injured in the mishap. It was pushing two in the morning when H.B. and Orb arrived. A hat-sized fire still burned near the chuckwagon. Some cowhands loitered near it speaking in hushed tones. A lantern hung from the wagon lighting a man leaning over near the injured boy apparently trying to comfort him. H.B. quickly dismounted pulling his bag with him. Both bags were rather weighty and full of medical gear and supplies. In moments H.B. was beside the young man placing an LED headlight over his head. Luckily, his own headache had dissipated thanks to Buster's potent brew. Gene Terry, the boss, stood next to Orb amazed at the emitting headlight and wiping tears from his eyes. The background whispering of the other cowhands ceased as they watched fascinated by the unusual display of light.

H.B. opened, cut away, and soon had a close look at the extent of the injury. Bill Terry breathed rather shallow, short puffs but was lucid and responsive. A makeshift bandage covered the gore in his side and oozed blood. His loss of blood was critical. He needed an immediate transfusion. The cow's horn had penetrated deeply, too, likely tearing internal organs in its path. Surgery was a necessity but near impossible under the primitive conditions, but it had to be done if the boy was to have any chance at all.

"Orb," H.B. said standing up. "I need all the men to line up and give blood samples. This boy needs a blood transfusion immediately. I need the chuck table covered with a sheet so we can place the young man on it. He requires immediate surgery."

Although Orb had grown accustomed to H.B.'s strange way of talking, he still was puzzled. He'd never heard the word "transfusion" and taking blood samples from other hands seemed highly irregular. Gene Terry snapped to and took control of the situation and lined up the cowboys as H.B. requested. Some of them complained about the procedure but complied when Gene threatened their firing. Thankfully, the boy's blood type matched two of the hands, including Gene Terry's, so H.B. started drawing three pints of much needed blood. The rest of the Terry's hands were dumbstruck, standing at a safe distance with unbelieving expressions. The flashing LED light and plastic canisters filling with other men's blood seemed extremely queer and highly irregular.

The surgery took just over two hours. H.B. worked with deft and steady hands. The trained trauma surgeon in him took over and he sailed through the work with a precision that even surprised himself. Orb was his assistant doing what he could do to pass the instruments that he knew nothing about. He watched H.B.'s skills in surgery with total awe and a growing respect. There was no longer any doubt in his mind that this tall cowboy knew something about medicine. In all his considerable years of experience, he'd never heard of siphoning one man's blood and draining it into another one. Plus, H.B. had several IV's, he called them, flowing and attached to the kid's arms emptying other strange liquids from small, clear bags into his body. It made for a mighty unusual sight. Gene Terry stood numbly by with his hands occasionally massaging his temples out of concern and fear for his son's life. He had already made a vow to himself that if he ever got his boy home safely, he'd never ride and boss another herd. There was plenty of ranching to be done in Bexar County without chousing these ornery horned beasts to points up north. This damned trail had already extracted from him far more than he could bear.

H.B. carefully stitched closed the wound, checked the boy's vital signs and walked to the fire a moment. He needed to clear his head and Gene offered him a fresh cup of coffee, following close at his heels. H.B. could see questions in his expression.

"Could I ask about his condition?" he queried almost apologetically.

H.B. had been trained not to overstate nor understate anyone's condition especially after a complicated surgery. However, only a six-inch section of the small intestine had been torn and the spleen slightly damaged. Other than that, the boy's insides had fared remarkably well considering the nature of the injury. Infection was H.B.'s major concern but with antibiotics that concern could be negated somewhat. He had a positive feeling about the lad. He was young and strong, a likely candidate for a full recovery.

"I feel he's going to be okay. The first couple of days will tell the tale. He'd lost a lot of blood and had a fair amount of internal bleeding. That's under control now and he appears to be stable. Overall, the surgery went very well."

"You think he'll be okay then?" Gene pressed again. His fatherly face was wrought up in worry.

"Yes," H.B. answered firmly. "My belief is that your boy will recover in time."

FOUR DAYS later H.B. left Gene Terry's camp to catch up with the Circle M herd. Orb had held up two days waiting and finally left, promising short drives. Gene Terry pumped H.B.'s right hand so hard when he left, he had felt a twinge of pain in his elbow. Bill Terry was recovering in splendid fashion. H.B. had left specific instructions regarding the boy. Gene would rest his herd another week before departure and only then for short drives. Bill would ride on a cushioned bed inside the chuck-wagon per his instructions. Pill form antibiotics were to be given for a month. The boy's color and vital signs were normal. H.B. didn't want him in a saddle for at least another month.

Patty Cake hit her stride and moved into her traveling gait. Gene Terry had given H.B. an additional horse for his medical gear and the gelding followed behind obediently, tethered to the saddle. By the end of the first day's ride, H.B. saw lounging cattle in the distance and the Circle M herd was just settling onto bed ground. H.B.'s appetite was piqued and Buster's stew tasted remarkably good. Orb welcomed him back with a grateful handshake while inquiring about young Terry's health.

"He'll be fine," H.B. said, working a mouthful of stew in his jaws. "They're sticking for another week before moving out. Bill needs a bit more rest."

CHAPTER

THIRTY-SIX

E tta turned crazy with grief. She had a wild demented look about her that set Cobb's teeth on edge. He'd scratched around the shed and found an old wagon sheet for wrapping the sodbuster's body in. He then attached the sheet to the traces using the mules for pulling. Etta followed along crying and carrying on the whole way. She shrieked at Cobb to stop if even if the slightest bump was encountered. Hell, Cobb thought, the man's dead. What can he feel? The half mile ordeal of dragging the body pushed Cobb beyond enduring as he had had no experience whatsoever in the finer art of dealing with a profoundly grieving woman.

"Slow down, slow down," she screamed over and over as they covered the route. "You're hurting my husband." The high-pitched, cutting sound of the scream unnerved Cobb to no end. Once in front of the soddy, Etta fell to her knees and pawed the dirt slinging soil into the air like a mad woman. Cobb fought her not to reopen the wagon sheet, to display the corpse, but her persistent wailing finally wore him down. Once opened, she fell on the body and would not leave it. Tears streaked new paths down her dirty cheeks and dripped onto Lum's stiffening body. She finally lay down beside the corpse, snuggling close as if she was bedding down and sobbed quietly with her arms entwined with his. The scene gave Cobb the creeps and he walked away to unhitch the mules cursing such foolishness under his breath. He could feel his own patience wearing thin, mighty thin. He had about made up his mind to just shoot the damn woman and kick them both into a shallow hole.

The long afternoon finally passed and darkness began to fall when Cobb reentered the soddy and found some dry cornbread to eat. His appetite was raging with few vittles to satisfy it. Etta still lay, moaning softly beside the corpse, with a cloud of expectant flies circling by the scores just above her head. Lum's middle was now swollen and distended. He looked to Cobb to be on the verge of splitting open like a ripe watermelon. The homestead's chickens pecked unmindfully around the two lovers, Etta oblivious to all goings on around her. Dusk fell and she remained frozen in place, showing no sign or willingness to move. Cobb tried approaching her but she rejected him absently mumbling in low, throaty moans. The dark night settled on the union of the two still tightly knitted together. One a dead and swollen corpse. The other an incoherent wife unwilling to acknowledge death even in such a ghoulish form. The eeriness of the woman clinging tightly to a corpse unhinged Cobb as he finally lay down on his pallet to rest.

Cobb Pickens lay there listening but hearing little except for the chirping of crickets. The woman only sniffled occasionally, clearing her throat of phlegm. Cobb's thoughts kept going back to try and figure why the man was such a damn fool in the first place scratching a living with a plow handle and suffering the indignities of viewing the ass end of a mule all day. What had it got him? Dirt farmers were funny people,

Cobb reckoned, working night and day pulling stumps, plowing, and seeding soil that may, and just as easily may not, produce a crop. It was a crap shoot at best. Who in the hell would put their faith in such a thin hope? He'd robbed his share of soddies over the years finding them mostly impoverished and too damned stupid to know the difference. He had rifled this entire dirt shanty and found nothing of value with the exception a half decent gold watch and a good-looking woman. The watch was likely some hand-me-down from some long dead relative. Nothing else. Those were poor returns, Cobb thought, for such tireless and unrewarding work. To sweat in a field all day and accumulate nothing for the trouble didn't make sense. Anyone not worth robbing couldn't command Cobb's respect. Later in the night still wondering about the woman, he walked out again carrying an old lantern for light, seeing Etta still holding vigil with the corpse. Cobb snorted his disapproval, turned on his heels, and slammed the old dilapidated soddy door in protest. It rattled a moment on its rusty hinges sending dust filtering down from the dirt ceiling. It made him sick to see a beautiful woman lying next to a dead man quivering like a scared rabbit. She was invaluable to him. A resource rich in possibilities which he fully intended to plunder in Dodge. Cobb considered again what a splash a beauty like her would make.

When Cobb next opened his eyes, a gray dawn was breaking outside. He kicked his light blanket off and walked to the little window peering outside. It was a small window with blurred and wavy glass but it appeared the woman was quiet and asleep. Cobb started a fire in the woodstove and put coffee water on, plans rolling through his mind. He was hungry and chewed on old, hard crumbly corn bread. A mouse scurried across the dirt floor and disappeared in a corner. Mouse turds lay near the cornbread showing the mouse had already breakfasted. Cobb drank his coffee slowly in no hurry whatsoever to walk outside. He was leaving these diggings today no matter what and if he had to, he'd tie the damn idiotic woman on a horse and lead her to Dodge. Surely, she'd come to her senses by then.

He poured the last half cup of coffee in his tin cup and walked out with renewed resolve. It was his intention to rattle some sense into this woman's head. She had carried this grieving thing way too far, in his opinion, and he was about to put a stop to it. He wanted an early start and no dead soddy's wife would change his plans. However, Cobb had another shock waiting for him. When he leaned over to shake the woman awake, he found her arm cool, actually cold to the touch. When he shook her again, he saw the reason for the coldness. On the dead man's chest was an old clasp knife with a blade open and coated with congealed blood. Cobb slowly raised the woman's arm and saw her right wrist cut deeply, sticky blood still oozing from it. The left wrist was cut the same. Apparently, Cobb surmised, the sodbuster carried the old knife about him and the woman had found it. It was sufficient to perform her desperate and pathetic act.

Cobb's first emotion was that of being soundly cheated. Something of great value had been stolen from him. To his mind, a very valuable piece of property in fact. Now he was left with two sorry corpses, with clouds of flies gathering on them, to deal with. He stood a moment letting his temper build and then exploded with curses as he disgustedly kicked dirt over the dead until they were sodded over from head to toe. Hell, they lived in dirt, plowed the dirt, why not give them what they loved the most? Dirt. Cobb shook his head in deep disgust and went to the shed and found a rusty spade with which to dig. He scratched out a shallow grave putting little effort in the project and rolled them in, face down, and spaded it closed.

The only witnesses to the funeral were a dozen chickens pecking around the place, clucking and scratching as chickens do.

Cobb quickly entered the soddy seizing the gold watch and a bedroll he'd found, and immediately saddled and left the premises. At the last moment, he decided to bring the mules along. After all, they were a matching pair and may be needed. The old soap bones of a horse was ancient and not worth stealing. The realization that there was still a lot of prairie to negotiate between the dead lovers and Dodge made the mule decision easy. Plus, whether he had to ride one or not, they'd likely fetch a few bucks in town.

THE NEXT FEW weeks passed without anything remarkable happening. Lori had called Hank and reported no real problem at their cabin. Some weekend boaters had apparently had engine problems and found themselves stranded. Thus, they had jimmied the door and used Lori and Ethan's radio-phone to call for assistance. Their neighbor, who checked on their cabin periodically, hadn't seen the note attached to the phone nor had he seen the hundred-dollar bill folded under it to pay for the damaged lock. They didn't leave their names but the note was sufficient evidence of explanation. It was the way of things in bush Alaska. Cell phone service didn't work in many remote areas thus necessitating, at times, such drastic actions. Nothing was found missing in the cabin so it was a calm and relieved Lori that Hank conversed with.

The razor wire around H.B.'s home was finally removed. Even the electrified cross fence separating the hundred-acre estate was taken down. Hank hired a back hoe operator to fill the many deep trap holes that covered the front fifty acres. The man just shook his head when Hank responded to the operator's question about "why" the holes were dug.

"Gophers," Hank said not batting an eye. That answer stopped any further inquiries.

He and Trey and Trent spent a whole day resodding the bare soil with new grass. The place took on the appearance of normalcy with the exception of the surveillance towers and surrounding fences. The occasional vehicle that passed by was only local farmers checking on their stock and pastures. Hank spent a couple of days cleaning Katy's house and straightening things up. She'd taken her two dogs to Old Bellville and they were happily living with the Germans. T-Bone, Hank's hound, enjoyed their departure. Katy's dogs were poster children of dog hyperactivity versus T-Bone's laid-back approach to life. He followed Hank faithfully not letting him out of his sight.

Hank drove to Bellville and picked up two pizzas. Trent wanted a six-pack of beer to go with it. He seemed unable to eat pizza without drinking beer. The Mitchell brothers were an interesting study in opposites. Trent had a free-ranging, loose personality, the Jake Spoon type. Trey was all business and more reserved. Yet both were professionals in the finer art of defense and exceptionally capable protectors of H.B.'s secret. Trent had taken Trey through the rift for a day of horseback riding on the ranges of the long ago past. On their return, Trey vowed a renewed commitment in the keeping of the secret.

"Dad gum," he said more than once. "What a sweet deal. I'd like to meet the man who created all this. I'd probably not understand a word of his explanation, but I'd like to give it a try."

"In most ways he seems to be just a regular feller," Hank said, after hearing Trey's statement. "Not remarkable at all at first. Yet there's something so extraordinary about him that the average Joe would likely miss it. He's a perfect example of how much a brilliant mind can achieve if left unfettered and free to ramble. The tall, razor wire fence around this place, which frankly shocked me at first, was put there by H.B. for a perfectly good reason – to keep the interference, the background noise, and the clutter of modern life away from him. His great mind needed silence and free spaces to think in and ultimately perform his miracles. Look at the teens, even pre-teens, and most adults in the world today. There's no silence, no real privacy left to ponder the great mysteries this universe has to offer. They're so plugged into a cyberspace, rat-tat-tatting little messages back and forth, searching for instant electronic entertainment, that there's no space for creative thought. The potential great minds, if they're any left, are awash in this worthless garbage. It makes you doubt your reasons for ever having served a country that's slipped into such decline."

Trent scratched his head in wonderment. He'd never heard Hank string together so many sentences. Both brothers nodded in agreement, however. All three men had fought for their country, two of the three had been awarded the Purple Heart – wounded in action. Yet, what had they risked their lives for? Freedom for the country they loved had been their battle cry as the bad guys' bullets whizzed by. Were they fighting for the freedom of Americans to be bond servants to media gadgets and a culture of crazed electronic lunatics? The new high-tech toys took many prisoners unwittingly and once captured held them in iron grips. Was this the America to give your life for? It was easy, when you thought about it, to doubt your reasons for such a sacrifice. Protecting H.B.'s secret was an easy choice. One man had stood alone, worked alone, and sacrificed all in achieving the seemingly impossible. He had done it in isolation, too. In silence and serenity. That was the place where a mind could work. Where a genius could operate.

"I've doubted my reasons for service at times," Trent answered after a long thoughtful silence had ensued. "For the very reason you just said, Hank. A standing army would be worth having to be able to protect H.B.'s secret. If we had all fought and even died to keep H.B. at work here, alone in his lab, it would have been worth our sacrifice. In a sense, the need of the one certainly outweighed the needs of the many in this situation."

"Truer words have never been spoken little brother," Trey said, scratching his head. "This is a marvelous contraption. Whoops. I guess I should call it a device. Where does this fit into the overall scheme of scientific discoveries?"

"Far above all of them," Hank answered. "It's incomprehensible, the science of this, when you try and put it in perspective. Mankind has no idea what's here and was never intended to know. Had H.B.'s wealth and reclusiveness not been widely publicized recently we wouldn't know about it either. It was a very personal secret to him. He let the cat out of the bag only because he wanted to get to that girl and couldn't wait any longer. That terminally ill young woman in Fort Worth drove his decision. That's why the knowledge about this must be exceptionally narrow and courageously protected. The world is unfit for and doesn't deserve knowing about it. It would only be grossly mishandled."

"Hell, don't let the politicians know about it," Trey snorted in disgust. "They'd just figure out a way to tax it."

HANK HAD ALWAYS TRUSTED his instincts. They had never failed him. They kept him alive on several occasions. These same instincts told him, now, there was a change in the air. A new, welcomed calmness permeated the hundred acres and Hank's good horse sense told him the war was finally over. Cutting the head off of the main snake had worked after all.

Shelly called Hank periodically chatting on and on about her new life. She was studying hard, she said, trying to make her first "A" in a college course. Her new red Ford truck was performing beautifully and she was taking it to Austin for the weekend. She wanted to see the state capitol and besides a friend of hers wanted to visit a boyfriend attending the University of Texas.

"Austin can be a pretty fast place, Shelly," Hank cautioned like a worried father. She certainly was a farmer's daughter and unwise in city ways.

"Nancy's a very conservative girl in matters of being fast," Shelly answered slightly defensive. "She's known this boy since high school."

"Well, like in any big city, Shelly. Just keep your nose clean and watch your step. Where are ya'll staying?"

"Her older sister's place. She's in law school at UT. Her roommate moved out so we have a bedroom."

"I've been traveling some," Hank reminded her. "If I miss your calls don't worry. Leave messages and I'll get back with you when I can. You know Trent's and Trey's numbers. Call them if you need something and can't reach me. They always know where I am."

Old Bellville was his destination more and more often. The county marshal, whom Hank had never previously met, was a frequent visitor of the bakery and he and Hank soon became acquainted. He was a steady fellow in his mid-thirties, stout-looking and friendly to a fault. He had a crooked grin that transformed his whole face for the better. He talked with a slight lisp but it didn't hamper his visiting habits whatsoever. Hank, on one occasion, told him about the stranger he and Katy had met on Katy's first visit through the rift. Tell Trotter was the marshal's name. Tell wanted the man's description.

"Bet I've got a poster on 'im," Tell said after listening. "Come over with me to the office and let's take a look see."

Hank followed him around the corner a half block from the bakery into a small office with a stack of posters scattered on an old, rough cut table. Tell's office desk consisted of the same, a pine table with a bull-hide chair. One large window fronted the office's meager accommodations. Tell, it appeared, spent very little time here. Mouse droppings were scattered about on the posters and Tell nonchalantly blew them to the floor. The jail consisted of one barred cell in the back of the already small, cramped room. An old cotton-tick mattress lay on a crude bunk occupying a majority of the space in the cell. Mice apparently had set up residence in the mattress as ticking balls were strewn about just below it. The whole place smelled of stale pee and musty old mice droppings. Tell thumbed through the posters passing them to Hank.

"Ain't much of a place," Tell apologized seeing Hank look around. "County won't provide much support. They barely pay me enough to stick around. The city constable does most of the town stuff."

Hank scanned the posters not seeing anything remotely resembling the greasy stranger they'd met. Rough sketches used by the law of 1885 weren't very effective identifiers. Some being so nondescript they could be just about anyone. Hank went through the stack quickly longing for fresh air. The dank office odors were making it difficult to breathe.

"No resemblance to the man we saw," Hank said, finally edging towards the door. Tell followed.

"They're some hard cases down around Houston way. They hang out a lot along the Brazos robbing unwary citizens. A ranger came through last week lookin' for a bank robber who robbed the Caldwell bank. He ain't come back through."

"The man we saw looked questionable," Hank answered. "Had I not been ready he'd have hit us I'm sure. I'd hate to think what he might do to a woman."

Tell nodded his head as he followed Hank back outside. The August heat pounded with a vengeance. Hank wiped his brow of sweat and tried clearing the smelly office air from his lungs. It was so hot and humid he could hardly think. Hank put his hat back on.

"I'm ridin' towards the Brazos this afternoon if you'd like to ride along. I could use the company," Tell said. "We might even run across the stranger you ran into."

Hank thought about the offer a moment and decided to accept. He'd been hanging around town for the past three days and even Old Bellville was closing in on him. Plus, he wanted to see more of the country from horseback. He stopped by his hotel room and picked up a few things and was mounted and ready to go within the hour. Katy walked over to see him off.

"Mr. Hargrove, you look mighty handsome astride that mare," Katy teased shielding her eyes from the sun. "When are you coming back?"

"I didn't ask but I've got plenty of vittles for a few days." He didn't mention his desire to find the stranger they'd met. Katy wasn't one, however, to be easily fooled.

"Watch you backside," she said, not enlarging on the statement. Hank knew her meaning. "This country sheriff is likely no more competent than the New Bellville ones. He's probably only good for throttling a few drunks. I doubt he's engaged in much gunplay."

"But I have, Katy," Hank said smiling. Usually, a smile could neutralize Katy's defenses, but she appeared unmoved.

"Oh, Hank, you know what I mean." Hank wasn't cocky but his self-assured attitude sometimes bothered Katy. "Back shooters don't necessarily need to see your face," she countered, frowning into the sun.

"Katy," Hank said, suddenly changing the subject. "Let's go gold huntin'."

"Gold hunting? Why? Where do you want to go?" The idea took Katy by surprise.

"The Klondike. Dawson City, Yukon. Let's speed up time just a little bit to, let's say, 1896 and head north just before the great gold rush. Maybe get there first. Wouldn't you like to find some gold nuggets? Do a little prospecting? If we hung around, we may even get to meet one of my favorite poets?"

"Who's that?" Katy asked.

"Robert Service. Spell of the Yukon, Rhyme of Remittance Man, Little Voices. You've heard of 'em haven't you?"

"Not sure," Katy answered. "I've not read much about the northland."

"How about it?" Hank pressed.

"Well, I might. What's got into you, Hank? Is this idea something that's just popped into your head?"

"No, I've been thinking about it for a good long while. Trey and Trent can handle H. B's place just fine now. Why stick around here? I'll get plenty of updated, fancy supplies from the other side and we can go well equipped. Take a steamer out of San Francisco to Seattle then to Nome or possibly Skagway. We could even go through the interior by dog sled during the winter if you'd like. There's a whole network of roadhouses through Canada. I'll youth up a bit and we'll head out. Well, Katy, how about it?"

"That sounds like a long trip to me," she said noncommittal. Katy rolled her eyes and offered a slight grin after some thought. She glanced across the street seeing Tell about to mount his horse.

"Are you goin' to make me an honest woman if we go?" She couldn't restrain herself from asking the question.

"Yes to the Yukon means yes to becoming an honest woman. Although I've always taken you for being an extremely honest woman."

"How about yes to the honest woman part and maybe to the Yukon idea?"

"Oh, they come as a package deal. The honest woman part comes first, here in Old Bellville, if you'd like. Then we'll mosey on north, taking our time."

Tell seemed to be having trouble tying his bedroll on just right. The idea of marrying Katy had been forming in Hank's mind for some time now. With H.B.'s place returning to normalcy the thought had grown significantly.

"Well, I won't decide to head north or marry you until we have a long buggy ride. After the buggy ride and a little courtin' I'll let you know. Mr. Hargrove, you best start layin' in your supplies for a long journey north just in case."

Hank laughed. Tell looked over wondering what was going on. Katy turned, took a few steps, and turned back to face Hank. A little grin formed on her face.

"Now you know I love moose meat, Hank. I suppose where we're goin' has moose?"

"The Yukon is loaded with moose, Katy."

"Well, don't get too cocky. You better remember you owe me a buggy ride and a picnic, too. You know how I love a good picnic."

"It'll all be just one big picnic, Katy. That's a promise."

Katy giggled, flipped her hair back from her face and

walked towards the bakery. She waved from the bakery door with a dreamy smile and disappeared within.

THE BRAZOS RIVER always reminded Hank of thin chocolate milk, with just a tinge of red. It was clay-banked and muddy. The river looked stagnant with little current to push it along. Brush and vines and undergrowth lined both sides of its banks and were often impenetrable by horseback. Hank and Tell rode east, almost passing directly by the rift window and the live oak housing the rift activation remotes. The long afternoon only grew hotter and the humidity was almost unbearable. They had ridden the better part of ten miles when they cut a trail. It was two riders heading in a southerly direction. Tell wanted to follow. They did follow, slowly, until nightfall and eventually set up camp on the west side of the river. Hank thought a cold camp with no fire would be wise but Tell had a skillet and wanted to fry some fatback. He soon had a too big fire blazing and a frying pan set up. Hank rolled out his bedroll next to his horse and chewed on a piece of jerky. Tell seemed oblivious to Hank's warning about attracting attention.

"They likely ain't bad guys," Tell responded to Hank. "They probably ain't close enough around anyways." Why had they followed their tracks then, Hank thought, if he wasn't suspicious?

The darkness settled and Tell stayed near the fire never letting it die down. He fed the hungry flames like a cold norther was about to hit. Hank stayed outside the fire's light listening to the night sounds but could hear little over the crackling bonfire Tell had carelessly built.

Evening had fallen to full darkness when Hank first noticed his mare's ears twitch forward. She was staring out into the blackness past Tell alerted by something. Tell had just rolled his own bedroll out and was cleaning the frying pan with dry grass when a shot rang out. Quickly followed by another explosion. Tell clasped both hands to his chest as he dropped the pan, eyes wide with surprise, and fell backwards barely missing the fire pit in his fall. Hank unsheathed his rifle and shot into the darkness emptying his Henry's chamber. Moving slightly, he then pulled his revolver and blindly shot where he'd seen the light flashes. After emptying it, he yanked his 9mm automatic pistol, grabbed two extra clips and moved into the undergrowth circling first to the west and then moving parallel to the river in a southward direction. He wanted to try and cut off the shooter's escape. After a few minutes movement, he paused listening for sounds. Crickets chirped so loudly he could hardly make out a sound above the din of their noisy music. He moved a few more feet and paused again. Then a thin sound, just in front of him, moved through the vines. It was two men and he distinctly heard their whispers. They were coming fast and none too stealthy. One sounded to be struggling to move. Hank had apparently hit one. One voice could be heard encouraging the other to move along. The other voice, cursed his partner under labored breathing. In mere moments they were only a few feet away moving directly into Hank's path. He raised his 9mm, waited a full minute for precise sounds, and emptied twelve rounds into the darkness before him. He heard the unmistakable thuds of lead piercing flesh followed by wounded men groaning. He jammed in a second clip and emptied it towards the moans. Then inserted the third clip and waited.

Hank moved twenty feet to his left and after a couple of minutes crept slowly, carefully again parallel to the fallen men.

Thankfully, the crickets' chirping had temporarily subsided. The downed men made no further sounds. Finally, after another four to five minutes of careful listening, Hank turned on a small penlight holding it far to his side and carefully moved to the fallen forms. Both shooters were stone cold dead. On examination, Hank found the pocked-faced greasy stranger that had confronted he and Katy was one of them. He appeared to have been struck in the torso by Hank's initial fire. They, now, were both riddled with multiple bullet holes.

Hank hurried back to camp and found Tell laboring for breath. Two rounds had hit him. One a high glancing blow to the shoulder doing little damage. The other bullet, however, had pierced vitals. It entered just under the ribcage and had not exited. Tell's lips were fringed with a skim of red foam. A lung shot, Hank thought, likely fatal without immediate medical attention. He was torn about what to do? He couldn't haul the man to Old Bellville tossed over a saddle without killing him. Old Bellville's doctor was an incompetent drunk anyway, according to Katy. Not much help there. Could he get his Dodge truck to this location? It was four-wheel drive and raised slightly. He'd taken it through rougher terrain in the past. However, he would be doing something highly irregular taking a wounded man from 1885 back through the rift for medical help. What would the Bellville Hospital think? Even if Tell lived, he could likely never return the man back to Old Bellville. The gunshot wound would raise suspicions and cops, incompetent or not, would be poking around asking questions. Tell could die any minute but he was certain to die without serious medical intervention. Working on impulse, Hank saddled his mare, dug a headlight out of the saddlebag, and started through the darkness for H.B.'s. Within the hour, he reached the oak housing the remote and hurried through the rift. He roused a sleeping Trent and both were ready to go in ten minutes.

The Dodge navigated the terrain thankfully without getting stuck. However, returning to the precise location was no easy task. It was a moonless night and every rolling hill and small gully looked the same. It took almost two hours to locate Tell. He was still breathing but unconscious. His skin was pale and cool to the touch. He'd lost a lot of blood, mostly internally. They rolled him carefully onto a sheet and lifted him to a foam rubber pad in the back of Hank's truck. Trent stayed with him holding the body in place while Hank drove back. The return trip, surprisingly, took only twenty minutes. Once back across the rift at 4:00. in the morning, Hank and Trent contemplated what to do.

"If we drop him at the emergency room someone will see us. That's much too risky. This guy's taken a bullet and we'd be the prime suspects."

"True," Hank agreed. "How about leaving him visible from the roadway, close by, and set off three or four flares? That should get someone's attention. I've already checked. He's got no identifying papers on him. We'll drop him on the opposite side of town and get attention."

"Let's be careful, Hank. We don't need any suspicions raised right now. Being truthful would get us thrown in jail and the loony bin all at the same time."

Within the hour and no traffic visible at the moment, they laid Tell down gently on the roadside grass near an all-night convenience store on the west side of Bellville. This was on Texas 36 so traffic would soon report what they saw. Hank set off three flares and they pulled out stopping at the convenience store to watch. Two cars passed by slowing, but not stopping to render aid. Hank was tired of wasting time and called to the young female clerk to come see the red flares. She gazed out the window puzzled by the red glow.

"Better call the police," he urged as she peered out. "Something's going on." She immediately dialed 911 as Hank and Trent drove off feeling they'd done all they could for Tell Trotter. Short of seriously implicating themselves, they'd at least given Tell a chance at survival.

CHAPTER
THIRTY-SEVEN

Orb directed the overall route north but veered considerably west. The Cimarron River, then the Arkansas, then crossing the north branch of the Santa Fe Trail, and bearing straight northwest from there. Twinks estimated the herd to be approximately fifty miles west of Dodge City at the time of crossing the Arkansas River. The country was rolling prairie, much the same terrain since crossing the Texas border, vast, empty grasslands where millions of buffalo had once roamed. They had long ago left the main cattle trails probing new country away from the settlements. The steers were trail broken, cooperative and fairly easy to handle. The skies remained cloudless, for the most part, and the ever-constant breeze cooled the hottest time of the day. The cowboys were light-hearted, finding the journey more enjoyable as the weather cooperated and the traveling became easier.

Next came the Smoky Hill River, the South Fork of the Solomon, then the North Fork, followed by Beaver Creek.

Beaver Creek's banks were lined with ripe plums and Buster made a plum cobbler, surprising the sugar-starved hands. Buster's health had dramatically improved and he was becoming his old self again. Cussing like the cantankerous old coot he really was. He openly favored H.B. now and always tried slipping him tender morsels and first bites. The hands tolerated it to a point but didn't like the obvious favoritism. They had the good sense to fear Buster and his ever-present 10-gauge. Horsefly, who mainly tended the remuda, gathered up enough courage to complain to Orb, but was cut off in mid-sentence.

"Hell, I ain't sayin' nothin' 'bout nothin' never again," he later told Bo Davis, the only confidante he had in the outfit. "Orb gave me the blackest look I ever seed."

The cowboys after stuffing on cobbler sat around the campfire watching the stars gather in the night sky. Buster rattled around the chuck cursing some pot for being uncooperative. Orb had ridden out to circle the herd and see it properly bedded. The bed ground was dry and grassy, a perfect combination for trail weary steers. The new moon had yet to rise and had little light in it anyway. Twinks shuffled cards trying to scare up a poker game. Most hands were too shy and broke to play the man. He rarely lost and if he did his irascible nature scared them. Nevershed looked skyward, stretched and yawned the way a full-bellied man will, and held a cup of steaming coffee in his paw. H.B. stood to his side, sipping his own coffee, when Nevershed offered some thoughts on the starry sky.

"It's a fer piece up yonder ain't it?" he mused, not directing the statement to anyone in particular. "I'm guessin' that bright one there," pointing to a large star with his finger, "is more'n a thousand miles up. What do you think, H.B.?"

"It's a bit further I imagine," H.B. said looking up. "The steady glow like that one's doing means it's a planet, not a sun or star. The twinkling means it's a star."

"Is stars suns?" Nevershed asked, with genuine curiosity.

"Yes, most of them. A few are whole galaxies, great masses of stars that just look like a single star from here."

Twinks overhearing chimed in. "Moon's not a star, is it H.B.? It's not really a planet either, is it?"

"To be considered a planet you must orbit the sun. Go around it. The moon circles the Earth so it's considered a moon. The moon doesn't generate light, only reflects the sun's rays. So, it couldn't be classified a star. Stars produce energy in the form of heat and light just like our sun."

Nevershed listened carefully apparently an interested star gazer. "How fer is the moon from us?"

"It varies slightly. Mostly around two hundred forty thousand miles average." The statement stunned the cowboys listening in. Even Twinks stopped his shuffling. He'd always guessed it to be a far piece but not that far.

"Reckon there's another place up their like Earth?" he finally asked, still contemplating the moon's distance. All ears were tuned to H.B.'s answer.

"Many places like us, I'm sure. I'm guessing the Creator didn't make it just for us to gander at. It's there for a reason just like we're here for a reason. Just a part of the big plan."

"Plan?" Travis Strayhorn said pricking up his ears. He'd always been a church-goer with his parents down near Brownsville but he couldn't rightly remember his preacher mentioning a "big plan." "What do you mean, H.B.?"

Twinks looked up at the tall cowboy waiting for his answer. Twinks had known a few smart men in his time but H.B. easily took the cake. Though he wasn't very talkative, he was confident in his knowledge and willing to give advice about things he knew. He apparently knew a great deal about the twinkling diamonds dancing in the far heavens above. Twinks, like most cowboys, had always been fascinated by the night sky. Men who spent their lives in the open invariably were. It was a full half of the world they lived in yet they couldn't grasp its complexity. However interesting it may be to look at, it was mysterious and far beyond the understanding of common men. Enlarging it to encompass God, the Creator was a new twist. He hadn't thought about the larger picture but he was primed to hear H.B.'s answer.

H.B. looked up drinking in the starry sky and there was a long gap of silence. "Well," he started thoughtfully, "every living thing has a purpose, a reason for being in my opinion. We humans like to think we're special and we are and we aren't. We're special because we know our existence is temporary, not permanent, at least not in our present form. We're special because of our reasoning powers. We have the ability to think out problems and come to solutions at times. We're uniquely special, too, because we even organize ourselves for the purpose of killing one another. We plan wars, execute battles, pre-plan the destruction and death of others of our species. That seems to be a pretty unique part of being a human being." Not a creature was stirring in the camp. Even Buster had walked over to listen. Twinks glanced around at the mesmerized audience, all in deep thought, trying to absorb some meaning.

Softening the approach, H.B. said, "The Creator made it all. The stars, the sky, the sea, the land, and the tiniest bug you've ever seen. Every blade of grass we cross on this prairie is from His hand, and with the creation, so too, was an intricate plan made. We are part of the plan. Remember, we aren't the plan,

JOURNEY THROUGH THE RIFT

we're just part of it. What you see shining above you is a part of the plan, too. A master plan none of us can know about completely. Most of what we see up there remains a mystery. However, that's for Him to know and for us to merely contemplate. One thing is for sure, nothing exists by accident."

Travis was struggling to understand H.B.'s meaning completely. He wasn't irreverent of God but had difficulty grasping the concept of an all-inclusive universe. Orb came riding up, breaking the trance of the men. Buster walked back to the wagon and Horsefly took Orb's horse, releasing it in the remuda. The unusual depth of the discussion kept the men quiet for a spell but soon Twinks had coaxed some of the boys into taking cards and the mood lightened. Orb walked over to H.B. after pouring coffee.

"We'll make Nebraska tomorrow," Orb said looking down into his cup. "That should put us, with luck, about a week out of Ogallala. We'll stick there a day or two resupplying and head for Wyoming. We'll follow the North Platte to the border, then hit Fort Fetterman and just above the Fort we'll follow the Bozeman Trail north."

"Sounds good," H.B. replied. He'd been looking forward to seeing the high country and the frontier that up to now he'd only romanticized about in his readings.

"We'll cross the Montana border sometime in early August. That should give us just enough summer to make it to the Blackfoot Agency."

The poker players laughed after Twinks made some wise crack. Buster walked over and stood by H.B. and Orb. He had wanted to thank H.B. for giving him the pills but hadn't found the privacy to do so. Impulsively he reached up and aggressively shook H.B.'s hand. The suddenness of the act caught H.B. by surprise. Then Buster quickly turned, as though embarrassed, and walked away without a word passing his lips. Orb was puzzled by the action but said nothing. He took another slow sip of Buster's dark coffee and stared into the fire.

THE YUKON TERRITORIES was a tough piece of real estate to negotiate. No doubt it would take some special preparation to be able to penetrate successfully the land of the midnight sun. Hank had been reading as much literature as possible about the gold rush of 1897-98. Author Pierre Berton's Klondike Fever particularly intrigued him. It chronicled the saga completely and was an interesting resource and inspiration. Hank carried a copy with him when he entered Old Bellville a couple of days later. He stopped by the bakery and enjoyed a pastry with Katy. She chatted happily. The conversation led her to ask about Tell, finally, and Hank whispered he'd tell the story later. She looked at him slightly perplexed. Katy had been yearning for the long buggy ride with Hank and cajoled him to make good on his offer. It was barely mid-morning with plenty of time left to pull off a nice afternoon picnic. The blacksmith has one for rent, Katy explained. Even has a top in case of drizzle. That didn't seem required as the sun was up and shining. He has a stout gelding to hitch it to, too, Katy pressed. Hank could see he had a picnic and buggy ride in his near future so he excused himself and wandered across the little square to the black-smith shop. Franz Schmidt was the proprietor and he was a horse of a man, hands the size of a catcher's mitt. He had a broad, flat nose, and spoke with even a thicker accent than the German girls. Franz had short, curly hair and was sweated down shoeing a rambunctious buckskin.

"Sure, sure. Plenty goot," Franz said to Hank's request for the buggy rental. Hank asked about a good buggy route and Franz thought the stagecoach trail towards Caldwell would be the smoothest. "Plenty goot," he said again fetching the harnesses. Within the hour, Hank parked the buggy in front of the bakery and walked in. Katy was grinning from ear to ear.

"Thought you might show up so I packed us some dinner."

Freda was all smiles peeking at Hank from behind the counter as she handed a customer his bread. The bakery tables were full of patrons with standing room only. Hot bread sales were booming not counting the thriving business of selling various pastries. Katy hustled off to a table to fill cups with coffee. She ran back into the kitchen for sugar, refilling someone's sugar bowl. The place was a low hum of steady conversation. The door continuously opened and closed as a steady stream of customers came and went. Helga came in from the kitchen and took over Katy's job. Katy walked in the back, to their living quarters, and took off her apron. She grabbed the picnic basket and walked back into the bakery grabbing Hank's hand and leading him out of the door. The noon sun was warm but it was one of those rare days where the humidity was low. Hank helped Katy into the buggy, climbed onto the seat himself and popped the gelding with the reins They started out the north road away from the town square at a smart trot. They met a couple of wagons filled with vegetables headed for the local market. After a mile north the houses thinned and gave way to gentle rolling hills. The stagecoach ran between Brenham and Bellville three times weekly carrying mail and passengers. It was a smooth route and well traveled. Katy leaned over against Hank taking his hand in hers.

"Isn't it marvelous riding in a buggy, Hank? Who could want for better transportation?" Her voice was girlish with excitement. She squeezed his hand even tighter.

"I have to admit I like it," Hank said. "Just a little slow I guess."

"Why would anyone want to travel any faster? That's what I don't understand. Over there everything's too fast for me. This is just the right pace."

The stagecoach trail led up a long, gentle hill topped with post oak growth.

"I haven't seen Tell Trotter today. Usually, he's good for a visit or two at the bakery. Didn't he come back with you?"

Hank popped the reins again. Franz's lazy gelding appeared ready to turn around and go back to his feed bag in the barn.

"Tell got shot, Katy. That stranger we saw our first day out and another outlaw shot him down. Tell liked his fires and practically staked himself out. I warned him not to build one but he wouldn't listen."

"Did you bury him?" Katy asked, assuming his death.

"No, he wasn't dead just bad lung shot so I took him across the rift. Hopefully, he'll make it. He wouldn't have survived for sure over here."

"What happened to the bad guys?" she asked.

"They died of accidental lead poisoning shortly thereafter." Hank chose not to elaborate any further. The gelding, with prompting, finally decided to reach a trot again.

Katy looked across the buggy seat, though the distance was merely inches, she felt as if a vast gulf had suddenly opened up between them. Her hand loosened almost imperceptibly on his. The beauty of the early afternoon, the rolling hills, the warm sunshine, a cooling breeze that had played a symphony of delight for her senses and now a troubling thought had taken hold. Try as she might to not let it have its way, the thought had formed a ring of defenses in her heart. To some extent the uncertainty she felt was of her own creation. A product of her dogged desire to hold onto something she feared she might lose. Yet, had she really won it? Was it just a game of bait and switch? Had she been too conniving for her own good? Had she sat the table too carefully, planned the catch too deviously, and sprung the trap too convincingly? She'd never really even kissed the man in passion. Maybe a peck on the cheek is all.

The word "love" had never been exchanged in any form or fashion. Yet, wedding bells had been discussed. Surely, she hadn't imagined that, but the price of the wedding was heading to the gold creeks of the Klondike. Not that going to the Klondike particularly bothered her. What bothered her was the question of whether she had bought him or had he bought her? Was the price too high for both of them? If this relationship would stand it had to stand on even ground. It had to be level from the beginning. She knew she wasn't Hank's first rodeo but she darn sure wanted to be his last. She deeply loved the man but aspects of him sometimes created a strong uncertainty in her. He wasn't the kind of man who needed a woman for self-actualization. He wasn't a petticoat chaser. Didn't need a female to make him something he wasn't on his own. His strong center of independence laid her bare, at times, with worries. His lack of neediness created her uneasiness yet that was what she most admired about him – his rugged independence. Thinking about it made her head hurt and she flinched when the buggy hit a bump in the road. Hank felt her hand jerk spasmodically.

"Katy, are you okay?" he asked, looking at her. Her eyes were moist and a small trickle of a tear rolled down one cheek. "Should I stop?" he asked, suddenly concerned. "I just didn't see the bump."

"Hank, it's not the dang bump that's bothering me."

Hank pulled off in a nice grassy area. They were a good five miles from town now. A pretty stand of oak trees stood just to the left of the road and he steered the buggy under the shade. The light north breeze moved the oak leaves making a low rattling noise as it passed through. Katy wiped her cheek with a finger and sniffled slightly. She despised cry-baby women and here she was tearing up. She didn't like the way she felt right now. It was unfamiliar territory for her. A deep, abiding love was hard in many ways. She'd tried to love her first husband but he'd categorically refused it. Usually, the rejecters of love do so in defense of the fact that they are unable to return what is freely given. Finally, the vessel of love one pours out day in and day out dries up. Passion finds outlets in other pursuits – hobbies, gardening, reading – instead of directing itself into the rocky regions of a dark and hardened heart. She had escaped to those places for many wasted years of marriage, but she'd grown her own strengths from it. Learned love's hard lessons and vowed not to take the step again. True love had a funny way of doing things to a woman's resolve, and now she sat beside a man she loved so much it hurt. She didn't want her past failure in love to taint this perfect moment, but it had.

"Hank, I'm sorry for this. I sometimes let feelings take me away."

"I don't mind that, Katy. I'm guilty of the opposite sometimes. I should let my feelings take me over once in a while."

A rather long pause ensued while they held one another's hand. Katy gathered her strength sensing her emotions still churning just below the surface.

"Katy, I first need to tell you something," Hank said, looking her in the eye. "And then I need to ask you something if that's okay?"

"Sure, I'm okay with that," Katy said, unsure of what might

be coming. She so hoped she hadn't spoiled the beautiful after-noon and the picnic completely with her tears.

"I'm good at some things, Katy. Other things I'm not so good at." He reached in the back of the buggy and carefully picked up a leather saddlebag he had carried along. Inside, Hank had carefully wrapped a fresh red rose from the other side of the rift. He'd placed it in a plastic bag with wet paper towels hoping it'd stay fresh. The flower clerk in Bellville had said it would. The moment of truth was fast approaching as to the freshness of the rose. His nervous hands pulled the bag out and he turned sideways away from Katy's curious eyes, and unfolded the wet paper towels. Surprised to see, the rose was tenderly fresh, glistening with moisture and radiant as the moment he had purchased it. Hank carefully stuffed the bag and paper towels under the buggy seat and turned with a broad smile to Katy, holding out the rose.

"My dearest Katy," Hank said, as Katy put her shaking fingers around the rose stem. "I need to let you know how very much I love you. I'd like to humbly ask you to marry me. I don't care if we live on Mars or Old Bellville or New Bellville. I don't care if we go to the Klondike or not. I want you to be my wife, to love and to cherish one another forever."

Katy was rendered speechless, for once, by the depth of Hank's sincerity. In one solitary moment, with a beautiful rose in hand, all her concerns and worries evaporated. Blown away with the breeze that cooled them under the shade of the oaks. His open love, kind eyes, and gentle proposal melted her heart and tears began to flow. The beautiful red rose glowed in her hand and small water droplets splattered from it as a result of her shaking hands. A faint feeling came over her as the surge of emotions reddened her cheeks. She gathered herself, momen-tarily, trying vainly to find a voice inside. Unaccustomed to be at loss for words, Katy found herself struggling to make a reply. She finally found language and pulled Hank to her joyfully.

"Yes, Hank, yes. I'll be your wife forever and ever. I love you. I love you so much darling. Where ever you want to go, I'll follow."

They embraced for a long moment as mockingbirds sung melodies in the high branches above the buggy.

THIRTY-EIGHT

P reacher Jim Davis delivered a moving wedding ceremony. Trent was Hank's best man with Trey as groomsman. Katy's dual bridesmaids were Freda and Helga. Lori and Ethan had flown the Citation down from Alaska to be present but only for a day or two. They had construction going on at their cabin and winter shows early in the northland. Preacher Jim's church held only eighty citizens in its pews and the standing room only crowd filled the back of the sanctuary. A little flyer posted in the bakery about the upcoming nuptials created an unusual amount of interest. Both local newspapers ran articles, too, which piqued the local gossip. All were well-wishers for the couple, at least for Katy, who seemed determined to change the social status of women in Old Bellville. Preacher Davis made over the couple with more words than needed to be spoken but his powerful style of delivery held the audience at rapt attention. Katy wore a beautiful wedding gown, simple to match the era, although purchased from a Houston bridal shop from across the rift. The Germans had matching gowns from the same Houston shop made-to-fit especially for the stout bakery girls. Church choir members, ten strong, sang "I love you truly" in the background with piano accompaniment. The honeymoon, promised by Hank, would be a railcar ride to Fort Worth and a few days' celebrating in the booming cowtown.

Though this was far from a fancy wedding, Katy had lobbied hard for a simple elopement.

"Let's just get Preacher Davis and ask him to marry us, Hank. I've walked the isle before and it didn't work. I'm afraid my many stains will spoil a white wedding dress."

Hank, believe it or not, was the one who held firm for a small but formal wedding. After all, he'd never been down the aisle he explained. A more traditional service struck him as the correct way to tie the knot. After the buggy ride, Katy was ready for an immediate "I do" with the preacher. Hank wanted at least a three-week engagement thinking that to be a more proper thing to do. Katy acquiesced in the end, but she struggled with all things formal, especially weddings.

Freda and Helga broke down halfway through the ceremony being so moved by the beauty of the event and the powerful voice of Preacher Davis. Katy threw her impassioned arms around Hank and delivered the most passionate post-wedding kiss anyone in the congregation had ever witnessed. The preacher grinned broadly. The choir sang sweetly. Even Lori teared up in the end. It was a definite first Lori said to Ethan as they waved at Hank's and Katy's departure on the train, that citizens from the other side had married across the rift. History had been made here and indeed it had. Trent and Trey had hurriedly left the church just after the wedding anxious to re-cross the rift and missed the bride and groom's train send-off. The estate was temporarily unprotected. Hank mentioned he would likely see them in a couple of weeks.

Katy was agreeable to a switch forward in time to 1896 and

a trip to the far north gold hunting. The long discussion about the remote possibility of something happening to the rift didn't dampen their enthusiasm one iota. They were where they wanted to be anyway and certainly wouldn't be saddened if unable to return to the modern era. Katy had grown especially fond of the age of twenty-five. A pure second chance at life wasn't a common event and both clung heartily and thankfully to the opportunity.

THE DELIVERY of the herd went off without a hitch. The Blackfeet Agency employees were grateful and cooperative. They had several thousand hungry mouths to feed for the winter and the steers meant sustenance for the locals. Pockets of buffalo still existed in the northern herd but they were scattered, some even escaping to Canada, thus finding enough protein to maintain families of various tribes a dicey proposition. The Indian agent would be faced with disaster trying to contain the Indians in peaceful pockets without the beeves. The chuck wagon and remuda, roughly 125 animals strong, were sold to Race Gilchrist of Helena. He was a rancher and needed new blood in his horse herd.

The thought of ranching in Montana intrigued Orb and had also captured H.B.'s fancy. They had crossed with the herd countless areas capable of sustaining large ranches. The land was there for the taking. Race Gilchrist was one of the first to be taking advantage of the open ranges and vast grasslands that abounded.

"What's it like ranching up here?" Orb asked, curious about the opportunity.

"Tough. It's not like south Texas where you come from, I'm sure." Race was almost as tall as H.B. standing next to him. He had pale, sky-blue eyes set far back under his prominent brow ridges. He'd brought four ranch cowboys along to help drive the horses and shepherd the wagon. "Good country, though. Rich grass and lots of it. Lakes freeze so you've got to locate close to moving water if you're in the high country. Cattle will eat snow but it's better if they've got water."

"We saw some great country back aways. Close to Sweet Grass Creek off the Yellowstone River," Orb said.

"I bet I know the place. Yep. That's great country. Makes for a much shorter drive to the government agents than having to push a herd all the way up from Texas."

"Think the cattle demand will stay high?" Orb asked, probing for information. It didn't make much sense raising cattle if you didn't have a place to sell them.

"Your herd is the fourth one they've bought. Plus, they contract everything I can raise. They'd do the same for you. Time's coming when this free land will be gobbled up. Rumor has it a half dozen prospective ranchers are snooping around about to locate. Best act now if you're thinking on it."

"Well, H.B. and I have talked about it. How many cattle do you need?"

"As many as you can get," Race answered, "and plenty of horses, mules, pigs, and chickens. Supplies are rather scarce and hard to get up here. Stock up before winter. Hard traveling once the big cold sets in."

"Think a thousand head would be a good start?"

"Darn right. Bring some small bulls for the heifers, though. Cuts down on the calving problems. They wander off quite some distance to calve in this big country so it's hard to be of help to a first calf heifer."

The Gilchrist cowboys had started the remuda and wagon

off and Race stood in his stirrups looking after them. "Am I gonna see you boys come next fall?" he asked smiling.

"Likely," Orb said looking at H.B. "Two or three of my men have agreed to help out. I think we've got the makin's for a ranch. H.B., here, said he'd partner up with me."

"Well, good luck. Come up and see me in Helena sometime. We'll break bread and talk over the cattle business if I don't see you delivering cattle here next fall. See you boys later." With that, he spurred up to catch the disappearing chuck wagon and horses.

Orb paid off the hands and they were collectively antsy wanting to get started for Silver Bow. They had a hundred eighty miles to cover. They could catch a train there and ride the Iron Horse south. Even Nevershed had decided to ride the railroad which surprised Orb. Nevershed had never been a man to take advantage of the iron horse.

Twinks Brady, Cody Meyer, H.B., and Orb were riding back down the same route they'd come. It was early September, and if they hurried they'd get through the high country before the first snows stuck. They'd already seen the first high country snowflakes drifting down so it was only a matter of time. Each man had a spare horse, plus H.B.'s five prize ponies, so they were well mounted and could push hard. Should make forty miles on a good day. Poking cattle slowed a trip but not this time. They'd spend a day, maybe, snooping around the Sweet Grass and Yellowstone River country area figuring out a ranch site, but other than that it'd be a fast trip.

NINETEEN DAYS later they camped on a small creek no more than fifteen miles northwest of Dodge City, Kansas. It had been a long day and they were too tired to push farther on. The men and the horses had fared well overall and the weather, though now close to October, had been tolerable – very cool but not uncomfortably cold. A snowflake or two had touched them near the tall country beside the Big Horn Range but not a drop of rain had fallen. This would be their last night's camp before Dodge and all were anxious to hit a town.

"I want a thick steak," Twinks said, tired of the short rations they'd been on. He sorely missed Buster's cooking. "My belly button's rubbing a hole on my backbone."

"A barbering would be good, too," Cody said. "I'm getting to smell a bit gamey. Bathin' in this ice water ain't for me."

Orb was making the last of their coffee and they finished the strips of dried jerky they'd purchased in Ogallala. Just ahead would be plenty to eat. They could look forward to that. Twinks for sure would forego coffee for a belt of whiskey. Right now, though not much of a drinker, a shot of whiskey even sounded good to Cody. Just as darkness settled, they witnessed the distant smoke of an approaching locomotive.

"Dern, that's a long way off ain't it," Cody said, watching the smoke rise in the evening sky. The wind had lain down and the hat-sized fire burned in a vertical fashion. Not a common sight on the plains where the breeze was constant.

"I'm tempted just to ride on in and settle down in a hotel room," Twinks said, grumpily rolling out his bedding. "These nights is getting too cool for me. My ol' bones are starting to creak. Liable to get the rheumatism. Ain't that right, H.B.? Cold ain't good for joints is it?"

"I know mountain men said they got rheumatism in the knees from wading in cold creeks fetching their beaver. Too much consistent cold probably's not good. It would take longer than a few cold nights to affect you."

"I might help you boys start a ranch in Montana but I need a cabin to sleep in. You boys are gonna put up cabins ain't you?" The matter about where'd he'd sleep during the long winter months had been preying on Twink's mind for some time. Sleeping in the open didn't seem logical in such extreme cold.

"Sure, we'll put up cabins," Orb answered. "Building's got to start as soon as we get the cattle there. That little creek just south of the Sweet Grass is loaded with timber. Grass is thick, and I bet it's well protected from the howling north wind. We'll have to put up pens and barns and cabins. We'll need lots of timber cut. That's why we need you, Captain. Somebody's got to keep guard so the young men can build."

"I can swing an axe," Twinks said, opening the possibilities of his doing manual labor. Orb was surprised by his offer. "My Pa and I used to chop cedar around Junction when I was just a kid. I'm an old cedar chopper from way back. I'd like to try my hand at it again."

"I've built a shed or two," Cody said, not wanting to be left out on the construction of the ranch. "I'm a little better than cut to shape, beat to fit, and paint to suit."

"I know an ol' log builder around San Antonio if I can find him," Orb said. "I'd sure like to convince him to come along. We'll have need of a man like that."

The idea of building a ranch from scratch in Montana had taken hold of H.B. The country was crisp, cool, and low in humidity. The skies there were a hue of blue not to be found in the southlands. Best of all, the mountains lay visible on the horizon and were a sight that particularly appealed to H.B. Elk and mule deer were prevalent and a pleasure to hunt. Sure, it had its weather but it was a land of plenty and ripe for settling. H.B. had no other obligations to fulfill.

"Need to leave in very early spring," Orb said, stirring his coffee. He saved a sack of sugar in his saddlebags for he liked his coffee very sweet. "I'd like to leave no later than mid-April, possibly earlier."

"I may just stay in Dodge and wait for you," Twinks offered. "I'm tired of traveling. I might find me a nice hotel and gamble for a spell."

"Well, don't let your hands get too soft if you're gonna use an axe," Orb said grinning. "Shuffling cards don't make calluses last time I checked."

WITH NOTHING LEFT to eat or drink, the group departed just at the crack of dawn, reaching Dodge just before noon. They galloped up to the Wright House, rented rooms, and made their way to the steak house. Normally packed during the peak droving season, in late September business invariably dropped off. A few patrons sat at the tables but it was less than half full. The air in the restaurant's ceiling had a blue hue from the cigar smoke. H.B.'s lungs were particularly sensitive and protested the smell. They found a corner table, near an open window, and H.B. welcomed the fresh air.

The horses were fagged out from hard riding and they'd stabled them first, requesting a generous bait of corn and oats. Orb didn't want to spend but a day in Dodge fearing early northers striking on the open plains. The horses needed rest and Cody's spare mount had started limping late in the day. He'd likely need replacing.

With stomachs full they wandered the streets all going to a bath house for a good scrub and trimming. The bathhouse served sweet brandy and fresh cigars. All but H.B. partook with enthusiasm. He did, however, finally opt for a little brandy and found it fairly agreeable. The Silver Dollar Saloon was just across the street and the piano player was already hard at work. They ordered a round of whiskey and stood at the bar recollecting the long trails they'd just crossed.

"Should make Fort Worth in less than two weeks," Orb figured. Even H.B.'s prime mounts were about worn down from the rigors of the Montana trip. "We should buy fresh mounts, if possible, at least two or three backups." All heads nodded to the idea.

Cody sipped his whiskey appearing to have trouble inhaling after each drink. Twinks tossed back the jigger and asked for more. Orb sipped his sparingly and H.B. eyed his drink with distrust. The Silver Dollar was an opulent saloon with ornate fixtures, heavy wooden chairs, and a large mirror, full length behind the bar. The barkeep was dapper-dressed with slick, greasy black hair and a matching pencil-thin moustache that sloped downward below his lips. The piano player plunked in the dim-lit back area where two tables of card players sat. Five men played at one, four at the other. The games looked to be high-stakes if the concentrated looks on their faces was any indication. Twinks longed for a game and the four-player table looked to be an open invitation. When his eyes covered the four-player table a second time, a flash of recognition sent his hackles up. What the hell? He blinked his eyes trying to blow the brandy and whiskey from his brain. Could it be? Still unbelieving he leaned over to Orb and whispered something. Orb's head snapped up staring at the players. Orb grabbed Twink's arm on reflex and held it a moment.

"Damn," passed Orb's lips. "That's him alright. Bastard's nested up right here in Dodge."

Cody spun around hearing Orb's statement and saw the man in question. Sure enough. There was Cobb Pickens holding a hand of cards oblivious to his observers. Twinks impulsively started towards him but Orb's grip tightened on his sleeve.

"What's your plan, Captain?" Orb asked, already knowing the answer. He hoped to contain Twinks, to think the discovery through just a bit. The man had no idea he'd been spotted so a plan, a trap could be laid carefully. It wasn't a point or even a discussion. It was a matter of when they'd get the renegade.

"The bastard tried to kill us, Orb. That son-of-a-bitch needs killin'," Twinks answered, reaching for his boot derringer. Both barrels fired at close range straight in the scoundrel's chest seemed a just reward. Words needn't be exchanged.

"Captain, I'm on your side here but let's think this thing through. No need to get rash and draw a murder charge. Bat Masterson, the new law here, won't cotton to you killin' an unarmed man deserved or not."

Orb still clung to Twink's sleeve hoping to settle him down. Dodge's Boot Hill cemetery was filled with righteous killers. Cobb wasn't worth hanging for. A good man needn't swap his life for such a sorry bastard. Twinks paused a moment, his eyes glaring with hatred. The bartender scurried away glancing at the derringer in Twink's hand as he went. The poker players, too far away to hear bar stool conversation over the clanking piano, remained preoccupied with their cards. Each focused on his own hand.

"His greasy renegades got what they deserved. Orb you know that," Twinks pleaded, quivering with his pumping adrenaline. "We need to take him out."

"Yes, we do," Orb agreed. "He ain't goin' nowhere though. You don't need a murder charge hanging over you. Let's visit with Masterson first. Tell the story. He'll be just as dead a day from now."

Twinks' black look lightened just a bit. He fingered the derringer desiring to use it while trying to focus on Orb's words. He had pictured Cobb's death in daydreams and night dreams. He'd witnessed his dying over and over again in his mind, broken into sweats thinking about it, and he wanted to see it through, damn it. Yet what Orb said did make some sense. Likely a murder charge would come if, indeed, Cobb was unarmed. The rap would be hard to beat with so many witnesses to the killing. The town council was trying to get a handle on the town's violence. That's why Bat Masterson had been hired. Twinks would be an easy target for a vigilante mob bent on establishing peace. Hanging one man for murder would be small potatoes for the town council in its pursuit of new-found respectability.

"Captain, let's step out for some fresh air," Orb said, looking at Cody and H.B. "I can't think in here with Cobb so close." They all turned and walked out, Twinks following reluctantly. They stood on the boardwalk taking in the sights of Dodge's one long street. Saloons and party houses dominated the business frontages showing a clear sign of catering to the rambunctious cowboy cliental. However, late September reflected a gentling down since the herds had stopped flowing in and, for the most part, the drovers were gone. Buggies and wagons now lined the main thoroughfare and the mercantiles were filled with shoppers and respectable Dodge citizens.

"Marshall's office is just down the street," Orb said. "What say we go pay him a visit."

Two doors down Cody found a shop and entered after seeing the rows of hard candy. His sweet tooth needed satisfying. He said he'd catch up later. Gingham curtains adorned the shop windows and colored candy lined the counters. The shop also contained a soda fountain selling various flavored soda waters. It all looked like heaven to Cody and he plopped down after ordering a sarsaparilla. The place was painted all white and glowed from the sun's reflection. Two young teenaged girls entered glancing Cody's way and giggled themselves up to the serving counter. They both carried parasols looking mighty ladylike for such young pullets. Cody stole a glance but didn't stare, feeling shy about their girlish giggling. He hoped it wasn't his appearance that inspired such laughter. He'd worn his nicest clothes to town but nothing was pressed and proper. Trail dirt penetrated even the wax paper he'd wrapped them in.

Bat Masterson was unusually accommodating, especially to former Texas Ranger Captain Twinks Brady. He'd heard of the captain's exploits and respected a man with a reputation in the field of law and order. Masterson had long, flowing black hair touching his collar and a handlebar moustache to match. He was a well-groomed fellow and his toilet water, liberally applied, permeated the office. He had been sitting at his desk fingering wanted posters when the group of three walked in. His lips looked sealed in a downward way, not inclined to smiling, but his attitude was light and easy. He had a reputation for being tough and unbending in applying Dodge law.

Orb told the story of Cobb Pickens with Masterson listening carefully. A deputy wandered in and the marshal shushed the discussion until he departed. Twinks filled in the empty spaces, if Orb paused to catch a breath. No emotion showed on the marshal's face as he nodded occasionally through the narrative. He asked questions, directed more at Twinks, regarding the men they'd killed on the prairie. He thumbed through the posters finding two with rewards they'd dispatched. Scar being the most sought after figure earning a bounty worth $500. The other two-bit outlaw was a character named Ringo who harassed herds usually through the badlands of Indian Territory. Ringo had a $100 reward on his head.

"Damn glad you got Scar," the marshal said finally. "He's been a hard one to run to ground. I'll inform the council and you'll get your money for these two scoundrels. Likely there're posters on some of the others in Texas. Might be worth checking with the sheriff in Fort Worth."

Bat Masterson slid his chair back and stood up stretching stiffly. Contrary to reputation, he was only of medium height and walked slowly to the window looking out. There was a pause in the conversation.

"Pickens has been a pain in the ass ever since he arrived. He rode in with two stolen mules I suppose but never got a complaint from anyone. He's a damn sorry gambler who intimidates the customers at the Silver Dollar. Thinks he owns the place and has run out the class folks. The owner hates him with a passion but won't confront him for fear of his own life. Quite frankly, I've been too busy keeping peace with the herds coming in all summer to pay him the attention he deserves." Masterson walked back to the center of the room facing H.B., Twinks, and Orb.

"I'd like to see him gone. Black Jack, the proprietor of the Silver Dollar, thinks he carries a boot gun, which I wouldn't doubt. I could arrest him on suspicion of murder but would have problems sticking the charges. Carrying a boot gun, if he has one, will only get him a couple of days in the hoosegow. So, I'm open to suggestions. I know one thing for damn sure. I want him gone from Dodge."

Twinks scraped his boot on the plank floor of the marshal's office thinking hard. He wanted a confrontation but didn't want Cobb to have a chance to get the drop on him. You never knew about a damn back shooter. He might stow the derringer under the table where it would be easy to get to. Cobb's methods wouldn't involve fair play in any case. You could forget gentleman's rules.

"We need to get him away from the card table," Twinks said almost to himself. "I don't trust the damn outlaw. He's slick and may have a firearm close by. This renegade needs killin', marshal. We could grab the bastard and haul him out of town if you want. That way no shootin' happens in the city limits. Where does he stay?"

"Palace Hotel," Masterson answered, eager to provide information. "Room ten upstairs, right next to the stairway. I've been let in a time or two checking his place over. He's a slob but we couldn't arrest him for that."

"We could waylay him easy enough," Orb suggested. "Catch 'im before he gets to his room. Haul him out of town and settle the score."

"That's okay by me," the marshal answered, leaning against his desk. "You can repeat the trick with every other damn tin pan gambler in Dodge if you want. Pretty quick we'd clean out the riff raff."

"We'll pass on that I reckon," Orb answered. Just then Cody opened and peered through the law office door like he wasn't sure he should come in. "He's one of my men," Orb said, as Masterson glanced up. Cody stepped close to H.B. and stood stiffly uncertain if he'd interrupted important proceedings.

"Pickens usually shuts his gambling off around midnight

and stumbles back half-drunk to his digs. That'd be as good a time as any." Masterson twirled his moustache with his fingers thinking about sweeping the vermin like Cobb out of Dodge. A few gambler disappearances should discourage their sorry fraternity somewhat. He wished like hell he could just put them all on the next train out.

"Tonight sounds good don't it Orb?" Twinks queried. He couldn't wait to get his hands on the bastard.

"Fine with me," Orb replied. "The sooner this thing's behind us, the better."

"Good. Then that's settled. I'm the only one on duty after midnight. Town quiets down then so it should be easy." Masterson walked over in front of Twinks and extended his hand. "Hope you might consider hanging around Dodge City. I could sure use a good hand like you, Captain."

"Oh, I ain't sure I want to law anymore," Twinks answered, shaking his hand. "I was thinkin' of playing a few card hands myself. I'm real fond of poker."

Masterson gave an unexpectedly hearty laugh shocking the four men somewhat. "Well, I take a hand or two myself at times. 'Course I like playing straight poker and not vying against card sharps."

"I'm the same," Twinks answered. "Straight, honest poker is my only game."

THIRTY-NINE

Cobb Pickens fought like a panther reared in the cedar breaks. He was stout as a damn bull and if he was snockered none of the four could tell it. Twinks first rode him to the ground only to find himself promptly pitched off and eating dirt. Orb came in with a swift kick but Cobb warded off most of the strike's force deflecting it with his right arm. His short and thick stump-like frame was a ball of fury showing surprising speed and agility. Cobb immediately stood up having knocked Orb to one side only to be tackled by Cody. He grabbed and tossed Cody like a flour sack into the side of a building. The thud was sickening and Cody melted to the ground moaning. H.B. threw a punch but missed his aim and was hit hard in his chest by Cobb's fist. The wind came out of H.B. as he staggered backward gasping for air. Twinks attacked from his backside again and wrapped his arms around Cobb's stubby neck. Cobb twisted like a coiled rattlesnake and soon loosened the hold enough to wriggle out. Twinks grabbed for his throat but got only a handful of Cobb's shirt collar. Cobb mimicked a cornered badger twisting and striking with lightning speed. Orb finally regaining his feet swung wildly getting a piece of Cobb's ear with his fist but took a hard right in return. Stars exploded in his head as he hit the ground momentarily stunned.

Twinks kicked Cobb as he turned around deep in the crotch and Cobb's eyes bugged out in response. Cobb grabbed his genitals just as H.B. hit the base of his neck with a solid blow. Cobb wheeled around facing his attacker when Twinks hit him at the base of the skull with a plank board Cody had broken loose hitting the wall. The board shattered and Cobb's muscular body trembled and shook momentarily not yet realizing its smaller head was hurt. Cobb staggered forward one feeble step and crumpled to the ground. Twinks grabbed several short ropes he'd brought and swiftly secured Cobb's hands behind him. They turned Cobb over and stuffed his mouth roughly with a rag and tightened a bandana around his mouth and head. Then Twinks cinched another rope from his ham-hock-sized hands under his crotch and back around his wrists.

H.B. checked on Cody finding him dazed but not seriously injured. The horses were tied close by and within moments Cobb had been pushed up and securely tied down in the saddle. Cobb was still about half rummy but was gaining his senses quickly. Twinks strapped additional ropes around him for good measure and within minutes they were moving down a back alley and out into the open prairie south of town. Cobb was trussed tight and unable to move as he gained full consciousness. He fought his bindings and cursed his assailants in unintelligible grunts unable to accept his defeat. His attackers, each having felt Cobb's wild, raw power, led the renegade southward toward a stand of trees along the Arkansas River. In fifteen minutes, a tree was secured, a rope hung, and Cobb's thick neck was circled within.

"Bastard don't deserve a proper hangin'," Twinks barked as he untied Cobb's boots loosening them from the stirrups. Cobb tried kicking Twinks but couldn't reach him. Twinks then mounted his own horse, grabbed the end of the rope and dallied it around the saddle horn. Cobb grunted and struggled as Twinks tightened the noose.

"Cobb, listen you bastard," Twinks yelled as Cobb twisted and contorted in the saddle. The rest of the men sat on their horses watching the spectacle. "You're fixin' to meet ol' Beelzebub himself. Tell the ol' hobgoblin hello from all of us. You damn sure fit better in hell than here." With that, Twinks spurred his horse and Cobb was elevated from his horse's back into the near branches above. His feet flounced and kicked and twitched as death came. Five full minutes later, Twinks dropped the rope and a corpse was all that was left of Cobb Pickens. They dragged the body down to the Arkansas and dumped it in. "Good riddance," Twinks announced as the current hauled Cobb away. "Sure, hope you know how to swim."

HANK HUNG around Old Bellville several days after their return from the Fort Worth honeymoon. The Gulf, Colorado, and Santa Fe Railroad's accommodations were adequate and, overall, the couple enjoyed the ride to the cattle town. The many stops along the way irritated Hank somewhat but he bit his lip not wanting to dampen Katy's enthusiasm for the trip. He and Katy occupied the largest room in the Tavern Hotel in Old Bellville now but Hank soon tired of the routine of going with Katy in the early morning hours to the bakery and then wandering the boardwalks looking for ways to fill his idle time. The Austin County Times and the Bellville Standard had cub reporters standing ready to interview Hank and Katy about their experiences in Fort Worth. Their short journey north had stirred the local gossip once again. News must be in short supply in the hamlet Hank thought if their trip was front page news. Hank tolerated the interviews. Katy beamed her way through them excitedly reliving every step they took. Locals apparently traveled little so the journey to Fort Worth sold a lot of newsprint. Hank and Katy took on an air of notoriety in the community which displeased Hank to no end. It seemed he could find no peace anywhere as the rankest stranger, if seeing and recognizing Hank, would call him by name and shake hands with far too much familiarity. It was during these first days of return to Old Bellville that Hank began to miss his little cabin on the banks of the San Saba River. It was peaceful there. Quiet and uncomplicated. The kind of life he enjoyed the most. Within a week of their return Hank was so restless he could bite himself. Katy was the first, of course, to notice Hank's unease.

"Hank honey," she said getting ready in the early darkness of their hotel room. Her appearance at the thriving bakery was needed by six each morning. "What's going on? You seem to be unhappy."

"I sure am," Hank said, not able to curb his feelings. "I don't like being the center of attention, Katy. I wasn't made to tolerate it. I might pull out for a few days and go visit my San Saba cabin on the other side. I certainly need away from here."

"Why, Hank, you know I'm not going to stop you from going, but you're not going anywhere without me. You haven't forgotten we're married have you?"

"Katy, you know better than that. What'll the German girls think with you gone."

"That's not my worry, darling. That's their worry. I'm not letting my husband slip off that easy."

"So, my days of freedom are over," Hank stated with a slight grin on his face. He had been in bed watching Katy dress.

"Darn tooting, they are. I'm tattooed all over you mister and don't you forget it. I've been through the ol' absent husband routine in my past life. That's not going to happen again."

"Well, just knowin' we can go anytime makes me feel better already. Really, the people here are awfully nice, Katy. Very well meaning. They're just a little overpowering for my tastes. I like a little anonymity. I'm not the famous type."

"You can thank your sweet wife for making you famous," Katy said, pulling her silk slip over her face and holding it just below her nose like a sheik's wife. Hank instantly warmed to her act. Katy's fresh beauty beamed radiantly and Hank fought the impulse to pull her back in bed. Katy in marriage was a much different Katy as Hank encouraged the playful side of her nature. He reveled in the act of her innocent flirtatiousness.

"You're about to be late for work, young lady," Hank said, motioning her over. She slipped towards him like a kitten coming for warm milk.

"Well, worse things can happen," she said, snuggling into his arms. "They just better start getting used to it."

Fort Worth glowed five miles away as the dusk settled over it. Street lanterns were lit giving the town a warm, inviting look. It was a welcome sight to the three tired men. They waded the Trinity River and struck the outskirts of town just as the darkness settled deeper over the community. It looked largely the same to H.B. Several new residences, however, dotted the north side of town as carpenters were apparently in a thriving profession. Cody, H.B., and Orb rode slowly down First Street gawking at the business establishments lining the road. Twinks chose to stay in Dodge having acquired poker stakes in the form of reward money. Bat Masterson needed an under-cover man to help him weed out the undesirables in the corrupt gambling society that had recently blossomed in Dodge. Twinks was the perfect man for the job. He could spot a cheat a mile off. Plus, he drew a deputy's pay now being on the city's payroll. It was a win-win for the captain. Wages and winnings. You couldn't beat that.

"See ya in the spring," he said, as they mounted that morning in front of Wright House almost two weeks before.

"Keep those axe hands primed and ready," Orb shouted, as they spurred up the horses leading three new mounts for spares. "Can't have no tender dainty fingers in Montana."

"Don't you worry none," Twinks shouted in reply as they trotted away. "These hands and fingers'll be ready when you are."

They rode up to Corley's Boarding House and H.B. gently rapped on the front door. A voice called to enter and the three of them did having just broomed themselves off on the front porch. The parlor glowed warm and golden with lantern light. Someone was coming out of the kitchen. It was Jessie Madelyn. She paused in mid-step and stared in disbelief at the tall figure standing before her. In response, she covered her mouth with both hands, and shrieking with joy ran straight into the arms of a very surprised H.B. He held his dusty hat away from her with one hand and patted her back with the other. He felt completely awkward and overwhelmed by Jessie's unexpected response. He had, of course, noted her pink cheeks, face filled out with healthy weight gain, and returned vigor. She had changed dramatically from his last memory of her.

Orb and Cody stood behind him with their mouths agape at the affections the young woman lavished on H.B. He had failed to mention a love interest in Fort Worth and they stood by, dumbfounded by the sight. Slowly, Jessie released H.B. wiping her eyes of tears. Elsa stormed out of the kitchen door wondering about all the carrying on. She stood there with a stern look of disapproval on her face wiping her hands on her apron. Her stare was fixated on the three men.

"Well, you men hungry?" she asked, finally noticing the tired appearance of the weary trail-dusty patrons.

"Why, yes, we are Elsa," H.B. answered formally, with just a sprinkle of sarcasm. "Thank you for your kindness."

They were led by Jessie to the dining room where bowls were set and filled with Elsa's tasty beef stew. Sliced tomatoes, radishes, even steamed carrots were presented as side dishes. Jessie fluttered around the table with excitement. Even Elsa was friendlier than was her normal habit.

"Dr. Fields just left to deliver a baby," Jessie said smiling. "Settlers living several miles east of town. It's her first baby so the expectant dad was no help at all when the time came."

The men ate two helpings each and Jessie showed Cody and Orb their rooms, their eyes plainly showing fatigue. She then led H.B. to his room, the same room where he had previously stayed, and picked up his hand at the door's entrance. Emotions bubbled over that she could not control.

"The only reason I am here holding your hand is because you saved my life. I am ever so grateful to you." Jessie's words failed her, momentarily, feeling a knot forming in her throat. H.B. stood close watching and waiting. "I missed thanking you before you left. I have suffered so over my callus behavior in failing to express my sincere gratitude. I owe you so much."

"Why, you're welcome," H.B. said uncomfortably. "You were on the edge, Jessie. Thank goodness you allowed my intervention. I was afraid, perhaps, we had waited too long. I can see you're completely well. I'm glad you finished the pills."

"Well, I tried giving Dr. Fields some of them but he refused. He has several ill patients, but he said you meant all of them for me. I finished the whole bottle several weeks ago."

She used the sleeve of her dress daubing her teary eyes. She sniffled clearing her nose trying to hold on to a scrap of her dignity. Her knees had suddenly gone weak and were trembling. Holding H.B.'s hand gave her a fluttery feeling but she wasn't ready to turn loose. H.B. felt embarrassed by her affections but maintained his poise. He was so tired he felt like he could sleep standing. His legs were like lead pipes dangling below his waist. They had pushed hard for the past three days to reach Fort Worth. It was mid-October and the first cold fronts were undoubtedly close behind. Orb was a man on a mission and a hard driver when cold weather was threatening.

Jessie finally realizing H.B.'s extreme fatigue, returned his hand. He braced against the door jam, suddenly needing to steady himself. The poor man was so tired he could hardly stand much less put up with an emotional woman like me Jessie thought. H.B. staggered to the bed after closing the door leaving Jessie standing just outside. She wiped tears and then ran to the sanctuary of her room, shutting the door and leaping on the bed, almost in the same motion. She wept softly for several hours mostly out of relief that H.B. had truly returned. Mostly because she had gotten to say what she really wanted to say. The shock of walking into the parlor and the image of him standing there in the doorway stayed firmly planted in her mind. The image wouldn't disappear and the sight was pleasant to file away and then pull out again to look at. She, too, liked his strong arm embracing her in his own shy, reserved way.

BREAKFAST WAS a gay affair the following morning at Corley's Boarding House. Dr. Fields had returned from maternity services and had a strong appetite. Black coffee was needed by all present to clear the cobwebs a bit. Orb, Cody, and H.B. felt revived for the most part but still saddle sore from too many hours of riding. Jessie had slept but barely in anticipation of daylight and seeing H.B. again. He just seemed much too young to be a doctor she thought as she waited on the hungry men. Elsa kept the stove hot cooking salt pork, scrambled eggs, and toasting homemade bread. Paula Jane came in and assisted where she could but Jessie wouldn't let her near H.B. She was stingy about letting anyone else wait on him. H.B.'s stomach was growling when he awoke and they all fell to like starved wolves. Finally, when everyone had reached their limit, Dr. Fields sprung the question he had waited so long to ask.

"Doctor, do you have any more of those wonderful miracle pills you gave Jessie? I have three or four patients suffering from pulmonary problems similar to what Jessie had. One is in an especially weakened state."

"Yes," H.B. answered. Jessie had finally sat down with her breakfast plate and was listening to the conversation. "You say you have four at this time?"

"Yes. One is almost bedfast now. She's a dear friend of Elsa's."

"I can give her an injection and follow up with pills," H.B. said. "She might need a jump start." Elsa was listening by the kitchen door. They had been friends for many years, Madge Talmidge, and Elsa. They had even attended the elementary grades together in a one room country school just outside of Austin. Those were the days when the Comanche were still lords of the plain. Austin, itself, wasn't immune from their raids. Locals kept loaded guns nearby at all times and still got butchered for their trouble. Before the moon waxed halfway and a few nights after were the most dangerous. The Indians stayed in camp on the bright nights patiently waiting for the Comanche moon, as it was commonly called, to arrive. Elsa's father had been scalped on one such night after being completely eviscerated. Thankfully, another settler had found him below the barn and spared the family from witnessing the carnage.

"I sure would appreciate some help especially with Mrs. Talmidge," Dr. Fields said relieved beyond belief. "Would you mind seeing her today?"

"Yes, I'd be glad to, but let's do it before noon if possible. We're leaving heading south early this afternoon." Orb was purchasing two additional mounts and leaving his played-out horses in Fort Worth. Cody was planning to do the same. H.B. would get home with his animals but they had suffered some loss of flesh. He planned to let them rest and recover across the rift. The hundred acres of rich coastal grass would soon flesh them out. He needed time to buy some cattle for the Montana ranch anyway. He wanted to contribute as much stock as possible for the drive north.

Jessie Madelyn wilted hearing the news of H.B.'s departure. She didn't own him though, that much she knew. She'd hoped he'd stay around for a few days. She had never really been able to visit with him in a state of good health. Her wretched illness had absorbed the moment.

"Sorry you're leaving so soon," Jessie said, trying to sound normal but unable to pull it off. Suddenly, the breakfast didn't taste good anymore. She picked at it now, mostly just stirring her eggs around.

"Weather's changing," Orb said, always with a pessimistic weather eye. "We don't want to get caught out in one of the early blizzards." He felt someone needed to mention the justification for such a short stay. His aching bones were ready to stop, too, but he had the long winter ahead to recover.

H.B. left the majority of his remaining antibiotics with Dr. Fields along with specific instructions. He even left some in an injectable form showing Dr. Fields the procedure for administering a shot. The whole concept of placing a needle in the muscle and dispelling the liquid there intrigued the doctor to no end.

"Use injectables only in dire situations requiring faster response to an infection. Pills take a day or two to become effective," H.B. cautioned. "I will bring a resupply to you on my return but use them only when necessary. So, keep the antibiotics for definite emergencies."

Dr. Fields readily agreed. H.B. had saved his reputation and perhaps, ultimately, his booming practice. He would be very stingy with them, indeed.

"When do you plan to return?" he asked, still hoping to learn more from the medical genius of this young doctor.

"Very early spring, late March likely. We're making an early start for Montana."

Jessie only got to speak with H.B. a few more minutes before their departure as Dr. Fields took up most of his time. She understood he was heading for Montana, and the idea of ranching had always fascinated her. However, starting a ranch wasn't woman's work according to tradition and that alone galled her. Why could men blow in and blow out of someone's life anytime they pleased? They were free roamers going here and there with the liberty of a red hawk yet she, just because she was a woman, had to remain confined and housebound. Dominated by a world of men. She felt like she was a prisoner bound to the nearest kitchen. Condemned to playing a menial, subservient role in the greater scheme of things. Cody appeared to be her age and yet he rode off free as a bird to light on whatever limb he wanted. What made him so different? She could sit a horse. Handle a buggy mare with deft hands and a gentle touch. She could walk, run if needed, pack water, plant soil, rear children, even comfort the sick, yet she couldn't just ride off into the sunset as men did. Watching the men gather their things, secure their baggage, and finally mount up cavalierly made her feel like she'd been kicked in the stomach. Why couldn't a young woman just mount up and ride off? She could pull a trigger. Her finger was strong enough. Yes, she was convincing herself as the men turned to leave. Yes, I'll learn to ride better and learn to shoot. Elsa can protest all she wants. She protested the garden yet we're eating my vegetables. They had said they'd return in the spring. H.B. had promised Dr. Fields to return. She had overheard the conversation. A different Jessie would present herself on their return in the spring. They would find a strong, competent woman capable of taking care of herself. She was weary of life's limitations. She'd even learn to rope. Why not? She could throw a rock almost as good as any boy could.

She waved from the porch as the three men rode away in the mid-afternoon. She'd told H.B. goodbye rather awkwardly but it was the best she could do. She held his hand again but he didn't seem too determined to hold her hand back. He's just shy as a colt she told herself as he mounted and gathered the ropes to lead his string of ponies. Cody and Orb waved smiling broadly and H.B. ducked his head and rode out of her life again.

Jessie swallowed a hard lump in her throat as the horses

kicked up dust in their hurried departure. She stood there feeling frustrated and useless. Watching the backsides of men go where they pleased wasn't such a pleasant experience. After all Corley's Boarding House wasn't her dream. It was her parent's dream. Its chains bound her now but they could not hold her forever. She would carefully plan her escape and fly away. It was a solemn, determined Jessie that turned away wet-eyed yet resolute as they melted into the distance. She knew freedom and adventure would never find her if she was going to just sit back and wait for it. Elsa could just go and pout herself into a tizzy for all she cared.

FORTY

K aty hugged Helga and Freda. All three girls' eyes were moist with tears. Hank was not so patiently sitting his horse waiting out the goodbyes and daydreaming of their future. Their plan was to return through the rift and supply themselves for a long journey. A journey that would eventually land them in the gold fields of the Klondike. Hank hungrily devoured the history of the era and knew the names of the famous creeks, the gold-bearing streams, and every minute detail of their discovery. He had no intention of changing the direction of history whatsoever. He just wanted to be a part of it. See Dawson City, Yukon, in its booming era. See Diamond Tooth Gerty's, maybe meet Carmack and Henderson, walk First Street watching greasy, dirt covered sourdoughs with their moose hide pokes drop thousands in gold into the slender purses of dance-hall girls and gaming tables. The very air glittered with gold it was told. Gold slipped from one man's hand to another hand like it was burning hot. The old miners pawed their fingers raw digging for weeks and lost their nuggets in one single glorious spree in town. Kings of Eldorado they were called, and rightfully so. So much gold was deposited in the sawdust floor of Dawson's Monte Carlo Bar that two children who panned the area beneath the floor netted twenty dollars a day for their efforts.

Dawson City existed as a metropolis for approximately twelve months from July of 1898 until July of 1899. Before this magnificent gold boom, it was a mere frontier berg of shacks and tents. After July of '99 it slipped slowly but inevitably into a ghost town of shadows and old memories. For one glorious year it was labeled the "San Francisco of the North." During this momentous period, it enjoyed almost every amenity available to civilized cities the world over. It was four thousand miles from civilization, in the shadow of the Arctic Circle, and a vast wilderness too huge to comprehend. Hank knew he wouldn't take Katy there without meticulous preparation. Just planning for it excited him. It was what dreams were made of. The stuff of legends.

Katy walked onto the boardwalk and Hank dismounted to help her into the saddle. She usually balked at his assistance but now wanted to appear ladylike. After all, several citizens including the bakery clients were watching, not counting the teary-eyed German girls. So, Katy accepted his help graciously. Katy wanted to revisit the German girls before departing north but Hank wanted to hold them to a tight schedule. Goodbyes could get lengthy and emotional so Katy eventually gave in. They'd not stop in Old Bellville in 1896 when they passed by. They couldn't show themselves perhaps even younger than they were presently to citizens who would have inevitably aged. The ultimate fate of the German girls would have to remain a mystery for now. Katy agreed to the plan, reluctantly.

The five-mile ride on a beautiful morning revived Katy after the sadness of saying her goodbyes. She'd return she promised the girls and fully intended to do so. Hank was a restless man in Old Bellville and she knew her new husband needed a change of scenery. It was late October and the air was cooler, finally overpowering the long months of torturous heat. The promise of cooler climes and less humidity actually appealed to Katy. Hank had warned of difficulties on the long trail but that didn't bother her. She had survived many difficulties through the years.

Hank whistled the old song Lorena, one of her favorites, as they rode along. It was the theme song of the John Wayne movie, The Searchers, which she always contended to be the greatest western movie ever made. Mocking birds fluttered in practically every tree and sang their melodies with the rapture of lovers. It was, indeed, a fine morning to breath the air, to feel the sunshine, and ride horses over the hilly south Texas terrain. Hank's eyes scanned each horizon as they always did when they rode. He didn't like surprises he always said. She hoped that statement didn't apply to her. The silly thought made her smile to herself. Hank was as set in his ways as she was in hers. Both were wily veterans, so to speak, and veterans of the field and flower, but she knew without a doubt, that they matched each other perfectly. That was a rare occurrence no matter how many lifetimes someone could live.

They reached the thick oak tree within the hour that held the rift remotes, locked hidden and secured in a safe. Hank punched in some code and quickly the rectangular rift opened and the darkened secret lab of H.B.'s appeared. It always reminded Katy of a massive high-definition screen constructed out of the thin air. All around it was 1885 in its still primitive state yet walk through and technology, cars, interstate highways, and electronic wizardry abounded. She knew she would age again and that wasn't much fun. Gaining forty years in one single step was hard to take, but it would only be a temporary thing. In a few days they'd leave again. Hank had said he'd roll back his age to twenty-five for the trip to the Yukon and Katy to maybe twenty-two. Wow. She could live with being a few years younger in 1896. That wasn't such a bad deal.

Stepping through the rift and leading their two horses took just moments. Katy opened the back door, led the ponies out, and secured them under the spreading limbs of one of H.B.'s massive live oak trees. She noticed Trey and Trent's pickups parked in the driveway. Both young men took their duties as guardians very seriously. She walked back in the darkened lab as Hank punched a series of numbers into the computer console and instantly the rectangular rift disappeared. She saw her reflection in the plate glass of the small office and observed her added years. Damn it, she said under her breath, barely moving her lips, but Hank heard it and offered consoling words.

"It's only for a few days, Katy, and I'll click you back to an even younger filly than you were in Old Bellville. You'll have your hands full with a twenty-five-year-old Hank. I was pretty rowdy at that age."

"Rowdy or randy?" she said, with a twinkle. "I've pretty much had my hands full with Hank at forty. I'm not so sure I can handle the Hank of twenty-five."

They both broke out in laughter. Then something rather strange happened. Hank saw it first behind Katy's shoulder. The rift reopened. What? Hank thought glancing back at the computer console. Katy turned around facing the opening and stared in disbelief. Hank stepped back out of the office and approached closer to the newly opened portal looking out. Katy followed. Sure enough. Someone was standing with several horses by the oak tree. Katy rubbed her eyes in disbelief. He was a tall cowboy type with a large hat on his head.

When he started walking towards them Katy finally realized who it was.

"That's H.B.," she said excitedly. "Just a somewhat younger version of 'im. I know his horses well. That's H.B. for sure."

In mere seconds H.B. stepped through the rift leading his horses and stopped abruptly, after spotting Katy and Hank standing in the shadows. His face took on a shocked expression. It was an expression now worn on a seventy-year-old H.B. That one step back through the rift was quite a humdinger, Katy thought looking at him.

"Well, Katy," H.B. managed to say. "I'm surprised to see you here. And Hank, how are you?" he offered, pulling his gloves off and extending his hand. Hank shook his hand, and Katy offered hers as well. Hank, quite frankly, was in awe of the man standing before him and had fully expected to never see him again. "I guess I best get these horses outside and let them go. They've had a few hard weeks."

Hank and Katy accompanied him out and unsaddled and released their horses along with H.B.'s. The horses trotted towards the sunshine and, after a good roll, settled down to some serious grazing. Trey and Trent came out through the front door with excited looks, Trent of course carrying an automatic pistol.

"The buzzers have gone nuts on the monitoring equipment," Trent said, trotting across the porch. He holstered the pistol after seeing it was Hank and Katy. He wondered who the tall cowboy was but didn't ask any questions. H.B. looked their way equally inquisitive about who the other two men were. Hank introduced everyone with Trent and Trey awed by the fact that the inventor of the rift, himself, had returned. Trey was most anxious to ask questions but was able to restrain himself for the moment.

H.B.'s eyes scanned his hundred acres seeing the security

poles with their electronic gadgetry attached. He, himself, had a few questions but was too starved to wait any longer for food. Katy led the way into the house asking if a noontime meal of ham and scrambled eggs would do. There was no disagreement among the men. H.B. went into the living room and spread his long legs on the leather couch looking around at his home with curiosity. Hank, Trey, and Trent followed and sat down. They'd been playing cards on the coffee table and Trent gathered them up and placed the card deck back in its carrier. H.B. audibly sighed and pulled off his tall, dusty boots. Hank could hear Katy humming and scurrying around in the kitchen. H.B. finally spoke first.

"Looks like there may have been just a mite of excitement around here," he stated. "Sorry to have run out on everyone like I did. I'm going back pretty soon though. I've got to buy some cattle for a drive. Planning on heading to Montana and start up a ranch with a few acquaintances of mine. Are Ethan and Lori back in Alaska?"

"Yeah," Hank said. "Alaska's their country and they hate leaving it for long. I've got some of those same feelings about my place on the San Saba," he added.

"Hank, I'm glad you've handled things so well. Trent and Trey," he said, looking at them directly, "thanks for helping out. It looks like a few changes have occurred since I left."

"Oh, just a few," Hank replied, smiling broadly.

"Any trouble to speak of?" H.B. asked, turning around to face Hank.

"Oh, not that much," Hank said nonchalantly. "Nothing that we couldn't handle."

H.B. turned a slow turn looking southward over his hundred acres. Hank paused watching him scan his estate but decided to ask anyway.

"What about the girl in Fort Worth?" Hank queried, curious about her condition.

H.B. seemed slightly taken aback by the question. He turned and looked at Hank with Trey and Trent watching closely.

"She's fine. I believe I'll see her again come spring.

CPSIA information can be obtained
at www.ICGtesting.com
Printed in the USA
BVHW032242291222
655301BV00001B/2